Emily Forbes is an award-winning author of Medical Romance for Mills & Boon. She has written over thirty-five books and has twice been a finalist in the Australian Romantic Book of the Year Award, which she won in 2013 for her novel *Sydney Harbour Hospital: Bella's Wishlist*. You can get in touch with Emily at emilyforbes@internode.on.net, or visit her website at emily-forbesauthor.com.

Lifelong romance addict **JC Harroway** took a break from her career as a junior doctor to raise a family and found her calling as a Mills and Boon author instead. She now lives in New Zealand, and finds that writing feeds her very real obsession with happy endings and the endorphin rush they create. You can follow her at jcharroway.com, and on Facebook, Twitter and Instagram.

Also by Emily Forbes

Bondi Beach Medics miniseries

Rescuing the Paramedic's Heart
A Gift to Change His Life
The Perfect Mother for His Son

Also by JC Harroway

Forbidden Fling with Dr Right

Mills & Boon Dare

The Proposition
Bad Business

Discover more at millsandboon.co.uk.

MARRIAGE REUNION IN THE ER

EMILY FORBES

HOW TO RESIST THE SINGLE DAD

JC HARROWAY

MILLS & BOON

First published in Great Britain 2022
by Mills & Boon, an imprint of HarperCollins*Publishers* Ltd,
1 London Bridge Street, London, SE1 9GF

www.harpercollins.co.uk

HarperCollins*Publishers*
1st Floor, Watermarque Building,
Ringsend Road, Dublin 4, Ireland

Marriage Reunion in the ER © 2022 Emily Forbes

How to Resist the Single Dad © 2022 JC Harroway

ISBN: 978-0-263-30139-7

09/22

MIX
Paper from
responsible sources
FSC® C007454

This book is produced from independently certified FSC™ paper
to ensure responsible forest management.
For more information visit www.harpercollins.co.uk/green.

Printed and Bound in Spain using 100% Renewable Electricity
at CPI Black Print, Barcelona

MARRIAGE REUNION IN THE ER

EMILY FORBES

MILLS & BOON

CHAPTER ONE

LILY LOOKED AROUND the almost empty bedroom at the bare walls and the pile of linen that had been stripped from the bed and dumped in the middle of the mattress. Daisy's possessions had been packed into boxes, ready to be moved to her fiancé's house at the other end of Bondi Beach, and for the first time in two years Lily would be alone in her house.

She hadn't stopped to think about how she was going to feel but seeing the barren room with all traces of her little sister removed was confronting. It signalled the end of an era. An end she wasn't ready for. She'd never lived here without company. She was happy for Daisy, of course she was, she'd found her person and was heading off to start a new life, but the empty room looked so final. So lonely.

Lily and Daisy had both made their choices, although the outcomes were very different, and for Lily her choices meant she'd have to get used to being alone.

She was an adult, she could manage, she reminded herself. She should be looking forward to having a whole house to herself, it was something she'd never experienced, but she was worried it wouldn't be to her liking.

She'd grown up sharing a bedroom with another sister, Poppy. Until the age of eighteen when she'd moved to Sydney to study medicine they'd shared a room, clothes and dreams. When Lily had moved into university accommodation, she'd still shared common spaces, if not a bedroom, with dozens of other students. She'd only moved out of there when she'd got married.

As a child she'd longed for a room of her own, space of her own. She should be looking forward to this next chapter, but she was acutely aware of the hole Daisy's departure was going to leave in her life. The hole Lily had filled by caring for her siblings. But all three of them were making their own way in the world now, forging ahead with their futures. They didn't need her any more and she didn't know how she would fill that gap without anyone to mother, without anyone to fuss over.

As the eldest of the four Carlson siblings she had always mothered her younger brother and sisters. Lord knew their parents hadn't been interested in raising their own kids, so Lily had taken on that role more often than not. She should enjoy having no one to think about but herself, she should be looking forward to this next chapter, but she could already feel the weight of her loss and her past decisions weighing her down.

She hoped they weren't going to crush her.

Too much time on her own would leave her with too much time to think and she knew where her mind would wander.

To Otto.

'Is that everything?' Daisy's fiancé's voice interrupted Lily's thoughts and she turned her attention away from the past and back to what was going on around her.

Daisy nodded. She'd been taping the last packing

box closed but she'd stopped what she was doing to look at Ajay.

'What about that one?' Ajay asked as he pointed at a flat white box perched on the top shelf of the wardrobe.

'That's not mine,' Daisy replied as Lily's heart skipped a beat. She hadn't looked inside that box for years but she knew exactly what it contained.

Daisy stood up and started to shove her bed linen into a large bag as Ajay picked the final box up from the floor. He waited until she was looking at him again. Mindful of her hearing impairment he made sure Daisy could read his lips, before he asked, 'I'll take this to the car and wait for you there if you're ready to go?'

Daisy nodded again before turning to face Lily. 'Are you sure you don't want to come to us for dinner?' she asked.

'I'm sure,' Lily replied. She knew the house was going to feel empty but Daisy was heading off to her new life, off on a new adventure with her fiancé and his son, Niki, and Lily didn't want to intrude. She would find something to occupy her time, something to keep her mind engaged, something to enable her to ignore the quiet solitude because she knew she wouldn't enjoy it.

She pasted a smile on her face as she hugged her sister and Ajay and waved them goodbye before returning to Daisy's old bedroom intending to remake the bed. Perhaps that would help it to look less lonely. Less empty. As long as she could ignore the indentations in the carpet where Daisy's chair and chest of drawers had been she might be able to pretend someone still occupied that room if the bed was made.

She crossed the room, intending to get the spare linen out of the wardrobe, but her attention was drawn to the white box that sat on the top shelf, taunting her. She reached out, planning to slide the wardrobe door closed, to put the box and its contents out of her mind. She'd make the bed another time, she decided. But instead of hiding the box away she found herself reaching for it and taking it off the shelf.

She sat on the bed and lifted the lid.

She brushed her hand over the tissue paper that lined the box. It crinkled under her fingers, daring her to remove it.

She knew this was the last thing she should be doing when her nerves were already stretched tight, when the loneliness was like a demon hiding in the shadows daring her to look his way.

If she ignored the shadowy corners in her mind, if she kept her gaze averted, her attention diverted, she could keep the demon at bay, but she wasn't strong enough.

She pulled the top sheet of paper off and ran her fingers over the fabric that had been hidden underneath, feeling the tiny, delicate, fabric flowers that were scattered over the material, separating the individual petals from one another.

She slid one finger under the folds of milky white fabric that lay beneath the flowers. Despite the warmth of the late summer evening the satin was cool to touch.

She knew she should resist temptation. She knew she should put the lid on the box and hide it away again. The past was the past, there was no going back.

But her hands weren't listening. They were working independently of her mind. She intended to pick up the tissue paper, to layer it back in the box but instead she hooked her fingers under the narrow straps of fabric and lifted the contents from the box.

She stood up with the straps looped over her fingers, as the skirt of the dress fell to the floor.

Lily stepped in front of the mirror and held the dress up against her.

The smooth satin of the skirt brushed over her bare legs as it hid her shorts. She swayed slightly and the satin swished over her hips. She pressed her hands tightly to her shoulders, holding the dress to her body, making sure she wasn't tempted to try it on. She knew it would still fit her but she had no intention of wearing it again. Anxiety, skipped meals and an occasional break from work to go surfing had kept her weight constant and her figure was pretty much unchanged from the last, and only, time she'd worn this dress. On her wedding day almost five years ago.

She took a deep breath and closed her eyes as the memories flooded back.

She and Otto had been married for nearly five years but it had been two years since she'd last seen him, since she'd said goodbye, and somewhere along the way even their conversations had dwindled to discussions about the house they owned, their jobs on opposite sides of the world and the weather.

She could blame the time difference or their busy lives for their lack of communication but if she was honest she knew she'd avoided picking up the phone in an attempt to block out the past, to block out the reason she'd left.

She had never imagined their relationship would deteriorate so badly. What did that mean for their future? Did they even *have* a future?

She'd thought Otto would come after her but, when he hadn't, she'd gradually begun to reimagine her life solo. That hadn't been her intention initially but now it looked as if it was the only way forward. She'd avoided Otto, avoided the difficult conversations, avoided talking about their loss. She knew it was too painful for her to broach that subject but she had no idea if Otto was as afraid of that conversation as she was or whether he was just oblivious to her pain. To her sadness.

She knew Otto was an optimist. He looked on the bright side of life—always looked for the positives, was always in good spirits. His attitude had always been 'why worry about the things you couldn't change' and he chose to focus his energy on the things he could control.

Otto had always been much more carefree while Lily was more serious. His personality had been a good foil for hers. Until one day when their differences had collided with each other instead of complementing each other.

Until the day that Lily's dreams of a perfect life, of children and a family of her own, had been shattered.

She wasn't pessimistic by nature but her positivity had taken a beating. She'd been distraught but Otto hadn't understood her devastation. His mantra was 'what's done is done, move on, put it behind you'. His life hadn't stopped, his focus hadn't wavered. He'd forged ahead on his path, insistent that they'd get past the loss. But she hadn't been able to. And one loss had led to another.

She hadn't been able to handle Otto's lack of support. She'd felt unsupported, misunderstood and miserable. And so she'd walked away.

She'd lost everything.

She opened her eyes, turning her back on the mirror, not wanting to look at the dress. It was a symbol of a future she no longer had.

She'd learned to compartmentalise her memories.

She'd locked them away. It was the only way she'd been able to get through each day. She'd wanted to talk to Otto but they had barely spent any time together after the incident. No, she needed to call it what it was—the assault. It was two years ago but she hadn't yet forgiven Otto for not keeping his word. If Otto had come home when he should have, she wouldn't have been assaulted and they wouldn't have lost their baby.

She had been more than five months pregnant at the time. She'd survived morning sickness, homesickness and immense fatigue all while starting a new job and had reached the point where she'd been enjoying the pregnancy and was excited about the future. She'd known Otto had been less excited, the pregnancy hadn't been planned, advancing their timeline, but she was certain he'd change his mind once he held his child in his arms. She delighted in reaching the milestones, in feeling her baby kick. Feeling the hiccoughs and watching as her stomach moved and stretched as the baby performed somersaults in her womb. She'd lain awake at night, uncomfortable but happy, dreaming of the life they would have, their family of three, and had been convinced it would all work out just as she pictured.

And then it had all gone wrong.

She knew it wasn't all Otto's fault. The blame lay with the man who had assaulted her, who had punched her in the stomach, stolen her bag and left her lying on the ground as he'd run off. But if Otto hadn't changed his plans, if he'd left work when he was supposed to, she wouldn't have been in the wrong place at the wrong time. She wouldn't have lost their baby.

Anger had become intertwined with her sadness, leaving her feeling bereft, adrift and alone. Unsettled and upset, she'd fled London, leaving Otto and their marriage behind. After two years she'd learnt to put the past aside in order to face each day. She hadn't forgotten what had happened but she was learning to live with it.

Forgiveness was a different story. She knew it was important but it was something she had struggled with. Perhaps one day she could learn to forgive if not forget.

She sighed. She hadn't wanted to give up on her dreams, on the idea of marriage and a family, but it was time she faced facts. Her marriage was over.

She didn't have to completely give up on her dream of a family but it was time to acknowledge that her dream was going to look different, *had* to look different. She could have a family but it wouldn't be with Otto.

She still wanted that perfect life and while she might not be able to change the past it didn't mean she had to give up on her future.

She folded her wedding dress and put it back into the box, covering it again with the tissue paper. For a brief moment she thought about seeing if either of her sisters wanted to borrow it. They were both engaged but while it would fit Poppy it would be too big for Daisy and was it bad luck to borrow a wedding dress from a marriage that hadn't lasted?

Technically Lily and Otto were still married, but her marriage and her life were in limbo.

It was time to face facts—Otto wasn't coming back.

In the back of her mind she'd always expected that he would come for her and she'd kept extending the timeline in her head. She'd made excuses: he was busy—working and studying for his fellowship, they'd been living on opposite sides of the world and the global pandemic had made travel to Australia from London all but impossible.

But Otto's fellowship was due to finish this month, international travel was back on the agenda and there was still no sign of him coming home.

She wondered what his plans were. Surely he would have told her if he was coming back to Australia? He had Italian parentage on his mother's side, he could decide to stay overseas, and the fact he'd said nothing made her think he was settled in England, that he'd given up on them. On her.

If he wasn't coming back she had two options. She could go to him or she could move on without him.

She still loved Otto. She'd never stopped loving him. But she'd blamed him for failing to protect her. He'd promised to look after her, she'd trusted him to do that but he'd let her down.

She knew she wasn't blameless either, she'd failed to protect their child and that knowledge had been hard to accept and she knew it had contributed to the situation she found herself in now. She knew she'd run away. She hadn't been able to cope with seeing Otto every day. He had been a reminder of her broken dreams. They should have been able to help each other but instead all Lily had felt was a gaping divide between her emotions and his, her needs, her feelings, her hopes and dreams and his.

And she hadn't been able to bring herself to return to London, to go back to Otto. She still struggled to comprehend how their fairy tale had gone so wrong. The past two years had seen them drift further and further apart until she felt as if there was nothing left any more. And, while they lived on opposite sides of the globe, she knew their problems were unsurmountable.

Should she go back now? Give their marriage a chance? Without realising, she shook her head. Since the day she'd announced her unexpected pregnancy it was clear they were on differing timelines and nothing had changed. Otto would have told her if he wanted a family now. She would have told him if she was prepared to wait. It was that simple.

It had taken her some time to come to terms with the loss of their first baby but she had never wavered from knowing she wanted to be a mother and the unexpected pregnancy had only made her want that sooner rather than later. And now that her siblings were all settling down her biological clock was ticking overtime. In the past few months her brother and two sisters had all found true love and Lily had been left reassessing her own future. Otto had stopped asking about her plans a long time ago but it was clear in her heart, if not her head, what she wanted. She wanted a family. It was that simple.

She had to move on.

She couldn't go back.

She couldn't face returning to the place where it had all gone wrong.

She'd failed him but he had failed her too. He'd let her down, he'd lost her trust and she didn't know if he could win it back again. Or if he even wanted to.

She had wondered if they would ever be able to resolve their issues but the more time that passed, the more unlikely that seemed.

In her head she knew it was too late for their marriage. Surely if they were meant to be together they would have found their way back to each other by now.

What was left to fight for? What was easier to give up? Otto or her dreams of having a family? What was more important?

Her heart ached but she knew the answer. It was time to move on. The time had come to move forwards.

She put the lid on and slid the box back onto the shelf, relegating her wedding dress to her past, the decision made but not made lightly.

She shut the wardrobe door and checked the time. It would be mid-morning in London. She and Otto needed to have a frank discussion but she couldn't call now. He would be at work but even if he answered the phone she wouldn't know what to say. She needed time to prepare.

She would delay for one more day. What difference would a day make now after two years? She'd use the time to make some notes, to sort through her thoughts, to prepare her argument.

There was a lot to resolve but it was beginning to look as though it would be better just to start again. She'd waited long enough.

She wiped a tear from her cheek with the back of her hand as she closed the bedroom door. It was time to take a leaf out of Otto's book and do something about the things that were under her control.

Otto was woken by the flight attendant serving his breakfast accompanied by the pilot's announcement that they were on schedule for their arrival into Sydney. He stretched his shoulders and adjusted his seat as he tried not to think about how much he'd paid for his spot in business class. He'd slept well, the expense had been worth it and if he was going to worry about the price he shouldn't have booked the fare. He could afford it. There were probably other things he could have done with his money, there always would be, but the ticket was paid for, what was done was done, and he wasn't going to feel guilty about the extra luxury and comfort.

He'd been raised to work hard. To save money, to not live beyond his means, to be charitable. Money wasn't for frivolous things. His upbringing had been religious, nothing extreme, but he and his brothers had been taught to look after others, to be charitable.

His mother had always made them put their own money on the plate at church, she'd instilled in them the importance of giving back. She had died when Otto was thirteen but he continued to be charitable as a way of honouring her memory. He still missed his mother but it was what it was. He'd learnt not to wish things were different, not to worry about the things he couldn't change. That mindset had come about as a direct reaction to his mother's death, a defence mechanism. He realised that wishing she hadn't been on the road at the same time as a drunk driver wasn't going to bring her back and so he'd learnt to worry about what he could control. To fix the things he could.

He shook out his napkin and tucked into his breakfast. Flying business class was a luxury but he refused to add more guilt to his conscience. He had enough already.

He'd worked non-stop for the past two years and he needed to take a break and if the only break he was going to get was on a long-haul flight from London to Australia that would have to do. Working hard had been a choice, a deliberate measure to combat loneliness. Finding himself with time on his hands—time he hadn't wanted—he'd filled those hours by studying, working and volunteering for extra shifts, offering to work on all the holidays, including Christmas.

Keeping occupied had served its purpose. It had left

him with no time to think about anything other than medicine but he'd reached a crossroads and he needed to take
stock of his life, to work out what he wanted to do next.

He could have stayed in London, he'd been offered a
position in the hospital there, but he'd also been offered
a position at Bondi General, replacing a surgeon who
was retiring. Receiving an invitation to his sister-in-law's
wedding had been an added persuasion, the extra push he
needed to set a date to get on the plane. But even without
that, when he weighed up his options, he knew he only
had one choice. He had to come home. There was one
thing he had to prioritise above all else.

His marriage.

That was assuming he still had one.

He hadn't seen his wife in almost two years. For the
past seven hundred and eight days he and Lily had had a
marriage in name only. They'd shared nothing but phone
calls since Lily had packed her bags and walked out of
their London flat.

He hadn't tried to stop her from leaving. She'd told
him she needed to go and he'd believed her. But he'd
never intended to let her go for good.

Living on the opposite side of the world from his wife
during a pandemic wasn't ideal and the time difference
and their busy schedules hadn't conspired to make it easy.
Their phone conversations had been brief, superficial and
never particularly satisfactory and the calls had become
progressively shorter, less frequent and less revealing.

Now, he had no idea what she was thinking. When
they were first married they'd spent hours talking about
their hopes and dreams but all of that had changed after
Lily left. They never discussed their feelings in their
phone calls and he wasn't sure how she felt about him,

their marriage, their past or their future now. Had the passage of time healed her wounds? The loss of their baby had affected her deeply. It wasn't something they talked about at great length but he knew she'd taken it hard. Should he have encouraged her to talk to him about it?

He knew he hadn't because he didn't want to upset her and because he didn't want to see the accusations in her eyes. He'd felt guilty. His actions had put her in a vulnerable position. He hadn't been the one to cause her physical harm but the emotional injuries had scarred Lily just as badly and he still felt guilty.

Would time have healed the wounds? Would she have forgiven him? Would she be happy to see him?

He'd felt so confident when he'd been making plans to return to Australia. He had visions of what his future would look like. But as the plane flew over the Australian continent he began to wonder if he was wrong.

He wasn't sure he believed that absence made the heart grow fonder. His feelings for Lily hadn't changed in the past two years, they'd always been powerful. He'd remained faithful to her, he had made a promise to her on their wedding day five years ago and it was a promise he intended to keep. But he didn't know if Lily would have done the same. Had their separation changed her? Maybe there was a time limit on absence.

He hadn't been able to fix her two years ago. She'd been broken and he'd had no idea how to put her back together. After losing the baby there was so much they'd never spoken about. Where did that leave them?

Two years was a long time. Was it too long? The loss of their baby had torn them apart. Did they have the tools to put the relationship back together? Did Lily want him back?

He hadn't told her he was coming back and he knew it was because he'd been afraid she might have told him not to bother.

His trepidation grew as breakfast was cleared and his arrival was imminent. He wondered what sort of welcome he was going to receive. Would Lily be pleased to see him?

He felt the descent begin and he looked out of the window at the city as the plane approached the airport. It was a glorious summer's day, the harbour shimmered under the sun's rays and the iconic bridge stretched over the water, curving against the blue sky.

He was home.

CHAPTER TWO

'LILY, INCOMING AMBULANCE. ETA three minutes. Male cyclist, hit by a car. Can you take that one?'

Lily nodded as the triage nurse raced past with instructions. She was treating a child who was suffering from heat exhaustion. He was dehydrated and had been vomiting but fortunately his temperature was not elevated into an alarming range. She finished setting up the IV fluids and quietly instructed the nurse to stay with the patient and to be alert for any seizures. She peeled off her surgical gloves and apron and exchanged both for fresh protection. The ED at Bondi General was busy and she knew it was a juggling act trying to prioritise their patients. School had returned after the summer holidays but the February heatwave continued to see people flocking to Bondi and the surrounding beaches and when things went wrong those same people came through the ED doors.

Lily's first thought was why did someone feel the need to go for a bike ride when the mercury was nudging a hundred degrees Fahrenheit?

The ambulance pulled into the bay. She recognised the paramedic who climbed out of the back as one who often worked with her sister Poppy.

'Hi, Alex, what have we got?' she greeted him as he pulled the stretcher from the ambulance.

'Fifty-two-year-old male cyclist, multiple injuries. LOC, right upper limb fractures, rib fractures, abrasions, lacerations. BP one hundred over sixty. Pulse ninety-eight. He's in and out of consciousness. GCS of eight.'

The cyclist's helmet, what was left of it, was tucked at his feet. He was fortunate that he'd been wearing one—without it, Lily suspected he might have been taken straight to the morgue.

Her initial thought about the ridiculous decision to go for a ride in this heat was replaced with another, more pressing thought given the seriousness of the patient's injuries. His injuries were extensive and as she and Alex pushed the stretcher inside she knew he was going to need more skills than she could offer.

'We're going to need a trauma surgeon,' she said to Julie as she and Alex pushed the patient into the ED and headed directly to a treatment room.

The patient was transferred to a bed and the ED team got to work. Nursing staff inserted cannulas to run drips and attached him to the monitors. Lily kept one eye on his vitals as she prioritised his injuries. His BP had dropped further and she wondered if he had internal injuries with associated undetected internal bleeding.

'Can someone organise to cross-match blood type and run some O negative now?'

Lily picked up a torch and checked his pupils for re-action to the light, starting her assessment at the head, deeming that the most critical and planning to work her way down his body.

His eyes remained closed when she finished, no response to verbal stimuli but as they didn't know his name that made things difficult. She applied pressure to his fingertip, squeezing firmly, and was relieved to see his eyes flicker open. The door opened as she released his hand.

'All right, someone catch me up.'

That voice from behind Lily was so familiar. It brought goosebumps to her skin and made her catch her breath. A silly reaction, she knew it couldn't be Otto. Her ears were playing tricks on her—she was imagining Otto's voice because he'd been in her thoughts.

She glanced over her shoulder to see who she'd mistaken for Otto and almost dropped the torch.

Her husband was standing inside the doorway.

'Otto!' Lily felt the blood rush from her head, making Otto's face swim before her eyes. She put one hand out, reaching for the bed to support herself as her vision blurred and her legs threatened to fold beneath her.

'Hello, Lily.'

Lily could feel her eyes bugging out of her head as her brain tried to catch up with what she was seeing. Her husband, who as far as she'd been aware was supposed to be on the other side of the world, was standing in front of her.

She squeezed her eyes shut for a moment, clearing her mind, half expecting when she opened them that he would have disappeared. Half expecting that she was imagining things.

But no, he was still there, in her ED.

She opened her mouth wanting to ask what he was doing, why he was here, but her powers of speech deserted her.

'Everyone, this is Dr Podgers, our new trauma specialist.' Julie was standing beside Otto, introducing him to the team.

Lily snapped her jaw shut, closing her mouth, waiting for her world to stabilise, hoping Julie wouldn't ask how they knew each other but fortunately there was no time for idle chat, they had a critically ill patient to manage.

Lily found her voice, and she could hear herself recounting the patient's history and assessment so far. Her head was spinning and she hoped she was making sense as she tried to process what was happening. No one corrected her summary so she assumed she must be giving the correct information.

Otto was standing beside her. She could feel the warmth emanating from his body, making her skin tingle. She wanted to look at him, still unable to believe what she was seeing, but she kept her eyes fixed on the patient, knowing she'd likely lose her train of thought completely if she looked Otto's way.

'GCS was eight,' she said as she watched one of the nurses removing road gravel from where it was embedded in the patient's upper arm. The cyclist had been wearing a short-sleeved Lycra riding suit, which was now dirty and torn and hadn't afforded him much protection against the metal of the car that hit him or against the hot bitumen of the road where he would have eventually come to rest. Lily kept her focus on those small deliberate movements as she spoke, ignoring the fact her husband—estranged, absent, she didn't know what to call him—was standing beside her. 'Blood pressure is still dropping. I'm worried about internal injuries. He's going to need scans.'

'Lily!' The nurse opposite her lifted her head, pausing her task to get Lily's attention.

The road gravel had packed a laceration, stemming the blood loss, but as the nurse had removed it the wound had opened up and blood was gushing from a now gaping hole. In a matter of seconds, the sheet was soaked in blood.

'Lacerated brachial artery. I need a tourniquet and an operating theatre. Now!' Otto shouted as the alarms on the monitors started beeping.

Lily grabbed a tourniquet and tightened it around the patient's arm as one of the nurses picked up the phone and called Theatres.

'You can use OR Three,' the nurse said as she hung up the phone and began to disconnect the monitors from the wall.

Lily checked that the tourniquet had stopped the blood loss before pulling up the cot sides. Otto had already kicked the brakes off and had moved to the head of the bed. There was no time to wait for an orderly with a bed mover.

'Let's go,' he instructed. 'Lily, keep an eye on that arm, make sure that tourniquet stays tight.'

Otto was already moving, pushing the bed in front of him, obviously expecting Lily to accompany him.

Adrenalin surged through her as she half walked, half ran, beside the bed, steering it out of the ED and towards the lift where one of the nurses was holding the door open for them.

They manoeuvred their patient into the lift. Lily squeezed in next to the wall and pressed the button for the operating floor. The doors slid closed and all of a sudden it was just her, Otto and their unconscious patient.

Otto had squeezed himself in next to Lily and she moved further into the corner, putting as much distance between them as she could. She gripped the rails on the bed side, grounding herself as she stared at him.

She couldn't believe he was back.

She couldn't believe he hadn't told her.

She felt ambushed. If she'd learnt one thing from her chaotic childhood it was that she coped best if she had a chance to prepare. She dealt in knowns, not unknowns. Even when working in the ED she dealt in facts, she knew the science. Years of study had taught her what to look for, she understood the signs and symptoms and they indicated how to treat her patients. She was always prepared. Always. But not today. His arrival had caught her by surprise and as she thought about his unannounced appearance her shock turned to anger. How dared he not let her know?

She was about to castigate him when the lift stopped. The operating theatres were only one floor above the ED and the short ride had saved Otto from a verbal tirade.

He reached out for the rail on the bedside as the doors slid open, his hand coming to rest on top of hers. The heat of his touch burned through her, searing her skin. She yanked her hand away as the theatre staff pulled the bed out of the lift and whisked the patient away. Otto followed them, issuing instructions, not even glancing Lily's way before he disappeared, leaving her alone.

Everything had happened so quickly and to find herself standing in the corridor alone was disconcerting. She leant on the wall for a moment, sifting through her feelings and recovering her equilibrium. She was astounded, confused and annoyed.

His return had completely blindsided her and the fact that he hadn't bothered to tell her he was coming home reinforced that she'd been right to start thinking about moving on. He'd shown her no regard. He hadn't warned her. He hadn't made time for her. He hadn't even looked back at her just now. He'd just walked away.

She had no idea why he was back or what his return meant but she intended to stick to her plan. She couldn't let his reappearance disrupt her. She needed someone who would support her when the going got tough. Life wasn't easy, she knew that all too well, and she deserved to have someone who had her back.

She returned to the ED and picked up her phone from the triage desk. She needed to get on top of things and put her plan in place.

Her hand was shaking as she typed in a message.

We need to talk.

The text was simple and unemotional and nothing at all like she felt but she had to keep her emotions in check. She'd made a decision.

She hit 'send'.

Otto turned the shower on full, letting the needles of water pepper his skin. He rolled his shoulders and felt the tension of the day and the fatigue of jet lag leave his body. It had been a stressful start to his new role.

His first official day had gone as expected professionally but not emotionally. After two years apart his intention had been to see Lily in private before he started work. He'd called her when he landed yesterday but her phone had gone straight to voicemail. He'd assumed she was at work and he'd left a simple message saying he'd call again later before jet lag had caught up with him.

Seeing her at the hospital today had thrown him off balance. He realised he hadn't mentally prepared himself for the possibility that he'd run into her at work first. A stupid oversight, he knew now. She was an ED doctor, he was a trauma surgeon, it was highly likely they would cross paths at work but he hadn't really considered that scenario. In his head, he had a vision of how their reunion would go and having it at work hadn't been the picture he'd conjured. It had thrown him. And it had obviously unsettled Lily.

He closed his eyes and put his face under the spray as he thought about the text message she'd sent him this afternoon.

We need to talk.

It was brief, hard to decipher. It felt terse but perhaps she'd sent it in a hurry. He found it difficult to read the tone of a text message at the best of times. No emojis, no clue. All he had to go on was her reaction to him when he'd appeared in the ED. Surprise. Shock. Both of which were to be expected given the circumstances. It wasn't an ideal start to his planned reunion and he owed her an apology for appearing out of the blue. He wouldn't call her. He needed to see her.

He walked to the shops, picked up a couple of things and then hailed a taxi.

The drive took him past Bondi Beach where the late afternoon sun turned the sea the same colour of blue as Lily's eyes and the golden sand of the beach was the colour of her hair. He had the window down and the scent of frangipani in the air reminded him of her perfume and, if he closed his eyes, the warm ocean breeze on his face could be mistaken for her soft breath on his skin as she lay curled into his side. Even after two years he could instantly recall how the weight of her head felt on his shoulder as they lay naked in bed, her long hair splayed across his chest, her fingers resting on his thigh.

In London he'd almost been able to ignore the absence of Lily. They hadn't been in the city long enough to establish a history of time spent together there and there hadn't been the constant reminders of her on every corner, but in Sydney everywhere he looked, everywhere he turned there was another memory. The beach, their favourite coffee spot, their local pub and the cinema where they'd seen their first movie together. The past was everywhere but what of the future?

He sighed as the taxi driver dropped him at the house on Moore Street. His house.

He had the keys in his pocket but it didn't feel like his house, or even their house, any more. He felt like a stranger. It was Lily's house now.

He stood on the front step and took several deep breaths to calm his nerves before pressing his finger to the doorbell.

The sound of the doorbell made Lily jump. She'd been on edge ever since she got home. No, ever since Otto had appeared at the hospital. She hadn't been able to work out what he was doing here and why he hadn't told her he was coming back. She hadn't worked out how she *felt* about him being back. She had so many questions but no answers.

She'd fled from the hospital the minute her shift had ended, wanting to put some distance between them, wanting time to clear her head but her thoughts had been going round in never-ending circles.

The doorbell rang a second time and she headed down the hallway. She breathed deeply, trying to calm her nerves, a sixth sense telling her that Otto was standing on the doorstep. She would have liked more time to compose herself but she knew she had to face him at some point.

She turned the handle and despite mentally preparing herself the sight of Otto standing on the step still made her heart race.

'Hello, Lil.'

He leant towards her and Lily panicked. Was he going to kiss her? She wasn't sure but she knew she wasn't ready for that. She was discombobulated enough. She turned her head and his lips grazed her cheek.

He smelt fresh, as if he'd just stepped out of the shower, and she could feel the warmth of his body. She moved back. Her self-control had never been good around him and she needed to keep him at a distance. She'd finally worked up the courage to raise a difficult topic of conversation with him, thinking he was thousands of miles away, and she couldn't drop her guard now.

She could see the confusion in his eyes caused by her avoidance of his kiss but he didn't question her. She'd longed for his attention two years ago, she'd longed for him to acknowledge her pain, their loss, to share the heartache and to comfort her but he'd shut her out. Throwing himself into his work and leaving her to deal with her grief and now the combination of shock and anger made her react without thinking. She hid behind the door, shielding herself from his affection and attention as she ran her eyes over him, taking stock, looking for changes in his appearance that she might have missed in one of their infrequent video calls.

He wore a short-sleeved polo shirt that was snug across his broad chest and exposed his arms. His arms were muscular, well-defined. She'd always loved his arms and they looked as strong as ever. His olive skin looked as if it hadn't seen a lot of sun lately, he was paler than she remembered, but she knew it wouldn't take long for his skin to tan in the Australian summer. He was still lean, she thought, as she looked for differences.

He was thirty-four, four years older than she was and she noticed some grey scattered through his dark hair, not much, but that was something new. It didn't detract from his looks, it was just a sprinkle, just enough to show the passing of time.

But despite the years that had passed he still looked good and there was no denying, in her eyes at least, he was still the most handsome man she'd ever seen.

'What are you doing here?'

'You said you wanted to talk,' he replied. 'Can I come in?'

His head was slightly angled as he watched her, his dark eyes questioning. The street was quiet but she was sure he hadn't come all this way to have a conversation on the front step. She nodded and stepped back.

'I thought you were still in London,' she said as her heart rate finally slowed and began to resemble something close to normal. Something that didn't make her fearful that it was going to leap out of her chest or, alternatively, suddenly give up altogether. 'When did you get back?'

'Yesterday.'

'*Yesterday!* Why didn't you tell me?' Her head wasn't spinning any more even if her mind was and she felt as if she were operating on autopilot as she turned and walked down the narrow passage, past a bedroom to her right until she reached the point where the house widened out, opening into the lounge room, which led to the kitchen. She didn't need to direct Otto, he knew this house better than she did. It had been his house before they'd met. Before they'd got married.

'I meant to. I called you when I landed. Didn't you get my message?'

'Yes. But you didn't say anything about being back. You ambushed me at the hospital.'

'I wanted to surprise you.'

Mission accomplished, she thought as she collapsed onto the couch.

'Shall I take these to the kitchen?' he asked and it was only then she noticed he was holding a bunch of lilies and a bottle of wine.

She felt like bursting into tears. Part of her wanted to fall into his arms, to let him soothe her soul, but he hadn't been good at that. That was one of the reasons she'd left London in the first place. Otto, the man who wanted to fix things, hadn't been able to fix her. She was still fragile. She couldn't deny she was drawn to him, that she still felt a physical attraction, that had never changed, but it was her emotional needs that he hadn't been able to meet.

She took a breath and held her tears in. She couldn't fall apart now. She'd had a plan before he'd rung the doorbell and she couldn't change course now. She had wanted to talk but a cosy catch-up wasn't what she'd had in mind. When she'd initially decided on her plan a face-to-face conversation hadn't even been on her radar. She'd imagined having this conversation over a video call with him in London. Would she be able to remain on track? Focused on the conversation she wanted to have now that he was here in person? She was already finding it unsettling to have him in the same room as her. It made the situation very real and far more personal than having a video call. It wasn't going to be as easy to keep a clear head when she could see him in the flesh. When she could see *all* of him, not just bits. When she could reach out and touch him. When she could smell his aftershave.

She was shocked and stunned but somehow, she held herself together. She shook her head as she tried to clear her thoughts. 'I wasn't expecting to share a bottle of wine,' she told him. 'I wasn't expecting flowers.'

'I didn't want to turn up empty-handed.'

She couldn't remember the last time he'd bought her flowers. They'd never had the money to spend on little luxuries like fresh flowers. She didn't want to refuse his gifts but she didn't want him bringing her flowers either. In her mind it complicated things and that made her response a bit terser than she intended it to be. 'I wasn't expecting you to turn up here,' she said.

'You said you wanted to talk,' he repeated. 'I assumed you meant in private. This seemed like the best place.'

She suspected the talk he envisaged was rather different from what she had in mind. She wasn't planning on sharing a bottle of wine and reminiscing about their past. Their paths had diverged a long time ago. She had a plan for her future.

'Just let me put these down,' he said, gesturing with the wine and the flowers.

Her heart was racing again and her hands were shaking. She knew that was caused by the adrenalin coursing through her, a result of the slight shock she was experiencing at his appearance, but she couldn't let herself be distracted by his presence. She'd made a list in preparation for the phone call she had imagined them having but she now felt woefully unprepared. She'd never imagined this conversation was going to be easy but it now felt almost impossible.

She needed to remember her plan. She was going to move ahead with her life.

Seeing her siblings find love had been the sign that made her realise she'd been living a lonely existence. She had put her personal life on hold for two years, she couldn't blame Otto, and she didn't, not completely, this was on both of them. It was time to reset her personal goals and work towards them.

Having Otto back in Australia wasn't enough. Not unless they were on the same path and she suspected Otto's path was now a long way from hers. Two years of heading in different directions would put them miles apart. In two years they hadn't spoken about what happened next and she couldn't rely on Otto to give her what she wanted. If he wanted a family he would have told her before now. If he didn't want a family yet then she needed a divorce.

It was time to let go of Otto. Of the dream of raising a family with him, of having his children. It was a dream she'd had from their very first date. She knew that was why she'd held on as long as she had. And it was a dream that was hard to let go of. Even harder now that he was back in her space. But she'd have to relinquish it if she wanted a chance of realising the dream at all. She needed someone to have her back and she wasn't sure if she could trust Otto to be there for her.

She needed to find someone who wanted to walk beside her into her future. Someone who was happy to share her path.

It didn't matter that he was there in person, she told herself as he came back, empty-handed, from the kitchen. That didn't change anything. He might only be back temporarily. He might have come back to ask *her* for a divorce. She needed to stay firm. She needed to stay resolute.

'I wanted to talk to you about getting a divorce,' she blurted out the minute he stepped back through the doorway. She didn't know how to break it to him gently. She worried that his presence would distract her and make her waver. She was worried he could change her mind. She had to stay strong. She'd made her decision.

Otto's blood ran cold and he could have sworn his heart skipped a beat, if not several. He'd been unsure of the reaction he was going to get when he arrived at Lily's door and he wasn't sure what he expected the conversation to entail but he knew for certain he hadn't expected divorce to be the first topic of discussion she would raise.

Her words punched him in the face. He was stunned. Completely blindsided.

He knew they had things to sort out. After two years apart he wasn't foolish enough to think they could act as if nothing had happened and they hadn't left each other in a good place so of course they had work to do, but divorce? He'd made a commitment to Lily for life when they exchanged wedding vows. She had too. You didn't walk away from that at the drop of a hat. She could argue that two years wasn't the drop of a hat but there were a lot of factors at play and divorce was not an option. Not in his mind.

He put his hand on the back of the couch to steady himself, relieved he'd put the wine in the kitchen—there was a good chance he would have dropped it on the floor after hearing Lily's bombshell.

He was struggling to breathe and little black spots

danced in the corners of his vision. He took a moment to force air into his lungs, to combat the feeling of utter terror that swamped him. He hadn't tried to stop her when she'd left him—maybe he should have but he knew she'd needed her family around her. He hadn't been able to fix her, he hadn't been able to give her what she needed, all he'd been able to do was let her go. But he'd had no intention of letting her go permanently. He'd assumed she'd come back to him. Maybe that had been a mistake. But he wasn't going to give in without a fight now. There had to be something he could do.

He forced his feet to move and somehow made it around to the front of the couch. He sank onto the cushions, facing Lily across the low coffee table. 'You want a divorce?'

She nodded.

'When did you decide this?'

She shrugged.

'What does that mean?' he asked, unable to decipher her gesture.

'I've been thinking about it for a while. Wondering what we're doing. What the point is of being married any more.' She wouldn't meet his eyes and he knew there was something else going on. Something she wasn't telling him.

'What do you mean what's the point? Marriage is a commitment. We made a commitment. To each other. You don't just give up on that and you don't get to make a unilateral decision.' He knew they had unresolved issues but he hadn't, in a million years, expected those issues to bring them to this. She was his wife. He loved her and he wasn't going to give her up quietly. There had to be something he could do. He had to fix this.

'I'm not,' she argued. 'I think we should talk about it, that was why I called and left you a message, but I think a divorce makes sense.'

He couldn't disagree more. 'Sense? How on earth does it make sense?'

She was frowning. A little crease appeared between her blue eyes. 'This can't come as a complete surprise. We haven't lived together for two years.'

'Because you left me!'

'You didn't try to stop me.'

When Lily had told him she wanted to go home, to leave London and return to Australia he hadn't argued. He was frantically busy with his work and study and Lily was spending a lot of time on her own. He figured she needed a break and he was happy for her to go, he didn't know how else he could help her. When he'd said goodbye, he'd done so assuming that she would return to London at some point. But he hadn't counted on a global pandemic. He knew she could have returned despite what was happening in the world—it wouldn't have been easy but it was far from impossible. She had a work visa. She could have come back at some point in the past two years. But she hadn't.

And he hadn't been in a position to go after her. Until now.

'I thought it was what you wanted,' he said. 'I thought you wanted a trip home.'

'It wasn't what I wanted. But I couldn't stay. I needed to come home.'

She was right, he hadn't tried to stop her from leaving but he wasn't going to take all the blame. He had been committed to his fellowship but he'd never wavered in his commitment to his marriage. But what about to Lily herself? Had he given her the attention she needed? He knew he hadn't made her needs a priority after she'd left, he'd focused on his work and had figured he'd make it up to her later. But the months had passed and they'd remained apart. He realised now that they'd each been waiting for the other one to come back and it seemed Lily had grown tired of waiting.

Well, he was here now. And there was one thing he was certain of. 'I didn't come back from the other side of the world to get a divorce.'

'I didn't know you were coming back.'

He'd been foolish not to tell her that he was coming home but he'd been frantic trying to speed up the process of moving and starting his new position. He'd decided to surprise her even though he hadn't been a hundred per cent certain of the reception he'd get but this was completely unexpected. She'd checkmated him with a surprise of her own.

'Can I ask you why you've decided now that you want a divorce? Why not six months ago? A year ago?' There could only be one reason, he suddenly realised as his stomach turned. 'Have you met someone else?'

Lily was shaking her head. 'No.'

Thank God, he thought, as a small semblance of hope returned. From the first moment he'd laid eyes on Lily he'd known he wanted to get to know her and from their first date he'd known he wanted to marry her. That meant spending the rest of his life with her but of the five years they'd been married they'd spent two of them apart. Was that too long? Or was this one case when time would heal all wounds? He didn't know the answer to that but he would find out.

He had no idea.

His biggest regret was that he hadn't known how to help Lily. He liked to fix things but he hadn't been able to fix her. He'd been at a loss. Her physical injuries had healed but the emotional wounds had been harder to treat. He knew his actions had compounded her emotional scars and so, to lessen his guilt over the part he had played, he'd let her go.

Now he was nervous, uncertain, and it was an unpleasant feeling. He always looked for the positives in a situation, practising mindfulness, something he'd worked hard on after his mother had died and he'd learned that even on a bad day there was usually something good to be found. He didn't mind a challenge but he felt as if he was three steps behind Lily and that put him at a disadvantage. But he refused to give up. He wouldn't give in. He knew he would fight for her but if she wasn't prepared to surrender he wasn't sure what he could do.

'Does the fact that I'm back change things?' His motto had always been not to worry about things he couldn't change but he wanted to change her mind.

'I don't know.'

She was fiddling with her wedding ring, spinning it on her finger. The movement caught his eye and buoyed his sprits. She hadn't removed her rings, surely that was a good sign?

Otto reached out and ran his thumb over the gold band on her finger. 'You're still wearing your wedding ring,' he said.

Lily's heart leapt and her breath caught in her throat. She resisted the urge to close her eyes, to curl her fingers around his hand, to pull him close.

The touch of his thumb on her skin sent her pulse skyrocketing. She knew there was no truth in the folklore that a vein connected her ring finger directly to her heart but it certainly felt like it to her. She hadn't counted on feeling so connected to him still and her physical reaction to him took her by surprise. Emotionally she was still fragile, still desperate to hear him acknowledge her pain, but there was no denying there remained a connection between them. A connection wasn't quite broken yet.

Which was one reason she still wore her wedding ring. It was a part of her. A part of her dreams, and taking off her rings was going to be the last step, the point of no return, and a step she wasn't prepared to take until they were divorced. Was she still holding out hope that they could fix things? Was she scared? Frightened?

She'd never wanted to remove her rings and, in a way, keeping them on her finger kept her safe. Despite being separated from Otto by oceans and time she hadn't been at all interested in other men and if she looked married it discouraged men from asking her out. She suspected that didn't bode well for finding a partner in the future but she'd take it one step at a time. And the first step was getting a divorce. She knew that while she remained legally married to Otto she wouldn't be able to move on. It wouldn't feel right.

'We're still married,' she said as she pulled her hand free and covered her rings, knowing she would have to remove them if she got divorced. That thought scared her a little. She'd have to join the dating scene. She hadn't really thought that through. In her head she had gone from married to Otto to having babies but she hadn't thought about *how* she was going to meet someone to have babies with. Ever since she'd met Otto she'd never looked at another man. Her attraction to him had been immediate and complete and every cell in her body still remembered him. Just like the day they first met.

She had been a final year med student. He was a registrar. Lily had noticed him the moment she'd stepped into the ICU. He was standing beside the specialist, she no longer remembered who the specialist was or what the patient's diagnosis had been and she didn't think she knew at the time either—Otto had captured her attention and that was it.

She had noticed him immediately and their eyes had locked but she hadn't been able to maintain eye contact. She'd looked away, forced herself to focus on the patient but she hadn't heard a word that anyone else in the ward round had said. She'd felt Otto's eyes on her the entire time.

He was tall, dark and handsome and exuded confidence but it was so much more than that. He didn't pretend that he wasn't looking at her but his attention hadn't made her uncomfortable. She was used to attention, she was tall, blonde, athletic and she knew she was considered pretty, but she wasn't confident and she didn't court attention. She usually tried to make herself less noticeable. But she was drawn to Otto. She had a sense that they were supposed to meet, that their paths were destined to cross. She would normally dismiss that feeling as ridiculous hippy nonsense born out of her childhood growing up in a commune, but the sense that their souls were speaking to each other, as stupid as it sounded, was too strong to ignore. She didn't *want* to ignore it and at the end of the ward round she found herself concocting a question and directing it to Otto, making sure he had to answer her. He'd offered to go over some case notes with her, they'd chatted and laughed, he'd invited her for a drink after work and they'd been together ever since.

He was funny, cute, confident and self-assured. He knew what he wanted and she found that attractive. Growing up, she'd been surrounded by drifters. No one on the commune ever seemed to have firm plans or any desire to achieve anything other than to get to the next day. They took everything one day at a time but Lily wasn't wired that way and she often felt as if she was the only one with goals, as if she was the odd one out.

She had one goal in mind. To get out of Byron Bay.

She'd studied hard with that goal in sight and when she'd been accepted into medical school at the age of eighteen she'd left Byron Bay and headed to university in Sydney. She hadn't looked back.

She'd felt a calling to medicine. When Lily was fifteen, her eight-year-old sister, Willow, had died after contracting mumps. Willow had been Daisy's identical twin, the youngest of the five Carlson siblings, and if Lily's parents had believed in childhood vaccinations, then Willow, in all likelihood, would still be with them today.

Daisy had also contracted mumps and had lost her hearing as a result of the viral infection. She was now profoundly deaf but Willow's death had impacted on all of the siblings in different ways and it had solidified Lily's ambition to become a doctor. She *wanted* to save lives. If it was in her power she would prevent any other family, any other siblings, from experiencing what she and her brother and sisters went through.

Getting into university, studying medicine, had become her focus. She'd had no plan for her life past finishing university. That had seemed a monumental goal at the time and it was all she could manage. She'd had one plan, one goal, and she figured she'd work out what to do next once she'd achieved that first step.

But Otto had known exactly what he wanted. In life. In his career. And he knew when he met Lily that she was the one for him. That knowledge had bolstered her confidence. She'd been buoyed by his adoration, his conviction that they were meant to be together. She'd been swept along by his belief that anything was possible as long as they were together.

And together they had a plan.

Until the plan went awry and she had fled home, alone.

But now Otto was back. Without warning, without reason. She needed to know what he was thinking. She needed some answers.

'Why are you here?' she asked. 'In Sydney.'

'It was time to come home. I'd finished my fellowship and I had a job offer here.'

There was no mention of her, his wife.

He hadn't come back for her, she realised. For them.

There was no them. Not any more.

'I'm taking Leo Atwill's job,' he continued. 'You know he's retiring?'

Lily nodded; it had happened suddenly but she knew Leo was retiring for health reasons. But Otto's announcement felt like a knife through her already bleeding heart. 'You came back here because of the job? Not for me?' She hated that she was asking but she couldn't stop herself.

'Of course, you were part of it.'

'Bu you didn't even discuss it with me?' How important was she if he didn't even bother to mention his plans?

'It all happened in a hurry,' Otto continued. 'There was a lot to organise but it seemed serendipitous that a job came up at Bondi General. I thought it would be nice to work together. You don't look like you agree?' he said, reading the uncertainty in Lily's expression.

She hadn't ever worked with Otto. She'd been a medical student, then an intern, then a registrar but they'd never worked together and she was kidding herself if she thought she was going to be able to work with him regularly without getting caught up in memories. Not even memories. Her reaction to his unexpected touch had nothing to do with memories and everything to do with chemistry. Neither her head nor her heart nor her hormones had forgotten him. How was she going to manage?

She would have to find a way.

And quickly. Otherwise, she would have to look for another job and she didn't want to leave Bondi General. She loved her work. She loved the fact she was close to home, close to the beach, that she worked with good friends not to mention her sisters. She wouldn't let Otto's arrival push her out but she knew it was unlikely that he would move. He'd just arrived.

She'd have to find a solution.

'Working together might make things awkward when we get divorced,' she said.

'I don't want a divorce,' he countered.

'We haven't lived together for two years. The courts would grant me a divorce on the grounds that we have been separated for more than twelve months.'

'Have you looked into it already?'

He sounded unhappy. 'No,' she said. 'But I know from other friends that's how it works.'

'But we're not officially separated,' he argued. He closed his eyes and tipped his head back, lifting his hands and running them through his hair. He let out a heavy sigh and opened his eyes, looking directly at Lily. 'You have to see this has come out of the blue for me. You've taken me completely by surprise.'

'I felt the same when you turned up at work today.'

'I didn't intend to spring my return on you like that. I wanted to see you before I started work, I planned to. I wanted us to have a private conversation but obviously it didn't turn out that way and I'm sorry. Look,' he implored, 'I realise we're not going to be able to sort this out tonight but do you think you could hold off making any decisions for now?'

'What are you suggesting?'

'Don't do anything. Sit tight. Don't file for divorce until we've had a chance to have a proper conversation. I'm jet-lagged and a bit shell-shocked to be honest. I need some time.'

'How much time?' She frowned.

'Can you give me three months?'

'Three months!' She'd thought he might say a few days but months! 'What will another three months achieve?'

'It will give us time to see how we feel. To see if we can fix things.'

Otto *always* thought he could fix things.

'Not everything can be fixed,' she retorted. 'Some things are too broken.' *She* felt broken. 'I don't know if I can give you months.'

'Why on earth not? When we got married you promised me a lifetime. Surely you can give me another three months.'

Lily took a deep breath as she tried to get her emotions under control. It was true, she'd made promises that she'd had every intention of keeping but things hadn't turned out quite like she'd expected. 'That was before,' she said.

'Before what?' he asked, as if he didn't know. As if he couldn't guess.

She could feel the old wounds beginning to gape again. Thoughts she'd worked so hard to suppress. Did she have to spell it out for him? 'Before we lost our baby.'

'Lily, if I could go back in time and change that, I would. You know I would.'

'Do I know that?' she asked. 'I have no idea what you'd do any more. Not after that. You didn't want children back then. You never wanted that baby.'

'That's not true.'

'Why would you go back and change what happened? I want a family,' she continued without giving him a chance to argue his point. 'That's why I need a divorce. I can't have a family on my own. I need to start again.'

'You don't need to start again. I'm right here.'

Did she dare believe they could make their marriage work? She knew they had things to resolve but if he was willing to start a family would she be prepared to work on their relationship? Could it be fixed? She wasn't sure but if he was ready to have a family she knew she'd be willing to negotiate her position. It wasn't to say they didn't have other issues to sort out, she still didn't know if she could trust him to support her if things went wrong, but what if he was ready to have a family?

'Do you want children?' she asked. 'Right now?'

He hesitated and she knew the answer.

'We agreed to wait until you were thirty-two,' he said. 'Until we'd established our careers.'

'I've changed my mind.' She realised she'd moved the goalposts but only after they'd been accidentally moved two years ago. That event had been enough to change her mindset.

'Why?'

She'd put her dreams aside for the past two years but now they were back in full force. 'I have a hole in my heart and the only way I can fill it is with a family of my own.'

'Lily, please, can't you give us a chance? Can't you give *me* one more chance?'

'I don't know.' Something was missing in her life and she needed to fix it. It was up to her.

All her life, responsibilities had fallen to her. As the eldest sibling she'd taken on the responsibility of looking after her brother and sisters. She'd never had anyone look out for her. She'd always relied on herself. When she'd met Otto she'd thought finally there was someone who would take care of her but he had let her down too. It was up to her to determine her future. 'I need to fix this,' she said.

'Won't you let me help? There must be something I can do? Tell me. Is there anything? What about counselling? What if we tried that?'

'What difference would that make?'

'I don't know,' Otto admitted. 'But I'm not just going to give up. Please, Lil, don't throw our marriage away. Three months and some counselling, that's all I'm asking for. Then, if you still want a divorce, I'll give you one.'

Lily knew she shouldn't give in. She was terrified that Otto would break her heart all over again but it wasn't as easy as she thought it would be to give him up. Not while he was sitting in front of her pleading for another chance. Not when she could see his face, hear his voice and reach out and touch him.

Now that the moment was here she was reluctant to give it all away. To give him away. Despite everything that had happened she knew she still loved him. Maybe, just maybe, if he still loved her too, she could convince him that adding children to their lives was the next step they should be taking.

She nodded. She knew she was risking everything but she also knew her heart would break no matter what she did. Did she want her heart broken now or in three months' time?

She closed her eyes. She didn't want to see the pain in Otto's dark eyes, she knew it was a reflection of her own. She didn't want her heart broken now, which meant she had only one option—she'd give Otto what he wanted. 'OK. Three months,' she agreed, crossing her fingers that the potential reward of a family of her own was worth the risk of heartbreak.

'And counselling?'

'I'll think about it,' she replied, buying herself a little time.

She didn't want to discuss her marriage with a stranger. She didn't want to discuss her failings as a wife because she knew, no matter how much blame she laid at Otto's feet, some of it had to lie at hers as well.

Was she prepared to open herself up to that?

CHAPTER THREE

LILY WAS ALONE AGAIN.

Otto had left, he'd gone back to his hotel. She felt conflicted about him staying in a hotel. This was his house after all, perhaps she should offer to move out? He should be able to live in his own house. But she knew she couldn't stay there with him.

She was finding it hard to keep her thoughts moving in an orderly fashion. Normally she was focused, able to compartmentalise, but Otto's arrival had her confused. Her mind was muddled and she found herself jumping between thoughts. Her head was telling her one thing but when she saw him, when he smiled at her or touched her hand, her heart told her something else altogether.

No, not her heart. Just her hormones. They'd get used to him being around soon enough, she thought as she sliced some lemon and added it to a jug of water, which she carried out to the deck, placing it on the table, keeping busy as she waited for her sisters. After Otto had left, the house had felt way too empty so she'd messaged her siblings and invited them over. Jet was busy but Poppy and Daisy were on their way. She needed their company—she was worried that if she was alone she might be tempted to call Otto and ask him to come back. It was much better to call her siblings while her mind was in turmoil.

Poppy had offered to pick up takeaway from Lao Lao's kitchen, Jet's fiancée's family restaurant, and Lily had happily agreed. As the eldest sibling she'd always taken on the role of looking after her younger brother and sisters and it was nice to have someone look after her for a change.

'So, I'm guessing you're about to tell us that Otto is back?' Poppy said as she helped herself to another dumpling from a container.

Poppy didn't meet her eye but Lily didn't miss the glance she shared with Daisy and she realised that her news wasn't going to be news at all. 'You knew that?' she asked, looking at Daisy, making sure she could read her lips, knowing Poppy would be able to hear her question while Daisy's hearing impairment would make that impossible.

'Ajay told me he'd met him at work,' Daisy said.

'He knew who he was?' Lily realised she'd been foolish to think she could keep her relationship to Otto a secret. The hospital grapevine was constantly working in overtime and with most of Lily's family connected to the hospital in some way her marital situation was bound to be discovered sooner or later.

'He knew your husband is a doctor named Otto…' Daisy said, leaving her comment to trail off and leaving Lily wondering why until Poppy filled in the gap.

'He might have heard Otto was coming back.'

'How?' Lily frowned. *She* hadn't even known. Daisy's fiancé, Ajay, worked in the emergency department with Lily—he would be no more privy to who was being hired than she was.

'I have a confession to make,' Poppy added. 'Ryder and I invited him to our wedding.'

'What? Why?'

'He's family. I didn't want to exclude him.'

'Our parents are family too but you're not inviting them.' Lily knew Ryder had suggested a couple of times to Poppy that she should invite her parents, worried that she might have regrets later, but Poppy remained resolute and her parents remained uninvited.

'I wanted Otto to be there. I thought you'd be pleased to see him.'

'He told me he came back because he was offered a position at Bondi General.' Lily was confused. 'He hasn't mentioned your wedding.'

'He didn't come back because of our wedding. When I invited him he said he was coming home anyway. He'd already accepted the job at Bondi General, our wedding just gave him a deadline.'

'Why didn't you tell me you'd invited him?'

'I assumed he would.'

'Well, he didn't.'

'I didn't realise he hadn't.'

'You're not pleased he's back?' Daisy signed.

'Maybe a year ago I would have been,' Lily replied, using her hands to communicate. All the Carlson siblings had learnt to sign after Daisy had lost her hearing as a child. Daisy often preferred to use sign language, particularly in a group situation, as she found it hard to follow multiple conversations if she had to lip read.

'What does that mean?' Daisy hands fired back another question.

'I feel a bit unravelled by it all, to be honest,' she admitted. A year ago her biological clock hadn't been ticking as loudly as it was now. Now it threatened to drown out every sensible thought in her head any time she found her mind wandering. A year ago she thought she could have looked at Otto without noticing the passing of time, without feeling the absence of children—not just the baby they'd lost but all the future children she wanted. She was running out of time but she didn't know if she was going to get what she needed from Otto. She had no idea if he was going to be prepared to meet her timeline. Was she wasting precious weeks by agreeing to counselling? By agreeing to give him those three months?

'I don't know what to think. What to do. What to say. I wasn't expecting him and I'm not prepared for this.' She realised that was one of the biggest factors contributing to her sense of upheaval. She hated feeling unprepared. All her life she'd committed time and energy to preparing for things—from tests, exams, job interviews and holidays, right through to Sydney and then London— she never went in blind. Her unconventional, chaotic and crazy childhood had taught her that she coped best if she knew what was coming, if she felt ready. Otto should have known that about her and she found herself a little irritated that he'd put her on the spot by arriving unannounced. She wasn't prepared in any way for his return.

'How is he?' Daisy asked, as concerned as always for everyone's feelings.

Lily shrugged. 'Fine.' Otto had an unwavering sense of optimism. Things had pretty much always worked out for him so why wouldn't he have a positive disposition? Even after her announcement she could tell he felt that this was just a glitch, a problem to solve, something to be fixed, and she knew he thought he'd be able to fix it. She wasn't so sure. But her sisters didn't know about the grenade she'd lobbed at Otto the moment he'd arrived home. She'd have to tell them.

'Maybe you just need some time to adjust to having him back,' Poppy suggested.

'Maybe…but I'd just made some big decisions and now he's back and it's messing with my plans.'

'What sort of big decisions?'

'I told him I want a divorce.'

'What? Why?'

'You can't divorce him. He's your person.'

Poppy and Daisy objected simultaneously.

'But what if he's not my person?'

'What do you mean?' Daisy asked.

'I know you think there's a person for everyone but there has to be more than one,' Lily argued. Plenty of people found love a second time around. Daisy's fiancé, Ajay, was a prime example. He'd been married before, happily married until tragedy struck, but he'd fallen in love with Daisy as well. But Lily wasn't going to give specific examples. She didn't want to remind Daisy of Ajay's past. She knew it as well as Lily did. 'And what if I chose the wrong person to start with?'

'No.' Daisy was shaking her head. 'I've seen you with Otto, we all have and yes, I know that some people are lucky enough to find love more than once but all of us fall hard and fast. I've decided that it's a Carlson trait. Look at Jet and Mei, Poppy and Ryder. They fell hard and fast and even with other relationships in between that love never died. Nothing else they found could compare to how things felt when they were with the one. I look at you and Otto and I see the same thing.'

Lily wasn't so sure. She used to think she and Otto were destined for each other but things had changed.

But what if Daisy was right? What if Otto was the only one for her? What if she was about to throw away her future? What if she never found happiness with someone else?

But she'd never know if she didn't try. 'We've been apart for almost two years,' Lily said. 'I can't waste any more time.'

'This is your marriage! You're not wasting time.'

Daisy might think Otto and Lily were meant to be but Daisy had always had a rose-coloured view of love. And just because Daisy thought the Carlsons were the type to give their hearts away once and only once didn't mean that Lily couldn't be the exception to the rule.

She and Otto had married quickly, they'd had a whirlwind courtship and then spent almost half of their married life apart. She had nothing to measure their relationship against. How was she to know if he was the right one for her, the only one for her?

How had they let themselves get to this point?

'Can you tell me what brought you here today?'

Lily perched rigidly on the edge of the sofa in the therapist's office, feeling as if she was getting ready to bolt for the door at any moment.

Poppy's fiancé, Ryder, had recently started work as a psychologist. He worked with at risk teenagers but had passed on a recommendation for a marriage counsellor. Lily had agreed to counselling, knowing she would recommend the same to her siblings or friends and knowing she owed Otto that much at least. She just hoped it wasn't a waste of time. She didn't think counselling would fix their problems but perhaps it would give them closure on their relationship.

She looked around the room, trying to calm her nerves. The space was decorated in neutral tones, with pot plants to soften the space and sheer curtains at the open window. The counsellor had positioned a small three-seater couch opposite her armchair and there was a second armchair to the right of the couch. It looked like a lounge room and was obviously decorated with the aim of relaxing its occupants but despite that Lily was on edge and she was aware of Otto's tension as well. But while she was stiff and uptight his unease made him restless. He'd chosen to sit on the couch with her, ignoring the single armchair. Was that habit, for show or did he really want to sit beside her? She didn't know.

She returned her attention to the therapist. What had Helen asked? Why were they here?

Lily had known they'd be asked that question but she found herself suddenly unprepared. She was nervous, anxious, tongue-tied. It reminded her of the feeling she'd experienced before oral exams in medical school. What if she didn't know the answer? What if she got one wrong and the lecturer thought she didn't know her topic?

She thought about her answer now. Was it wrong to open with 'I want a divorce'?

Was that still what she wanted? She had agreed to give him three months. Perhaps it would sound better if she said she wanted a fresh start. But was that too ambiguous? Did she want a fresh start with Otto or with someone new?

She sighed. A fresh start with Otto wasn't possible. Not after everything that had happened. It wasn't easier to start again but it would be less painful. She couldn't look at Otto without remembering what she'd lost.

'Otto? Lily? I need to know why you're here today,' Helen repeated.

Lily flinched.

She was here because Otto had asked her to come. Because she'd told him she wanted a divorce. She needed to be honest. She owed it to herself and to Otto.

Otto and Helen were both looking at her, waiting for her to speak. Why did she have to go first?

'I want a divorce,' she said. She'd wanted to sound so certain, so sure of herself, but her mouth was dry and her voice was barely above a whisper. Her future without Otto had been so much easier to imagine while Otto was on the other side of the world. It was *a lot* harder when he was sitting beside her.

'And I don't,' Otto stated.

Lily couldn't help but notice how determined he sounded even though there was nothing he could do to prevent a divorce, nothing except try to change her mind.

'I am used to seeing couples who have differing points of view, it goes with my job, and I appreciate you've both taken time to come to see me today,' Helen replied. 'So that I can understand your situation, can you tell me what you are hoping to achieve through counselling?

'Maybe it would be easier for you if I explain how I see my role,' she continued when neither Lily nor Otto were forthcoming with any more details. 'My role is to help you work through what your issues are. What your needs are. To help you work out if these are things that you can work on, if these are things you *want* to work on. It might be behaviours that need to be modified, it might be expectations. And that will be the case for both of you. I hear you already have differing points of view. This is your opportunity to work out if you are prepared

to consider working together on your marriage or if it's
time to step away. We will not be apportioning blame.
Marriage is a partnership and you have to work together
if you want it to be successful.

'I will give you things to think about,' Helen said,
'things to talk about, but I cannot give you the answers.
I can't tell you what to do nor can I make the decisions
for you. It is up to the two of you to determine where you
go from here. If I can start with you, Lily. You said you
want a divorce.' She paused, waiting for Lily's response.

Lily nodded.

'I'm a counsellor, not a divorce lawyer. Why have you
chosen to come to counselling?'

'Otto asked me to.'

'Why did you *agree* to come?' Helen rephrased her
question.

Coming to counselling was a way to assuage her
guilt for her part in all this. She'd blamed Otto but she
was the one who had walked away from their marriage. It had been easier to walk away, to try to outrun
her sorrow, than to confront their issues and she felt
guilty for that.

Staying in London would have meant seeing Otto
every day. Being reminded of everything they'd lost.
Being reminded that there were still only two of them
when there should have been three and that she was partly
responsible for that. Running away had meant she could
avoid thinking about what had happened, to some degree. Putting some distance between her and Otto had
let her forget what had happened, if only for short peri-
ods of time. But some respite from her guilt, her sadness,
her loss, was better than none at all. Some respite had

allowed her to function. Running away had enabled her to avoid admitting to her role in the tragedy.

She was still avoiding it.

And that was why she had agreed to come. It was easier to agree to counselling than it was to apologise for her part in all of this.

Was it also easier to ask for a divorce than to ask for forgiveness? Was it easier to ask for a divorce than to apologise?

It must be.

'If you've already decided you want a divorce, I take it you're not interested in saving your marriage?' Helen asked when Lily gave no response. 'What do you need from me?'

Did she want to save her marriage? She would have said yes two years ago, even one year ago, but now? Now she felt their paths had diverged too much. She wanted babies. He didn't. It was as simple as that. 'I thought maybe you could help us to communicate better with each other.'

'Has that been an issue?'

Lily nodded again. 'We seem to have difficulty discussing the important things. Like divorce. If Otto and I don't agree that a divorce is the best thing for us, then that's a difficult conversation to have. I thought you might be able to help us with that process. I don't want to fight. I don't want to argue. I just want to move forward with my life. I thought counselling might give us closure.'

Lily could feel Otto tensing beside her. She didn't need to be looking at him to be aware of his reaction. Every one of her nerves was still attuned to him. Physically they were connected, it was emotionally where she felt the divide. His physical reactions were always obvious to her but his thoughts were harder to decipher.

'Otto?' Helen asked. 'Why did you choose to have counselling?'

'Definitely not to help us get divorced. The opposite. I hoped it would help us work out a way forward—together.'

'You understand that might not be possible?'

'Yes.'

'Tell me about your situation,' the therapist asked. 'How long have you been married?'

'Almost five years. That has to be worth something, doesn't it, Lil?' Otto looked at her, his brown eyes dark and imploring.

Lily couldn't hold his gaze. She could see his pain, she felt it too, but the pain they shared wasn't lessened by sharing. Seeing him was a reminder of everything they'd lost and she couldn't trust him not to break her heart all over again.

He'd promised to take care of her. To love her always. And she felt he'd abandoned her at the first obstacle. In their marriage vows they'd promised to support each other but when things went wrong it hadn't brought them together, it had torn them apart. She turned back to Helen. 'But Otto has been in London for two years. We've been living apart.'

'That was your decision, Lily,' Otto said.

'Otto,' Helen interrupted. 'Let Lily talk. You will have your turn.'

'He didn't even tell me he was coming back,' Lily continued, ignoring Otto's comment. He was right, she had chosen to leave but he hadn't come after her, he'd chosen to let her go. 'That's just one example of our lack of communication. We used to be able to talk to each other.'

'What changed?'

'Lily stopped talking,' Otto replied as he turned to face her. 'You shut me out. You wouldn't tell me how you were feeling.'

She'd been scared to start talking, scared she'd lose control and wouldn't be able to recover. Scared of where she would end up.

'I was feeling the same way every day, alone with my sadness, alone with my grief, alone with my loss.'

'It was *our* loss, Lily,' Otto stressed, before telling Helen. 'We lost our baby at twenty-one weeks. That was when things changed.'

Helen was silent for a beat or two before asking, 'Do you want to talk about your loss, Lily?'

Lily shook her head, the irony not lost on her. She wanted to talk to Otto but she wasn't ready to talk to a stranger about their baby even if she was a counsellor. Lily's grief was still too raw to share with anyone else. It was personal. It was between her and Otto.

Lily knew it would be difficult for counselling to help her if she wasn't prepared to unpack some of her emotional baggage but then, she hadn't really expected counselling to help anyway. If she could learn how to find forgiveness, that would be a start.

She was aware that Helen was observing them. It made her nervous. What was she looking for? What did she see?

'You were in London together?'

Lily nodded.

'But you came back alone?'

'Almost two years ago.'

'Why did you do that?'

'I needed things that I couldn't get in London.'

'Like?'

'Comfort. I needed comfort and company.'

'But Otto was there.'

'Physically, yes. But not emotionally. We weren't communicating. I barely knew anyone and after our loss I felt even more alone. Adrift. I needed my siblings and I needed the ocean. This ocean.' She waved one arm in the direction of the Pacific Ocean. She and her siblings had spent their childhoods in the ocean, swimming and surfing. It was where she found calm, it was where her soul was restored. 'I needed to see it. I needed to be in it. And I needed to see the sun, to feel it on my skin. This is my home. I needed to come home.'

'Did you intend to go back?' Helen asked.

'I don't know.' She'd been so intent on leaving she hadn't thought about what came afterwards. About how long she'd stay away. She hadn't really intended not to go back but she hadn't returned either. She'd been in limbo. And she'd stayed there for two years. There were too many painful memories in London.

'You said you and Otto used to be able to talk to each other?'

Lily nodded.

'Do you agree, Otto?' Helen asked.

'Yes.'

'I'm going to give you some homework. Do you remember your first date?'

'Yes,' they answered simultaneously. Lily could feel Otto looking at her but she refused to meet his gaze this time. She didn't want to share that moment. She needed to block out those memories if she wanted to move forwards.

'Where did you go?'

'We went for a drink at a bar near the hospital where we met,' Otto replied.

'Good. I want you to go out together. I want you to talk to each other as if you've just met. Get to know each other again. Listen. Put everything that has happened aside, just for the moment,' Helen added, probably in response to Lily's expression.

'What is the point in that?' Lily asked.

'It's an exercise in listening. I don't want you talking about big things, things that require debate or discussion. I want you to talk about simple things. Practise your listening skills, show an interest in what the other person is saying without having to think of an argument. Without conflict, without agenda. Talk about what you do in your spare time, about your hobbies, the movies you like, your favourite places to visit. Think about all the things you wanted to know about each other when you first met.

'You need to open the lines of communication but you need to choose a neutral topic,' Helen continued. 'Something that isn't associated with your relationship, something that isn't raw and emotional. Something that won't lead you to judge each other's feelings. You can work your way up to those big discussions once you feel that you can trust each other to be honest. Once you know you can listen without judgement. When you can listen without assuming how the other person is feeling. I want you to start over.

'Do you think you can do that, Otto? Lily?'

Lily nodded. She wasn't sure but she was prepared to give it a try. She had never been given a homework task that she hadn't completed and she couldn't agree to counselling and then refuse to commit to the process.

'There's a bar across the road,' Otto said as they left Helen's office. 'Shall we go there?'

'You want to do this now?'

'Why not?'

Lily could think of a million reasons why not, including the fact that she would prefer time to prepare mentally for the homework Helen had set them. She'd prefer time to think about some safe, neutral topics of conversation and to find a safe, neutral venue. A wine bar wasn't what she had in mind. 'You want to go to a bar? This isn't a date. It's an exercise.'

'That doesn't mean we can't enjoy ourselves, that we can't have fun. You do remember how to have fun, don't you?'

She was too embarrassed to admit that maybe she didn't. Otto was always the one who brought the fun to their relationship. She was much more serious. Her life before she met Otto hadn't been a lot of fun and life without Otto *definitely* hadn't been fun. But she wasn't going to tell him that.

'Come on, let me buy you a drink.'

He grinned at her and held out his hand and she could feel her resistance folding. She'd have to work on strengthening her resolve if she hoped to execute her plan. She couldn't afford to let Otto back into her life. There was too much at stake.

But she had agreed to the homework so she crossed the road but ignored his outstretched hand. Not that Otto seemed to mind. She could tell by his expression that he was taking her acquiescence as a victory to him. She'd let him have this one but the battle was far from over.

There was a small courtyard at the back of the bar and Otto found them a table for two under the vines. It was a lovely evening to sit outdoors, warm and still. He passed her a drinks list. 'What can I get you?' he asked.

'I'll have a gin and tonic, thanks.'

'Would you like anything to eat?'

She shook her head. Having something to eat would take longer and she would find it more difficult to escape. One drink would be enough.

'Where shall we start?' Otto asked as he returned from the bar with their drinks.

'I don't know, this feels so pointless.'

'What does?'

'Having to sit here and make small talk,' she said. 'I already know everything about you.'

'It's homework, Lil. Do you want to go back to Helen and tell her you didn't do it?'

She'd always been studious. She knew she wouldn't. And Otto knew that too. 'No.'

'We've got two years of catching up to do. I don't really know what you've been up to although Jet tells me he is a father, which makes you an auntie.'

'You've spoken to Jet?'

'We've stayed in touch.'

Lily knew Otto had spoken to Poppy but she didn't realise he 'kept in touch' with any of her siblings on a regular basis and hearing it was Jet was doubly surprising. Lily sometimes wondered if Jet would keep in touch with his own sisters if they didn't make an effort but Otto had always got along well with her family. His willingness to embrace her siblings was one of the many things she'd found attractive about him and that didn't seem to have changed. She wondered what else about him hadn't changed. There were some things she wanted to stay the same and others she needed to know had evolved.

'So, I have a niece.'

She nodded. 'I guess you do.'

'And An Na is what…seven?'

'Yes. She's amazing and Daisy is going to be a step-mum to a two-year-old, Niki.'

'I've met Ajay. He seems like a good bloke.'

'He is. Daisy is madly in love.'

'So all three of your siblings are settling down.'

Lily nodded. 'It's been a whirlwind five months.' And it had reignited her desire for a family of her own and had put her on the path to asking Otto for a divorce. 'It's ironic, isn't it?'

'What is?'

'I'm the one who desperately wants kids and Jet and Daisy will both have a family before me. Poppy probably will too.'

'You've got a family. You've got me.'

Lily shook her head. 'You know what I mean. I want kids.'

'I do too.'

'But not right now.'

'No.'

'Why not?'

'I want to get my career established first. We've talked about this.'

'Are you prepared for it to cost us our marriage?'

'I'm hoping it won't come to that,' he replied.

'It will unless one of us changes our minds. Otherwise nothing will be resolved.'

'Let's see what happens,' he said.

She knew he was expecting her to change her mind. He should know better.

The timely arrival of a waitress at their table broke

the thread of the conversation. She delivered some small share plates—flatbread and dips and salt and pepper calamari with golden fries. Lily pinched a chip from the bowl. If she had her mouth full she wouldn't be expected to talk.

'I thought you weren't eating?' Otto teased as he pushed the bowl closer to her.

'They smell so good,' she said.

'I ordered extra… I knew you'd want some. You always did prefer to eat off my plate.'

That was true. No matter what she ordered when they ate out she always ended up preferring whatever Otto had ordered. He'd always been happy to share and there were plenty of times where he'd even swapped orders with her. She'd forgotten how generous he was in some ways.

'What do your parents think of becoming grandparents?' Otto asked as she sampled the calamari.

Her parents were far from typical and if Lily hade ever entertained a notion of them changing their ways she was yet to see any evidence of it. Even the arrival of grandchildren wasn't enough to bring out their nurturing side.

'They haven't met An Na yet.'

'No?'

'Dad had a cerebral aneurysm about the same time that we found out about An Na.'

'You didn't tell me.'

Lily thought he could add that to the long list of things she'd never told him. She didn't have a close relationship with her parents—growing up on a commune hadn't fostered close ties and she disagreed with a lot of their beliefs. Her strained relationship with them meant they rarely entered into her conversations, with Otto or anyone else. She shrugged. 'He's recovering well but they haven't been down to Sydney. They don't seem in any hurry to meet An Na or Ajay's son, Niki.'

'They're still living on the commune?'

'Yes.'

'Have you seen your dad since his aneurysm?'

'The four of us did go up to Brisbane while he was in hospital but that was a few months ago. It was an interesting visit. Dad was quite forthcoming about their history, it was a bit of a revelation actually, and he apologised for some aspects of our childhood but while I appreciate the fact that he acknowledged their actions impacted us it didn't really atone for their behaviour. It doesn't excuse some of the things they did. Living on the commune was an easy way to opt out of responsibility and that is fine if you've only got yourself to think about but they had five children. Even if they were living in denial in the early years you'd think after Willow died they might think about the consequences of their choices and decisions and how that affected us. I'm not convinced they did their best in raising us and apologising now doesn't change that. They haven't changed either, they are still each other's priority. The four of us are a long way down their list and I don't think the arrival of grandchildren is going to change them. I don't think they'll necessarily want any involvement with grandchildren or that my siblings will want them involved.'

'Will they be at Poppy's wedding?'

'No.' They hadn't been at Lily and Otto's either.

'You know Poppy and Ryder have invited me. Is that OK with you?'

'It is.' Lily wasn't going to tell Poppy who she could

and couldn't invite. 'We're working together anyway. I can't avoid you.'

'Do you want to?'

The honest answer was no but she knew it would make her life a lot easier if she did keep her distance. She'd be able to keep a clearer head for a start.

As he waited for her answer Otto reached across the table. 'Hold still,' he said as he stretched out one hand. 'You've got aioli on your face.'

He brushed his thumb over her cheek, running it across her skin from the corner of her mouth. His hand was warm, his touch gentle and it made her breath catch in her throat, made her forget the question.

It was so long since anyone had touched her like that— gently, with familiarity—and it felt so intimate. Her body still knew him even if her mind was trying to forget. It was the same when he'd run his thumb over her wedding ring. She'd missed that sensation. Would she find that connection with someone else or was Daisy right? Was Otto her person?

No. If he didn't want kids he wasn't her person. He couldn't be.

Lily stood up. It was time to go. The things she liked about Otto hadn't changed. He could still make her laugh. He could still make her pulse race. He still made her feel alive but she knew they still had hurdles to get over. What she didn't know was if they were hurdles she had the energy to jump or if they were barriers she couldn't control. Were they hurdles Otto had to take down or ones she had to learn to live with?

That was a dilemma for another day but she knew she didn't have infinite days to answer the questions. She had a biological clock and it was ticking. And she knew it would get louder as Poppy and Daisy started families of their own. She was thirty years old. She was torn and confused and she wasn't sure she could continue like this for three months. She'd go mad.

CHAPTER FOUR

'INCOMING AMBULANCE,' JULIE announced to the ED. 'Jet ski accident. Teenager with suspected spinal injuries.'

'I'll take it,' Lily responded. 'Who's the trauma surgeon on call?' she asked, knowing it was better to forewarn the specialist, knowing in this instance it was unlikely they wouldn't be required.

'Otto. I'll page him now.'

Of course, it would be Otto, Lily thought. She hadn't seen him since the re-enactment of their first date two days ago because she'd been on days off, but it was becoming obvious that it was going to be impossible to avoid him at work.

She took a deep breath to calm her heart rate. There was always a spike of her pulse whenever an ambulance was expected as adrenalin kicked in when an emergency was announced. It mattered not that she felt confident in her skills—that fight-or-flight response was triggered every time and flight was not an option. But she knew her heart rate had escalated more than normal and she knew that, along with the flight response preparing her to deal with the emergency, there was an element of flight response as a reaction to knowing Otto was on his way.

She changed her gown, replacing the dirty one with

a fresh one, along with fresh gloves. She could hear the approaching siren and she hurried to the ambulance bay, leaving the ties of her gown undone. Someone would do them up for her outside.

Otto followed her out of the hospital. She saw him in her peripheral vision as he strode out to the ambulance bay, his inherent confidence evident, looking as though he'd been working at Bondi General for years, not days.

She listened as he greeted everyone by name. She knew he would have made a conscious effort to get to know the names of colleagues. He was good at making friends. His father was a defence force doctor and Otto had moved frequently as a child and he'd become adept at making friends easily out of necessity, but he was a social person by nature too. He enjoyed company, the bigger and louder the crowd, the better. Lily was happier in a small group of close friends or family.

'Hey, Lil.' He greeted her last. She frowned at his intimate abbreviation of her name. She'd asked him to keep their relationship a secret for now. Her colleagues knew she had a husband but she didn't need them to know it was Otto. Not yet, not while they were sorting out their relationship. There was nothing to tie them together, neither of them had worked at Bondi General before they'd moved to London and she practised under her maiden name so keeping their marital status private was going to save them from being the subject of any gossip. As a schoolgirl she'd been gossiped about on plenty of occasions because of her family's living arrangements on the commune and she'd learnt to avoid giving people any ammunition.

'Otto.' She kept her response brief. Despite not wanting to advertise their relationship she was annoyed that he'd greeted her last. As if she wasn't important.

She was still conflicted. Irritated on one hand, drawn to him on the other. She couldn't pretend that the sight of him didn't set her heart racing.

She turned her back slightly. If she avoided looking at him she'd give her pulse a chance to slow down.

'Do you want me to tie your gown?' he asked, obviously seeing the loose ties as she'd turned away from him.

His arrival had distracted her and she'd forgotten to ask someone to do it for her. Before she could answer, before she could say no, he had stepped behind her. She jumped as his fingers brushed the nape of her neck. She had to force herself not to close her eyes as long-forgotten memories of his warm hands on her skin threatened to overpower her. Her body remembered him and she could feel herself wanting to sway towards him. She took a deep breath, clenched her fists and tensed the muscles in her legs as she fought to stay still.

Did his fingers linger a little longer than necessary on her shoulders? Or were her senses heightened? She wondered how she was going to extricate herself from the situation when she felt his hands drop away.

'All done,' he said as the ambulance pulled into the bay, allowing her to take a step forward, putting some distance between them and enabling her to recover her equilibrium.

She breathed out and let her shoulders relax as her future sister-in-law climbed out of the driver's seat.

Otto greeted Mei as if they were old friends and Lily wondered when they'd met. It must have been in the past couple of days. He hadn't said anything about meeting

Mei when they'd gone for their 'date'. Why hadn't Jet and Mei included her when they caught up with Otto?

But she knew why. Because of the bombshell she'd dropped on Otto.

That didn't stop her from feeling irritated. She had never been one whose emotional responses had easily seesawed but since Otto had reappeared in her life her emotions seemed to be in a constant state of flux.

Jet was *her* brother, which made Mei *her* family. Why did Otto get to spend time with them?

The answer was simple—Otto and Jet were friends, and she couldn't do anything about that.

But what would that mean for her future? It was just another thing she hadn't considered.

When she'd decided she wanted a divorce Otto had been overseas. Having him back in Bondi was a scenario she hadn't thought about and it was obvious there was going to be a flow-on effect—to her at least. But she'd have to deal with that later, she thought as she switched her mind to their patient as the back door of the ambulance was opened and the stretcher was unlocked.

'Patient is a nineteen-year-old girl with head and suspected spinal injuries,' Mei told them as the stretcher was unloaded from the vehicle. Lily could see the girl had been intubated and immobilised to protect her spine from movement. 'She was a passenger on a jet ski with a group of friends,' Mei continued. 'There were multiple watercraft, she came off and was hit by the jet ski that was travelling behind. She was possibly hit in the head. Her friends dragged her from the water before lifeguards reached them. GCS of seven.'

That wasn't good. Three was the lowest possible score

and a Glasgow Coma Scale score of between three and eight indicated severe traumatic brain injury.

'Oxygen sats were eighty-nine per cent but climbing with treatment.' Mei continued to relay the patient's vitals. 'Pupils were equal and reactive.'

'Let's get her inside,' Otto instructed. 'Do you know if she's had any alcohol?' he asked as he helped Mei and Alex push the stretcher into the ED.

'I'm not certain,' Mei replied.

Lily knew alcohol could adversely affect the outcome in patients with a TBI. 'Do you know her name?' she asked.

'Chelsea.'

'All right,' Otto directed. 'Let's transfer her on the count of three.'

They slid her carefully onto a hospital bed, five of them working together, and Otto barely stopped his assessment. 'I need blood tests, including alcohol levels, a full blood count and I want her ABGs monitored,' he said as he connected the patient to a ventilator.

She observed and listened to Otto as he communicated with the staff and his non-responsive patient. He was confident and assured, directing the staff clearly, concisely and politely. He worked without ego and was obviously good at his job and Lily found his professional demeanour attractive. But she didn't *want* to find new things about him attractive. It was hard enough that her body betrayed her every time he was nearby, she didn't need her mind confusing her too.

'Lily, can you repeat the GCS, please?' Otto asked as he connected a monitor to Chelsea's ventilator to measure her exhaled carbon dioxide levels.

Lily ran through the tests for verbal performance,

motor responses and eye opening. Chelsea had no verbal response, but that was to be expected given that she was on a ventilator. She did withdraw from pain when Lily forcefully squeezed her trapezium muscle but her eyes remained closed in response to the painful stimuli.

'GCS is five.' That wasn't good news. Mei had earlier reported a score of seven.

Otto looked up. Lily could see he was worried but there was no sign of panic. He picked up a torch and checked Chelsea's pupils. 'Left pupil five millimetres, nonreactive. Right, two millimetres and sluggish,' he recounted. They all knew that the information indicated raised intercranial pressure meaning that Chelsea most likely had bleeding in or around her brain.

'Theatre?' Lily asked and, when Otto nodded, she lifted the phone and repeated the same procedure as on Otto's first day in the hospital, only this time she made sure she wasn't the one accompanying Otto in the lift to Theatres. Drama seemed to be following Otto, she didn't plan on doing the same.

'Chelsea didn't make it.'

Judging by the expression on Julie's face, Lily expected her to be the bearer of bad news but this was worse than she feared. Her first thought was that it was a tragic outcome for Chelsea's family, an afternoon of fun on the water had ended in tragedy with one life lost and plenty of other lives would be changed for ever as a direct consequence, but then her mind went straight to Otto, as it had been doing all afternoon.

Chelsea had certainly been in a critical condition when she'd been brought to hospital but sometimes the odds were in the patient's favour and sometimes they weren't.

The news that she hadn't survived shocked Lily but her sympathy lay with Otto.

How would he be feeling?

She knew he would be hurting. She knew it hit him hard when he lost a patient and she knew he hated having to be the bearer of bad news to a grieving family but she was conflicted. He'd never admitted to struggling emotionally when it had been the two of them suffering a loss. When they'd lost their own baby, he'd kept a stiff upper lip, he'd never showed any outward signs of despair or distress. She'd never been able to tell if his stoic countenance had been his way of coping or if the loss had not felt real to him. Had it been an intangible concept? She had been the one who had felt the baby move and grow inside her. She felt as if she'd known, almost from the moment of conception, that she was pregnant. She'd felt different. But she understood how foreign it might feel to a father, to Otto. That until he could hold the baby in his arms it might not feel real. But she had no idea about his mindset really. He'd never shared his thoughts or feelings with her about that time of their life.

But even if he wouldn't verbalise his feelings, she knew Chelsea's death would have affected him. What she didn't know was what, if anything, she should do next. Should she leave him to it? Should she seek him out? Was it any of her business any more?

She hated to think of him having no one to turn to if he needed a shoulder. A friendly face. Some support. Could she offer that to him?

She was the one who knew him best.

He had no one else.

She called past his office at the end of her shift but it was empty. One of the cardio-thoracic administration staff members told her that he'd left for the day. In the past he would have sought her out after a day like this, he would have wanted her company. Knowing he hadn't looked for her felt strange, upsetting, but she knew she couldn't have it both ways, not after she'd raised the topic of a divorce. She had no right to be hurt. He'd be hurting more than her.

She could have left it there, she could have gone home, but having decided to find him she now felt compelled to do so. If she found him and he didn't want her company he could tell her as much. She knew where he would have gone. He would need to let off steam and, like her, swimming cleared his head. He would be at the beach. What she didn't know was which one, but she'd start at Bondi. It was the closest.

She walked down to the beach, covering the few hundred metres in no time. She stopped near the lifeguard tower and leant on the railing that separated the parked cars from the beach. The elevation gave her a good view of the kilometre-long stretch of sand curving from the ocean pool in the south to the headland in the north. But it wasn't the sand she had her eye on. She swept her gaze over the ocean. It was after six but the summer heat was still intense and the beach was still busy but the real swimmers were few and far between and it didn't take her long to spot Otto. He was out past the breaking waves, swimming parallel to the shore and heading south towards the lifeguard tower.

The afternoon sun was warm on her back as she watched him swim. His strokes were even, smooth, hypnotic. She didn't mean to wait for him but she was still standing by the railing when he turned towards the beach.

She could have left then but her feet weren't moving and she was still there when he came out of the water.

His chest was smooth and pale. He hadn't had time yet to catch any sun. His swimming shorts clung to his thighs. He might be pale but he was in good shape. Superb shape, she thought as she took in the semi-naked sight of him.

He hadn't seen her and she watched as he walked up the sand towards her. He looked good. Better than she remembered. Had she forgotten or had she stopped paying attention?

He'd left his towel in front of the tower and he bent down to retrieve it, throwing it over his head and rubbing his hair dry. She remembered how he never bothered to dry his skin after a swim and sometimes even after a shower. She felt a blush steal across her cheeks as she recalled how, after showering, he'd stand at the mirror, naked, while he shaved or wander around the house naked while his skin dried. He would let the water evaporate from his body but he always dried his hair. It was sticking up now, stiff with salt.

He threw his towel over his shoulder and looked up. He smiled as their eyes met and she waited to see what he would do next.

He made his way across the sand and jogged up the stairs beside the lifeguard tower, coming to a stop beside her. 'Are you looking for me?'

She nodded. 'I wanted to check how you were.'

'You heard about Chelsea?'

'Yes. It sounded pretty awful.'

Otto wondered what it meant that Lily had come to find him, that she was checking in with him. Could he take it as a good sign? He wasn't sure. He didn't want to get his hopes up or make assumptions. He'd keep the conversation on a professional level.

He nodded. 'It was. She had severe trauma with a massive amount of cerebral haemorrhaging and I suspect spinal cord damage as well.' They'd tried their best but sometimes there was nothing that could be done. They were doctors, not magicians. 'If she'd survived, she'd have been severely disabled but that doesn't make it any easier for the family. The news is still devastating for them.'

It had been devastating for him as well. He knew he'd found it particularly hard today because he was already feeling unsettled. Lily's bombshell had disturbed him and he didn't need another wave to swamp his already leaky boat. He felt as if he was just holding on as it was. But none of those feelings were things he wanted to talk about. Talking about it wouldn't change what had happened and he'd learnt not to spend his energy worrying about things he couldn't change.

He'd come to the sea to clear his head. The ocean was calming and he'd missed it while he'd been in London. Swimming laps in a pool wasn't the same and it had been good to be back in the sea. It was good to see Lily too but he didn't need her help. The swim had given him time to reset and he wasn't going to dwell on what had happened. Chelsea's death didn't sit well with him, of course it didn't, he hated losing patients, but he knew that sometimes it was inevitable. He'd done his best and that eased his conscience and he had to put the events of the day behind him. Tomorrow was another day. Tomorrow he'd be back at work doing it all over again, hopefully with better outcomes.

The lifeguards were packing up the beach, taking down the flags, bringing in their boards, putting the warning signs away. It was time to go. 'I left my phone and keys in the tower with Jet. I'd better grab them before they lock up for the night.'

Lily looked at him quizzically before she nodded. 'You sure you're OK?'

'Yeah. I'm OK.'

He wasn't. But not for the reasons Lily thought. He hated losing patients but he'd learnt to accept that he couldn't save everyone. He wasn't infallible, he wasn't perfect. He could accept that. It was one reason why he'd chosen trauma as his speciality. He didn't have time to build relationships with patients, which meant it hurt less if things went badly. As a trauma surgeon he could deliver bad news and then move on. He could provide fleeting comfort to a family in their time of need without providing counsel. He didn't need to become invested in their heartache, he didn't need to share their experience of loss and grief, he didn't need their grief to stir up reminders of his own. He didn't want to remember how he'd felt as a teenager after losing his mother.

It didn't mean that losing a life wasn't difficult but as long as he had done his best he could accept the inevitable and ultimately he knew he saved more lives than he lost. He'd learnt to accept the losses that came with the job, but he couldn't accept losing Lily. He couldn't accept that their marriage was over. He wasn't prepared to accept that divorce was inevitable.

Coming back hadn't turned out as he'd expected and he still didn't know how to fix things but in his mind their marriage was salvageable and he wasn't giving up until he'd figured out how to save it. So, even though his world was unsettled, even though *he* was unsettled, he told her what she wanted to hear. 'I'm OK.'

Lily looked as if she was about to close the gap between them. As if she was about to reach for him. His spirits lifted and he almost stepped towards her but the look on her face stopped him. There was kindness in her expression but no love and he knew she was offering the comfort of a friend. He could see compassion in her eyes but also pity. He didn't want her pity. He didn't want to show any weakness. That was something that had been instilled in him and his brothers by his father. He admitted it wasn't necessarily healthy but it was a habit that was hard to break.

The lifeguards were pulling down the shutters on the tower windows, putting the tower to bed for the night. Otto knew they'd be locking the door next. He didn't need Lily's pity. He didn't want it. It was time to go. He stepped away and said, 'I need to go, I'll see you at work.'

'I've got the day off tomorrow,' Lily replied. 'I'll see you at our next counselling session.'

Frustration and longing, fear and disappointment churned in his gut as he watched her walk away from him. He didn't want her pity but he wanted her. He wanted to go after her. To tell her he was sorry. To ask her again for another chance but he knew his words would be wasted. He knew it was actions she needed from him. He'd have to figure that out. And figure it out quickly, he realised as he headed into the tower.

'A few of us are going to grab a meal at the pub. You're welcome to join us,' his brother-in-law extended the invitation as he handed him his phone.

'Thanks, but I'll give it a miss. I've had a tough day at work.' He didn't want to go out for beers with the boys.

He'd wanted to go home with Lily. He wanted to curl up beside her, to hold her in his arms. To bury his face in her hair, to feel her curves under his hands. He knew that would ease the stress of the day.

'You sure? A beer might be just what you need.'

But Otto knew he wouldn't be good company. The swim hadn't really helped. Not in the way he needed but a beer wasn't the answer. 'Maybe another time.'

Should he arrange to catch up with Jet independently? he wondered. Should he ask his advice? He and Jet were friends but Jet was still Lily's brother. Who would he prioritise? Would he take Lily's side? Would he think Lily's request for a divorce was warranted?

Otto decided he wasn't ready to hear Jet's opinion. Not yet.

Admitting he couldn't solve his own problems didn't come easily. Admitting he was wrong was even harder.

'How are you both?' Helen asked as Lily and Otto sat down for their second counselling session.

As Otto sat beside Lily again on the small couch she thought she should have chosen the single chair, but she couldn't move now. That would look like an obvious slight and there was no need for that. Instead she picked up a loose cushion and held it on her lap as a mini shield. Against what she wasn't quite sure.

'How did your exercise go?' Helen continued once they were settled, if not comfortable. 'Did you manage to complete it?'

Lily nodded.

'And how did you feel afterwards?'

Lily didn't reply. She'd felt a tumult of things. She'd felt sad. She felt as if she'd wasted time. She felt as if she'd made poor decisions even when she knew she hadn't. She wasn't sorry she'd married Otto but she was sorry she was getting divorced. Not because she thought it wasn't the right thing to do but because she had never wanted it to come to this. But she couldn't see any way around it. Not yet.

She'd agreed to counselling but she now thought it was a mistake. Unless Otto agreed to start a family there was no way of saving their marriage. She wasn't sure if she could sit through counselling, waiting for him to make a decision. She wasn't sure she could bear it. She wasn't sure if her heart could take it. Spending time with him, raising her hopes, only to have them dashed if he didn't change his mind. It would break her. Again.

'I don't feel like it achieved anything.' Otto spoke up. 'We had a perfectly civilised drink and conversation but at the end of the day nothing has changed. I think it's safe to say Lily hasn't changed her mind and neither have I. We're still diametrically opposed.'

'The point of the exercise wasn't to solve your differences,' Helen reinforced. 'It was to practise talking and listening. Did you do that?'

'Yes,' Otto replied. 'Finding general topics of conversation wasn't difficult.'

They'd spent far longer together than Lily had anticipated and she wondered if Helen would be surprised to hear how easily the conversation had flowed. If it would surprise her to hear how much Lily had enjoyed Otto's company. She didn't think anything they'd said or done yet was unexpected and she didn't want to be just like any of the hundreds of couples Helen might have counselled over the years. Lily wanted to be different. More complicated. More challenging. More important. She wasn't sure what that said about her. She'd always been competitive and obviously nothing had changed—even if she was getting divorced she wanted to be doing it well. Would that shock Helen?

'What did you talk about?'

'Nothing important,' Otto said.

Lily frowned in disagreement and Otto's comment prompted her to speak out. 'We talked a little about work but mostly we talked about our families. Both of those things are important. To me, anyway.'

'Are you both close to your families?'

'I'm close to all my siblings,' Lily replied. 'I see one or more of them every day.' Her relationship with her siblings brought her immense joy. Her relationship with her parents, on the other hand, was much more complicated. But Helen didn't question her about her parents. Lily didn't imagine that it had gone unnoticed that she hadn't mentioned them and she found herself wondering what significance Helen put on that.

'And, Otto? How about you?' Helen had paused before addressing Otto and Lily wondered if that had been deliberate. If she was waiting to see if Lily added any more information.

'You want to know about my family? How is this important?' Unlike Lily's relationship with her siblings, Otto's life was completely independent from his family.

'How you were raised has a big impact on a lot of things,' Helen replied. 'It shapes you. Your family and how you were brought up will influence how you see the world and will influence your expectations of relationships.'

'My family is scattered all over the world so seeing them recently has been difficult.'

'Would you usually see them frequently?'

Otto shook his head. 'I have two older brothers but we're not in regular contact. We get along when we're together but in our day-to-day lives there's no need for contact. I speak to my father occasionally.'

Lily could hear the tension in Otto's voice and she knew he was unconvinced that trawling through his childhood was necessary. Even though she knew, they both knew, the research said differently she was inclined to agree with him, but she knew that was only because she was as reluctant to talk about her childhood as he was. She was happy to talk about her siblings but there was a lot to unpack in her history. While the spotlight was on Otto she was OK, but she knew Helen would turn it on her at some stage.

'And your mother?' Helen asked Otto.

Otto shook his head. 'My mother died in a car accident when I was thirteen. Three months later my brothers and I were in boarding school.'

Lily could hear the pain in Otto's voice. She knew he'd never forgiven his father for sending them away. For not acknowledging their grief. Otto used humour to mask his pain but Lily suspected that could only work for so long. Helen had been on the money—family had a lot to answer for.

'And how often did you go home?'

'That would depend.'

'On what?'

'On where home was. My father is a doctor in the defence force, we moved every three years. Sometimes it was easy to go home, sometimes it was easier not to.'

'And before you went to boarding school. Did your mother work?'

'That also depended on where we were living. She did some volunteer work but she gave up her career to support Dad in his and to raise us. Dad was the head of the household but no one argued with Mum either. They presented a united front to us and there was no dissension in the ranks. Our upbringing wasn't strict, as such, but we definitely had structure. Rules were set and expected to be followed. As the youngest of three brothers, I guess I had a tendency to push the envelope but my brothers and I mostly had each other's backs. We got into mischief but we learned to get ourselves out of it. I don't know if that was Dad's influence or if it was by necessity to save Mum's sanity. Dealing with three boys couldn't have been easy.'

'But your mother had the primary responsibility of raising you?'

'Yes. I guess they had fairly traditional parenting roles. Until she was killed.'

'Do you have similar expectations about marriage and family dynamics? About who would support whom?'

Otto paused and looked at Lily. 'I don't know that I ever thought about it specifically. I guess I imagined we'd support each other.'

'So when you got pregnant had you talked about what the future would look like? How you would raise the baby?'

'No,' Otto admitted. 'The pregnancy wasn't planned.'

'Were you planning on having a family at some point?'

Otto nodded.

'But you hadn't discussed the details? Who would raise the children? Did you assume it would be like your family? Did you expect Lily to stay at home?'

'I didn't plan on Lily giving up her career.'

'Were you planning on giving up yours?'

'No. That was a conversation for another day. Maybe we'd get help.'

'From whom? Your family? Lily's?'

Otto shook his head. 'No. Our parents couldn't be counted on.'

Listening to Otto answer Helen's questions, Lily realised again how much they'd both assumed things would work out. For someone who liked a plan she couldn't believe how naïve she'd been. Yes, their pregnancy was unexpected but she couldn't believe that at no point had they talked about the logistics of raising a family and what that would mean. It had all been dreams and hopes. Nothing concrete, nothing tangible.

'And when you moved to London, was that for your work or Lily's?'

'We went for my work. But Lily was happy to move.'

'How did you broach that topic? Was it a fait accompli that Lily would go too? Did you have to put your career on hold, Lily?'

'No. I had a job at the same hospital.' Otto was right. She had been happy to go. She had seen it as an adventure, their first real adventure together and she'd wanted to support him. But unfortunately, things hadn't turned out as she wished.

'And how did you find the move?'

'Harder than Otto did if I'm being honest.'

'In what way?'

'Otto was used to moving and having to start over. He moved house every three years and changed schools often whereas I'd only moved once before, when I came to Sydney for university at the age of eighteen. He's more outgoing than me and good at making friends.' Otto had learned to use humour to break the ice and make friends. He was funny and people liked to be around him. He was a good foil for Lily, who had a tendency to take life very seriously.

'I'm not as socially confident,' she added. And she wasn't, by nature, a risk-taker. Otto was always eager to try new things, he was much more spontaneous than she was and she knew that she relied on him to make her push herself. To make her test her boundaries. 'And I missed my siblings. We were close growing up, we still are, so being on the other side of the world from them was tough.' Poppy was only twenty-two months younger than Lily and Jet was sandwiched in between. They'd been inseparable growing up and she'd missed them more than she'd anticipated, especially after she lost the baby.

'Where did you grow up?'

'In Byron Bay. My childhood was probably the polar opposite of Otto's,' she said as she saw Otto smiling. They both knew their families were like chalk and cheese. 'I grew up on a commune.' Lily took satisfaction in seeing that, finally, something she'd said surprised Helen and Helen's expression made Lily more forthcoming with information than she had intended. 'My childhood was chaotic and unconventional. Structure and order were non-existent. We had virtually no supervision. No boundaries. No rules. Now I crave order, structure, routine.' She did not like surprises.

'Your parents didn't adopt traditional parenting styles?'

'Not at all. I virtually raised my siblings. My parents weren't interested in that.'

'How many siblings?'

'Four.' She still counted Daisy's twin, Willow, even

though she'd been gone for fifteen years, lost to a preventable infectious disease.

'And you're the eldest?'

'By eleven months.'

'Are your parents still married?'

'My parents are together but they never married.'

'Being married isn't important to them?'

'It never seemed to matter. My father is the single most important thing in my mother's life. He always came first for her. Before any of us children. If she had to choose between him and us she would choose him. Every time.'

'And how do you feel about that?'

She felt a lot of things. Hurt. Upset. Angry. But they weren't feelings she wanted to share. Once again, she could see the irony of her reaction. She was in counselling, she was supposed to open herself up, she was supposed to expose herself, reveal her thoughts and feelings in an effort to communicate better but some things were too painful. 'It made me determined to ensure that my children will know they are special, wanted, important and loved,' she said, censoring her reply but speaking to Otto as much as she was answering Helen.

'And how do you feel about marriage? How important is it to you?'

'It's very important.' She'd only intended to get married once but wasn't that what everyone thought?

'You said you've been living apart for two years but you have only just brought up the topic of divorce. Why is that?' Helen asked. 'What was the trigger? If marriage is important there must be something more important to prompt this decision?'

'My marriage was important but having children of

my own is more important. It was looking like I couldn't have both.'

'We had planned to wait until you were thirty-two. You're only thirty,' Otto interrupted. 'We have time.'

'We might have had time but we'd also have to be in the same place. You were in London, I was in Sydney, things between us were strained, I didn't know where we were headed.'

After the assault Lily had learned to block all thoughts of having babies from her mind. She couldn't face the idea of something going wrong again but seeing her siblings with children of their own and spending time with Niki and An Na had reawakened her desire. Her biological clock was ticking and she needed to satisfy it. If Otto wasn't coming back she needed to look at her options. 'I need to find someone who wants what I want. I can't do this alone.'

'You don't have to be alone, I'm right here. We can try again.'

Lily tried to explain. 'I know we had planned to start a family when we got back from London but when I got pregnant unexpectedly it felt like the right time for me. And then that was taken away.' She was speaking to Otto now. She'd forgotten that Helen was in the room. 'I realise I'm changing the goalposts but seeing my siblings settling down, seeing Jet and Daisy with children has reignited that need in me to have children of my own and time is ticking. My biological clock is ticking.'

'Lily, I promise you, we can fix this. I can fix this.'

'Why do you think everything can be fixed?'

'Because usually things can. Together we can work this out. It's not easier to end our marriage.'

'I didn't say it was easier. Just that it might be better.'

CHAPTER FIVE

'LILY, PLEASE DON'T throw our marriage away yet.'

She remembered what Daisy had said about the Carlson siblings having one true love and it was tempting to let Otto persuade her to hold on to that ideal. She knew not everyone was lucky enough to find love once, let alone twice, but Lily was still hurting. She felt as if she'd failed. At marriage. At being a wife. At being an expectant mother. She'd wanted Otto to protect her as he'd promised but she hadn't protected their baby.

Lily knew she hadn't caused the placental abruption that had ultimately resulted in the loss of her baby but she'd replayed the events of the assault thousands of times and she knew she should have reacted differently. If she hadn't put up a fight, if she'd just let the man take her bag, the outcome could have been different. It was a fact that was hard to come to terms with, almost impossible to accept. She had failed her own child.

She shook her head. She and Otto were two trains at the same station but on parallel lines and she really had no idea how to get them onto the same track. 'Too much time has passed. Too many things have been left unsaid.'

'This is your chance to say those things,' Helen told them. 'But carefully, mindfully. In small snippets.'

'I'm struggling with putting my thoughts and feelings into words,' Lily said. 'I find it hard and Otto's not great at asking questions.'

'Is that true, Otto?'

'Probably. If someone needs something from me I expect them to tell me, otherwise I guess I assume everything is fine.'

'In that case I have your next assignment in mind, then. I want you both to write a letter to each other.'

'About what?'

'Your feelings. The hurt. The slights. The things you are finding difficult to verbalise.'

'Why?' Lily asked.

'How is this going to help?' Otto asked.

'It will give you both time to process your thoughts. It should help you to clarify what your issues are. To work out where and why things started to go wrong.'

'Where do we start?'

'What was the turning point?' Helen said. 'The point where your paths began to diverge?'

'When I got pregnant,' Lily said.

'When we lost the baby,' Otto replied.

Lily was amazed. They couldn't even agree on that! She'd just outlined her thoughts as to when things began to go wrong. Hadn't Otto been listening or did he really see things so differently from her? If that was the case what hope did they have of reconciling?

'The pregnancy upset things for us,' Lily said. 'That was no one's fault—' she apportioned blame for other things but not for the pregnancy '—but I feel like that was when we started having different expectations about where we were headed.'

'All right,' Helen said, 'start there.'

'And then what? We swap the letters? Give them to each other to read?'

'No.' Helen shook her head. 'You read the letters to each other.'

'Read it out loud?'

'Yes. You told me your goal for therapy was to improve your communication skills. I know you could each read the letters in private but I want you to talk about things. Writing down your feelings will help you to own them, to understand them, and then you should find it easier to verbalise them to each other. I would suggest that when you read your letters to each other you give yourself time to process your responses. Don't feel you have to discuss what the other person has written, unless you want to. Once you've written the letters it then becomes an exercise in listening to each other. That's just as important as talking. I'll leave you with that homework and see you at the same time next week.'

'Are we able to push that session out by a week?' Lily asked as they stood up. 'My sister is getting married next weekend and I have a lot going on with that.'

'Of course,' Helen replied. 'The timing of these sessions is completely up to the two of you.'

'We might need to push it out even further,' Otto said. 'I'm away at a conference the following week.'

'You're going to the conference in the Hunter Valley?' Lily asked as they left Helen's office. There was an Emergency Medicine conference taking place just after Poppy's wedding. Lily was registered to attend but she hadn't given it much thought as yet. Her brain space was occupied by too many other things—mostly Otto.

'Yes. Last-minute change. I'm taking Leo's place. He's decided he's not well enough.'

'He was a keynote speaker. Have you got something to talk about?'

Otto nodded. 'I'm working on it. I can present Leo's session but there's also some pretty cool new technology that I want to mention. Some new technology that can connect to your phone and record a heart tracing.'

'You're serious?'

'Yep. It's pretty interesting. Not something we'd use in the hospital but it might be something to have in more comprehensive first-aid kits.'

'I'll make sure to attend your session, then.'

'You're going to the conference?'

'Yes.' She nodded. 'The hospital is sending Ajay and me.'

'Bondi General ED.' Lily picked up the phone at the triage desk and her stomach dropped as she listened to the ambulance dispatcher as he relayed details about the incoming patients.

'Julie! Ajay! Two incoming ambulances,' she called out as she hung up the phone. 'MVA vs pedestrians.'

'Pedestrians *plural*?' Ajay asked.

Lily nodded. 'Elderly driver. Reports say she hit two pedestrians, an adult and a child.'

'Any other details?'

'No.'

'OK, three patients coming our way. We don't have any patients rating one or two at the moment so I'll free up some hands,' Julie said as she began marshalling staff.

'You take the first ambulance, Lily, and I'll wait to see what we're dealing with,' Ajay said as they headed for the ambulance bay. As the senior ED doctor Ajay got to make that call.

The first ambulance swung into the driveway and Lily could see Poppy at the wheel.

She switched off the engine and jumped out, giving an update as she moved quickly to open the rear doors. 'I've got two patients on board. A mother and her six-year-old son,' she said as she pulled the door open.

Lily could see a patient strapped to the stretcher. An adult. The mother.

Alex, the second paramedic, was sitting cradling the child, who was wearing a school uniform and had his left arm in a sling.

'I need a wheelchair,' Alex instructed as he climbed out of the ambulance still holding the child. One of the nurses pushed a chair over to him and Alex carefully lowered the boy into the seat. 'This is Bailey,' he said. 'He's being very brave but he's complaining of a sore right arm. Suspected greenstick fracture of his forearm. Nil pain relief.'

Alex's tone suggested that Bailey was not the patient of primary concern, which left the mother. 'Take him inside,' Lily instructed the nurse, 'but stay with him and nil by mouth.' Bailey's assessment could wait for the moment. But as Raina started to push Bailey towards the ED he began to cry and looked back over his shoulder to his mother.

Lily could see the mother lift her head although the movement was made difficult by the cervical collar that had been placed around her neck. She was strapped onto the stretcher otherwise Lily was convinced she would have jumped up and followed her son. 'I need to go with him.' Lily could hear her distress.

'He's fine. The hospital staff are with him,' Poppy reassured her. 'You need to stay as still as possible.'

'Can I call someone for you?' Lily asked. 'Your husband, partner? A grandparent?' Bailey was going to need someone to support him while his mother was being treated.

'Natalie's husband is on his way,' Poppy said as she and Alex pulled the stretcher out of the ambulance. 'Natalie was struck by the car. Witnesses reported the force of impact threw her into the air and she landed on her left side. She is reporting back and pelvic pain. Possible pelvic or abdominal injuries.'

The patient had been put on oxygen and Lily could see an IV canula in her arm but she was surprised that Natalie wasn't clutching the little green whistle that was often given to administer pain relief.

'No pain relief?'

Poppy shook her head. 'She's five and a half months pregnant.'

Lily could feel the colour draining from her face. A pregnant woman with possible abdominal injuries sustained through a traumatic incident. There were myriad possible consequences of this accident but the first one that sprang to Lily's mind was the potential for placental abruption. She was aware that Poppy was watching her, waiting for her reaction.

'Why doesn't Ajay take Natalie?' Poppy suggested, knowing where Lily's mind would be going. 'The second ambulance is on the way with the driver of the vehicle. You can take the elderly patient.'

Lily knew there was no likelihood of the elderly patient being pregnant but before she could respond she felt a hand on her forearm, a light touch only, and then a familiar voice. 'Lily. It's OK. I'm here. We've got this.' Otto was beside her, speaking at a volume low enough that his voice wouldn't carry to the patient. He'd obviously heard the description of the accident and he too would know where Lily's thoughts had headed.

Otto waited for Lily to look at him, to acknowledge that he was there and together they'd take care of the patient. Lily looked into his dark eyes as he nodded, very slightly, reassuring her that, at least this time, he was beside her, offering his support.

She nodded in reply. She knew she could rely on him in the ED. She never doubted his professional support, he always gave a hundred and ten per cent to his patients and, by association, to his colleagues. It was only personally she felt he'd let her down.

Had she been too harsh? Too critical of him? Was she expecting perfection? No one was perfect, she knew that, least of all her, she thought as she heard Otto address Poppy. 'What do we need to know?'

'Natalie, aged thirty-six, struck by a car and fell, landing on her left side. Complaining of back pain and left hip pain, able to weight bear with discomfort. BP one-forty over ninety. Heart rate ninety-five BPM. Soft tissue swelling and contusions. Twenty-four weeks pregnant. Third pregnancy. No previous complications.'

'Any abdominal or vaginal bleeding?'

'Nothing visible. She's on oxygen as a precaution. Nil pain relief.'

Otto grabbed the end of the stretcher and looked to Lily. 'You good?' His gaze was intense and helped to settle her thoughts and she knew he was deliberately trying to calm her. She knew there were a number of possible scenarios, multiple possible outcomes for Natalie and perhaps she was being fatalistic but, from her experience, her thought process was reasonable. If Otto thought she was being overly dramatic he kept that thought to himself and focused instead on getting her attention back to the job in front of them.

She nodded. Forcing herself to be positive. Forcing herself to concentrate on the here and now. On this patient. There was no time for memories of the past.

'All right.' Otto increased the volume of his voice and spoke to Natalie. 'Let's get you inside, Natalie. Can you tell me what happened?'

'I was dropping my daughter off at childcare and was taking Bailey to school. We'd just come out of the building. There's a pedestrian crossing in the car park, right out the front, and we were walking across when a woman drove straight through it. She didn't stop. I pushed Bailey out of the way—are you sure he's OK? Where is he?' she digressed, obviously more concerned about her son than herself.

'He's OK,' Lily reassured her. 'He's with the nurses, they'll look after him.'

'Do you remember what happened next?' Otto asked, trying to get Natalie to focus. 'Did you hit your head?'

'I don't think so. The car hit me on my right-hand side. I went flying and landed on my left side.'

'And the pain is in your back and left side?'

'Yes.' Natalie's eyes were darting left and right and Lily knew she was looking for Bailey.

'Your husband is on his way to take care of your son,' Lily reminded her patient. 'I'll let you know when he gets here.'

'Any abdominal pain? Any cramping?' Otto asked as

they pushed her into a cubicle and Lily started connecting Natalie to the various monitors.

'No.'

'Have you felt the baby moving since the accident?'

'I'm not sure.' Lily could hear the fear in Natalie's voice but at least she now seemed able to concentrate on Otto's questions. 'My back and hip hurt so much I'm not sure what else I can feel.'

'And the births of your other children, did you have vaginal deliveries or C-sections?'

'Normal deliveries. I'm not in labour. I know what that feels like,' Natalie said, misconstruing Otto's question. 'This pain is different. I can't be in labour,' she said, obviously thinking that Otto was worried she was going to give birth prematurely. 'I'm only twenty-four weeks.'

'I know,' he reassured her. 'I'm just gathering the details.'

'Lily, can you check the foetal heart rate for me, please?' Lily was testing Natalie's motor responses when Otto interrupted her. Natalie had normal limb strength with moderate discomfort on moving her legs but Lily didn't think she had sustained any significant injuries to her extremities. She stopped the assessment to attach a heart-rate monitor around Natalie's abdomen. Her hands shook as she fastened the Velcro strap. She took a deep breath but it did nothing to steady her hands. She was finding the situation distressing and Otto's calming presence wasn't enough to settle her nerves. Or perhaps it *was* helping, perhaps she'd be worse if he weren't there. She finally managed to fasten the strap, pleased that Natalie wasn't in a position to see her hands, but the tremor hadn't escaped Otto's gaze. She saw him watching her.

'All good?' he asked and she knew he was referring

not to their patient but to her. She nodded, determined to get through. She had a job to do.

'Kevin.' Otto took her at her word and continued issuing instructions, this time addressing the nurse. 'Can you cross-match blood type?'

'Natalie, I need to feel your uterus.' Otto pressed gently on Natalie's abdomen. Lily could see there wasn't much give, her belly was hard, and Natalie winced. 'Is that hurting you?' Otto asked.

'Yes.'

'Foetal HR one-fifty and irregular.' Lily's voice wobbled as she passed on the information and Natalie looked up at her sharply.

'Is the baby OK?'

'A little distressed,' Otto responded, jumping in to save Lily from having to answer. 'That's to be expected given what you've both been through.'

Natalie's eyes were wide. She looked from Otto, to Kevin before speaking to Lily as the only other female in the room. 'I need to go to the toilet.'

'Kevin, can we have a bed pan, please?' Otto said before Lily could react.

Kevin helped Natalie to remove her underwear. Natalie's movements were laboured, restricted by pain and Lily could see Kevin was trying to avoid causing her any more discomfort as he helped her.

Kevin dropped Natalie's underwear in a stainless-steel bowl instead of leaving them on the bed and Lily could see the pants were stained with fresh blood. Her heart rate skyrocketed but, with shaky hands, she managed to remove the bowl. She made sure she kept the underwear out of Natalie's sight while letting Otto see the blood. She tried to keep her expression neutral, not wanting to increase Natalie's distress, but she could feel her own anxiety escalate. She checked the monitors. Natalie's blood pressure was dropping but her heart rate was still high.

Kevin whisked the bed pan away as Natalie finished with it and Lily looked to Otto. His return look said 'don't jump to conclusions' but she couldn't help it.

'Natalie, you've got some vaginal bleeding. I need to have a quick look at that. Dr Carlson will stay in the room, everyone else can step out for the moment. Is that OK with you?' Otto glanced at Lily when he mentioned her name. Lily knew he was silently checking with her that she could manage, not that she had a choice—she was the only female member of staff in there, she had to stay. Lily forced herself to block all thoughts of the past from her mind, forced herself to focus on Natalie as she tried to avoid jumping to conclusions.

'Is the baby OK?' Natalie repeated.

'I won't know until we have a look.'

Lily noticed that Otto didn't answer Natalie's question directly, instead he deflected and deferred his answer, choosing to turn up the volume on the foetal heart-rate monitor instead. 'Can you hear that?' he asked. 'That's the baby's heartbeat.' Lily hoped the baby's heartbeat stayed nice and clear and strong. She hoped Otto's demonstration didn't go awry.

The exam room cleared and Lily stood beside Natalie's shoulder as Otto examined the patient.

'I want a sonographer and an obstetrician,' Otto told Lily. Lily could hear the concern in Otto's voice and knew he was worried. She knew he was thinking of placental abruption. She was well acquainted with the condition. Better acquainted than one could ever wish to be.

She wasn't sure how much longer she could keep a brave face. She flicked her gaze to Otto, looking for reassurance.

He nodded his head, just a slight movement but it was a confident one that managed to convey, *You're OK. You've got this.* He mouthed, *You're doing well*, knowing she'd be able to lip-read. She'd picked up the habit from Daisy. She wasn't nearly as proficient but she could decipher common words and basic phrases. She breathed out, exhaling audibly, and the tightness in her chest eased.

'Natalie, I want to take you for an ultrasound scan.'

'What for?'

'Just to check the placenta.' It was less frightening to say that than to say he was worried about the baby and, technically, what Otto was saying was true. If there was placental abruption and if it was severe, there was nothing that could be done to save the foetus.

'Is my husband here yet?'

'Lily, can you go and see if Natalie's husband is here and check on Bailey at the same time? I'll wait with Natalie.'

Lily knew Otto was offering to wait with Natalie for Lily's sake. So that Lily wouldn't need to answer Natalie's questions. She knew he was getting her out of the room deliberately, trying to protect her, to give her a chance to take a breath, to reset. Had he recognised she'd reached her limit? Did he think she was about to go to pieces?

She stepped out and concentrated on breathing. *Don't think about it*, she told herself. *Don't think about London. Don't think about our baby.*

She should be able to cope, she should be able to deal with these patients and these presentations and she was convinced that usually she would manage. She wasn't sure if having Otto there was making the situation better or worse, easier or more difficult. Having him there was keeping her anchored but his presence also stirred up the memories that were never far from the surface of her mind. Seeing Otto in the flesh brought everything back more vividly and the memories had been bombarding her. Two years had passed but the pain was still sharp, raw, acute. It still took her breath away. But it was more than pain. There were so many emotions. Guilt. Regret. Blame. Anger. Confusion. And, since Otto had returned, all those feelings were much closer to the surface of her mind than they had been for a while.

She was finding it difficult having to mix Otto and her memories with her professional life. Too many parts of her life were coinciding, colliding, and she wasn't able to get any relief. Divorcing Otto might fix one problem in that it would give her an opportunity to begin the journey to motherhood again, but she wasn't sure if she could keep working with him. He was a good doctor, an excellent one, and professionally she knew she could manage but would she be able to separate her personal feelings, her emotional side, from her professional side? Would being divorced make it any easier?

She sighed. That was going to be up to her but she suspected it wouldn't help.

Maybe she'd been approaching therapy the wrong way, she thought as she checked to see if Natalie's husband had arrived—he hadn't—and then went to get an update on Bailey. Maybe instead of opening up the lines of communication she should be looking for closure. Maybe she should be learning how to forgive, forget and move on.

Perhaps forgiveness was the key. She had to forgive Otto for what she saw as his part in their loss, and for what she saw as his failings as a husband, but she had to forgive herself for those same things too. She'd failed as a mother and a wife and she wasn't going to be able to move on without making a conscious decision to put the past behind her.

And Otto was part of her past.

When Lily returned to Natalie's treatment room with news of Bailey, Natalie's husband had arrived and Natalie had had the ultrasound and had been taken to Theatre.

Natalie's husband was going with Bailey for his X-ray and Otto was waiting to speak to Lily. He closed the door and she knew from his expression what he was going to say.

'She's going to lose the baby, isn't she?' Lily asked. Somehow she thought it would be less confronting if she said the words rather than having Otto tell her but the words caught in her throat and came out as a sob, a cry for help.

Otto nodded and opened his arms, offering her a hug, knowing exactly what she needed. Why was it that he knew what she needed now? Why hadn't he been able to give her the comfort she needed two years ago? she thought as she stepped into his embrace. Despite the regret she felt over what had transpired before, she wasn't going to refuse comfort. She needed a hug. She needed human contact after the day she'd had.

'She had a severe placental abruption,' Otto told her as he wrapped his arms around her and held her close.

She leant her head against his chest as memories of years past rushed back. Memories of hours spent lying in his arms, of feeling his warm skin under her hands, his sculpted muscle under her fingers, his breath on her body, his lips on hers. She closed her eyes as she fought to contain tears of regret. Now that she was in his arms she couldn't remember why she'd refused to return to London. Was she about to give away the person she needed? Was she ever going to be able to replace him?

She wound her arms around him as his embrace tightened. Did he need the comfort, the reassurance, as much as she did?

'Are you going to be OK?' he asked.

No. She didn't think she was but answering truthfully wasn't going to help anyone. What could Otto do about it? She had a job to do. She nodded. Accepted his hug for just a few moments longer as she composed herself before going back to work.

She had no idea how she got through the rest of her shift, it was all a bit of a blur, but she knew she hadn't made any mistakes. If she'd thought she was in danger of making errors she would have left for the day. It was better to be at work, better to stay busy. She knew the memories would be worse if her mind were still.

At the end of her shift she walked home, thinking about Otto. She wondered if it was wise to go home to an empty house, alone with her thoughts, alone with her memories, but what other option did she have?

She didn't need to talk about the day but she did need company. She could see if one of her ED colleagues was free for dinner, or one of her sisters, any of them would provide her with company but she didn't want to have to explain her day. She wanted someone who would understand what she'd been through without needing to hear it and she knew none of them would get it in the same way as Otto did.

She needed Otto but she needed the old Otto. The one she'd had before they'd lost their child. Before they'd stopped communicating.

While she accused Otto of not wanting to hear what she had to say, of not listening to her, she knew she was partly to blame. She'd been distraught but also angry and guilt-ridden and that maelstrom of emotion had made her shut Otto out. He'd rightly accused her of doing that but after they'd lost the baby she'd needed comfort. She hadn't wanted to relive the experience, hadn't wanted to relive the emotions, hadn't wanted to feel guilty but she had wanted to hear Otto say he didn't blame her. She'd resented the fact that he hadn't tried to comfort her verbally or physically, that he seemed happy to exist in silence and in solitude. She knew she couldn't hold him solely responsible for the breakdown of communication in their marriage. Their marriage had ceased to exist as a partnership, they'd become two individuals sharing a house, and they were both to blame.

Lily lay on the couch as the evening settled around her. She kept thinking she should get up and do something but she couldn't think of anything to do. It was too late to go for a swim or a surf and she didn't have the energy anyway. She probably should just go to bed but she knew she'd just lie there staring at the celling, not sleeping. She'd spent the first hour crying but her tears had eventually stopped although she could still feel where the salty tears had dried on her face, leaving streaks on her skin. She was about to get up to wash her face when there was a knock on the front door.

She ignored it.

There was a second knock. And then she heard Otto calling her name.

She got up. She needed a hug, she needed company, and Otto was there, almost as if he knew she needed him.

She opened the door and stepped towards him. It was

automatic, a response born out of old habits, and Otto opened his arms and held her close. She shut her eyes and felt herself relax in his embrace. She wasn't going to cry any more but it felt so good to be held.

'Why are you here?' she asked, her voice muffled against his chest.

'Because you're my wife,' he replied as if that was all that mattered. Maybe it was. 'And I was worried about you.'

'I'm OK.'

'You're not,' he said as he released her and stepped back to look more closely at her. 'I know you think I've got zero emotional intelligence when it comes to your feelings, but I know how hard today was for you and I wanted you to know I'm here for you. You say I don't listen or ask how you are. I'm here, doing both. Have you eaten?' he asked.

She hadn't even thought about eating. She shook her head. 'I'm not hungry.'

'You need to eat. You need some carbohydrates, comfort food,' he said as he bent down and picked up some shopping bags that were at his feet.

'What's all that?'

'Ingredients. I'm going to make you spaghetti carbonara.' He wasn't taking no for an answer and Lily realised she was hungry and Otto was a good cook. Otto's Italian mother had been an excellent cook and she'd passed on some of her culinary skills to her sons before she died and Lily had always loved his pasta dishes.

He followed her inside, poured them each a glass of wine and sat her at the kitchen bench while he cooked. He knew his way around the kitchen and he chopped and fried and stirred and sipped his wine while he chatted about things that had happened during his day, avoiding the topic of Natalie, letting Lily add comments when she felt like it, but mostly she was just content to sit quietly and watch him work. She enjoyed sitting listening to the sound of his voice. It was calming and reassuring. It wasn't the subject matter that was relaxing, he could have been reading her the weather forecast, it wouldn't have mattered, but there was something comforting about the domesticity of the two of them together in the kitchen.

Otto fried the guanciale while the spaghetti cooked before draining the water and adding cheese, eggs and a sprinkle of pepper to the guanciale and pasta.

His movements were smooth and measured, almost automatic. He moved around the kitchen in the same way Lily imagined he moved in an operating theatre—calmly and confidently.

'You still enjoy cooking your mum's recipes?' she asked.

'I do. Cooking was something I have really strong memories of doing with Mum. It keeps me connected to her.'

'Can't you see yourself making those same connections with children of your own?' she asked as he placed a bowl of pasta in front of her. She couldn't stop herself from asking the question. She knew she was having difficulty accepting that he didn't want children yet. She'd always been able to imagine him as a father and she couldn't understand how he couldn't see that, how he couldn't want that experience yet.

'Eventually.'

'Eventually?' Was he going to continue to delay until it was too late for her? Why had she agreed to give him these three months if nothing was going to change?

'Let me explain. I know we planned to have a family but, when those plans became a reality, I admit I struggled.'

'Why?' She'd known he hadn't been as excited as she had been about the unplanned pregnancy but he'd never explained why.

'After Mum died I taught myself not to worry about things I couldn't control. It was how I processed her car accident, by accepting there was nothing I could do to change that outcome, and it became a rule for me to live by. The only time I found myself struggling to live by that rule was when you got pregnant. There were so many things I couldn't control, so many ways I could let our child down, but they weren't things I could ignore, they were things that I felt were my responsibility to manage. But I didn't know how I was going to manage and I freaked out. What if I couldn't do it? What if I let you down?'

'We were doing it together. It wasn't just up to you.'

'In my head, you were my responsibility. Our child was my responsibility. Maybe my letter will explain it better.'

'Your letter?'

He nodded as he cleared their plates. 'I think I should read it to you,' he said.

'Now?'

Otto nodded.

'Why now?'

'I know you're sad. I know you're thinking about London. About our baby. I'm hoping that if we can talk about it, it might take some of the pain away.'

'You think talking about it is going to make me feel better?'

'I hope so. I think Helen is right. We do need to talk

about what happened. Writing down my thoughts helped me to understand how I was feeling and also helped me to understand how you might have been feeling. I think you need to hear it.'

'You brought it with you?'

'It's on my phone.'

When Lily didn't object Otto took his phone from his pocket. He hoped he was right. He hoped that if he could explain his thoughts and feelings to Lily it would help her to understand that the issue hadn't been that he didn't care but that he hadn't known how to help her. He was hoping he could help her now.

He'd come past the house without warning, needing to check on her, but unsure of his reception. When she'd opened the door he could see she'd been crying but getting her to open up was proving more and more difficult. Despite the counselling sessions she still kept her cards close to her chest. He thought perhaps if he went first, if he exposed his vulnerabilities, she might be able to do the same.

He poured her a second, smaller glass of wine and began talking.

'The other day, in Helen's office, you said that our problems started when you got pregnant. That surprised me. I didn't think that was the turning point. In my mind it was when we lost the baby. The first thing I had to do when Helen gave us that homework was to work out where to start so I listened to you and went back to the day you told me you were pregnant.'

They hadn't been in London very long, just a few weeks, and they were still finding their feet when Lily had delivered her news. Otto could still remember how shocked he'd been and he knew he hadn't reacted as Lily had hoped.

'We were still both settling into our new routines, new jobs, a new flat. We were working long hours and getting used to the lack of sunshine at the beginning of an English winter. I'm not making excuses, just acknowledging that we had a lot going on. We were already dealing with a lot of changes and I admit, when you showed me the pregnancy test you'd done, my first thought was, *This is too soon* and I know I didn't hide that thought very well. At all well. It was clearly written on my face.

'You accused me of not wanting the baby and that wasn't true. I wasn't happy about the timing—' they'd agreed to wait until he'd finished his training, until they had established their careers '—and I was worried about how we'd manage. I was going to be working long hours and studying on top of that. We were away from home, away from your siblings, away from any of our support networks. It was going to be tough.

'I knew you were excited and I knew you wanted me to be excited too and I knew you were upset with me because it was obvious that I wasn't. I was scared.'

'Scared?'

He nodded. 'I didn't know how we were going to manage. I had all sorts of thoughts—some were premature, I admit. My head went straight to the nine months ahead. How would we cope? We had no help. We'd be down an income. How would I manage to work and study with a new baby in the house? How would I support you emotionally and financially? How would I support a family? I had no idea how to do it all and that knowledge terrified me. I knew I would let you down. I wasn't ready. I wasn't prepared. It was a scenario I wasn't expecting at that point in time and I accept that I didn't handle it well.'

He'd been convinced that a pregnancy would derail their plans but Lily had been adamant that they'd figure it out. He wasn't so sure. 'I couldn't change my path. I knew you were going to have to be the one making sacrifices, you would be the one putting your career on hold.'

'That was a decision I was prepared to make. That I was happy to make,' Lily said.

'I didn't want you to resent me later for continuing with my plans, my career.'

'You would rather I felt like you didn't want our baby?'

'That was never the case. I know things were a little wobbly for a while. You were emotional. I was terrified. But I calmed down, I realised people managed to raise families with a lot less than we had. I realised you were right, we'd figure it out as we went along, and I started to think of all the positives. I loved you—' he still loved her '—and I got excited about the prospect of fatherhood. Of raising a child with you. I went from being scared to being excited. I was still nervous but confident I could do it. That I could support you. That we could raise a child. I thought we got through those first few weeks unscathed. I thought our relationship was back on track. We were building a future.'

What he hadn't realised was that they'd been building a house of cards and when Lily lost the baby their house came crashing down.

'And then we lost the baby. I know you think I didn't grieve but I was trying to stay strong for you. I didn't think it was helpful if we both went to pieces but I can see that by hiding my grief to protect you it appeared that I wasn't grieving at all. I was and I was also dealing with my guilt.'

'Your guilt?'

He nodded. 'You were right, I hadn't been ready for fatherhood initially and that knowledge weighed heavily on my conscience when we lost the baby. I felt we were being punished for my thoughts and I also felt responsible that you'd been put in harm's way. I felt guilty because I let you down. You and our baby. If I hadn't taken the position in London, you wouldn't have been in that situation. If I wasn't working such long hours you wouldn't have been out late at the shops. I felt I should have protected you better. I blamed myself. And whenever I thought you wanted to talk I felt guilty all over again.' And every time Lily looked at him all he could see in her eyes were recriminations.

'I thought you were ignoring our loss,' she said.

'In my mind what happened, happened and there was no way to change that. Talking about it over and over wouldn't change anything.'

'I thought you were ignoring me,' Lily said. 'I gave up trying to talk to you about it. It was easier to leave.'

'I know I shut you out and I'm sorry. I didn't know how to fix you. I thought you needed to see your sisters. That you needed some sunshine. I thought time would heal your wounds but I always thought you'd come back to me. I assumed we'd be able to put our loss behind us and move on. That we'd get back on track. Our original plan had been to wait until after London before we started a family. I thought we could go back to that plan. I didn't expect not to see you for the next two years. I didn't expect a pandemic to keep us apart. I didn't expect a lot of things. If you could have travelled, would you have come back to me?'

'I don't know. I could have travelled. I wasn't sure if I wanted to. I didn't know if you wanted me back and I wasn't sure if I was ready to see you. You stopped talking to me. You stopped looking at me.'

'All I thought I could see in your eyes was accusations. I didn't want to see my faults, my failings in your eyes.'

'I thought you blamed me,' Lily said.

'Blamed you? No! Getting assaulted wasn't your fault.'

'Not for the assault but for losing the baby.'

'You lost the baby *because* of the assault. Because of the trauma. It wasn't your fault. You shouldn't even have been at the shops.' Otto knew that if he had left the hospital when he was supposed to he would have been the one at the shops, not Lily. He had stayed at work because an interesting case had come in, he'd put his work before his pregnant wife and he still hadn't forgiven himself for that. 'It was my fault, not yours,' he admitted.

CHAPTER SIX

LILY HAD BLAMED him too. Not completely, she knew she couldn't lay all the blame at his feet, but she had certainly laid some of it there.

She'd asked Otto to pick up some tea from the shops on his way home. It was the one thing that helped with her morning sickness, which seemed to strike at any time of the day or night, but Otto had called to say he'd been held up at work so Lily had gone out instead. The shop was two blocks away and despite the cold she'd decided it wasn't worth getting in a taxi, so she'd been walking alone along the dark and icy street when a young man had run past and grabbed at her bag. Lily had held on to it, refusing to let go. Instinct, she'd said later. Stubbornness. She hadn't wanted to let the boy get the better of her. She hadn't thought about the baby. She'd only thought about her bag. And that knowledge was something she had to live with now.

The thief had pulled hard on her bag but Lily hadn't given in. Not until he'd punched her in the stomach. She'd thought about the baby then as she was doubled over in pain. She'd loosened her grip on her bag and, as the thief yanked it out of her hands, she'd stumbled and slipped on the icy footpath, falling heavily and hitting her head.

Even thinking about it now was still overwhelming. She recalled the shock of the punch, the pain in her abdomen and her absolute fear for her unborn child as she lay bloodied and bruised outside the shop.

Witnesses had come to her aid. She'd sat up gingerly, her hands cradling her belly. She remembered feeling relieved as she'd felt the baby moving. She'd sustained a concussion but she hadn't been concerned about a head injury, her only concern had been for her child, but feeling the movement had convinced her that she'd escaped serious injury. Until the bleeding started and her world imploded.

She'd been rushed by ambulance to the hospital, the sirens and flashing lights adding an extra layer of panic to her fear. She'd prayed to the God she didn't believe in as she was taken to hospital but it had made no difference. The doctor diagnosed a placental abruption and there was nothing that could be done to save her baby.

Whether it was the punch to her stomach or the fall she would never know but her baby paid the ultimate price.

Outwardly, apart from a few bruises, nothing looked amiss but internally, both physically and emotionally, Lily was damaged. She'd never imagined she could lose her baby and she needed someone to bear the brunt of her devastation, someone to absorb her guilt, someone to take the blame.

Otto had become her scapegoat. If he hadn't stayed at work, if he'd come home when he was meant to, she wouldn't have gone to the shops. Eventually, when he began to avoid her, when he refused to talk about the baby or about what they were going to do next, her resentment built into anger.

'I needed you to tell me it would be OK. That it wasn't

my fault.' He should have blamed her but she wasn't ready to admit that she felt guilty too. She had been happy to let him shoulder that burden.

'I didn't know that was how you were feeling. You never said anything.'

She shouldn't have needed to. But, deep down, she knew she was also at fault. Even if the thief had to take the lion's share of the blame she knew she and Otto were both partly responsible due to their actions. She should have just let go of the bag. Why hadn't she? If she'd just let it go everything would have been fine.

But she couldn't go back. She couldn't change her actions.

How she wished she could.

'Lily?' Otto reached out and held her hand. 'I'm sorry I let you down. Can you forgive me?'

She realised she'd reached a place of acceptance and forgiveness. She couldn't continue to blame Otto or herself for what had happened. They were not responsible. The person at fault was the man who assaulted her.

'Yes.' She nodded. 'We could repeat our exact same actions from that night a hundred times and the same situation would never arise. I think I've finally accepted that.'

'Do you think we can try again?'

That was a question she still didn't know the answer to. She was worried he still wasn't ready. That they were still on different tracks. 'We can't just pick up where we left off. We can't go back to how we were before I got pregnant. We're not the same people any more.'

'I know that but that doesn't mean we can't find our way back to each other. We're not beyond saving.'

But she was worried that they were.

Unless he changed his stance about having children she couldn't see the point in staying married. She loved him and she worried she'd never find that type of love again but even though her anger had gone there was still a lot of pain. She could forgive him but she was afraid he could break her heart a second time.

Perhaps it was better to call time on their relationship now.

She looked at their hands, at their intertwined fingers, and remembered what they'd shared. Remembered the love they'd had and wondered if he loved her still. What if she never found love again? Did she want to navigate the world alone?

'Lily? Tell me what you're thinking. Talk to me. Tell me how you're feeling,' Otto implored.

She knew it was time for some honesty. The point of counselling had been to open the lines of communication and she knew there was a lot they needed to talk about, but she also knew she didn't have the energy or the fortitude to begin what would be a difficult conversation. It had already been an emotional day and she was feeling fragile. But there was something she could tell him. 'I don't know what the future holds but I don't want to be alone.'

'Tonight or always?'

'Both.' She knew she wouldn't sleep. She would toss and turn, thinking things over, thinking about today, thinking about their baby, thinking about Otto.

'What can I do?' he asked.

'Will you stay with me until I fall asleep?'

He hesitated and she thought he was going to say no. But he nodded, slowly. 'I'll do the dishes while you get ready for bed.'

Lily chose an old T-shirt, one of her own, and climbed into bed a few moments before Otto joined her. 'Will you lie with me?' she asked. She knew she shouldn't make that request but it might be the last time that she would share a bed with him and she knew that letting him go wasn't going to be easy.

He slid under the covers and lay behind her. She closed her eyes and snuggled back against him as his body moulded around hers and his arms wrapped around her.

She could feel him breathing, she could feel the rise and fall of his chest and the warm puffs of air against her cheek as he exhaled.

'I'm here. I've got you,' he whispered, and she felt him press his lips to the side of her head, just behind her ear.

Her nerve endings flared under the warmth of his lips. It would be so easy to roll over. To press her lips to his, to taste him, to love him, but she resisted the temptation. They weren't on the same page, not yet, and she would only confuse things, for both of them.

She concentrated on the rhythm of his breathing, matching her breaths to his, letting her heart rate slow and her thoughts quieten, until she slept.

For the first time in weeks Lily woke feeling refreshed. Despite her fears that she wouldn't sleep, that she'd toss and turn and relive the events of the day, and of the day two years ago, she'd slept soundly, dreamlessly, and she knew it was because of Otto.

She shouldn't have let him lie with her but she'd needed comforting and it had felt so good. So familiar. He'd been fully clothed, there had been no hint of anything sexual, she'd fallen asleep almost immediately and had only woken once and when she'd found herself still wrapped in his arms she'd gone straight back to sleep. But he wasn't beside her now. At some time in the night he must have left without her hearing him and she missed him already.

She stretched and rolled over and was lying facing the door, contemplating whether she needed to get up, when Otto walked into the room.

'Good morning,' he said as he placed a cup of tea and a plate beside her bed.

Lily breathed in the scent of freshly buttered toast. 'Good morning.' She'd had no idea that he was still in the house but she was incredibly pleased to see him. 'I didn't realise you'd stayed all night.'

'I didn't want to move in case I disturbed you. You seemed to be sleeping soundly and I think you needed it.'

'It was the best I've slept in ages. I slept like a log.'

'I didn't realise logs snored.'

'I didn't!' she protested.

'No, you didn't.' He smiled at her and her heart melted. How she wished the past two years had never happened. How she wished they could go back in time to before it all went wrong. To when they had their life together in front of them. Oblivious to what was to come, they had lived each day in a state of blissful anticipation, full of the naivety and hopefulness of youth. In the certainty that they were leading charmed lives and they had the world at their feet.

Oh, how those dreams had then shattered into a million tiny pieces leaving her alone to try to salvage what remained. Alone to try to pick up the few bits she could and piece them back together into what became a poor imitation of the life she'd dreamed of. She was still trying to piece it together but the pieces continued to slip through her fingers. She couldn't hold on to them all.

What if Otto was the glue she needed to make things work? To fix things. That would be ironic. He always said anything could be fixed. What if he was the missing piece?

He glanced at his watch. 'I need to get to work. Are you going to be OK?'

With a dozen small words he smashed her brittle illusions.

He wasn't the glue.

He had to go to work.

Work still came before her. Nothing had changed but she knew she shouldn't have expected it to. Not now. Otto didn't owe her anything more. She was the one pushing him away. She was the one who had raised the topic of divorce. What did she expect? That he'd drop everything to stay by her side? She knew she was being unreasonable. She didn't even have time to spend with him today, she had prior commitments that she couldn't get out of, didn't want to get out of.

She nodded in response to his question. 'I'll be fine. I'm spending the day with Poppy and Daisy.' It was the eve of Poppy and Ryder's wedding and the sisters had a full schedule. They were picking up Poppy's wedding dress, going out for lunch and then having pedicures. It was more than enough to keep her mind occupied. In the bright morning light with the cloudless blue sky outside her window it was a new day. She'd be OK.

'And tonight?'

'Girls' dinner with Poppy, Lily and Mei and then Poppy is staying here.' She smiled. 'Something about not wanting Ryder to see her until the ceremony tomorrow. Aren't you supposed to be having drinks with the groom and Jet?'

'I'd forgotten about that with everything else that's happened in the past twenty-four hours,' he said. 'So, I'll see you at the wedding, then?'

She nodded.

'Call me if you need me,' he said before he left, easing her hurt feelings a little.

Perhaps work wasn't the only thing that was important but while she appreciated the offer she knew she wouldn't call. She had to put the past to bed. They'd made mistakes, she'd made mistakes, but there was no going back. She'd forgiven him and now she had to move on.

But last night had left her conflicted. She'd missed their intimacy. She'd missed him. But she couldn't let a few hours spent wrapped in his arms influence her decision if nothing was going to change.

Otto's arms were light, they were missing Lily already, but his heart was heavy. Lily had forgiven him but she wasn't prepared to give him a second chance.

Last night might have been the last time he had the chance to hold her. That was why he'd stayed all night. He couldn't bear to let her go.

But it was safe to say things were not going according to his plan. He needed to work out what was going wrong.

He placed a call to Helen, hoping she had a cancellation and would have time to speak to him.

'Hello, Otto, what can I do for you?'

'I need some advice. Counselling isn't working the way I imagined.'

'How is that?'

Helen always answered a question with another question. It was infuriating but he knew why. It was a technique employed to make them work out the answers for themselves. 'I've shared my letter with Lily but she seems reluctant to tell me how she feels.' He heard the irony in his statement. Having difficulty talking about feelings wasn't something only Lily struggled with. He found it difficult too. Growing up with brothers and then going to a boys' boarding school didn't exactly help to develop the skills needed to share his innermost thoughts. 'I don't know if she is going to let me back into her life. I'm not sure that she's going to change her mind about the divorce. How do I fix this?'

'You might not be able to.'

'I have to. It's what I do.'

'Why is that, do you think?' Helen asked.

'Are you going to make this about me?'

'It's about both of you but, yes, currently it's about what you can do. It's about what you can control.'

'I have to get her to change her mind. I have to find a solution.'

'She might not change her mind. That was something we discussed at your first session. I think when you talk about fixing things you need to think about what you can control. You can't control Lily. You can't control her thoughts or her actions. All you can do is manage your own expectations about how you want your relationship to go.'

'I can't lose her.'

'How do you think Lily got to this point?'

'She feels I let her down.' She'd made that much clear.

'How?'

'I wasn't there when she needed me.'

'It's not Lily's mind you have to change. You can't control that. You can't change the way she feels. She's entitled to her feelings, even if they differ from yours. You have to accept that and work out what you can do. What you can control is what you do going forwards. You need to show Lily that you have her back. She wants a partner. Someone who is there always. Not just through the good times. Yes, she likes your spontaneity and humour. She sees it as a good foil for her more serious personality but she needs to know that you'll be there for her in the tough times. Can you do that?'

Otto nodded. Helen's words resonated with him and he recognised the truth in them. He knew Lily felt that her parents had let her down. He knew she felt the weight of responsibility of raising her siblings and that she'd looked to him as someone who would share the burden of responsibility, not add to it. He was supposed to take care of her.

He would do better. If Lily would give him a chance

'Are you ready?' Lily asked Poppy, as the wedding car pulled up on Queen Elizabeth Drive in front of the Bondi Pavilion, opposite the circular Bondi lifeguard tower.

'Definitely.' Poppy smiled. 'I've been waiting a whole lifetime for this moment.'

'You look beautiful,' Daisy signed as the driver opened the door for Poppy and all four siblings climbed out of the car.

Poppy's dress was a simple design, a fitted bodice with narrow straps, that plunged to her waist at the back. The skirt was full from the waist and fell to her ankles, but the simple style was elevated by the fabric, which was adorned with thousands of tiny sequins, which would shimmer and shine in the lights at the evening reception.

She carried a bouquet of white poppies interspersed with tiny daisies and lily of the valley in a nod to her sisters. Lily and Daisy were wearing pale blue linen dresses, also sleeveless, which finished mid-calf. All three of them had bare feet in preparation for the beachfront wedding ceremony.

It was just after seven on a mild, late summer evening. The lifeguards had pulled down the shutters on the tower, closing it up for the night. They'd roped off an area in front of the building and had chairs positioned on the beach forming a sandy aisle down the centre of the rows. The wedding guests were mingling but took their seats when they spotted Poppy, leaving Ryder standing at the water's edge waiting for his bride.

Jet, dressed in linen trousers and a pale blue linen shirt to match his sisters' dresses, kissed Poppy's cheek and offered her his arm before they made their way down the steps beside the tower.

Ryder wore a white linen shirt, sleeves rolled up to his elbows, pale linen trousers with the cuffs turned up and bare feet. He was grinning broadly as he watched Poppy walk down the sand towards him.

Lily looked around at the assembled guests as the celebrant welcomed everyone. The guests, a mixture of paramedics, lifeguards, a few of Ryder's new work colleagues and some of Daisy and Lily's hospital colleagues who had befriended Poppy, made a large gathering. Considering neither Poppy nor Ryder had lived in Bondi for long they had made a lot of friends. Mei, Ajay and Otto stood on the left of the aisle with An Na and Niki. They were Poppy's family until she was united with Ryder's, enlarging her family further.

The three dark-haired in-laws were such a striking

contrast to the blonde Carlson tribe and the idea of opposites attracting seemed so obviously at play that it made Lily smile. Her gaze landed on Otto, standing so straight, tall, dark and handsome, and her thoughts skipped back to their wedding day, when Otto had been waiting for her at the front of the church his family had attended since before he was born. Otto was watching her and her heart missed a beat when he smiled at her, bringing her back to the present and the recent memory of being wrapped in his arms as she'd fallen asleep. She dropped her gaze as she felt the blush stealing across her cheeks. She was reluctant to let Otto see where her thoughts had gone. She didn't know what to make of her feelings and until she did she didn't want him to attach any significant meaning to last night.

She let her gaze continue to roam over the party. Ryder's parents and younger sister stood with him. His parents were divorced but seemed to have been able to put aside their differences for Ryder's sake. His mother's new partner was among the guests but Lily was yet to meet him. Mei's parents had also been invited but Pete and Goldie Carlson were not on the list. Lily wondered now if Poppy had made the right call by not inviting their parents. Increasingly of late she had been feeling that time was running out. But that was her sentiment, not Poppy's, and she knew it was, at least partly, related to her biological clock.

Lily returned her attention to the ceremony. Poppy and Ryder's vows were heartfelt and sincere and both of them included plenty of references to the family and friends who had gathered to witness the occasion. It was a celebration of Poppy and Ryder's love and the celebrant was well aware of the importance of the guests in the couple's life together.

'Poppy and Ryder are making a commitment to each other here today but all of you are part of that commitment too,' she said. 'By accepting an invitation to their wedding you are making a commitment to support them in their life together. You are promising to be present in their lives, not just for the good times, the weddings, the parties, the celebrations, but for the hard parts too. There is no doubt they will experience difficult times, hopefully these are few and far between, but when they do, your role as friends and family is to support them. Today, you become part of their team as they go forwards into their life together.'

Lily knew how important family was and her thoughts returned to her own. Was their family too badly fractured to be put back together? Their family dynamics had always been unusual—was she wishing for something that was impossible? Even if the siblings' relationship with their parents was repaired, could it ever be the one she imagined? She doubted it.

It wasn't something that had bothered her before. She'd never had a close bond with her parents and her siblings had been enough for her. She knew they would support her as the celebrant was asking them to support Poppy and Ryder but once they had their own families was it realistic to think they could remain as close? Would their partners become their priority? Or the families they would be making together?

That was what she'd hoped to build with Otto. A family of her own. She couldn't expect her siblings to prioritise her over their own families and her parents weren't part of her life. Her family was fractured and she had kept her friends at arm's length since her return from London. Some had been Otto's friends first and she didn't want to see them or answer their questions—she left Otto to deal with that. A lot of her friends were having babies and she found that painful. She didn't want to talk about babies, her marriage or her failure as a mother. But if her siblings had less time to spend with her, where would that leave her? Who would she have for support?

She used to think she had Otto. She knew it was her fault that she didn't have that any more. She knew she'd pushed him away. And then run.

The ceremony was wrapping up and Lily took Poppy's bouquet as the bride and groom exchanged rings.

Poppy was radiant. Lily hadn't ever seen her this happy and she felt a twinge of regret mixed with sadness. She wished her relationship with Otto hadn't gone pear-shaped but she didn't want to be sad, not today. She took a deep breath and reset her attitude as Ryder and Poppy shared their first kiss as husband and wife. She would let Poppy and Ryder's happiness restore her spirits.

The wedding reception was in full swing. The party had all the right ingredients—a gorgeous venue, generous hosts, delicious food, music and guests who were ready to celebrate. Ajay and Daisy had offered to host and Ajay's house was a perfect location. It sat at the opposite end of Bondi from Lily's house, perched on the northern end with an amazing view down the coast. The twinkling lights of Bondi sparkled on the right, the sea was a vast expanse of midnight blue on the left and the curve of the sand in between glowed white in the moonlight. It was magical.

Mei's parents and Ajay's housekeeper-cum-nanny,

Mrs Singh, had organised the catering and professional wait staff were kept busy offering platters of food to the guests and topping up glasses. There was nothing for Lily to do except enjoy herself but despite her resolution it wasn't as easy as she would like.

Otto was mingling in the crowd, happily chatting to friends, acquaintances and strangers. It was something he was adept at. He had always been far more extroverted than Lily. She was happy looking for reasons not to talk to other people, preferring to keep her cards close to her chest, but tonight, Otto's extroverted personality left her feeling ignored. She sighed. What did she expect?

She was acutely aware of where he was at all times and he was currently talking to Poppy's paramedic friends. She watched him, envious of his confidence, and she watched the women he was talking to, aware of the attention Otto was receiving from the female guests. Was she really ready to give him up? The conundrum of her head versus her heart rose again and she turned away, still not a hundred per cent certain she was making the right decision.

The DJ had set up on the deck that looked along the beach towards the centre of Bondi. Ajay had strung festoon lights above the deck and as the dance music started up, guests began to move outside.

Niki, Ajay's two-year-old son, had fallen asleep on a couch near the kitchen and Lily used him as an excuse to escape for a few moments, to give herself some breathing space. She picked him up and carried him to his room. He was sleeping soundly and didn't wake as she got him ready for bed. She tucked him under his covers and sat with him for a while, thinking about Otto, thinking about their past, thinking about the daughter she and

Otto had lost. She would have been about the same age as Niki, just a few months younger. They could have grown up together.

She watched Niki sleep. Watched his chest rise and fall, watched his eyelashes flutter against his cheek, as she pictured her own daughter. Niki was dark, like his father. In Lily's mind her own daughter was always fair-haired, like all the Carlsons, with Otto's dark eyes.

She breathed in and closed her eyes as pain pierced her chest. The heartache was just as acute, just as raw, as it was every time she let the memories surface.

'Lily?'

She opened her eyes, quickly wiping away a tear, when she heard her name.

Otto was standing in the doorway, his lean frame silhouetted by the light from the passage. 'What are you doing sitting in the dark?' he asked her. 'You're missing the party.'

'I just needed a minute,' she said as she got up and joined him in the passage, pulling Niki's door behind her but not shutting it completely.

'Are you OK?' Otto was looking at her closely and she hoped she'd removed all traces of tears from her face.

She nodded. 'Yes. Just reliving the past.' She knew from his expression that he thought she was mad to be looking backwards, so she clarified her answer. 'I was wondering if I should have done things differently.'

'Things like?'

'Whether we should have invited my parents to our wedding.'

'Why on earth are you thinking about that?'

How did she explain? 'I was thinking about what the celebrant said about family. I've seen Mei's parents' relationship with An Na and Niki with Mrs Singh and also Ajay's parents when they visited from Fiji. I never knew my grandparents and seeing my niece and nephew with theirs was the first time I'd really seen what a normal, healthy intergenerational family relationship can look like. When I have children of my own one day I want them to know their grandparents, which made me wonder if my relationship with my parents is irreparable.'

'Of course, it's not,' Otto replied. 'Everything is fixable.'

But she knew that wasn't true. 'I don't know. Family can be complicated. My family is definitely complicated.'

'You won't know until you try,' he said. 'But, for now, come and dance with me. Tomorrow is another day.'

'You're not going to offer me a solution?' she asked, amazed he wasn't trying to fix things immediately.

'I thought you didn't want me to do that any more.'

'Maybe…but I can see on your face that you want to say something.'

Otto grinned and her heart skipped. He really was devilishly handsome when he smiled. 'I was just thinking that if I wasn't already married I'd marry you tomorrow and invite your parents to the wedding. I would insist and you would thank me later.'

'You'd marry me tomorrow?'

'And the next day and the next,' he said as he held out his hand, 'but, right now, we are celebrating with Poppy and Ryder. Come and enjoy the moment. Don't hide away giving the impression that you're miserable. Smile and dance,' he gently reprimanded.

He was right. She had vowed to enjoy herself. To be supportive of her sister and her new husband. She shouldn't be sitting alone in the dark.

'Tomorrow you can go back to wanting to divorce me,' he said with a wink as he took her hand in his.

She let him have her hand, let his fingers close around hers as he led her out onto the deck, let him take her in his arms as the DJ played a slower song. It seemed like all the guests were dancing and the crowded space meant he had to hold her close. She wasn't complaining. When she was in his arms divorce was the last thing she was thinking about.

'I shouldn't have said I *wanted* to divorce you,' she replied. 'I really meant I *needed* to.'

'You're talking in past tense,' Otto said. 'Are you changing your mind?'

Lily didn't know what she was doing. She couldn't think straight. But one thing hadn't changed. 'I feel as if I'm getting left behind,' she said. 'As if I might miss my chance to have children if I wait any longer. I want a family. That's what this is about.' She was envious of her siblings, all happily coupled together and embarking on the rest of their lives while she was in a holding pattern.

She sighed. She had a lot of regrets and she was worried that letting Otto go might be another one to add to her list but she couldn't see any other way to get what she wanted. She'd missed being with Otto but she would acclimatise.

'For the moment, I am still your family,' he said. His hand was warm on her skin and his voice was a whisper in her ear, sending a tingle along the length of her spine. 'I've missed this.'

She hadn't been honest with him for a long time. Maybe it was time that changed. 'I have too,' she replied.

'Don't let me go,' he said as he pressed his lips to her temple.

Lily's knees went weak and she clung to him for support. 'I won't,' she whispered. 'Not yet.'

He was her husband, her family, but she knew she wouldn't feel her family was complete until she was a mother. But she wanted a night off from thinking about that, from letting herself be consumed by those dreams. She wanted to remember what it was like to be held by her husband. She wanted to spend one more night in Otto's arms. She wanted to share her bed with him, she wanted to feel loved just once more before she said goodbye. But maybe dancing together was as close as she was going to get.

She closed her eyes and concentrated on how it felt, in case it was the last time. She committed every sensation to memory. The warmth of his hand, the touch of his fingers, his familiar scent of cedar and spice, the feel of his shirt against her cheek, the softness of his breath against her forehead and the beat of his heart under her ear.

As Otto held her in his arms and guided her around the dance floor Lily felt the pain of the past two years start to ease. With each beat of the music her spirit lifted as she lost herself in the sensation of being with Otto. Her body felt alive, her heart was light and for a few hours she let herself dream of a future with Otto. A bright, shiny, happy future where they had resolved all their differences.

They stayed on the dance floor until the final song of the evening, until the time came to farewell Poppy and Ryder. The guests crowded around the bride and groom to say goodnight but Lily and Otto found themselves in a corner of the deck, out of the spotlight and out of sight.

'Do you want to say goodbye?' Otto asked.

He still had her hand in his. Lily didn't want to let

go, she wasn't ready to break the spell. She didn't want the night to end. She didn't want her dream to give way to reality.

She lifted her head and looked him in the eye as she shook her head. 'In a minute.'

He smiled and held her gaze, his brown eyes dark and intense in the dim light. She was standing still, transfixed. He let go of her hand and she wanted to reach for it, to hold onto it, to hold on to him, but before she could move she felt his arms go around her waist as he pulled her closer to him. One hand was on the bare skin of her back, the heat of his fingers intense against her spine.

His other hand was under her chin. He pressed lightly under her jaw and she tilted her head as her body melted against him.

Otto bent his head and Lily closed her eyes in anticipation of the kiss she was certain was imminent. His lips brushed over hers, the gentlest of touches, so soft she wondered if it was nothing more than her imagination. Was he not sure of the reception he would get?

His mouth met hers again and she welcomed his kiss. His touch was firmer this time, more definite. Her lips parted voluntarily and she heard herself moan as his tongue explored her mouth. The outside world receded; it was condensed into this one spot, this one man.

She was aware of nothing else except the sensation of being fully alive. She wanted for nothing except him.

She felt her nipples harden as all her senses came to life and a line of fire spread from her stomach to her groin. Her heart was racing in her chest as she deepened the kiss. She was dizzy, light-headed, her breaths not deep enough to get oxygen to her brain. She needed to breathe.

Otto's fingers trailed down the side of her cheek sending a shiver of desire through her as they broke apart. He studied her face as if committing each of her features to memory. He didn't need to worry, she thought, she wasn't done with the night yet.

'Why don't you say goodbye to Poppy and I'll give you a lift home?' he asked.

She nodded. She'd let him take her home and she'd invite him in. What happened after that was up to Otto but if he accepted her invitation she knew it would lead to sex. At least she hoped so. She knew she was flirting with danger but it had been so long since she'd had sex and sex with Otto was always good.

The opportunity was hard to resist.

Impossible.

If it happened, she would add it to the memories she was making tonight. It might turn out to be another regret but she wasn't going to think about that now. She'd worry about that tomorrow. What had Otto said? 'Tomorrow is another day.'

He sat in the back of the taxi with her, his arm around her shoulder, holding her close as if he was afraid she would disappear if he let her go. He didn't know she had no intention of going anywhere, not tonight, not without him.

'Would you like to come in?' she asked as the taxi pulled up in front of her house. Their house.

He looked at her, a question in his dark eyes.

She didn't speak, she just nodded.

He paid the fare as she hopped out onto the footpath. The pavement was still warm from the heat of the day under her bare feet and despite the dancing she could feel grains of sand clinging to her calves as she climbed the steps to the front door.

She suspected there was sand sticking to other parts of her body as well.

Otto joined her as she turned the key. She let them into the house and handed him the keys. 'I need a shower, I'm covered in sand,' she said as she headed for the stairs. She climbed two steps before stopping and turning back to him. 'You're welcome to join me.'

CHAPTER SEVEN

SHE WASN'T GOING to play games. She wanted Otto to know where she was at but she'd barely finished the sentence before he was behind her.

She walked up the stairs and, knowing his eyes would be on her hips, she made sure to sway them just a little more.

She walked into her en suite bathroom and stretched her arm out, turning on the taps. While she waited for the water to warm up she undid her bra strap through the thin fabric of her dress and slid her arms out before pulling the bra from inside her dress. She remembered how Otto had always been astonished by her ability to remove her underwear without removing her clothes and she took pleasure in teasing him with that memory now.

She wasn't disappointed with his reaction. He stood, watching her undress, silent but not immobile. She dropped her gaze to his groin. She could see the effect she was having on him and it emboldened her.

'Are you sure about this?' he asked. His voice was husky and deep, laced with desire.

She nodded and he took a step towards her but she held up her hand, making him wait.

She reached back and checked the water temperature

before sliding the straps of her dress from her shoulders and letting it drop to the floor. She stepped out of her underwear and stood naked before him. She watched as his eyes darkened as he took in her naked form. His lips parted as he breathed deeply.

Lily smiled and lifted her hands to her hair. She pulled out the pins that had been holding it up, letting it fall around her shoulders before stepping into the shower. She turned her back to him and lifted her face to the spray, letting the warm water run between her breasts, waiting for Otto to join her.

Otto had watched, mesmerised, as Lily's dress slid to the floor. Automatically his eyes had followed the movement as gravity took hold and his gaze was now focused on the dress where it lay in a pool of blue around Lily's ankles. His eyes travelled upwards, up the length of her bare legs, long and tanned, to her slim hips, to the small triangle of blonde hair at the junction of her thighs.

He couldn't speak. A severe lack of blood to his brain had robbed him of the power of speech. But he could admire. So he did. Lily was naked and she was gorgeous.

His gaze travelled higher, over her flat stomach and her round belly button to her full breasts and erect nipples.

She was perfect.

He could see her pulse beating at the base of her throat, her lips were parted, her mouth pink and soft, her eyes gleaming.

She was glorious.

She lifted her hands to her hair and pulled out the pins, dropping them on the vanity as her hair tumbled around her shoulders.

She turned her back and stepped into the shower.

Otto watched her profile as she stood under the spray and lifted her face to the water. His eyes followed the path of the water as it flowed over her breasts and down the length of her thighs. Her skin was tanned and golden with the exception of her bottom, which was pale and smooth and round.

She turned her head, looking over her shoulder at him, her blue eyes large and wide, watching him as he watched her. She said nothing but when she smiled he couldn't resist any longer. There was only so much temptation he could stand.

He only had one thought. *Do not let her go again.*

He stripped off his clothes as quickly as he could and joined her in the shower.

He hadn't wanted to let her go on the dance floor and he wasn't going to let her go now.

He stepped in behind her and ran his hand over her rounded bottom. Her skin was warm, slick with moisture. She tilted her head to the side and he pressed his lips to the curve of her neck. He moved his hands to her narrow waist, sliding them across her belly and up to her breasts. He ran his thumbs across her nipples, feeling them peak under his touch. His erection hardened further, pressing against her back. He slid one hand down her body, his fingers sliding between her thighs, parting the soft folds of skin between her legs, seeking her centre.

She moaned and leaned back against him, letting him take her weight as her legs could no longer support all of her. He continued to massage her nipple with his left hand as the fingers of his right hand circled the hard little nub of her sex.

She was panting now as she thrust her hips towards him.

'Tell me what you want, Lily.'

He had a good idea of where this was heading but he had to hear her say the words. He had to know she wanted it as much as he did. He didn't want to take advantage of her but he did want to take her. To claim her. To have her. Right here, right now.

Lily's voice was husky and breathless as she replied. 'I want you to make love to me.'

He didn't need to be asked twice.

He spun her around to face him and pulled her close.

It was only a matter of inches before he could bend his head and claim her mouth with his.

Her lips were soft and forgiving under his. He teased them apart with his tongue and she opened her mouth willingly. Her mouth was warm and moist and he felt her arms wind around his neck.

His hands moved lower, cupping her buttocks. She moaned and thrust her hips towards him and he could feel her groin press against his erection. He held her to him, pinning them together.

He nudged his knee between her legs and she spread them apart, willingly, granting him access. His fingers found the centre of her being, as if they had a memory of their own, and he massaged and teased her. She arched her back and he felt her tremble.

'Oh, God, Otto, do it now,' she pleaded.

He scooped her up, lifting her effortlessly. She parted her thighs further and wrapped her legs around his waist as she clung to his shoulders. He thrust into her, deep and smooth, his hands on her hips as he lifted her up and down, sliding her along his shaft.

She tipped her head back, exposing her throat to him,

long and slender. But he didn't want to see her throat. 'Look at me,' he commanded.

Their eyes met, unblinking. Her lips were parted.

She bit her bottom lip and closed her eyes.

Her lip came free and she was breathing fast.

She opened her eyes and fixed him with her blue gaze. 'Do it now. Please, Otto.'

She held her breath, only releasing it as she climaxed. He felt her shudder as her hold on him tightened and finally Otto let go as well. He exploded into her soft centre, satisfied and spent for the moment.

He had fought hard to hold on, there had been no slow build up, he'd waited for this moment for two years and it had been hard and fast. He'd take it slow next time, he vowed.

He'd make sure there was a next time.

She clung to him as he turned off the shower. He never wanted to let her go.

He reached out and grabbed a huge, fluffy towel and wrapped it around them both.

He carried her to her bed, refusing to put her down despite her protests. She was long and lean and sexy as hell and he was going to make love to her again. If she'd let him.

The towel fell away as he laid her on the bed. Her skin was shiny, warm and slick. He could feel his desire stirring again and knew he wasn't finished.

He rested his hand on her stomach and his fingers spanned her waist as he bent his head and took her breast in his mouth. Lily breathed in sharply, a little gasp of air, and arched her back, lifting herself closer to him.

He flicked his tongue over her taut nipple before he lifted his head and said, 'I don't think we're done yet.'

Lily wrapped her hand around his erection in silent reply as she opened her legs and guided him inside her. Otto closed his eyes and lost himself in the heady sensation of being with Lily.

They made love slowly this time, savouring each moment. Sex between them had always been amazing, something that two years apart hadn't changed. If anything, it made it sweeter.

They climaxed together for the second time. Spent. Satisfied. Exhausted.

Otto fell asleep pressed against Lily's back with one hand cupping her breast and her head resting against his shoulder. He held her close, never wanting to let her go.

Now he was home.

Lily woke to the sensation of Otto's lips on her cheek. She smiled as she opened her eyes, anticipating a satisfying start to the day. 'Good morning.'

'Good morning, sorry to wake you,' Otto apologised as Lily felt her expectations being dashed. 'I need to go and work on my presentation for the conference.'

'Now?' she asked. The conference was scheduled to start tomorrow afternoon. She would have thought he would have sorted out his talk already.

He nodded and kissed her again, on the lips this time, which sort of made up for the fact that he was heading out of the door. 'I'd love to stay,' he said, bolstering her spirits, 'but I have to get this done. Although I have a suggestion. I thought we could head up to the Hunter Valley later today, take the wine train. Have a night in the resort before the conference starts.'

'Together?'

'Yes, together.'

Lily wondered what door she'd opened by sleeping with him. Was it closure she was after or a second chance? If it was closure she was after then going away with him was probably not the best idea. She wasn't sure what she wanted any more but she had a ready-made excuse, which might buy her some time to figure things out. 'I've got lunch with my siblings today.' Poppy and Ryder had checked into a hotel for their wedding night before they left on their honeymoon and the Carlson siblings were catching up for lunch first.

'The train doesn't leave until four,' Otto said, refusing to be dissuaded. 'You have lunch with your siblings. I'll book two train tickets and pick you up on the way to the station.'

'Do you really think that's a good idea?'

'No. I think it's a great idea,' he said as he sat on the side of her bed. 'We can spend some time together without interruption. You promised to give me three months, we've got another two. Think of all the fun we can have.' He placed his hand on her knee and his thumb rested on the soft skin on the inside of her thigh. He dragged his thumb slowly towards his fingers and Lily's nerve endings trembled under his touch as her eyelids fluttered. 'I can spend the next two months convincing you not to divorce me and you can spend the time seeing if you can resist me. You know we're good together.'

'It's not that simple,' she said as she resisted the urge to grab him and pull him into bed with her. Resisted the urge to let her actions make a mockery of her words.

'It is that simple,' he replied as his hand slid further up her leg. 'You'll see.' Lily's breathing was slow and deep and she fought hard to keep her eyes open. Fought hard to stop herself from begging him to come back to bed.

He was grinning, obviously totally aware of the effect he was having on her. 'I'll pick you up at three.'

Lily loved a plan but Otto had always been able to get her to go with the flow. He was the only one who had ever been able to convince her to wing it and she loved his spontaneity. It was such a good foil for her seriousness. She trusted him to bring the fun and he was right, it was only a couple of days in the Hunter Valley that he was asking for and she had promised to give him a couple more months.

She smiled slowly, deciding to let him convince her, hoping she wasn't making a mistake. 'OK, I'll see you at three.'

Otto congratulated himself on getting Lily to agree to come away with him. He was hoping to remind her of the good times they'd shared. To remind her of all the reasons why she shouldn't divorce him and, after last night, he was convinced that if she gave him enough time he'd be able to win her back. He needed to get her away from other distractions—work especially. He was doing his best to follow Helen's advice. To give Lily what she needed.

He was convinced that what she needed was him and he just needed time to show her that.

They were on board the wine train. Lily was flicking through a magazine reading while Otto worked on his presentation. He was having a final check and was about to suggest they go to the dining car for a glass of wine when a man burst through the connecting doorway into their railcar.

'Is there a doctor? We need a doctor. Is anyone a doctor?' The man ran through the carriage, looking left and right as he shouted, but he didn't stop.

Otto stood up and put his hand out, waylaying the man. 'I'm a doctor. What is it? What's happened?'

'There's a lady in the next car. I think she's having a heart attack.'

Otto closed his laptop and picked it up as Lily stood. 'We'll come with you,' he told the man.

They followed him out of their carriage and as the door into the adjacent carriage slid open Otto could hear the sound of a person in distress. They passed rows of passengers who looked to either be trying to pretend nothing untoward was happening or craning their heads, not bothering to hide their curiosity, as they tried to see the cause of the disturbance.

The woman's cries got considerably louder and as Otto got closer he saw she was clutching her chest as she sat doubled over in pain. She was in an aisle seat, effectively trapping the other passenger against the window. The passenger beside her looked as though he'd rather be anywhere else.

'Are you travelling together?' Otto asked the man beside the woman.

The passenger shook his head, eyes wide. Otto could have guessed by his terrified expression that the woman was a stranger to him and he had no idea what was going on. He wasn't going to be able to give Otto any details.

The woman looked to be in her mid-fifties, moderately overweight and her skin had an unhealthy pallor. Otto's immediate thought was that she was having a heart attack even though it could be any number of things.

Otto looked for the emergency stop button before wondering about the wisdom of pulling that when he had no idea where they were. The view out of the window was of countryside, barely a house or a shed could be seen. He turned to the young man who had alerted him to the patient. 'I need you to go and find a staff member. I need a first-aid kit, whatever they've got, and I need to know how far we are from a hospital.' The young man didn't move. 'Go that way.' Otto pointed in the direction opposite the one they had come from. 'There'll be someone in the dining car.' The man nodded and took off and Otto turned back to the patient.

He introduced himself and Lily, explaining they were both doctors before asking, 'Can I examine you?'

She nodded, unable to speak. Despite the noise she was making it was obvious she was struggling to breathe. Otto needed to calm her down. If her airways were compromised she needed to conserve her energy. Crying was using precious energy that could be better spent trying to force air into her lungs.

'Do you have any history of cardiac problems?' he asked, aiming for questions that only required yes/no answers.

She shook her head but Otto knew that didn't mean he could rule out a heart attack. People didn't necessarily know they were a candidate for a heart attack before they had one.

Lily had her fingers on the woman's wrist, feeling her pulse. 'Rapid but regular,' she told him.

Treating a patient in an emergency outside a hospital environment was not easy, despite what television shows might imply. The risk of dying increased dramatically outside a hospital setting. He wasn't a miracle worker but he'd recently lost a patient and he did not want to be in that position again so soon.

The young man returned with a rail employee. Her name badge read 'Carys' and she was carrying a small black bag that Otto assumed was the first-aid kit, although he'd been hoping for something a little larger.

'How far are we from a hospital?' he asked her as she handed him the bag. They'd been on the train for over an hour, they were well out of Sydney but Otto had no idea of their exact location or what medical care was nearby.

'We're twenty-five minutes from the nearest town with a hospital. We can stop the train but the nearest ambulance will be in that same town.' Which meant there wasn't much point in stopping. The train was travelling at speed. They were better off continuing to move. 'Do you want to stop? Do you know what's wrong?'

No and no were his answers but he didn't want to sound too defeatist. 'Not yet,' he replied, as he unzipped the first-aid kit, wondering how well it would be stocked. Would it have anything useful in it? He couldn't afford *not* to check it out. He had nothing with him.

A list of medications was taped inside—anti-nausea medication, nitro-glycerine tablets, an EpiPen and a bronchodilator inhaler were all listed and he committed those items to memory.

'Can you clear everyone from the car?' he asked Carys. He didn't need bystanders especially when there was no one who could give him any helpful information.

He pulled out a stethoscope and a blood pressure monitor, hoping the battery was charged. A thermometer lay underneath.

He handed the blood pressure cuff to Lily and she wrapped it around the patient's upper arm before inflating it.

'I'm just going to listen to your breathing,' he told the

woman as he slipped the buds of the stethoscope into his ears and held the bulb over her shirt. He glanced at the blood pressure monitor, surprised to find that both her blood pressure and pulse were within normal limits for a middle-aged woman. His gut instinct had been that she was suffering a heart attack but her heart wasn't going crazy. That was good news, but her cries of discomfort coupled with the crackling of her shirt was making it impossible to hear any breath sounds through the stethoscope.

'I need to slide this under your shirt,' he explained as he slipped the stethoscope between her chest wall and her shirt, but the change in position didn't elicit the result he was after. There were still nil airway sounds.

Her skin was turning slightly grey and Otto was concerned.

He assumed there would be a defibrillator on the train but these were only useful in a cardiac arrest, and then only sometimes. A heart attack was a different ball game. The woman was conscious and breathing so a cardiac arrest was unlikely. A heart attack was still his first thought but he knew other conditions could be causing chest pain and shortness of breath. A cold, indigestion, asthma, pneumonia or a virus were all possibilities.

Lily was quietly gathering as much information as she could without a verbal history. She was pointing the thermometer at the patient's forehead—the reading was normal, so Otto crossed pneumonia and a severe virus off the list. By a process of elimination he narrowed the problem down to one of two things: an asthma attack or a heart attack. They weren't similar in presentation but her symptoms weren't really typical for either.

He still wasn't sure that it *wasn't* a heart attack. It was impossible to get any history from her and yes/no questions were only going to get him so far.

'What do you think's going on?' Lily asked.

'It looks like a heart attack and unless I can stabilise her we'll have to call an ambulance and stop the train.'

'What do you need?'

'I'd like an emergency department. I'd like to be able to do an ECG. But I'll have to treat her with what we've got and see what happens.'

He turned to Carys. 'Can you call an ambulance? Find out where they can meet us. We should assume we're going to need them.'

The young girl nodded. 'I'll have to go and find out exactly where we are.'

Otto nodded as Lily asked him, 'That device you were telling me about, the one you're discussing at the conference, that records a heart tracing and sends it to your phone, have you got that in your luggage?'

'Yes.' He'd completely forgotten about the machine. 'You are brilliant.' In this situation having that machine at his disposal was more than he could have wished for.

'Do you want me to get it?'

He'd only ever used it in a training environment but it was the worth a shot. It should give him an idea of what the woman's heart was up to. He nodded. 'It's in my bag on the overhead luggage rack.'

While Lily was gone he took a nitrate tablet from the first-aid kit and slipped it under the patient's tongue, deciding to treat her as a heart attack patient in the interim. If she wasn't having a heart attack the tablet wouldn't do any harm and if her symptoms didn't ease he could administer the bronchodilator inhaler to open up her airways. Again, that wouldn't cause any problems if it wasn't required and he had to do something.

He'd just given his patient two puffs of the inhaler when Lily returned with the portable device. Otto attached the leads, syncing it with his phone, which was in his pocket.

The trace was normal.

It still didn't exclude a heart attack but it did reduce the urgency of treatment and Otto's diagnosis was now leaning towards asthma. As he let out a sigh of relief, his patient started to stabilise. Her breathing slowed, she opened her eyes, unclenched her hands and was able to speak, albeit with difficulty.

She reported a history of severe asthma and the effort of saying a few words brought on further shortness of breath. Otto handed her the inhaler as he listened again to her chest and this time he heard breath sounds.

'Do you have an inhaler?' he asked, thinking it was unusual for an asthmatic patient not to carry one with them.

Maria, she'd said her name was, replied, 'I do but I used it in the taxi on the way to the train station and I think I must have left it on the seat when I paid the fare. I couldn't find it in my bag when I needed it.'

Lily rechecked Maria's blood pressure and pulse and announced they were both closer to normal limits. Otto was confident that Maria's symptoms were asthma related but he insisted on sending her to hospital just to be thorough. He was satisfied with the outcome as he and Lily handed Maria's care to the paramedics. They had worked in unison, their skills complemented each other, and as the ambulance departed Otto's thoughts returned to the previous evening. He and Lily had been in unison then too. He was beginning to feel optimistic about the future. Surely Lily had to agree that their relationship was worth saving? That their marriage was worth fighting for?

'That wasn't quite the start I envisaged for our mini-break,' Otto said as they checked into the hotel.

'I don't imagine it was, but Maria was lucky you were there,' Lily said as the receptionist handed her the room keys. Otto had been given Leo's room but they'd cancelled the booking, agreeing that two rooms were unnecessary. 'We never got that drink on the train,' she said as Otto picked up their bags. 'Shall we have one on the terrace?' Past the reception desk she could see a terrace, which overlooked an ornamental lake and the eighteenth hole of the golf course that was part of the resort where the conference was being held.

'Maybe later,' he replied. 'I've got other things planned for us now. Starting with a massage for you.'

'Really?' she asked. 'Is there a day spa here?'

'I assume so but that's not where you're going. I thought I'd be your masseur.'

He was smiling at her, confident she wouldn't refuse his offer. And he was right. His massages were the best. His surgeon's hands were skilful, supple and strong, able to find all the right spots to achieve the desired outcome. Which Lily knew was sex. His massages always ended in lovemaking. A massage from Otto had always been one of her favourite forms of foreplay.

They found their room and Otto hung the 'do not disturb' sign on the door before closing it. He laid a towel on the bed while Lily lifted her hair and pulled it into a ponytail and then a bun, getting it out of the way. She knew Otto would loosen it again later. He loved to run his fingers through her hair and she had no objection.

She wondered if this was wise. Letting herself knowingly be seduced again. But she wasn't going to put a stop to the interlude. Why deprive herself of pleasure?

She reached for the zip at the side of her dress and undid it slowly. She slipped one strap from her shoulder and then the other and let the dress fall to the floor.

Otto's eyes were dark and intense now. All traces of lightness had vanished as he watched and waited for her.

She reached her hands behind her back and unhooked her bra, sliding it along her arms and dropping it to the floor.

She turned her back and bent forwards, removing her underwear before lying face down on the bed, head turned to one side. Otto draped a towel over her hips and buttocks, covering her legs.

A fan spun lazily overhead and the movement of cool air on her skin brought tiny goosebumps out on her arms. Then Otto's warm hands were on her skin. Running over her shoulders and down her spine. Back up to her shoulders and along her arms. The pressure of his palms and fingers was light to begin with, feather-light. Teasing her and creating goosebumps for a different reason now.

His pressure intensified as he ran his thumbs up alongside her spine. First one side, then the other, finishing at the base of her skull. He massaged the individual muscles around her shoulder blades, then her arms, before returning to her shoulders.

His hands moved out wider, out to the curve of her ribs. His fingers brushed the sides of her breasts and she felt her nipples peak in response. His hands moved lower, to the small of her back, to the little dimples at the top of her pelvis where the bones joined her spine.

He flipped the towel, drawing it off her hips to cover her back, exposing her buttocks and legs. He worked on one buttock, then the other. Kneading in small circles. His hands moved down her legs. First left, then right. He bent her knee and massaged her calf, then foot. Left foot, right foot, back up the right calf. He found tiny knots in her calf and worked them until they were free.

He rested her leg on the bed and moved her knees apart. His hands were on either side of her left knee now, his fingers splayed on the inside of her thigh. The nerves in her thigh trembled at his touch, igniting a spark of desire that shot deep into her belly. She forced herself to lie still, knowing the anticipation was almost as delightful as the fulfilment that was coming her way.

His thumbs pressed into her hamstring as he ran his hands up the back of her thigh, only stopping at the point where her thigh met her groin. His fingers brushed the gap between her thighs and Lily's stomach twitched in response. She could feel the moisture gathering between her legs. She wanted to push herself against his hand but before she could move his fingers had slipped across her sex and he was now running his hands down her right leg, back to her knee to start all over again on the other side.

She moved her leg slightly wider, giving him more room. She was breathing heavily now and struggling to stay still.

He flipped her over and ran his hand up the inside of her thigh. Lily closed her eyes as her knees dropped apart and Otto slid one finger inside her. She could feel she was wet and warm. Swollen. Ripe.

His thumb found her sex and circled it slowly. Lily

arched her hips and pushed herself towards him. But she didn't want to come this way. She wanted him inside her.

She lifted one hand and placed it on his chest. 'Wait,' she said as she sat up. 'I want to do this together.'

She could see he was as eager as she was. His erection strained against his trousers. She reached for him, sliding her hands under his T-shirt. She trailed her fingernails lightly over his skin and heard him moan. She held onto the bottom of his shirt and stood up, pulling his shirt over his head, exposing his flat, toned stomach.

His hands moved to the button on his trousers but Lily was faster. She snapped open the button and slid the zip down. She could feel the hard bulge of his erection pressing into her, straining to get free.

He stepped out of his shoes, not bothering to untie the laces, as she pushed his trousers to the floor. They joined his shoes and shirt in an untidy heap. He was naked except for his boxer shorts. Lily slid them down and Otto stepped out of them. Her eyes travelled over him.

He was glorious.

He grinned at her and winked. He knew he looked good and he was confident enough to admit it. His confidence was sexy. He was sexy. Lily suspected she would never meet another man who could send her pulse skyrocketing with just a wink and smile as Otto could. When he was standing before her, gloriously naked and clearly admiring her in the same way, she wondered if getting divorced was the stupidest idea she'd ever had. Was she making a huge mistake? Was Daisy right? Was Otto the only man for her or was it just her hormones making her second-guess herself?

Well, either way, she wasn't backing out of this opportunity, she thought as she took his hand and pulled him onto the bed.

She lifted her hand to pull the elastic from her hair.

'Let me do that.' Otto's voice was husky with desire. Lust coated his words, making them so heavy they barely made it past his lips.

She dropped her hand, leaving her hair restrained. He reached for her hair and pulled the elastic free. He wound his fingers through her hair, loosening the strands as he spread her hair out, letting it fall over her shoulders before burying his face in it.

His fingers rested at the nape of her neck and his thumb rested on her jaw. It was warm and soft, his pressure gentle. He ran his thumb along the line of her jaw and then his thumb was replaced by his lips. He kissed her neck, her collarbone and the hollow at the base of her throat where her collarbones met.

His fingers blazed a trail across her body that his mouth followed. Down from her throat to her sternum, over her breast to her nipple. His fingers flicked over the nipple, already peaked and hard. His mouth followed, covering it, sucking, licking and tasting.

The fingers of his other hand were stroking the inside of her thigh. She parted her legs and his fingers slid inside her. His thumb rolled over her clitoris, making her gasp. He kissed her breast, sucking at her nipple as his thumb teased her. She arched her back, pushing her hips and breasts towards him, wanting more, letting him take her to a peak of desire.

Still she wanted more. She needed more.

She rolled towards him and pushed him flat onto his back. She sat up and straddled his hips. His erection rose between them, trapped between their groins. He lifted his head, taking her breast into his mouth once more. She closed her eyes as she gave herself up to the sensations shooting through her as his tongue flicked over her nipple. Every part of her responded to his touch. Her body came alive under his fingers and his lips and her skin burned where their bodies met.

She lifted herself clear of him, pulling her breast from his lips. Air flowed over her nipple, the cool temperature contrasting with the heat of his mouth. She put her hands either side of his head and kept her eyes on his face as she lifted herself up and took him inside her. His eyelids closed and she watched him breathe in deeply as her flesh encased him, joining them together.

She filled herself with his length before lifting her weight from him and letting him take control. His thumbs were on the front of her hips, his fingers behind her pelvis as he guided her up and down, matching her rhythm to his thrusts, each movement bringing her closer to climax.

She liked this position. She liked being able to watch him, she liked being able to see him getting closer and closer to release. His eyes were closed but his lips were parted, his breathing was rapid and shallow, his thrusts getting faster.

She spread her knees, letting him in deeper inside her until she had taken all of him. Her body was flooded with heat. Every nerve ending was crying out for his touch.

'Now, Otto. Now.'

He opened his eyes and his dark gaze locked with hers as he took her to the top of the peak.

Her body started to quiver and she watched him as he too trembled. He closed his eyes, threw his head back and thrust into her, claiming her as they climaxed together.

When they were spent she lay on him, covering his

body with hers. Their skin felt warm and flushed from their effort and they were both panting as he wrapped his arms around her back, holding her to him. She could feel his heart beating against her chest. She could feel it as its rhythm slowed, gradually returning to normal.

She tipped her head back and kissed him. 'That was some massage. Thank you.'

'My pleasure. Does this mean you're not going to divorce me?'

'Not today.' She smiled.

CHAPTER EIGHT

OTTO STEPPED OFF the podium at the end of his presentation and made his way to where Lily waited at the back of the room.

'Congratulations, that went well,' Lily said. He was an impressive public speaker. He knew his topic and had the confidence, charm and charisma to hold an audience.

'Thanks, I always prefer to get it out of the way early and then I can enjoy myself,' he said as he walked beside her and out into the foyer. 'Speaking of enjoying ourselves, what are you doing for lunch? Do you want to play hooky with me for the rest of the day?'

'You're not going to stay for any of the afternoon sessions? Some of them sound interesting.'

His expression implied that he had other things on his agenda and his next words confirmed that. 'Some of them do sound interesting but they're all being recorded, which means we can watch them later. There's no roll call, there are no exams,' he said when he could see her wavering. 'No one is going to notice or care if we're here or not. Half the doctors will be playing golf.'

'You want to play golf?' she said. 'That sounds horrendous!' Playing hooky went against the grain for her and if she was going to miss the conference, it needed to be for a better reason than a round of golf. A *much* better reason. Another massage, for instance, could persuade her.

'No,' he laughed. 'I do not want to play golf. I want to take you on a picnic.'

'A picnic?' She'd been hoping for something a little more R-rated. Was it terrible that she was slightly disappointed?

'Do you have a better suggestion?' he asked with a half-smile, making her blush. 'It's a shame to waste such a glorious day by being inside at either the conference or in our room, I'll make it up to you later.'

Lily grinned back at him. 'In that case, then, a picnic sounds like fun.'

Otto called an Uber and had it drop them at a winery that sat at the top of a hill a short distance from the conference resort. He collected a rug and a picnic basket from the cellar at the restaurant and took her across the lawns to a spot out of sight of the winery buildings but with amazing views over the Hunter Valley.

'Did you arrange this in advance?' Lily asked as Otto spread the blanket on the ground.

'I did.'

'Were you that confident I'd say yes?'

'I was pretty confident.' He grinned and took her hands and pulled her down onto the blanket beside him. 'And now,' he said as he opened a bottle of wine and poured two glasses, 'I intend to spend the afternoon reminding you of all the reasons why you don't want to divorce me.'

She never *wanted* to divorce him, she just didn't think she had another option if she wanted a family, but the more time they spent together, the more difficult she found it to imagine her life without him in it. But she was mindful of falling under his spell, of letting herself get swept away by the intimacy and company without thinking about the consequences. Without sorting out their issues.

He had been honest with her, now it was her turn. She needed to clear the air otherwise she knew they wouldn't be able to move forwards.

'There's something I need to tell you,' she said, 'in the interest of full disclosure.'

'Should I be worried?'

'No. It's about the letters Helen asked us to write. I think I need to read you mine.' She'd started writing it as soon as Helen had suggested it. As much as she hadn't been certain it was a good idea, she hadn't considered *not* doing it, but she had found it difficult. She'd stopped and started and hadn't completed it until after Natalie had been admitted to hospital with placental abruption. Until after the night she had spent sleeping in Otto's embrace. Until *after* she'd forgiven both Otto and herself. She'd needed to find forgiveness before she could find closure.

'Putting words on paper made me realise a few things about our relationship. I still think our issues started when I got pregnant but we were both to blame for the failings in our marriage and I needed to accept that some of the fault lay with me. You weren't as excited as I was when I got pregnant, I knew that, and I felt like I was going through the pregnancy on my own. You were busy, focused on your work and study, and we spent very little time together. I knew the timing of the pregnancy wasn't ideal but I felt like you were disengaged and choosing work over me. I knew you were going to be busy while we were in London, that was the whole point of going, but once I got pregnant I expected things to be different and I was upset that they weren't. And then after the assault things got worse. We spent almost no time together and we weren't communicating at all and I realise now there are things I should have told you. Things I should have said. After the assault I was distraught but I was also angry and I took that out on you. For a long time I blamed you. For staying at work instead of coming home. For not comforting me. For not supporting me.'

Otto shook his head. 'You were right to blame me. I did all those things and I've regretted each and every one of them.'

'No, it wasn't fair. We both made mistakes but those mistakes weren't the reason I lost the baby. The man who assaulted me caused that but it was easier to blame you than to accept that I had failed.'

'I don't understand. Why do you think you failed? What mistakes did you make? What did you do?'

'It's what I *didn't* do. I didn't let go of my bag. I should have. I don't know why I didn't. A stupid reflex. Stubbornness. Surprise. Something made me hold on to it but if I'd just let go, he would have left me alone. I wouldn't have been physically assaulted; I wouldn't have fallen. I would have just been a victim of a bag theft instead of a victim of assault. I would have been a woman who lost her bag instead of a mother who lost her baby.' Silent tears rolled down her cheeks and she brushed them away impatiently. She didn't want to look as if she was asking for sympathy. She was admitting her part in the trauma, she was taking responsibility.

'Lily, no.' Otto reached out and wiped the traces of tears from her face and Lily's heart skipped a beat. 'None of what happened was your fault. You don't know that you wouldn't have fallen. He still could have pushed you, punched you, hurt you.'

'I know that now but at the time I felt like I'd failed as a wife and mother and that was hard to deal with.'

'I had no idea you felt like that. Why didn't you say anything?'

'I was afraid of how I felt. Guilty. Lost. A failure. I was scared that if I didn't keep quiet I'd find myself admitting to those emotions and then you'd blame me. I wanted you to comfort me. To tell me you still loved me. To tell me the placental abruption wasn't my fault. But I was afraid you wouldn't tell me that and I couldn't stand the thought that you'd agree with me. That you'd think I caused our daughter's death.'

'Lily! I never thought that.'

'I could see it in your eyes. You couldn't even look at me.'

Otto shook his head. 'That was my guilt you could see. I thought it was reflected back at me every time I looked at you and it ate away at me. That's why I avoided coming home. That's why I avoided you. Because I couldn't bear to think I'd let you down. I don't blame you. Believe me, if I could go back and have that day again I would do things differently, we both would, but the blame lies with the man who assaulted you, not with you. If he hadn't snatched your bag, if he hadn't pushed you, it would have just been a night like any other. A night when I got home late and you were annoyed with me but we would have forgotten all about it.'

'I know that now,' she said, knowing he was right. It had taken her a long time but she'd forgiven Otto, she'd forgiven herself. 'But I still owe you an apology. I wasn't being honest about my feelings.'

'It doesn't matter...' he began to say before Lily joined in. 'What's done is done,' they said in unison.

Otto smiled and took her hand. 'What does matter is that I love you. I always have and I always will. What does matter is I don't want a divorce. I should have supported you then and I promise to support you now. Will you give me a chance to make it up to you?'

'What are you suggesting?'

'That we give our marriage another shot. Properly. I move back in and we start again. What do you think?'

Was this the moment she'd been waiting for? The moment when forgiveness of their past mistakes, the mistakes that had torn them apart, would turn into a second chance? A chance of a future together?

There was no way of knowing unless she was prepared to take that chance. Unless she was prepared to trust Otto.

She took a deep breath and nodded. 'I think that sounds perfect.'

Otto pulled her to him and kissed her. His kiss tasted of dreams and promises and Lily prayed that this time they would be fulfilled.

He topped up their glasses and proposed a toast. 'Here's to us and our happiness together. We have another life in front of us, we can learn from our past but not let it define our future.'

Lily touched her glass against Otto's and smiled as she pictured that future and the children she was sure were going to be a part of it. 'To our future.'

Lily and Otto walked into Helen's office and for the first time Lily knew she was smiling as they entered. Unlike the previous sessions, today's appointment wasn't filling her with dread. For the first time in months, she was completely happy and she was looking forward to advising Helen that this would be their final session. Otto had moved out of the hotel and back into the house. Their house. And she was enjoying the rebuilding phase of their relationship. She was enjoying having someone to have dinner with, someone to exercise with and someone to share her bed with.

She and Otto were back on track, she thought as she sat on the small sofa beside her husband.

'Is my job done?' Helen asked as they sat. 'You're giving your marriage another chance?'

'Why do you say that?'

'Your body language has changed. You look more relaxed, Lily, less wary. You're sitting much closer to Otto and you haven't picked up a pillow to put on your lap,' Helen said with a smile.

She was right. In all the previous sessions Lily had felt the need to use a pillow as a barrier, some protection against the attraction she still felt for Otto. But she didn't need that protection any more. She was embracing that attraction. She was embracing their relationship.

'We've made some progress.' Otto smiled.

'You're having sex?'

Lily looked sideways at Otto and smiled as Otto answered for them both. 'Yes.'

'You've resolved all your differences?' Helen asked. 'You've had an open and honest discussion about what went wrong?'

They both nodded.

'That's good. Have you talked about what happens next for you both?' Helen continued. 'What you want your future to look like?'

Lily shook her head. They'd talked about the past and the present but expected the future to take care of itself.

'I assume everything will go back to the way it was,' Otto replied.

'Which was?' Helen asked.

'We spend some time together, just the two of us, making up for the past two years, getting our relationship back on track. Once we're back on track and our careers are established, then we start trying for a baby.'

Once again, they were at cross purposes and Lily could see her plans crashing down around her. She'd assumed they'd be starting a family now. She'd made assumptions. Perhaps that was a mistake. She turned to Otto. 'You know I want children now. Isn't that what our renewed relationship is all about?'

'You haven't discussed this?' Helen sounded dumbfounded.

'I assumed we were on the same page,' Lily said. She turned to Helen. 'How do we resolve this?' she asked.

'It sounds like you still need to work on open channels of communication,' Helen told them. 'It's a positive that you are still physically attracted to each other and while that's great, sex is an important part of an intimate, monogamous relationship, sex without emotional connection is just sex,' she said. 'Sexual chemistry is important but it isn't enough if you don't share the same goals and similar values. You need to acknowledge that your feelings can, and will, differ from each other and you need to acknowledge that is OK. It's impossible for two people to think and feel exactly the same way about things. You need to respect those differences.

'If a relationship is going to work you should expect to share similar views and goals, but to expect someone else to always share your views on everything is unrealistic. If a relationship is going to work you should be able to deal with challenges together. You don't have to agree on everything but at the end of the day your fundamental beliefs have to align. It's up to both of you to work out what the fundamentals are. You have to decide which differences you are prepared to accept if a relationship is going to last and which differences are non-negotiable. You can walk away without having those conversations but if you want to give your relationship a chance, even if it's being able to move forwards with a different type of relationship between the two of you, then you need to have conversations around that. What are your non-negotiables?'

'I want children,' Lily said.

'So do I,' Otto replied, 'but not yet.'

'When?'

'I assumed we'd wait until you turned thirty-one before we started trying for a family,' Otto replied. 'Just like we'd planned.'

'That's another year away! You know I want children now. We both know that a previous placental abruption increases the risk of having another. I want to try to fall pregnant before I get much older in case something else goes wrong.'

'Lily, I want to be around when we have children. After being sent to boarding school I promised myself that I wouldn't be an absent father. Right now I'm establishing my career. We agreed to wait until you were thirty-two before we had a family. That means aiming to get pregnant next year. I want to be around to help with our children.'

'I can manage.'

'But I don't want you to manage on your own. I want to be there to form that bond.'

'There will never be the perfect time,' Lily retorted. 'There is always something else you want to do, another box to tick, another challenge to meet. What if you keep putting it off?' She was worried he'd keep delaying. She was worried he'd want to wait for ever.

'Marriage is about compromise,' Helen told them. 'Who is willing to compromise?'

Lily wasn't sure if she was. She knew the compromise would be at the expense of an imminent pregnancy and that might be more than she was prepared to give up.

She reached for her bag and stood up. 'I need some time to think about this,' she said. She needed some fresh air, time to clear her head.

'Lily, wait.' Otto had followed her out of Helen's office and he stuck his arm out as the lift doors were closing. 'I'm not letting you go again,' he said as he followed her into the lift. 'We need to sort this out. You want trust. I want truth. I don't want a divorce. I don't want someone else making a family with you. I love you. I always have.'

The lift doors slid closed and Otto faced her. 'If you don't love me, tell me now. If you want a divorce, tell me now. If you want to give our marriage another chance, tell me now and we'll figure this out. Today. We can't get the last two years back but we can have a future. If you don't want a future with me, tell me now, and I will walk away and you can get on with your life.'

The idea of watching Otto walk away made her feel physically ill.

'I don't want someone else to be the father of my children either. I love you too. I don't want a divorce but I do want a baby. If we stay together I can't understand the point of waiting. And I'm worried that you'll keep delaying starting a family.'

'I think we need some time where it's just the two of us. I don't want the added pressure of you trying to get pregnant while I'm starting this new job,' he said. 'I want the next pregnancy to be different from last time. I want to be there to support you through it. I don't want to be at work all the time. I don't want you to feel like you're doing it on your own. Not the pregnancy part. Or the raising our baby part, but I'm willing to compromise. Instead of waiting until next year, can you give me until the middle of this year and then we'll start trying to get pregnant? That's only a few more months. We could have a baby by the middle of next year and I'd be able to have time off. I want to be part of it. I need to feel I'm part of it.'

'How do I know you won't change your mind?'

'I need time to prove that to you. I'm asking you to give me that time. Meet me halfway. Please. I want to be the father of your children,' he pleaded as they stepped out of the lift. 'I'm just asking for a little more time.'

She could give up her dreams of a pregnancy in the near future or she could give up Otto. The decision was hers.

Lily yawned and stretched. It was good to be busy, it kept her mind off the subject of her ticking biological clock and off babies.

She'd chosen Otto. She didn't want a future without him and she didn't want to have babies without him so she'd chosen her husband and hoped she'd be able to live with the reality of delaying her family. But it was easier said than done.

When she was busy she could block out thoughts of

babes and pregnancy but in the long hours of the night she tossed and turned. Her mind was restless and she imagined she could feel her empty womb aching. She was exhausted. Even though Otto slept beside her she was edgy, unable to still the thoughts, and the lack of sleep was making her tired and grumpy. She'd lost her appetite and she was feeling emotionally fragile. This wasn't how things were supposed to be.

She breathed deeply in an attempt to get some oxygen to her brain. The air in the ED felt stagnant and smelt stale. Perhaps she should pop outside while she had a moment, she thought. But before she could stand the phone on the triage desk rang, startling her.

'Incoming patient,' Julie announced, as she replaced the receiver. 'Male in his twenties, multiple injuries, a fall at Ben Buckler.'

Lily stood up quickly, before her blood pressure could stabilise, and she grabbed at the desk as the room spun around her.

'Are you all right?' Julie asked.

'Yes,' she said as her surroundings steadied. 'Just a bit light-headed. I think I stood up too fast.' The ED had been busy and she'd missed lunch, that wasn't uncommon, so perhaps her fatigue was also having an impact on her blood sugar. She should probably have something to eat but that would have to wait.

The ambulance pulled up and Poppy emerged from the rear. She 'd been back at work for a month since returning from her honeymoon but she hadn't lost that glow of happiness of the newly married. Lily knew that, in contrast to her younger sister, she was looking tired and worn out. She felt, and looked, as if she could use a holiday.

'Patient is unconscious, has multiple fractures and

suspected spinal injuries and will need a mental health assessment,' Poppy said. The steep, unforgiving cliffs of Ben Buckler at the northern end of Bondi Beach were a frequent spot for accidents and some deliberate mishaps as well.

Lily started pushing the stretcher into the ED as Poppy continued her summary but something wasn't right. Lily could see Poppy's lips moving but it sounded as though she were talking underwater.

Her vision was blurry. She squeezed her eyes shut, trying to clear her vision, but when she opened them there were black spots in her view and then the room began to spin.

'Lily? Lily, can you hear me?'

Lily opened her eyes.

'Where am I?' she asked as she realised she was looking up at Poppy. The last thing she remembered was walking into the ED beside the trolley.

'You're in the ED.'

That was good. 'Why am I lying down?' she asked as the ceiling came into focus behind Poppy's head.

'You fainted.'

'Fainted?' She wasn't a fainter. She'd only fainted once before. Her blood sugar must be really low, she thought as she sat up.

'Slowly,' Poppy warned.

'I'm fine. I skipped lunch.'

'Do you want me to get you something to eat?'

The thought of eating made her nauseous. 'No.' She shook her head. Carefully. 'What are you doing here anyway? Shouldn't you be back on the road? And what happened to our patient?'

Poppy shrugged. 'Ajay's taking care of him and I was owed a break. So unless Alex and I get a call out I thought I'd wait here until Otto gets out of Theatre.'

'You told Otto?'

'Why wouldn't I tell Otto?'

'You didn't need to bother him. I'm fine.'

'He's in Theatre anyway.'

Of course he was busy, Lily thought. It was lucky she was fine otherwise what would he do?

'What's going on?' Poppy wanted to know. 'I thought the two of you had sorted things out.'

Lily hadn't been able to bring herself to share the latest dilemma with her sisters. She was still trying to process it herself. 'So did I,' she admitted, 'but it turns out we were both making assumptions about our relationship.'

'Meaning?'

'I thought being back on track meant that we wouldn't get divorced and we'd start a family. Otto thought it meant we wouldn't get divorced and we'd start a family in a couple of years. He did offer to meet me in the middle. He suggested that we start trying to get pregnant in six months instead of next year but I'm still not sure. I get that I can't have children right now without Otto, it's not like I have another man waiting in the wings, I know it would take time to find someone, establish that relationship, before I could have kids, but what if Otto changes his mind? What if he wants to put things off again?'

'You don't trust him to keep his word?'

That was the big question. She wanted to trust him. She had to trust him if they had any hope of a future. But how was she going to do that? 'I'm going round in circles in my head. I'm not sleeping. I'm tired and anxious and confused. I'm not myself.'

'Are you sure it's just emotional stress? What if it's something physically wrong. You just fainted. Do you want me to get Ajay in here? Maybe he should order blood tests?'

'No. I'm sure I'm fine.'

'Could you be pregnant?' Poppy asked.

'Pregnant!'

She was about to say, *Don't be ridiculous. I'm not pregnant*, but was it completely out of the question?

'When was your last period?' Poppy asked.

She had to think. Before the conference. Before Poppy's wedding. She could feel the colour leave her face as she fought back a rising tide of nausea. 'Six weeks ago.'

'I think you should do a test.'

'I can't be pregnant.' As if saying that would make it true.

'Why not?'

'Because Otto isn't ready.'

She knew it was too soon in their rekindled relationship. As if things needed to get any worse!

Otto took the stairs two at a time, burst through the last door and sprinted into the ED.

'Where is she?'

Julie was at the triage desk and her eyes were wide as he raced past her. 'Exam room four,' she called out.

Otto's heart had lodged in his throat the minute he'd received news that Lily had collapsed. He was furious that the information had been withheld from him until after he'd finished operating even though he understood why. He would not have been able to concentrate if he'd been advised earlier and professionally that would not have been acceptable but, personally, if anything happened to Lily, he would be a broken man. As long as she was OK, he would give her anything she wanted, he vowed. Do anything she wanted.

'Lily!'

She was pale but it wasn't the colour of her skin that worried him. It was the look on her face. She looked petrified.

Oh, God. What was wrong? She'd obviously had bad news.

'I'll wait outside.' He hadn't noticed Poppy until she spoke. She looked at Lily and then left the room. Why was she waiting outside? What was she waiting for?

Otto's fear escalated. 'What is it? What's wrong?' He rushed to Lily's side, kissed her cheek and took her hand. If she'd had bad news so quickly it must be terrible. Anything minor would take longer to find.

Lily was trembling.

He sat beside her and wrapped an arm around her shoulders. Was she cold? Frightened? In shock? Where was a doctor? Who was going to tell him what was going on?

'Lily, you're frightening me. Tell me what's wrong.' He knew this was his moment. The moment to show her he was beside her one hundred per cent. His moment to support her in whatever way she needed. 'Whatever it is, we can handle it. Together.'

Her eyes filled with tears and Otto's heart froze in his chest.

'Lily?'

'I'm pregnant.'

'What?' It took him a moment to process what she was saying. It wasn't what he expected. 'Pregnant?'

She nodded.

He laughed. 'Oh, thank God.'

Lily was frowning. 'You're not upset.'

'No. I'm relieved. You looked terrified and I was expecting bad news. Something life-threatening. Pregnancy isn't terminal.'

'Maybe not. But it is permanent.'

'What does that mean?'

'I'm keeping the baby.'

'Of course we are.' He let out a sign of relief. An unexpected pregnancy was nothing compared to all the ailments he'd imagined could have befallen Lily.

Lily frowned. 'Are you sure? You said you weren't ready for children.'

'I know. But the idea was beginning to grow on me.'

'Really?'

He smiled and sat on the edge of the bed. 'Spending the past month with you, and seeing you with your niece and nephew, I began to see what you saw. What our life would look like. Chaotic, disorganised, sure, but also fun and filled with love. I knew I wasn't going to be able to control everything and that's OK. If I've learnt my lesson, I can accept that some things are out of my control. Like how much I love you.' He leant forwards and kissed her. 'I don't need to control everything. I just need you. All that matters is that you're OK. All I could think of after I heard you'd collapsed was that I would do anything, give you anything, as long as you were safe. I couldn't handle losing you but I reckon I can handle a baby.

'Are you sure? You're not going to freak out? You're not going to tell me it's too soon? That we have things to sort out? That you have a career to establish?'

'Lily, I want children with you, I want a family with you, and if it's sooner rather than later then that's OK.

I love you and I promise I will be here for you and our children. One hundred per cent. I apologise for being an arse. I was worrying about things that didn't matter, things that could be sorted.'

'Things that could be fixed,' Lily said with a smile.

'Exactly.' He smiled back. 'And that's my speciality. Fixing is not controlling.'

'I'm sorry I doubted you. I assumed I knew what your reaction was going to be.'

'I would do anything for you. I don't want to lose you. I never wanted to lose you. I love you. I always have and I always will. That has never changed.'

'And what if things go wrong?'

'We have to believe that things will be OK, but if they're not then I hope we've learnt something from counselling. We'll talk to each other, support each other. We're going to do this together. Today and every day. We're a team. And this baby will be the newest member. This baby is our future.' Otto put one hand under her chin and tipped her face up so she was looking at him. 'I want you to look at me and see someone who will take care of you and our family. I want you to look at me and see someone who loves you, today and every day. I want you to look at me and see someone who is ready for the next chapter in our life together. Our life as a family. Speaking of which, there is something I've been wanting to discuss with you.'

'Yes?'

'I think we should renew our wedding vows. Make our promises in front of our friends and family as we start the next phase of our life together. What do you think?'

'I think that sounds perfect.'

'And I also thought we could invite your parents.' He

paused, waiting to see if Lily had any strong objections, but when she stayed silent, he continued, 'It might be the chance you've been waiting for, the opportunity to build a relationship. Knowing we're about to start our own family might be the catalyst that's needed. What do you say? How does that sound?'

'It sounds like you want to fix something.' She smiled.

'Only with your permission.'

She nodded. 'I think that's a good idea,' she said as she reached for him and took his face in her hands. She pulled him closer and kissed him. 'I love you. And I will tell anyone who wants to hear it and I will happily marry you all over again.'

EPILOGUE

'AN NA WILLOW CARLSON-CHEN! Be careful!' Mei called out to her daughter, who was jumping into the pool, narrowly missing Niki, who was splashing about with Lily's father. Pete had made a good recovery following his brain aneurysm sixteen months earlier. He'd committed to his rehabilitation, working hard to restore his balance and strength, motivated by his desire to get back on a surfboard.

The entire Carlson clan, including Lily's parents, Pete and Goldie, had descended on Poppy and Ryder's new house to celebrate Naming Day for the children.

Lily, Mei and Jet were watching the antics in the pool and Jet was laughing as An Na resurfaced, spluttering. 'Our poor child. She's been lumped with a mouthful of a name.'

'It's all out of love,' Mei said.

An Na had officially been given her auntie Willow's name along with a hyphenated surname. The Carlson siblings had agreed to give any daughters 'Willow' as a middle name, a connection to their sister, Daisy's twin, who had been taken from them too early. Today was a celebration of not only An Na's name but also the baptism ceremonies for Poppy and Ryder's five-week-old son, Teddy, and Lily and Otto's daughter, Posie Willow Sofia Rodgers, who was three months old and had been named for her aunt and paternal grandmother.

Lily looked around the garden at her family, in awe about how much had changed in a year. Two babies, two more weddings—Jet and Mei and Daisy and Ajay had all married—and Poppy and Ryder had bought a house. Lily knew how much that stability meant to Poppy and to see her sister, all her siblings, so happy and settled only added to her own happiness.

'Dad, Dad, come in the pool with me,' An Na instructed and Jet willingly obliged. He was a soft touch for his only daughter. As he said, he came into An Na's life late and had to make up for lost time.

'Are you ready to have more kids?' Lily asked her sister-in-law as she lifted her own daughter from her breast, where she had been feeding, and listened for the little satisfied burp.

'Not just yet. I've got a few more years of med school to go along with juggling my shifts with the ambulance service. I don't think I can put much more on my plate. I know there will be a big gap between An Na and any siblings but she'll have plenty of cousins.'

Lily found it incredible to think that eighteen months ago the four Carlson siblings had no children in their lives and now there were four between them.

'Goldie,' Mei called out to her mother-in-law. 'Come and sit with Lily. I'll bring the food out.'

Lily looked up to where Otto and Ryder were cooking the barbecue and Ajay and Lily's mother, Goldie, were ferrying plates from the kitchen to the outdoor table, ready for lunch. Poppy had gone inside to change Teddy and Daisy was preparing salads. There was constant movement between people but there was always some-one to talk to or to lend a hand.

Goldie sat down in the chair vacated by Mei. 'Can I hold Posie?' she asked and Lily happily passed her the baby. 'She is so beautiful,' Goldie said.

Lily didn't disagree. Her daughter was divine. Fair haired and dark eyed, just as Lily imagined.

'I wish I could remember how it felt to hold you in my arms when you were a newborn but I am so grateful for the chance to hold my grandbabies,' Goldie said.

It had taken some time but, thanks to Otto and his pen-chant for fixing things, Lily and her siblings were gradu-ally mending their relationship with their parents. Otto had got the ball rolling when he'd organised a renewal of their wedding vows and invited Pete and Goldie. He had listened to Lily when she'd said she felt they should have invited them the first time around and that invita-tion had been the catalyst that brought them into their grandchildren's lives.

Pete and Goldie had been young parents themselves, with no experience and no family support. By their own admission they hadn't known what they were doing and Goldie, in particular, had found the weight of respon-sibility too much. Now they were able to enjoy being grandparents, with all care and no responsibility. It was perfect for them and Lily was enjoying getting to know her parents as people, without expectations.

'How are you?' Goldie asked.

Lily knew it was a loaded question but she kept her answer simple and honest. 'I'm good. Tired but happy.'

'Otto said you're starting to think about going back to work? That seems soon.'

'I won't be going back for a few months but I have to start thinking about childcare.'

'What are your plans for that?'

Lily knew her mother wouldn't be offering to help. Pete and Goldie lived in Byron Bay, an eight-hour drive north of Sydney. They were able to visit for special occasions but not available for regular babysitting and Lily and her siblings were fine with that. They weren't sure they were ready to hand over any major child-minding to their parents; they hadn't exactly been model parents when raising their own family. 'Poppy, Daisy and I are thinking about sharing a nanny for Posie, Ted and Niki, although I'm not sure we've convinced Mrs Singh to share Niki,' she replied, 'and then we'll cover any gaps in our shift work rosters between us.'

'You're very lucky to have the support of each other. If I hadn't had the support of the commune I don't know how I would have managed.'

Until recently Lily hadn't thought her parents had managed at all but she hadn't known the full story. Goldie had run away from home, fallen in love with Pete and had Lily when she was eighteen. She'd then fallen pregnant in rapid succession with Jet and then Poppy and had suffered with undiagnosed postnatal depression after Lily's birth before another bout of depression after Daisy's twin, Willow, had died. Goldie's history went a long way to explaining why she'd always seemed so disconnected from her children's lives but forgiveness was an ongoing thing and the revelations were taking some adjusting to. Lily was getting there sooner than Poppy and Daisy but she was mindful that everyone needed to process things in their own way. Perhaps not all the bridges could be repaired.

Lily knew it was Goldie's history of depression that made her check in on Lily's well-being. She also knew that Otto had been watching her closely for any signs of postnatal depression but Lily knew she was fine. In hindsight, she knew she'd suffered depression after the assault that had caused the loss of her first child but having Posie had been the best thing for her. She hadn't forgotten her first daughter, but Posie and Otto's love had put her back together again.

'Mum, would you be able to make your salad dressing?' Daisy asked as she approached, reaching her hands out to take the baby. Goldie stood up and passed Posie over as Lily smiled. It was lucky Posie was a placid baby who had no qualms about being passed around.

Holding babies suits you, Lily signed as Daisy took the empty seat. Her youngest sister had always had a Madonna-type soul. *Are you and Ajay talking about babies yet?*

'Ajay would like more children and I'd be happy with that but if it happens it happens and if not,' Daisy said with a shrug, 'I already have everything I wanted. I found my person and he came with a bonus in the shape of Niki. I don't need anything more.'

'Lunch is ready,' Otto said as he joined them. 'Do you want me to put Posie down for a nap?'

'Thank you,' Lily said gratefully. She never minded holding her daughter but even she could admit that it was easier to eat a meal when she wasn't trying to juggle a baby.

Otto lifted Posie from Daisy's lap and snuggled her into his shoulder. Lily never tired of watching him with their daughter. Posie adored her father and he adored her. Like Daisy, Lily had everything she ever wanted although she would happily have another baby. But she had time. Otto wasn't going anywhere and neither was she.

It turned out that Daisy was right, she thought as she stood and kissed first Posie's cheek and then Otto's.

There was only one man for her.

* * * * *

HOW TO RESIST
THE SINGLE DAD

JC HARROWAY

MILLS & BOON

To Becky, my horse-loving, welly-wearing,
Land Rover–driving friend.

CHAPTER ONE

WATCHING DR AARON BENNETT speak from the main lecture-theatre podium of London's City Hospital gave Stella Wright serious crush flashbacks. Of course she had fancied him. Who wouldn't? But, where her ridiculous teenage obsession had been abstract, that of the shy fourteen-year-old she'd once been, now she struggled to focus on his lecture to this year's intake of general-practitioner trainees.

Like an expensive single-malt whisky, Aaron had only improved with age. He sported a head of sandy blond hair that had the tendency to flop over his aristocratic brow. His dark-framed glasses made his bright blue eyes—ones she had once considered *dreamy*—appear more intense. He wore a fine-knit V-necked jumper over his shirt, and when he had turned his back on his audience to point at the screen, Stella had almost drooled at his toned backside. In fact, his entire look brought to mind a sexy professor fantasy that Stella should in no way indulge.

She dragged her eyes away. She was long ago done with charmers and Aaron Bennett epitomised the definition. Or at least he had during his twenties and early thirties in their Cotswold village of Abbotsford.

With a reputation as a charismatic playboy, he'd regularly blasted back into their sleepy village for a weekend of hedonistic fun, always driving a fast sports car and bringing with him a gaggle of friends looking for a wild party at the country estate his parents still ran. His notorious reputation had been the talk of the town, every eligible woman and mother alike wondering when the local heartthrob would settle down. Return home for good and take up his place in the small community.

To everyone's surprise, he eventually had.

And now, here in London—Stella's home these past nine years—he seemed somehow out of place, even though he himself had trained and worked in the capital.

Of course, she hadn't heard a word of what he'd actually said for the last five minutes since she'd first drifted off into a lust-filled daydream and then been reminded of another Cotswolds smooth-talker, one who'd done such a good job of breaking her heart, she'd sworn off relationships at the tender age of eighteen. Which was why, when he closed his laptop at the end of his lecture and said her name, Stella almost slid from her seat to disappear beneath the desk.

'Could Stella Wright please see me? Thank you.' He swept his gaze over the doctors filling the auditorium.

In case her friends were watching and wondering what she had done to upset the teacher, Stella forced her face to freeze on a benign smile, while her insides tumbled over themselves to make sense of his request. What could Aaron Bennett want with *her*? Yes, they came from the same small village, where his family descended from a long line of landed gentry. She knew all about his tragic past, which like Stella's own notoriety had no doubt been prime village-gossip fodder. But they'd never actually spoken to one another.

Fourteen- or fifteen-year-old Stella would have swooned. It was a good thing that twenty-seven-year-old committed singleton Dr Stella Wright's swooning days were over.

As Aaron fell into conversation with one of the keener registrars, a gorgeous blonde Stella knew well enough to guess had approached him with an intelligent question that had nothing to do with his backside or dreamy eyes, Stella headed for the stairs and raked her scattered wits for something to say other than *Hi, I used to have a crush on you.*

For goodness' sake, he was one of her educational supervisors. Her past and irrelevant infatuation with Dr Delicious should serve only to remind her of the momentous reasons she'd left Abbotsford for the big-city lights of London in the first place. Why she'd followed in her sister Darcy's footsteps and moved here, reinventing herself in the process.

Heartbreak Harry, as she'd named her ex.

Stella cast a glance at Aaron. Had he remembered her from Abbotsford, heard the gossip?

Still in conversation with the blonde, he seemed completely oblivious to Stella. Perhaps he didn't know she existed. Well, that suited her just fine.

She paused halfway down the steps to reply to a group text from her GP trainee friends, who were about to scatter across the country for the final eighteen months of their training.

Clubbing tonight—last night before we all disperse.

Stella smiled, a spasm of nostalgia pinching her ribs. She was staying in London. She loved living here. The vibrancy, the constant bustle, the anonymity of being one person out of millions. But she would miss her crew. Who would go clubbing with her now? Her sister was recently all loved up, so she had no hope of dragging Darcy out on the town.

Just then her friend Tom called out from the front of the lecture theatre, where there was a bottleneck at the exit.

'Stells.' He waved, snagging her attention away from Aaron's broad shoulders. 'Pre-drinks at the pub tonight? Wear your dancing shoes.' Tom offered a playful wink, a shimmy to a tune only he could hear and left the lecture theatre.

Tom didn't do subtle. There was no way Aaron had missed their interaction.

Prickles danced over her skin, a sensation of Aaron's observation that should have been uncomfortable but instead left her wondering if he was still single or remained unattached after the death of his wife.

She looked up, sucking in a breath as her stare collided directly with his. He had been watching her, his conversation seemingly abandoned as he stared intently.

A small smile twitched her cheeks while she battled the incendiary effects of that direct eye contact. It could have only lasted a second or two, but it was long enough for Stella's pulse to skyrocket and her breath to trap under her diaphragm as if she had a stitch.

Had she imagined a tightening of his facial muscles between his brows, the thinning of his lips? Was he judging her penchant for having a good time, letting down her hair, dancing?

Clearly they had little in common beyond coming from the same village.

Stella lingered over the last few steps to the front of the auditorium, waiting for him to wind up his conversation.

The other doctor headed for the exit, leaving her and Aaron alone. The vast theatre, which could easily seat three hundred people, shrank to the size of a broom cupboard. The closer she stepped, the more attractive he became. Nerves accosted her stomach at his tall, imposing masculinity. Their differences—the age gap and the country-boy, city-girl chasm—seemed increasingly trivial.

'Dr Wright, thanks for waiting behind,' he said, his deep voice confident and full of warmth. He tossed his glasses onto the podium and held out his hand.

'No problem,' she croaked, shaking his hand firmly in order to boost her wobbling confidence. Alone with her and up close he seemed to have morphed into the hottest man she'd ever met.

With his glasses removed, his bold blue eyes were more vibrant. His biceps and pecs were clearly demarcated beneath his jumper. His tie was ever so slightly askew, lending him a roguish, devil-may-care vibe that tied all of his attractive qualities together with a bright red bow, a combination that packed a considerable punch to Stella's poor neglected libido.

She swallowed. Time to get a grip. His hotness was completely irrelevant.

a) He had looked disapproving at her clubbing plans.

b) Despite no trace of a dad bod, Stella knew from her parents that he had a young son.

c) Perhaps the most important factor of all: Stella hadn't dated since Harry.

'I won't keep you long.' He dropped her hand.

Stella wiped her palm on her trouser leg as discreetly

as possible, praying like crazy that he hadn't felt the jud-
ders zapping along her nerves as they touched. This close
she could smell his aftershave, which was woodsy and
fresh and made her homesick for autumn walks through
the countryside and roaring fires on a cold day.

'What's this about?' she said, the flash of what looked
like guilt or sympathy on his face raising her defensive
hackles. Was he recalling what he knew of her from the
small talk that had once circulated in Abbotsford?

She felt like a germ swimming in a petri dish.

Privacy was scarce in village life, and Stella had left
the Cotswolds for university under a cloud of unjust gossip that still had the ability to make her shudder with
shame. Not because the rumours had been true—beyond
being young and naive and falling head over heels for
the wrong man with a young son and a complicated past
he'd lied about, she'd done nothing wrong. But because
she couldn't for the life of herself fathom that she'd once
been so gullible, so lovestruck, so pitiable.

If only she could forget the humiliation of not only
having her tender teenaged heart broken for the first time,
but also being unfairly vilified as some sort of Lolita-
esque home-wrecker...

'I'm afraid there's an issue with your GP placement,'
Aaron said without reference to Abbotsford. Perhaps he
didn't recognise her after all.

Stella winced at the bedside manner of his tone. 'What
issue?'

Aaron's stare roamed her face as if peeling away her
layers of armour, one by one. Did he have to look at her
with such...intimacy?

'I'm afraid your assigned GP, Dr Roberts at Ealing

Health has suffered a serious medical emergency and will no longer be able to accommodate you at his surgery.'

Stella covered her mouth in shock. 'Is he okay?' *Poor Dr Roberts.*

'He suffered a myocardial infarction yesterday,' Aaron said, 'and underwent coronary artery stenting this morning, but obviously he isn't expected back at work for some time.'

Stella nodded, realisation dawning. She was due to start her GP placement at Ealing Health on Monday. Dr Roberts was meant to supervise her training for the next year and a half.

'So what happens now?' she asked, her skin tight with prickles. 'Presumably I'll be placed at my second-choice surgery in Hammersmith.'

'I'm afraid not.' Aaron's lips flattened, drawing Stella's gaze reluctantly from his piercing and perceptive eyes. Idly she wondered if he'd be a good kisser. He must be to have earned his reputation.

He cleared his throat, drawing Stella back to the conversation. 'They already have a GP trainee there.'

'So where exactly will I be placed?' Stella's blood started to roar in her ears. She empathised with poor Dr Roberts, she truly did, but there had to be a suitable alternative. The powers that be at the Royal College of General Practitioners must have a plan B for this kind of unfortunate eventuality.

Aaron frowned, his lips twisted with frustration, a move that did nothing to diminish his rugged good looks. 'As most of the placements have already been finalised, you've been assigned to my practice in the Cotswolds.'

Stella's mouth fell open. 'What…? But…' No. Abbotsford was a part of her previous life, a life she'd abandoned when she'd wrapped up her tattered heart, left behind tragic small-town Stella and moved permanently to London. She had abandoned the misty-eyed and gauche teenager she had been, grown up, reinvented herself. Here she was fun and free Stella with a career she adored, a buzzing social life and an enviable shoe collection to complement her party outfits.

Aaron rubbed his hand along his cleanly shaven jaw as if he was as irritated with the arrangement as she was, which inflamed her further.

'I'll go anywhere else,' she pleaded. 'There must be somewhere else.' She was being rude, but his news couldn't be any less welcome.

'I'm afraid not.' His polite smile was tight. 'But bear in mind that I didn't ask for a trainee either.'

She flushed and then qualified, 'What I mean is that I specifically requested to be assigned to a London practice. I'm more likely to receive a broad experience in the city and this is where I plan on living and working. I've no interest in a village practice.'

She had left village life behind.

At her unintentional put-down, the corners of Aaron's eyes crinkled, his irises chilling two shades icier.

He crossed his arms over that broad chest and this time her keen eyes caught a glimpse of golden chest hair behind the loosened collar of his shirt. 'That may be the case, but there is nowhere else at such short notice.' Now his expression sported as much frustration as Stella felt coiling in her stomach.

Her heart sank, the bad news in no way softened by the flare of lust running through her veins.

No, no, no. She couldn't work for her ancient crush, and she couldn't spend the next year and a half living in the village that featured at the centre of her most shameful regret.

Perfect.

Aaron's lush lips moved. Instead of imagined kisses, Stella listened as he confirmed her worst fears. 'I'm afraid, Dr Wright, that, like it or not, we're stuck with each other.'

CHAPTER TWO

AARON STAMPED HIS feet in order to drive some blood into his frigid toes and pressed the phone closer to his ear to hear over the chatter of some rowdy passers-by. The streets around City Hospital were conveniently littered with long-established aptly named pubs: The Surgeon's Arms, Nightingale Inn, and his personal favourite: The Crown and Canker. It was Friday night. Spirits were high.

'Okay, Charlie. Dad will help you build a castle in the morning, I promise,' he said to his five-year-old.

'Will you be here before breakfast, Daddy?'

'Of course I will. I promise.' He winced. A slither of that special brand of guilt reserved only for parents snaked down his spine. 'Does Grandma have our favourite cereal, the one that makes our muscles strong and our brains smart like a superhero?'

His son's boyish chuckle warmed him through, as it never failed to do. If only it could permanently drive away the constant fear that he was making a hash of raising his son solo.

'Yes, Daddy. See you at breakfast. Goodnight. I love you.'

'I love you too, Champ.'

Aaron spoke briefly to his mother, confirming that

he'd be back in Abbotsford first thing in the morning and then hung up the phone. For a handful of seconds he stared at the blank screen, paralysed by familiar remorse. He tried to minimise his nights away from Charlie. He'd made a promise to his tiny days-old son that he'd always be there for him, be both parents rolled into one, so that the boy would never want for anything. The only reason he'd taken the GP lecturing position at City Hospital was because he could make a difference, give something back to the general-practitioner training programme and limit his absence from home to one night a month.

It was silly, but to Aaron the time away seemed interminable.

He slipped his phone into his pocket, struggling with the sense of failure and regret that became heightened whenever they were apart. But no amount of self-flagellation changed their circumstances.

It was still just the two of them. The Boys' Club.

Snapping from his trance, Aaron ducked out of the dreary mid-November weather and inside the warmth of The Crown and Canker. The sweet smell of real ale and wood smoke accosted his nostrils and provided a sense of nostalgia akin to a comforting embrace. He cherished every moment of being a single dad, but after a long week at work, he couldn't deny himself his one vice: a pint or two of good beer in good company.

And tonight, more than ever, he wished to forget the new distraction in his life, one he certainly didn't need: Stella Wright.

He'd instantly spotted her familiar name on his list of GP trainees. The first time he'd seen her at City Hospital, back in the summer, when he'd attended his interview, he'd recognised her, despite only previously knowing her from afar. She was the kind of woman you noticed. Strikingly attractive, her kaleidoscopic green-brown eyes bright with intelligence and that ready, infectious laugh that had seemed to demand his attention. Just like today, she'd been with the tall redheaded man who'd beckoned her from the front of the lecture theatre. Was she out with him now, laughing, drinking, dancing? Clearly they were a well-matched couple.

No wonder she despised the idea of leaving London.

Sleepy Abbotsford and a hick GP like him had little to offer a young, vibrant socialite like Stella Wright.

I'll go anywhere else.

Oh, her plea had kneed him right in the groin, because he harboured similar reluctance. The last thing he wanted was an unwilling trainee messing with his ordered existence. He had vowed, after losing his wife, Molly, only days after she'd given birth to their only child, that providing Charlie with stability and more love than he could ever need would be Aaron's number-one priority.

He sighed. There would be no avoiding the issue when she arrived in his GP practice on Monday morning. He'd have a major complication to manage, one with mesmerising hazel eyes, a captivating smile and a stimulating personality. One who unconsciously reminded him that he was more than a rural GP, a father, a son. He was also a man, a part of himself he'd sidelined for the past five years.

Fortunately for him, not only did Stella likely have a boyfriend, but Aaron had also become a pro at multitasking since Charlie's birth. If he focused on his priorities—Charlie and his work—he could keep any attraction he felt towards Stella the way it should be: irrelevant.

Dodging a raucous crowd who appeared fully com-

mitted to celebrating the start of the weekend, Aaron
scanned the crowded pub. He spotted his old friend, Joe
Austin and Joe's girlfriend, Darcy—who just happened
to be Stella's sister—in a nook near one of the windows.
Aaron waved, stretching above a sea of heads and weaved
through the Friday night revellers, his spirits rising in the
buoyant atmosphere.

This was exactly what he needed tonight. Forget Stella
Wright.

He arrived at Joe and Darcy's table, his stomach
swooping to his boots. Stella sat with them. He hadn't
spied her from across the pub. Now his blood surged with
adrenaline, both thrilling and dreaded.

Their eyes clashed like a high-speed collision. Hers
were defiant, challenging in a way that heated his blood.

'You made it,' said Joe, grinning in welcome and rising to his feet.

'Yeah, sorry I'm late.' Aaron dragged his stare away
from Stella, whose lips had flattened with disapproval
the minute he joined them, and greeted Darcy. 'Lovely
to see you again.' He kissed Darcy's cheek.

'You remember my sister from Abbotsford, of course,'
said Darcy, seemingly unaware of the frosty atmosphere
surrounding him and her sister.

Aaron shrugged out of his coat. 'A little, yes.' He offered Stella a nod of recognition and a tight smile that he
hoped concealed the rush of turmoil her presence created.

Of course their age difference, he at least fourteen
years her senior, meant he hadn't been familiar with
Stella when they'd both lived in Abbotsford beyond
knowing that she existed. He had vague memories of
Darcy's younger half-siblings, of there being three Wright
sisters, but then he had left home for university, become

too absorbed in his own life and only returned to the village to live six years ago.

'But we met properly earlier today.' He cast another glance at Stella, finding her mouth pursed with displeasure in a way that told Aaron she hadn't been aware that he was invited this evening.

'Oh,' Darcy chuckled, glancing at Stella with mischief in her eyes. 'Did you know that she had an enormous teenage crush on you back in the day? Hanging on every word of the gossip from your famous weekend parties.'

'Oh, please.' Stella dismissed her sister with an eye roll, her expression feigning boredom. Only the flush colouring her high cheekbones gave away any discomfort.

'Is that right?' he said, disregarding the increased thrill of his pulse and the renewed rumbling of fascination this news provoked. He placed his coat on the window seat lining the ancient bay window, a spot that would position him directly opposite Stella, and smiled benignly at the woman who had all but told him earlier that his small country practice was lame.

She had certainly outgrown any interest in him.

He dragged in a strengthening breath like the ones that he had employed to help him ignore her presence in his lecture. Until her supervisor's ill-health had forced Aaron's hand, forced him to speak with her directly. Forced him to invite her to his quiet country practice where he reigned, controller of his predictably stable universe. And Charlie's.

Stella tossed her dark hair over one shoulder and turned her apathetic gaze his way. 'I didn't know you were joining us tonight…that is, joining *them*.' She pointed to her sister and Joe, who watched their stilted interaction with barely concealed amusement.

What was it about her that drew his curiosity? So she was the first woman in years to ignite a spark in his libido. That meant nothing. Even if she wasn't with the guy he'd seen her with on more than one occasion, he had his life just the way he wanted it and he wouldn't risk disruption to the status quo for something as trivial as sexual attraction. Especially not for a woman who would not only be his trainee, but who also thought his life, his practice, probably even he himself were dull and provincial.

Aaron shrugged. 'Is it a problem?' He had come here to relax, to catch up with Joe. He refused to spend the night trading gibes with Stella, even if it was the most exhilaration he'd had in ages.

She shook her head. 'I'm not staying.' As if to prove her point, she stood, scraping back her chair on the ancient floorboards. 'I'm here with people. We're going clubbing later.' She tilted her chin as if expecting some comment.

He didn't need her reminder to know that she likely viewed everything about him with derision, or that in addition to their age difference, their personalities, their interests couldn't be more different.

He hid his sigh of relief, grateful that she would soon be leaving. She looked far too sexy in her little black dress, and he wasn't used to noticing members of the opposite sex. But there was no ignoring Stella. He looked down to where her long, slender legs ended in a pair of gravity-defying heels—clearly he was a weaker man than he would have thought.

'I see you're wearing your dancing shoes.' He couldn't help but badger her, if only to keep her at a distance.

Stella nodded, defiance pursing her lush lips. 'Yes.' She gave his outfit—jeans, a navy sweater and boots—

a return once-over that made his body temperature rise a few degrees.

'You're welcome to join us, if you like.' Amusement sparkled in her eyes. 'Although Darcy and Joe have declined. Fuddy-duddies.'

It was issued as a challenge, one he was only too happy to decline as Joe and Darcy merely sniggered. 'No, thanks. My clubbing days are over. But enjoy yourself. As you probably recall, there aren't any nightclubs in Abbotsford, so it's sensible to get your fix before Monday.'

Mock horror widened her eyes. 'How will I ever endure such a sleepy backwater?'

He grinned. 'Oh, we find a way to make our own fun.' Aaron looked away from the tantalising sparks of fire, for which he liked to think he could take credit. For a man who avoided complications, who relished the quiet, predictable life, he was having way too much fun sparring with this woman.

'Unfortunately for her,' he said to Joe and Darcy in explanation, 'Stella will be joining me as my trainee at the practice from next week.'

At his reminder that she'd been far from enthusiastic earlier, Stella opened her mouth as if to speak and then closed it again, her eyes narrowing.

He took advantage of her temporary speechlessness. 'Well, it looks like it's my round. Can I get anyone a drink?' With Joe and Darcy's order fresh in his mind— Stella had declined—he made his way to the bar, putting some much-needed space between them.

He'd just about reached the front of the queue when someone jostled him from behind. Aaron glanced over his shoulder at the same moment someone grabbed his arm.

'Oh, sorry.' A red-faced Stella braced her hand on his

bicep while she corrected her balance. She looked none too pleased that she'd been forced to touch him rather than wobble from her heels.

Aaron took advantage of the fortuitous split second and inhaled the delicious scent of her perfume, enjoying the heat of her body so close and the blush staining her cheeks.

'Did you change your mind about the drink?' Aaron asked, glancing down to where her hand still rested on his arm. He dared not think about how long it had been since a woman had touched him; he was already ancient and out of touch in this woman's eyes.

Stella snatched her hand away. 'No, I didn't. I just came over to clarify a few things with you.'

Ah, she'd come with an agenda. Why bother if she found him so…objectionable? Perhaps he made her nervous. She certainly seemed a little jittery, her eyes darting around the pub as if seeking out an escape route.

'Oh?' He stared into those amazingly spangled eyes, feeling a little like the man he'd been at Stella's age— single but never short of the company of a beautiful and fun woman, confident that he was master of his own destiny, cramming pleasure into every second of his free time. Awareness of her warmth still invading his personal space, of the way her dress clung to her breasts and of the way she made him feel twice as alive as he'd been before she appeared in his consciousness, forced him to redirect his stare to the selection of spirit bottles behind the bar.

Off-limits, way off-limits.

She was too young for him. She would be working for him, no matter how much they both begrudged that twist of fate. And, as always, Charlie needed all of Aaron's spare energy.

'The concerns I voiced about my placement have nothing to do with you personally,' she said, a soft aggrieved huff passing her full lips. 'I hardly know you.'

Said lips were slicked with some sort of shiny gloss. Aaron couldn't help but wonder how it would taste. He needed to focus on her grievances, not indulge inappropriate fantasies.

'It's nothing to do with your practice specifically,' she continued as she did her best to keep her body as far away from his as possible in the crowded bar, a feat that involved shifting her weight from one foot to the other in time with the flow of bodies around them.

'It's not even about the lack of dancing facilities.' Her mouth twitched as she held his stare.

He dragged his eyes away from the temptation of those lips, delighted to discover her sense of humour. It only increased her attractiveness.

She sobered then. 'I had a plan. A plan that doesn't include returning to Abbotsford.'

Aaron nodded in sympathy, his mind abuzz. So it was the place that offended her, not him. But that made no sense. Her parents still lived in the village. She'd grown up there. Would it be so terrible to spend time in a place so familiar? Now he wished that he had paid more attention whenever he heard mention of the Wright family over the years. Maybe then he would understand her reluctance.

Perhaps it was related to the man he had seen her with.

He swallowed the foreign taste of jealousy, his gaze flicking to the very guy, whom Aaron had spotted in conversation with a group of late twenty-somethings at the other end of the bar.

'It's just that when you've been expecting one thing

and looking forward to the next stage of your career...'
she shrugged '...and then it's suddenly snatched away...'

He wasn't unfeeling. He could understand that she
wanted to be close to the man if they were an item. He
himself had trained in London and never imagined that
he would return to Abbotsford so soon, until he'd met
and fallen in love with local woman Molly.

His life had been perfect for a while. Until he'd messed
it up.

'Yes,' he said, his throat raw with guilt, 'life is great
for disrupting best-laid plans.' No one knew that better
than him. Healthy women weren't supposed to die after
giving birth to healthy babies in modern, first-world hos-
pitals.

'Anyway,' continued Stella, 'as you pointed out, you
are just as stuck with me as I am with you.'

She stared as if expecting him to wave a magic wand
and reassign her to another practice. If he could do that he
would have done it before even telling her of the change
in placement. With his commitments to the educational-
supervisor role and to his personal life, he had no desire
to foster a reluctant and disappointed trainee who pushed
his buttons and left him...restless.

Aaron winced. 'Yes. I apologise for the way that
sounded. What I meant was that with my lecturing time-
table, I had no intention of taking on a registrar this year.
Although, as you yourself insinuated, my quaint country
practice likely has little to teach you, anyway.'

He should stop goading her, otherwise Monday would
be unbearable. They were polar opposites personality-
wise, and she would clearly struggle to respect his professional opinion. It was doomed to complication, something
he avoided at all costs. He'd had enough of that in his life,

and he owed it to Charlie, and to Molly, to make their son's upbringing as normal and drama-free as possible.

So what the hell was he doing?

Stella narrowed her eyes as if he'd insulted her rather than voiced the facts. 'You know, until we met this afternoon, I believed the hype about you, your reputation as one of the Cotswolds' nicest and best GPs.' She fisted a hand on her hip.

'Thank you,' he deadpanned. A wave of heat and shame flooded Aaron's body. There was something about this woman that made him uncharacteristically adversarial. To make amends, first thing tomorrow, he would appeal to the powers that be to find Stella a more mutually acceptable placement.

'Look.' He adjusted his tone in surrender. 'I can understand that you don't want to be so far away from your boyfriend.' Aaron tilted his head in the guy's direction. 'Let me see what I can arrange, okay? If you really hate the idea of a rural practice in Abbotsford, I'll apply to the college to have you reassigned as soon as possible. It's not our intention to make your GP training torture, after all.' He managed his most cordial smile, dismissing the way she seemed to have awoken him as irrelevant.

'Tom's not my boyfriend.' Stella frowned.

Aaron's heartrate soared, as if one obstacle had been removed. But there were plenty more; best he remember that.

'He's just a friend,' she said, lifting her chin. 'I'm single and my preferring to stay in London has nothing to do with a man, I assure you.'

Except her emphasis, her dismissal made it sound exactly that. The knowledge he was free to find her as attractive as he liked inflamed him. This was bad, bad news. She was hard enough to ignore when he had designated her neatly out of bounds, but now that he knew they were both single, his imagination was free to wander. Right down Lust Street.

Nope, not going there. But a little harmless sparring could surely be returned to the table. He couldn't have her thinking him dull as dishwater.

'Don't be too emphatic,' he joked, his lips twitching with mischief. 'Or you'll have me wondering if your reluctance to work for me is from fear that your ancient crush will resurface.'

He needed to stop this inappropriate informality, but it had been so long since he'd even noticed members of the opposite sex, let alone wanted to talk—no, spar—with one. And he would need to employ humour and every defence known to man in order to keep her at arm's length once they were working side by side.

'I would never change my life for a relationship.' She huffed, unimpressed in a way that made him desperate to shock her and watch her reaction.

'And as for my ancient crush,' she swept her stare from his eyes to his toes and back, 'you shouldn't put too much store in what my sister says. Fifteen-year-old me was also madly in love with every member of the boy band of the moment and several cartoon characters, so don't take it too personally.'

Aaron chuckled. *Touché.*

Then she upped the ante, leaned close as if about to impart a secret. Aaron's body reacted to her proximity as if his libido was responding to a flashing green light. If it wasn't for Charlie and the fact that he'd had his chance at happiness and messed up, big time, he'd would have been seriously afraid for the week ahead.

Stella's breath tickled his neck. 'See you Monday, boss,' she whispered and sauntered off, leaving him confused, conflicted and neck deep in the delusion of possibility.

He abandoned the view of her retreat, the inevitable sinking feeling putting things back into perspective. This round, he would concede her the final word, because he and Stella could never be anything more than a fantasy.

CHAPTER THREE

MONDAY MORNING PUT paid to a weekend of repeatedly chiding herself for getting carried away and bicker-flirting with Aaron in the pub on Friday night. As penance, Stella had donned her most professional demeanour along with her thick tights, tweed skirt and cashmere jumper. She needed the armour if she was to survive working for Aaron, and, far from the sleepy rural practice she had imagined, Abbotsford Medical Centre was a busy place.

Much to Stella's disappointment, from the moment she had walked through the door, Aaron had been polite, formal and utterly appropriate in return.

No more hot looks she wasn't sure that she'd imagined but that made her flustered. No more flirtatious banter back and forth. And his gaze never once dropped below eye level, so her comfortable but flattering outfit was utterly wasted.

She sighed, watching him talk to their latest patient, a six-year-old girl named Gabby.

She had discovered that he was one of two partners at the practice, which served Abbotsford and a clutch of surrounding villages. The building itself had been refurbished since Stella had been a patient, and there was a practice nurse, a team of receptionists and two health visitors. Stella had spent the morning sitting in on his first surgery of the day, and this afternoon she would join Aaron's minor-surgery clinic.

So far, she had been pleasantly surprised by the variety of cases she'd seen. They'd referred a young woman with Wolff-Parkinson-White Syndrome to the specialist at Gloucester General Hospital for an ablation procedure, admitted an elderly farmer with an infectious flare-up of his chronic obstructive pulmonary disease and confirmed three pregnancies. Gabby was their last patient for the morning.

'Gabby, this is Dr Wright,' he said, drawing Stella into the consultation. 'She's going to have a look at your sore throat, okay?' Gabby nodded, big, tearful eyes wary.

Ignoring Aaron's imposing presence just behind her, her body's memories of his strong muscles under her hand and the warm, delicious scent of him in the pub when she'd stumbled at the crowded bar, Stella stooped to Gabby's level where the girl sat on her concerned mother's knee.

'Can I gently feel your neck and then shine a light inside your mouth?' she asked, smiling and showing Gabby the princess and dinosaur stickers stuck to her torch.

Gabby nodded and Stella checked her neck for lymphadenopathy, carefully palpating the swollen lymph nodes on both sides.

'Open wide,' she said, taking a quick look at the girl's very inflamed throat.

'So what's your differential diagnosis?' Aaron asked Stella, smiling reassurance at the girl. 'Don't worry, I'm just quizzing Dr Wright, but you are going to feel better soon.' His attention returned to the computer monitor, his hands clacking at the keyboard keys in a totally sexy way. Was it even possible to type sexily?

Aaron did.

Stella washed her hands at the sink in the corner as she reeled off her answer. 'Viral pharyngitis, Group A streptococcal infection, scarlet fever, acute rheumatic fever and infectious mononucleosis.' She shot mother and daughter a sympathetic smile, knowing that it was likely neither of them had had much sleep the night before. 'As Gabby is pyrexial with swollen and purulent tonsils and cervical lymphadenopathy, I favour streptococcus in this case.'

'Excellent,' said Aaron, his impressed smile doing silly things to her pulse. 'Gabby, Dr Wright and I are going to give you some medicine to take, which will hopefully make you feel much better. In the meantime...' he addressed the mother '...keep her fluid intake up—ice lollies work wonders—and she needs plenty of cuddles and rest.'

He glanced at Gabby. 'Would you like me to prescribe cartoons, too?'

The girl managed a nod and a shy smile and Stella joined in, a small sigh trapped in her lungs. Aaron in GP mode would lift anyone's spirits. Even she felt better in his presence and she wasn't even sick. He showed just the right blend of compassion, confidence and explanation. She could tell from his interactions with this morning's patients that he was well respected, trusted, even treasured around these parts.

It would be easier for Stella if he matched her previous impressions. Playboy Aaron she could dismiss, no matter how attractive charismatic and charming. Except he was no longer the dashing young Romeo, haring around the village in his MG convertible, a pretty date at his side.

To stop herself from drooling over Aaron dressed in crisp chinos, a checked shirt and a soft-looking blue sweater she wanted to rub herself all over, Stella recalled his elderly predecessor from her own childhood, Dr Millar. He'd been cut from the same cloth as Aaron, always bearing a warm smile that never failed to make her feel instantly reassured, a silly dad joke and a sympathetic ear.

But just as Aaron seemed to have changed, the Stella who had once lived, once belonged in Abbotsford had been different—trusting and hopeful on the cusp of adulthood. And then Harry had taken her heart, promising to take tender care of it for ever, before stomping all over the vulnerable organ and inviting the entire village to witness his handiwork. She'd gone from belonging to both him and to Abbotsford to being adrift in one fell swoop.

In the nine years she had lived in London, it had been easier to stay away and pretend that she didn't care than to return home for the weekend with all its reminders of how naive she'd been at eighteen. More than naive: disposable, rejected, mocked.

To stop her destructive train of thought, she locked her attention back on Aaron, who was collecting the prescription from the printer. She'd quizzed her parents last night when she'd arrived in Abbotsford, learning that he was still decidedly single, despite an almost constant campaign to lure him into a relationship by the village matchmakers and every hot-blooded single woman in the region. He also sent hearts and ovaries aflutter with his fanatical devotion to his little boy.

She observed him out of the corner of her eye and exhaled a discreet sigh; his magnetism, his maturity and dependability were exhausting. She was, after all, only human.

He signed the prescription and stood, passing it over to Gabby's mum. Stella perved another glimpse of his sexy backside, which looked as good in today's chinos as it had in Friday's jeans. She decided he was too perfect. There must be a catch, not that she was worried for herself. If he kept his word and applied for her transfer, she'd soon be away from his particular brand of temptation. But the local women deserved a fighting chance at resisting him, surely.

As Gabby and her mum stood to leave, there was a tap at the door.

Karen, the practice nurse, poked her head through the opening, her face serious. 'Aaron, we've just had a walk-in. It's urgent—can you come?'

Aaron excused himself to their last patient and nodded to Stella, indicating she should follow him. They hurried to the adjacent treatment room.

Stella's adrenaline spiked. She forgot all about fancying Aaron, about being back in Abbotsford, about everything except assisting the person in need of urgent care.

Inside the treatment room, a man in his early sixties sat perched on the examination couch, his fingers curled over the edge with a white-knuckled grip.

'Keep the oxygen mask on, Stan.' Karen replaced the mask over his nose and mouth. 'He's had chest pain since he woke this morning,' said Karen. 'Oxygen sats are ninety-two per cent.'

Aaron rushed to the man's side and took his pulse.

For a split second a flash of recognition gave Stella pause—the patient was Stan Mayfield, Harry's, uncle—

but one look at his grey complexion, the sweat beading over his skin and his laboured breathing and she flew into action, wheeling the ECG machine she spied in the corner of the room over to the bedside.

'Call an ambulance, please, Karen,' Aaron requested calmly, encouraging Stan to lie back on the couch while he unbuttoned his shirt. That completed, he took the stethoscope from around his neck, placed the earpieces in his ears and moved the diaphragm over Stan's chest in order to listen to the heart and lungs.

'Does the pain radiate anywhere else?' asked Stella as she stuck electrodes to Stan's sternum, left chest, wrists and ankles in order to obtain an electrical trace of the heart.

Stan nodded, his eyes wide, terrified. He held up his arm, clearly too breathless to speak but indicating that the pain was spreading down his left arm.

Stella tried to comfort him with a hand on his shoulder, compassion nudging aside her adrenaline and automatic actions.

'I'm worried that you're having a heart attack, Stan,' said Aaron, his gaze flicking up to collide with Stella's. 'Dr Wright is going to take an ECG, and I'm going to give you some aspirin and something for the pain. Remind me, are you allergic to anything?' Aaron moved to the locked drugs cabinet and inserted the key from the set he kept clipped to the belt loop of his trousers.

Stan shook his head as Karen re-entered the room. 'Ambulance on its way.'

'And the only medication you're on is the anti-hypertensive I prescribed last month, Stan, right?' Aaron confirmed.

Another nod.

Stella pressed the button to take the ECG. Her respect for Aaron flew through the roof. Could he recall the medical and drug history of each of the two thousand patients registered to the practice? He'd grown up in this village. He lived here with his family. He likely knew everyone. Stella could understand how that could be an asset.

And sometimes, as in her case, a curse.

'Some aspirin, please, Karen, and morphine,' said Aaron, leaving the drugs to the nurse and joining Stella to look at the ECG tracing the machine produced. Stella pointed to the obvious ST elevation on the electrocardiogram, indicative of cardiac ischaemia. Aaron met her stare and nodded his agreement.

Stan was indeed having a heart attack.

Karen handed over the syringe and vial of morphine, which she and Aaron checked together, while Stella inserted an intravenous cannula into the vein on the back of Stan's hand. With the painkiller administered, Stan's pallor improved, his agitation lessened and his respiratory rate dropped closer to normal.

Stella stood back, feeling suddenly out of place, out of her depth, even though she knew she could have diagnosed and treated the medical emergency independently had Aaron not been here. Her bewilderment wasn't about the medical emergency. It was the wake-up call of treating someone she knew from her past life. Her pre-London, broken Stella life. A life she never wanted to revisit, but here she was anyway.

Stan had shown no sign that he recognised Stella, but seeing him again reminded her of that deceived, guileless girl she had been. She might have reinvented herself in London, taken her heartache and pretended it didn't matter, become a carefree party girl too happy-go-lucky for relationships. But the reality was that it had hurt too much to be eighteen-year-old Stella. And back here, her worst fears solidified.

She would always be that artless version of herself in Abbotsford.

The ambulance arrived, a flurry of activity as a brief history was shared and Aaron swiftly completed the paperwork and then called ahead to the accident and emergency team to let them know to expect an acute myocardial infarction.

The drama dealt with, a wave of shivers struck Stella as the adrenaline dissipated from her system.

As if he noticed her shaken composure, Aaron took her elbow and led her to the staff room.

'Time for tea,' he said in a no-nonsense tone, ushering her inside the deserted room, which was comfortably furnished with sofas, a flashy coffee machine and a reassuring array of healthy-looking potted plants.

Aaron wouldn't have missed her freak-out. He was a smart, perceptive, intuitive doctor.

He would ask questions. If he were any other man she might offer a full explanation.

Only, to him, there was none of her ugliness that she wanted to expose.

CHAPTER FOUR

'YOU DID VERY well this morning,' Aaron said, dropping her arm and flicking on the kettle. 'Tea or coffee?' He opened a large jar and placed an assortment of biscuits on a plate and then deposited them on the coffee table in front of Stella.

Stella craved the return of his touch, his warm, capable hand giving comfort she hadn't expected, even though it was probably just his doctor's compassion on display. But ever since that very first handshake back in London she'd battled this fierce attraction.

'Tea please.' Her voice sounded embarrassingly timid. She cleared her throat and reached for a chocolate digestive, needing the blood-sugar hit after the shock of seeing someone she knew, albeit from her past, in an acute medical emergency.

Poor Stan.

Perhaps it was the realisation that if Stan still lived locally, it was likely that Harry and Angus did too. Why was that only now occurring to her? She should have asked her parents if her ex was still living in the next village. What if they walked through the door one day? What if she bumped into them around about? She was over Harry, but that didn't mean that she wanted to relive his offhand dismissal, how easily he had cast her aside.

'Are you okay?' Aaron took a seat next to her so they both faced the stunning view of the rolling hills and a scattering of honey-coloured stone cottages for which the whole area was known and adored.

Stella nodded, taking a grateful sip of her scalding tea and reasoning that, after nine years, she might not even recognise eleven-year-old Angus.

'Yes. Sorry... I just...' She took a deep breath, sifting through her emotions in order to best explain herself without giving too much away to a man who unsettled her, made her crave his approval and his touch. A man she knew instinctively that she would struggle to keep at arm's length, as she normally could with men she found attractive and compelling. Not that she had ever found a member of the opposite sex this compelling.

She met his concerned stare, her mind trying and failing to come up with a good enough excuse for her behaviour. She didn't want Aaron to think she was... unhinged or unprofessional. But nor did she want to inform or remind him of her past errors of judgement, the consequences of which had played out publicly on the Abbotsford stage.

'I understand,' he said in his reassuring voice, his eyes searching and soft. 'Seeing acute medical emergencies in the community is nothing like dealing with them in hospital, where you are part of a team and have every imaginable drug and medical device to hand. You'll get used to it. And you were still part of *our* team.' His mouth stretched into a sympathetic smile that made her feel worse.

She wanted him to look at her the way he had in the

pub on Friday. With heat and speculation and challenge and clear interest.

He took a biscuit, polishing it off in two bites. How could watching a man eat a biscuit be a turn-on? A bubble of light-heartedness filled Stella's chest, a miraculous feat considering the way her emotions had to-and-froed this morning.

She shook her head to both clear the erotic image of Aaron eating a chocolate digestive and to contradict his assumption. 'It's not that... I mean, you're right; it is different.' Just not in the way he meant.

She'd visited her parents here over the years, of course, usually for just a few days, and each time she had feared the possibility of being recognised or seeing someone she knew who was linked to her ex. But this was different. Her placement with Aaron meant living here for an extended period. No matter how much she'd tried to prepare for her return to Abbotsford, she had been unexpectedly rattled by seeing Stan.

She looked up, met Aaron's quizzical stare, her stomach churning anew. 'It's just that I know him. Well, knew him. Stan. Mr Mayfield. It was a bit of a shock, that's all, although I don't think he remembers me.'

'Oh... Well, you're not really a local any more.' His teasing smile was designed to lighten the mood, she could tell. But, overcome by being back in a place associated with her most painful and humiliating memories, Stella swallowed down the absurd urge to cry all over him and his snuggly jumper.

He sensed her distraction, his expression becoming serious. 'You know, I'm a good listener, if you wanted to talk.'

She met his calm blue eyes, her pulse pounding at the

realisation that despite their differences, despite how she felt about this traineeship and working with him, she respected him as a doctor. She even respected him as a man. Having been on the receiving end of it, she tried never to indulge in gossip, but you could hardly move in Abbotsford without hearing someone compliment Aaron Bennett, awesome single dad, brilliant GP and all-round nice guy. And now that she'd spent time with him, she understood the hype.

She didn't want to confide in him, except he had that bedside manner people warmed to, drawn into a confessional aura that made you believe that your secrets would be safe in his hands.

Would he understand how simply being back here reminded Stella of her worst pain and her biggest regrets? How, after Harry's betrayal, she'd vowed that she'd get smart, be done with relationships and never make herself that vulnerable to pain again?

If he hadn't touched her arm again, she likely would have kept the lid on the most shameful time in her life. But he did touch her, his fingers flexing on her forearm as if he couldn't help himself.

'It's okay,' he said in a low, soothing tone.

Stella's body shook from the collision of panic and desire. She sighed. She did owe him some sort of explanation after he had plied her with chocolate.

He probably knew the gossip version of the scandal that had driven her so far away from home, anyway. Better that he heard her side of events rather than that of the village grapevine. Better that she explained herself rather than give him the impression that she couldn't deal with her job.

Tired of tying herself up in knots, Stella took a deep

breath. 'Before I moved away, I used to date Mr May-field's nephew.' She searched his blue eyes to ascertain if he already knew that information, seeing only mild surprise.

He nodded for her to continue, his hand slipping from her arm, his intent gaze clear of judgement or morbid curiosity. 'I don't think I know Stan's extended family. Most of them are registered at the practice in Chelten-ham, I believe.'

Relief left Stella on a long exhale that Harry and Angus were unlikely to be patients of Aaron's. She wanted to say more, but for her sanity, for her pride, she needed to steer things back onto a professional footing.

'How do you deal with it?' Stella asked, feeling mar-ginally better for the tea and biscuit. Only now that her adrenaline had waned, she became hyper-aware of Aaron once more, his warmth next to her, the solid physical size of him, his calm, unfazed disposition. Why did all of his attributes add to his charms?

'Deal with what?' His mug, which was emblazoned with the words *My Dad is a Superhero*, made her lips twitch with an indulgent smile that tugged at her heart-strings.

She tried to imagine him as a father. He still carried that air of confidence he'd had as a young man, gadding around the village in his vintage sports car, bringing home a bevy of besotted female nurses only too willing to be the woman of the moment and causing a few rolled eyes in the post office.

'Living in such a small community,' she clarified. 'You know everyone you treat and they know you. Your past. Your mistakes.'

Stella shivered as she recalled walking into the village

shop soon after the rumours of her split from Harry had begun, hurtful, soul-crushing lies that had only added to her heartbreak. Unbidden, the worst of the tittle-tattle surfaced from her darkest memories.

'Has she no shame, splitting up a young family?'

'She's very young, but then, she should have known it wouldn't last.'

'Of course he would go back to the mother of his child.'

Stella hadn't been the other woman, she'd just been deceived and double heartbroken. If only she'd had two hearts to absorb the devastating impact.

How could people believe that she'd stolen her ex from his baby mama when the reality was the opposite, that Harry had lied to Stella and strung along both of them? She had tried to ignore the stares, the loaded silences, to enjoy her last summer at home before leaving for uni. After all, she knew the truth. Her family knew the truth. Harry knew the truth.

And that had been the worst part. The piece of Stella still in love with him had hoped, dreamed, prayed that Harry would set the record straight in the community and come to her defence.

Only he hadn't. His disloyalty had amplified the pain of his rejection.

'That's true,' Aaron said, watchful. 'But everyone makes mistakes. We're all human.' His eyes clouded, perhaps with his own memories.

Stella's human fragility had certainly taken a battering nine years ago. Confused, raw and trying her best to put on a brave face for her parents, she had left for London, where, after crying every night of Fresher's Week, she realised that she could become someone new. A clean start where she called the shots.

She had left sad Stella behind and never looked back. Until now.

'So how do you distance yourself?' she asked, keeping things work-focused. 'How do you socialise with people that you know intimately? As a doctor, you sometimes see people at their worst. How do you then make conversation in the pub as if you're just another acquaintance?' Wherever she worked as a GP she would need to master this skill. She definitely needed it here.

Aaron brushed a biscuit crumb from the leg of his chinos. 'I have a young son, Charlie, so I'm not too much of a regular at the pub.' He quirked his eyebrows, his smile, the intensity of his stare reminiscent of his playfulness on Friday. 'As you already know, my nightclub days are over.'

Stella laughed at his attempt to lighten the atmosphere.

'But you're right.' He placed his mug on the table and leaned forward, resting his elbows on his knees in the way he did when he talked to the patients. 'Being a country GP has its challenges and limitations.' He spread his hands in a gesture of vulnerability. 'I only have a few close friends that I trust with my personal stuff, together with my family. Otherwise, I try to be a private guy. Most patients respect that, even here in a small community.'

'Don't you find it…lonely? Isolating? My experience of growing up here is that everyone knows your business. I found it claustrophobic.' She needed to shut up, but he was so easy to talk to.

Recalling his sad expression earlier, Stella wondered if he was lonely personally too? Five years was a long time to be alone. She shouldn't care about his solitude, about the fact that he was probably still in love with his wife. She had no desire to think of him in any way beyond strictly professional. Except her body hadn't read that small print. It lit up when he was close, craving those casual infrequent touches or the clash of his expressive eye contact.

Stupid Stella.

It was never going to happen. She worked for him and he would consider her too young. They couldn't be more different. He was the country mouse to her town mouse. He had a son and Stella wasn't sure that she even wanted children. She certainly wasn't on the lookout for a relationship, so his loneliness or lack thereof was completely irrelevant.

Only all weekend, while she'd spent time with her sister Darcy doing some of their favourite London things as a farewell—a spot of shopping on Carnaby Street, a trip to their favourite Knightsbridge tea shop and cocktails and dinner at a funky basement club in Mayfair—she hadn't been able to stop thinking about Aaron Bennett.

The real man twice as attractive as the fantasy.

Oh, no...this was bad. Her crush had no business reawakening, especially now when it came in adult form, complete with sexy daydreams and impossible cravings.

How dared he be so sexy? So distracting? So... Aaron?

'All GPs have to be good at compartmentalising,' he said, dragging her mind from the gutter. 'Once I leave the practice, I try to forget work and switch on the other parts of myself. Charlie helps me with that. Five-year-olds need lots of attention.' He grinned in that indulgent way that told Stella he loved being a dad.

Stella's rampant imagination saw Aaron the father: playful, nurturing, patient. Why was that so unfairly arousing? And how could she switch it off? He was a dad, like Harry. Another red flag she should heed. After failing to be enough for one man, despite her bond with his son, she had no desire to find herself unfavourably compared to Charlie's mother, Aaron's wife.

He stood, collecting the mugs and loading them into the dishwasher. Break time was over and Stella needed to pull herself together and stop lusting after a man she didn't want.

'At the end of the day,' he said, his eyes haunted and vulnerable as he returned to the conversation Stella had all but forgotten, 'we all have regrets and we're all entitled to privacy. Remember that.'

He left the room, leaving Stella more conflicted than ever. What regrets was Aaron harbouring and how could she hold herself distant, as he advised, until she could flee from both the way he made her feel reckless with need and the way he reminded her of her own bitter mistakes?

CHAPTER FIVE

AARON PULLED AWAY from the kerb, all too aware of how Stella's light floral scent filled his car and his growing obsession with the way she smiled, her happiness and how she made *him* feel: as if a part of him he hadn't even realised was missing had returned and wanted to steer the ship.

Well, there was no way he would allow his libido to take charge. She was fifteen years younger than him. His trainee.

But it was more than mere attraction, as rampant as that was. As much as he respected his GP partner, Toby, Stella seemed to bring a breath of fresh air and renewed energy to the surgery, as if she'd flung open the windows to invite in the cool, autumn-scented air.

On her second day Stella had again sat in on his morning surgery, impressing him with her astute diagnostic skills and the way she questioned everything, wanting to learn as much as she could from the experience, when he knew her heart wasn't in this particular placement.

She seemed to have recovered from her minor wobble after treating someone from her past. It was only when she'd questioned him about keeping a professional distance from the patients he lived alongside that Aaron realised how out of her comfort zone she was here in what he considered a little corner of paradise, a place he was privileged to live and work. That she had rocked up anyway and was giving the job her all showed her tenacity, determination, courage.

But what had made her feel claustrophobic all those years ago and was it anything to do with this ex she had mentioned? He wished she'd opened up to him more, confessed the deeper reason she was so spooked. Yesterday he hadn't wanted to push her too hard, to pry. He'd even resisted asking his parents if they remembered Stella from nine years ago. No one liked to be the subject of gossip—he understood that on a personal level.

After Molly died he had been the talk of the town for a while. Fortunately, he had been too consumed by grief and guilt to care. He'd had Charlie to focus on.

Aaron cast a side eye at Stella, who sat in the passenger seat, reconciled that she would tell him what she wanted him to know, if and when he earned her trust.

They'd just finished a house call and were now headed back to the practice for afternoon surgery.

'I remember Mrs Taylor,' she said, glancing at him with a relaxed smile. 'She used to be a music teacher at the school, didn't she?' Her voice carried a tinge of sadness, compassion for the retired woman, who was receiving chemotherapy for stage two ovarian cancer.

'Yes. She taught me piano for a while, actually.' He smiled in her direction, reluctantly returning his eyes to the road, because the green blouse she wore today brought out the sparkle in her eyes. He didn't want to crash because he couldn't stop staring at a woman he should not be thinking about that way.

'Do you still play?' The curiosity in her gaze heated

the side of his face. To look at her would be to confirm what he'd see in her expressive eyes, what he felt growing stronger within him every moment they spent together and most of the moments they were apart: a constant, undeniable lure he was struggling to keep at bay.

But fight it he must until a new placement could be found and she moved back to London.

'A little—I'm trying to teach Charlie "Twinkle, Twinkle, Little Star".'

'That's adorable.' As he caught her lips curling into that wondrous smile of hers, he recalled what he'd come to think of as their *moments*, because this felt like another one.

What the hell? He should be convincing himself that he'd been mistaken, that a woman like Stella would have no use for a man like him. Except he couldn't forget their spark of chemistry on Friday night when she'd uttered a low challenge, for his ears only.

'See you Monday, boss.'

Her proximity when she'd leaned close to taunt him had set his body aflame for the first time in years. The shock that he had seriously considered kissing her was profound enough to render him on his best behaviour since.

But then they'd shared their second moment in the staff room yesterday when she'd haltingly confided in him about her reservations about returning to Abbotsford. Their differences, their working relationship…none of it had mattered in the face of her vulnerability. He had wanted to know exactly what made her tick, to understand her fears and dreams, to be alone with her. Not as her supervisor; not as Dr Bennett. Just Aaron, a man who'd, out of nowhere, reacted to this woman and needed to sort fantasy from reality in his mind so he could return to normal.

Well, his new normal anyway, the suspended state he'd inhabited since Charlie was born: get through each day knowing that he'd done everything he could for his son. Mostly that meant putting his own needs second, but that was a small price to pay for the mistake of his past.

Dragging his gaze from Stella's profile and from all thoughts of shared moments, he returned his thoughts to his son.

'I just need to make a brief stop to pick Charlie up from school before we head back to the surgery.' His responsibilities grounded him once more. Fatherhood had become the best role in the world. That his libido felt nineteen again paled into insignificance, especially as it was directed at this particular woman. He wasn't a teenager, or in his twenties, or even in his thirties. Stella Wright needed to remain off limits, because not only had she reawoken his sexual urges, she had also reawakened his guilt.

Aaron didn't deserve such light-hearted and frivolous feelings as lust after letting down Molly and Charlie in such a devastating way. He'd had his shot at happiness. He'd had it all and his wife, his son's mother, had died because he had been careless.

'Of course. No problem.' she said.

Normally Aaron managed to drown out his self-recriminations. But today, perhaps due to Stella's presence, memories gripped his throat in a choke hold.

Charlie's conception had been an unplanned slip-up. He and Molly had only been married a few months, and they had both wanted to wait a couple of years to start a family. She'd just opened her interior-design shop in

Cheltenham and they were enjoying married life together, decorating the run-down old farmer's cottage they'd bought, establishing Aaron's growing practice, living the life of a couple before children.

Then one giggly, wine-fuelled night, a shortage of condoms and a miscalculation of Molly's likely ovulation date had changed everything. Nature had overtaken their careful planning.

Oh, they'd both been excited about the baby after the initial shock. They'd made new plans to share the parenting responsibilities so they could still both commit to their respective careers. But with Molly's death, his guilt and shame had roared to life. Aaron should have known better. He was a doctor, for goodness' sake. He should have been more responsible. Not only had he lost the woman he loved, but also his recklessness had condemned his son to life without his wonderful, kind and funny mother. Every child deserved to know both of their parents. If he'd been more careful, if Molly had become pregnant a few years later, as they'd planned, perhaps she'd still be alive.

Oh, he understood on an intellectual level that the rare postnatal complication she had suffered had nothing to do with timing. But his wisdom didn't help. His beautiful Charlie, with his mother's energy and sense of mischief, served as a constant reminder of Aaron's deepest regret.

'Does he enjoy school?' Stella asked.

He seized the lifeline, wondering how long he had been silent.

'He loves it.' Aaron forced himself to smile, to return to the present moment. To be what he needed to be: Charlie's dad. 'Walking home has become our routine, boys' time where we chat about our day before I have to head back to work for a few hours.'

'Perks of being the boss.' Stella smiled as if infected by the image of his rapscallion son, who was active and full of probing questions. Then she quickly looked away, out of the window, her expression falling contemplative as if she had suddenly remembered that she didn't actually like children. But that couldn't be true. He'd seen her interact with a few at the practice. She was a natural.

'Yes. I'm very lucky to have a job near home where I can walk him across the fields after school.' Rather than rebel against life in Abbotsford without Molly and resent being the much talked-about widower, Aaron was endlessly thankful for this close community. They had rallied around him and his newborn son when they'd come home from the nearby hospital. Baked goods and casseroles had arrived on the doorstep with reassuring regularity. Offers of babysitting had flooded in. As Charlie grew, people delighted in seeing him out and about, always cheerful and engaging.

To Aaron it was heartening and bittersweet, as if Molly's death had made Charlie different, special somehow, when Aaron wished he could turn back time so his son had two parents.

'We're also lucky to have such supportive families near by. I'm never short of a babysitter.' He tried to repay people for their kindness and consideration by being the best GP he could be.

'So who cares for him after school?' Stella asked, her gaze wary as if she was only making polite conversation.

'My parents or Charlie's other grandparents; sometimes his aunt, Molly's sister.' Aaron had never mentioned to Molly's family that the timing of Charlie's conception hadn't been exactly planned. He didn't know what Molly had told them about her pregnancy. He was just grateful that they'd never once openly blamed him for their daughter's death.

He blamed himself enough.

'I'm glad you have help,' said Stella. 'Raising children is the hardest job in the world.' She expelled a small sigh that he wondered if she was even aware of.

She had spoken generally rather than with first-hand knowledge. As far as Aaron knew, like Stella and Darcy, the middle Wright sister, Lily, had no children.

'You're welcome to join us on our walk, if you'd like. Charlie has been asking about my new work colleague.' At the slight stiffening of her body he added, 'Or you can head back to the surgery and familiarise yourself with the cases booked for this afternoon if you prefer.'

He didn't want to force his rambunctious five-year-old on her if she only tolerated children, but nor did he want to exclude her, especially when he enjoyed every second of her company more than he should.

Stella chewed her lip, clearly dithering.

'Not fond of small children, eh…?' His stomach sank, although how Stella felt about his son didn't matter. He had avoided relationships these past five years, focused on raising Charlie. They were a two-for-the-price-of-one combination that would put many women off.

He cleared his throat, irritated by his foolish disappointment. He wasn't looking for a relationship. He and Charlie had a good thing going, a routine, stability. He wouldn't jeopardise that.

'They can be a handful,' Aaron joked, trying to lighten the atmosphere and rectify the direction of his thoughts. 'Don't worry, Charlie doesn't bite, but it's no big deal. I want you to see what life as a rural GP, something I know you don't aspire to, is like, but there's certainly no obligation on you to participate in my extracurricular activities.'

She shook her head as if clearing a silly thought. 'No, it's not that. I like kids as much as the next person. I'd love to join you actually. I'd like to see how the school has changed since I attended, and I could do with a breath of fresh air. Aside from my parents, obviously, stunning autumnal days like this one are what I miss most about Abbotsford.'

She stared out at the view—there was one around every corner—her small smile wistful.

'Oh?' he asked, intrigued anew by her complexity. One minute she acted bored by the pace of life here— bemoaning the lack of nightlife, feeling claustrophobic— the next she seemed fully at home in the village where she'd grown up. It was almost as if she was fighting her natural inclinations, acting as if she didn't belong for some reason.

But why would she do that? Perhaps it was linked to the ex she had mentioned. But that was a long time ago. Surely she'd fallen in and out of love a few times since then, in her search for Mr Right?

'I used to ride a lot as a kid and into my teens,' she elaborated. 'I spent hours riding Gertrude, my pony, out for a hack through these lanes and across the fields.'

'Now, there's something you can't do in London.' He could imagine Stella ruddy-cheeked and mud-splattered as easily as he could imagine her in skyscraper heels dancing with her arms over her head in some nightclub.

He swallowed at the memory of her long legs and shapely thighs, a tight black dress... He shouldn't be imagining her at all.

She shrugged, as if she'd merely swapped one rush for another.

Aaron understood. He'd once been desperate to move away from the predictability and expectations of home, to spread his wings and experience a different way of life. But unlike Stella, he'd always known that he would end up back here. He'd been raised to be heir to the Bennett estate his parents currently managed, which comprised the manor house, farmland and a handful of rented cottages.

'Do you ride?' Stella asked.

He shook his head. 'But Charlie is desperate for a pony, ever since he saw that animated movie with the talking horses.' So far Aaron had managed to dodge that particular demand. He shook his head. 'Never going to happen.'

'Are you overprotective, then?' she asked, looking at him with that hint of fascination that warmed his blood and had him craving their next *moment*.

'I prefer the term vigilant.' He frowned. 'It's something I never understood about parents until I had my own tiny human to love and nurture and keep alive. You never want anything to harm them, not a scraped knee or a broken heart.'

His insecurities tightened his chest, as if he'd run too far on a frosty morning. What if he made a complete hash of parenting? What if Charlie grew up hating him for the error of judgement that had led to Molly's death? What if he lost Charlie too as suddenly and pointlessly as he'd lost Molly?

'You're right. You want the best for them, all the time.' She nodded as if she knew exactly how he felt. Again he thought Stella must have some first-hand experience.

Then as if realising she'd said too much, she mumbled, 'It certainly must be a lot of responsibility.'

'And joy. Laughter. A steep learning curve.' He hesitated for a second but then ploughed on. 'You sound as if you have experience of children beyond professional exposure.'

He wanted to understand her reticence for being here, part of the Stella puzzle that clearly brought her some sadness, and he sensed it was connected. It wasn't his place to ask any more than it was his place to wonder at the softness of her lips or the intelligent depth of her hazel eyes, but there it was all the same, like an itch he couldn't scratch.

Outside the school, Aaron parked the car and turned off the engine, aware that his breath was trapped in his chest while he waited for a clue to the parts of herself she kept well hidden.

For a second, her stare moved from his eyes, to his mouth. His mind immediately returned to thoughts of kissing her. Did she fancy him in return? Had she, late at night when sleep evaded her, imagined his touch and if they would be good together, physically?

Need roared to life, waking every cell in his body. But it went beyond lust. He liked Stella. He wanted to know her. He wanted those moments.

She drew in a breath, as if preparing to share some intimate part of herself, but at the last second, she seemed to change her mind.

'Not really,' she said.

An answer that only left him with more and more questions.

CHAPTER SIX

AARON'S HANDSOME FACE lit up as the bell rang and older children began pouring into the school yard.

'Here they come.' He jumped out of the car and strode over to the school gate, where a cluster of parents and older siblings waited. Stella exited the car too but loitered near the back of the waiting crowd, feeling as if she needed a hat and some dark glasses to conceal her identity.

Did anyone here know her? Or were the prickles of apprehension dancing over her skin merely a reaction to the fact that every moment spent with Aaron seemed to bring them closer together? Make him more relatable, more complex and more human than her stamina could endure.

As he had talked about his son, his expression and the tone of his voice, even his body language shrouded in vulnerability, she'd struggled to tear away her gaze. Stella understood his sentiments and concerns with every beat of her heart. She too had loved a little boy with the ferocity of a parent, even though they hadn't been biologically related. Aaron's clear devotion to his son had brought the feelings rushing back until she could barely breathe.

For a few indulgent but foolhardy seconds Stella welcomed the memory of that other little boy, from another time: Angus. The soft, silky tickle of his fine hair against her face, the adorable toddler scent that she loved to inhale—a combination of baby shampoo, playdough and banana—the innocence of his trusting embrace, his small arms clinging to her neck as if she'd never let him fall, hurt or even cry.

She couldn't bear to think that the toddler she'd loved as fiercely as if he were her own had pined for her, even for one second.

When Harry had abruptly called things off via a cold, unapologetic text listing the reasons she knew were lies—that she was too young for him, that he needed to put his son first and try to make it work with Angus's mum—she hoped for the two-year-old's sake that Angus hadn't missed her one jot, certainly not with the soul-wrenching grief she'd experienced for him.

With the pain fresh under her ribs, Stella willed the bittersweet memories away, blinking at the sting of tears. Angus hadn't been *her* little boy, even if, for a while, she'd felt as close to him as she had to his father, Harry, the man she'd fallen head over heels in love with that final year she had lived in Abbotsford.

She cast a furtive glance around to see if any of the locals were looking her way, but all she saw were the large number of interested glances cast in Aaron's direction by the mums at the gate. One even hugged him and dragged him into her little huddle of chatting parents with an air of ownership that had others rolling their eyes.

Before Stella could examine the hot flush of jealousy, there was a bustle of small people, a cacophony of excited squeals and the collective triumphant waving of art in the air as the younger classes emerged.

Aaron crouched down to the eye level of a little boy with sandy blond hair the exact shade of his own, a golden field of corn or the very honey-toned stone that made this region famous.

Stella's stomach did flips at the vision. They were so alike. And she had been correct in her prediction that fatherhood would increase Aaron's sex appeal.

Warm currents shifted low in her belly. Aaron the man and doctor was hot enough. The addition of his fathering skills placed him beyond tempting, a combination potent enough to make any red-blooded woman get in line for a shot at bagging a hot daddy doc.

But not her. She had no intention of *bagging* anyone. If only her body understood that where Aaron was concerned.

She should have headed back to the practice. Not only would she have avoided the discomfort of wanting to tear at his clothes, but also sharing this seemingly innocent everyday moment with Aaron felt like an intrusion somehow, as if she was inappropriately elbowing her way into his life the way her accusers had claimed she'd done with Harry.

Aaron turned to seek her out, his face still wearing the indulgent smile for his son. He waved her over.

Stella tried to pull herself together as father and son spoke for a few minutes. The boy glanced in Stella's direction, thrust both his backpack and creative work at Aaron and ran off across the playground towards the rear gate of the school, which bordered rolling fields that lead to Bennett Manor.

Stella joined Aaron, her pulse tripping over itself despite her attempts to stay aloof and unaffected, to deny her attraction, which grew more and more rampant by the hour. Becoming emotionally embroiled was something she normally avoided by only casually dating. It kept her distant so that she didn't feel or grow attached. In Stella's experience, which was admittedly limited, feeling only led to pain, inexplicable rejection, isolation.

'He likes to exert his independence by racing ahead,' said Aaron in explanation as they fell into step, side by side, following behind a highly energetic Charlie.

Stella breathed a sigh of relief that Aaron hadn't made a big deal of her presence, and that Charlie hadn't peppered her with a hundred questions on who she was and why she was accompanying his father on today's walk home from school.

She certainly had no answers for the boy. This might be the stupidest thing she'd ever done. Hadn't she learned her lesson with Harry and Angus?

'He is full of beans.' She smiled despite herself. She didn't want to feel anything for Aaron or his no doubt adorable son.

Pride shone in Aaron's sexy grin. Of course, it only heightened the blue of his eyes and dimpled his cheeks. She needed a barrier to his potency, a distraction, and she needed it fast.

'Does he take after your wife?' she blurted, more as a reminder to herself that Aaron was likely still in love with Charlie's mum.

He shot her a side glance, his face falling but quickly recovering as if he was well versed in discussing his loss.

Stella winced, hating that she'd voiced the first thing that came to mind. 'I'm sorry—I heard about her death at the time, from my parents.'

A flare of shame heated her cheeks, because she knew all too well how it felt to be talked about. 'It's a small village. Like I said, everyone hears about your business, don't they?'

'I guess you're right about that,' he said. 'And thank you. Did you know Molly?'

Stella vaguely recalled a tall woman with amazing glossy brown hair and a wide, infectious smile. 'Not really. My mum liked her; said she had a great eye for interiors.'

Aaron's lips curved, a return to that smile that made him instantly approachable, engaging and oh, so kissable. So inappropriate, given he was talking about his wife, the mother of his child.

Aaron glanced at Charlie, who had his arms outstretched like an aeroplane and was swooping back and forth across the field. 'He has her zest for life and her sense of humour.'

Stella tugged her coat across her chest against the dampness of the impending dusk, which had seeped into her veins.

She had once imagined that she'd found that type of connection, lasting love with Harry. Yes, she had been young, just turned eighteen when they met. But she'd fallen hard and become starry-eyed for the slightly more mature twenty-three-year-old who had driven a battered old Land Rover and would stand in the rain waiting for her to finish stabling Gertrude just so he could give her a lift home.

He'd swept her off her daydreaming feet, and when he'd confessed that he'd had a two-year-old son she'd been excited to meet adorable Angus. They'd spent so much of Stella's after-school time together that Stella had fallen in love with both of them. Twice the risk equalled twice the pain when it had ended and she had found herself instantly excluded, alone and grieving.

Then the rumours had surfaced. The gossip. How young selfish Stella had tried to steal Harry and Angus away from his ex, a woman Stella had never met, never even thought about, because Harry had never mentioned her. When he had dumped Stella, the truth emerged, Harry cruelly confessing that he'd never stopped sleeping with Angus's mum all the time he and Stella were together, and that they wanted to give being a family another try.

Stella had felt used, stupid, immature, as if for Harry she had been nothing more than a distraction, a stopgap, a way to make Angus's mother jealous and want him back. The worst part had been that Harry had simply dropped his bombshell and moved on, reunited with his ex and picked up where they left off as if Stella had never existed. As if her deep feelings, her love, were irrelevant. As if she were a nobody.

Realising that she'd fallen silent and that Aaron was watching her, she picked up the conversation. 'It must still be hard for you at times. Does he ask about his mother?'

Aaron nodded, his eyes darkening with shadows. 'There have been one or two tricky moments. Mother's Day, birthdays, Christmas. Other children's simple curiosity, prompting Charlie to think that he's different. I struggle with that.'

Stella's sentimental soft heart clenched for Aaron and his son. Children were naturally inquisitive and quick to sense that they stood out in any way. No matter how blessed and privileged your life, human beings were designed to fear exclusion. Stella knew what it felt like to be a curiosity here. To be the recipient of pointed fingers and whispered unfair judgements.

'And of course, being a single parent, I'm paranoid that I'm doing it all wrong.' Aaron glanced her way. 'How is my dad-ranking on the village grapevine?' His mouth was tugged by that self-deprecating smile she'd come to expect as predictably as the sunrise.

She reluctantly looked away. 'I think you're doing all right. I've never heard a bad word spoken about you. And you seemed fairly popular with the village mums back there.'

He tossed his head back and laughed. 'You're not jealous, are you?'

Stella found herself grinning at the delicious sound of his glee. Then she rolled her eyes. 'As if.'

'You sound disappointed that I'm not some deplorable villain.' He waggled his eyebrows and Stella couldn't help but laugh, too. He was right. It would be easier for her wayward desire and her Aaron crush if he acted a little more despicably.

'Just because we're two very different people, who want different things, doesn't mean I don't respect you professionally,' she said.

'Well, that's a start, I guess.' His mouth twisted in a half-smile.

Stella's gaze latched on to his sensual lips, increasingly erotic images of them kissing sliding through her brain.

In lieu of an ice-cold shower, she needed an antidote to his magnetism.

'Do you mind me asking how Molly died?' She didn't want to cause him pain, but there was a professional curiosity that she knew he'd understand. And more importantly, the fact that he was likely still grieving, still in love with his wife, should help keep her rampant hormones in check.

'I don't mind,' he said, his lips pressing into a flat line. 'It was a long time ago. She went into cardiac arrest soon after delivering Charlie. She'd barely even held him.'

Shocked, Stella stopped walking.

He raised his chin as if girding himself to utter the words, his stare strained but unguarded. 'Amniotic fluid embolism.'

Stella reached for his arm the way he had comforted her yesterday, horrified for such a tragic and unfair loss. 'I'm so sorry. That's rare, isn't it?'

Aaron nodded. 'They managed to revive her, but she never regained consciousness after the arrest.' His gaze fell to her hand on his arm as if disturbed by her touch.

'That's awful. Tragic.' She dropped her grip and started walking again, putting a few feet of distance between them so that she could breathe, pull herself together and stop thinking of him in a sexual way.

Their steps synced once more. This time Stella made certain to keep her distance.

'She was transferred to ICU,' he continued as if forcing himself to continue the tale. 'She died two days later.'

Chills gripped Stella's frame, her empathy and compassion drawing her to him to a dangerous degree. She hugged her arms across her chest, floundering and, for the first time in years, fearful. For herself, for how easily she could become embroiled in her feelings where Aaron was concerned.

'I don't know what to say other than I'm sorry again.'

Aaron shrugged, but Stella saw his pain lurking behind his eyes, which seemed to display his every feeling.

'It was a horrible time, obviously, but I couldn't dwell on the tragedy, the bloody waste and unfairness of it all with Charlie to look after.'

Stella swallowed, gazed over at his profile. He glanced sideways and offered her a sad smile. 'Don't worry; we're okay. Charlie and I are a team. Boys Club.' He raised his fist and pumped the air.

She smiled, trying not to remember how she had once been a part of Harry and Angus's team. Until she hadn't. Because it had all been an illusion. A joke where only she was ignorant of the impending punchline.

'And we are lucky in so many ways,' Aaron continued. 'That's the message I try to instil in him. He has many people who love him, and he lives in a wonderful place to grow up.'

'It is that.' Stella's smile stretched, a flood of nostalgic childhood memories warming her through.

For the first time in ages Stella indulged her imagination of her own future and how it might look. She'd spent so long avoiding emotional entanglement in order to protect herself, she'd never given much thought to her desires for a family. Did she truly never want children of her own? Did her job, a job she loved, really provide enough to fulfil her? Would she always be content with big-city life, even when her friends started to settle down and perhaps move away to raise their own families?

She had once wanted all of those things until Harry had belittled and humiliated her, forcing her to change.

She became aware of Aaron's gaze.

'Earlier, you gave the impression that you might have experienced village gossip in a negative way,' he said with a compassionate smile that made her feel exposed.

'Mmm, just teenager stuff.' Stella reared back from

sharing too much. She'd kind of assumed that everyone, including Aaron, knew her business. But even in the few days she'd known Aaron on a closer personal level, rather than from afar, she deduced that he wouldn't toy with her emotions. He was too kind, too upstanding, too honourable.

With a sigh she hadn't realised she'd held inside since she first drove past the *Welcome to Abbotsford* sign, she offered him half an explanation. 'I was young. Naive. The ex I told you about yesterday—stupidly I fell in love. Trusted the wrong person. Made a fool of myself.'

'None of which are crimes,' Aaron pointed out with a small frown.

'No. But sometimes guilt or innocence is irrelevant, especially when the tale is juicier when the facts are omitted. But that's ancient history.' She tried to change the subject away from her. 'I'm not a heartbroken eighteen-year-old any more.'

'So you left Abbotsford amid a cloud of rumours. I can understand how that hurt, but you should know that I've never heard any of this before. I hope that reassures you that maybe the past is where it belongs.'

Of course, respecting people's privacy was a vital part of his role as a GP, but she had come to understand that discretion and integrity were inherent facets of Aaron's personality.

'I'm sure you could ask around for all the details,' she said absent-mindedly. 'There are probably lots of people who recall the *scandal*.' She made air quotes around the last word, with bravado. The last thing she wanted was for him to see her in a negative light, not when she worked for him and when her feelings for him were so conflicted.

'If you want me to know you'll tell me.' He stepped closer so that their arms almost brushed.

Something intimate passed between them, as if they were the only two people in the world, trading their deepest, darkest secrets. As if they could become friends.

Except friends didn't want to know how their chums looked naked.

Stella cleared her dry throat, kept her eyes front.

They approached the low stone wall that bounded the house where Aaron had grown up. Stella had only been inside once for a Christmas party where all the village children had been invited to meet Father Christmas underneath the biggest Christmas tree Stella had ever seen.

She paused at the gate, clinging to her self-imposed boundaries. 'I'll...um...wait here for you.'

Aaron turned to cast her a speculative gaze. 'Okay, although you are very welcome to meet my parents. They'll probably remember you.' He smiled so that she knew he meant because she had grown up here rather than because she was still an infamous homewrecker.

Before she could make an excuse, Charlie came running from the back of the house towards them.

'Daddy. Grandma made spaghetti for dinner, my favourite.'

As if he'd completely forgotten Stella's presence, Charlie peered up at Stella from behind his father's muscular legs.

'Who are you?' he asked in that direct way that only small children could pull off.

'My name is Stella. I work with your dad.'

I also fancy your dad something chronic.

Charlie's blue eyes widened and his chest puffed out. 'My daddy is a doctor.' He stepped from behind Aaron's legs and struck a series of martial-arts poses as if fighting an invisible villain.

Stella hid her delight behind pressed-together lips.

'Are you a doctor too?' he asked, as if remembering that she was still there, an unknown grown-up who warranted investigation.

'Yes, I am.' Stella nodded, trying to unsee the undeniable resemblance, including matching dimples when they smiled, between father and son. Despite Aaron's concerns, Charlie was clearly a confident, well-adjusted and imaginative little boy, and, as Stella had predicted, adorable.

Her heart gave an involuntary lurch that she wanted to run away from.

'Are you kissing my daddy?' Charlie asked out of nowhere, as if this was a perfectly reasonable question for a new acquaintance.

Stella flushed hot, no doubt displaying a fetching shade of beetroot red. Could they both see how much she *wanted* to kiss Aaron? How the thought endlessly occupied her fantasies?

The man in question merely emitted a low, indulgent chuckle at his son's question.

But then his eyes met hers and time seemed to stop.

He arched an eyebrow, his eyes full of challenge. This was probably the look that had once lured all those pretty nurses to succumb to his charms, leap into his sports car and attend his infamous house parties.

She looked away from Aaron's intense, very adult stare. 'Um…' *Awkward.*

'No, I'm not.' Her skin prickled, too hot, too aware, too close to the man who clearly still possessed all of the moves.

Oblivious to the stifling cloud of lust and panic engulfing Stella, Charlie continued his explanation as if for the dim-witted adults present. 'My friend Johnny said ladies and men kiss. That's how they get babies.'

Aaron's eyes once more locked with Stella's as she issued a nervous laugh. He obviously shared her mirth, his mouth twitching in that sexy way that felt like a secret, unspoken adult communication.

As if granted permission to think about exactly how adults made babies, Stella acknowledged in a rush that she absolutely wanted to have sex with him.

Oh, no, no, no.

Could Aaron tell the direction of her thoughts and how turned-on she felt?

'Johnny doesn't know everything, Champ,' said Aaron, his intense stare still holding her captive as he ruffled his son's hair. 'Why don't you say bye to Dr Stella, and you and I will talk about babies at bedtime, okay?'

'Bye, Dr Stella.' Charlie took off at the speed of light, leaving a fog of thick, cloying tension wrapped around her and Aaron. Wave after wave of exhilarating lust buffeted her poor, weak body in the silent moments that seemed to stretch for ever.

This was very bad indeed.

'Johnny knows *everything*.' Aaron raised his eyebrows. His smile was cool, relaxed, but the expression in his eyes was beyond suggestive. Carnal. Intent.

Then his gaze swept to her mouth.

Stella's pulse buzzed in her ears. Was he going to kiss her?

Did he want to have sex with her, too?

Her feet shuffled, her senses alive with anticipation that she tried to squash. What the hell was happening?

She couldn't seriously be thinking about Aaron Bennett's soft-looking lips, wondering if he kissed with the same all-consuming confidence that he wore as well as the fine wool jumper moulded to his deliciously contoured chest.

Kissing Aaron was not allowed. Sex with Aaron was the worst idea she'd ever had. Even standing here in a puddle of loaded silence with him was highly reckless.

Stella laughed another nervous chuckle. 'I'll…um… wait here.' Her voice cracked.

Aaron hesitated, his body inching closer. Then he sighed. 'Give me a few minutes to get him settled.'

She nodded, resolved. 'Then we should…um…get back to work.'

Even if he didn't, she needed the reminder that they were working together, that no matter how tempted, she would never know if Aaron's kisses would be demanding and animalistic or slow and seductive.

And she was one hundred per cent okay with that.

Wasn't she…?

CHAPTER SEVEN

On Friday, Aaron arrived at the village pub, the Abbotsford Arms, for the school fund-raising quiz. The Parents' Association planned to update the school playground equipment and he wanted to support the event. It had nothing at all to do with the fact that he had mentioned it to Stella in the hope that she too might come along.

As the warmth of the pub interior defrosted his cold cheeks and fingers, his gaze swept the patrons for the woman he couldn't scrub from his mind, even for a second. Because that moment by the gate had been a game changer. He could no longer deny how much he wanted her or the way she looked at him in return. With hunger.

Stella stood at the bar talking to another woman around her age. She wore skinny jeans that showed off her great legs and a chunky-knit jumper that couldn't quite hide the curves of her gorgeous breasts.

A slug of heat detonated in his chest, spreading through him as if his blood was laced with narcotics.

He paused near the door, collecting his thoughts and examining his obvious excitement. Ever since Charlie brought up kissing that day, he hadn't been able to stop imagining her lips against his, her taste, if she would make sexy whimpers in her throat as their bodies met.

Was he totally insane, or just deluded?

He scrubbed hand through his hair and tugged his scarf from his neck. He'd been quite good at this dance back in the day. Flirting, seducing, fun and frivolous sex. But what the hell was he thinking now? Aside from a couple of tame dinners that had ended with polite good-byes, he hadn't dated since Molly's death. It had been a long time since he'd shared a proper kiss, or any other intimacy, with another woman.

He knew his abstinence wasn't entirely healthy, but he'd been so focused on raising Charlie, compensating for being his son's sole parent, that his physical needs had been the least of his priorities.

But Stella and her throaty laugh and her figure-hugging jumpers seemed to have bumped the demands of his sex drive up to the top of the list.

'You decided to come?' he said to Stella as he arrived at her side and took in her warm, soft scent. He kept his arms glued to his sides to stop himself from touching her: her elbow, her hand, that small freckle on her cheek.

Those same cheeks pinkened as if he'd caught her out, exposed how she too felt about the whole kissing plan.

'Yes.' She smiled. 'Do you know Amy? She runs the riding school.'

Pretending that he hadn't noticed the breathless quality of Stella's voice, he greeted the other woman with a warm smile.

'Of course, I recognise you now.' He'd once talked to Amy about gently introducing Charlie to riding. The kid never stopped talking about ponies and practically galloped everywhere. Aaron just hadn't plucked up the courage to take him along yet. He could almost hear Molly's reservations.

Wait until he's older...

'Amy and I were at school together,' said Stella, her tongue unconsciously swiping her bottom lip as she looked up at him with that searching stare that seemed to ask a hundred questions whenever their eyes met.

She felt it too, this continual force drawing them towards a collision, like gravity. But what should they do about it, if anything? He wasn't getting any younger and he was essentially her boss.

'Well done on dragging her back to Abbotsford,' said Amy to Aaron. 'I've just this minute persuaded her to volunteer for Ability Riding while she's here. Get this city girl back into the saddle, literally.'

Amy grinned and Stella rolled her eyes. But the glow of enthusiasm around her told him she was as delighted as her friend to be associated with horses again.

The urge to touch her, kiss her, intensified. Aaron's body was also keen to get back in the saddle, but they worked together. Even a temporary fling without emotions could complicate things.

'I'm not planning on being here that long,' Stella said with a concerned frown in Amy's direction. 'So don't rely on me long-term.' At Amy's look of surprise, she added, 'Aaron has applied for a transfer back to London for me.'

Reminded of her plans to leave as soon as possible, Aaron tried to swallow down the violent rush of disappointment that he had no right to be feeling. But it was a perfectly timed reminder that no matter how many moments they shared, no matter that he couldn't stop thinking about her, that he wanted to kiss her, touch her, hear her moans of pleasure, she would soon be out of here.

She'd made it clear from the start that this wasn't the practice, or the place for her. Only he'd started to see glimpses of how being here brought out different aspects of her personality, flashes of fond nostalgia.

No matter how well her desire to return to London fitted with his aim to stay emotionally detached, Stella has settled in well at Abbotsford Health Centre. She had a warmth, a compassion that made her an excellent GP. She knew many of the local families that his practice served. Aaron knew that, despite her time away in London and her reservations about this ancient gossip, she'd be seen as one of them if she ever decided to come home and work in the village for good.

He met Amy's eye and offered a resigned smile.

Sensing both Amy's and Aaron's confusion, Stella blurted out more of an explanation. 'It's been great to be back, actually. It's just that I've lived there for nine years. I've grown up there in many ways, and that's where I always saw myself established.'

She flashed vulnerable eyes at Amy. They were clearly good friends. Amy likely knew all about this local guy, Stella's ex.

'That's funny,' Amy said, 'because until Harry broke your heart, you always dreamed about living in a country mansion like the one in Aaron's family. You planned to keep chickens and pigs and grow vegetables, while being a doctor on the side, of course.' Amy smiled fondly.

Stella laughed, nodded and avoided looking at Aaron.

Protective urges built inside him like steam. This Harry guy was the ex associated with the rumours. What had he done to her? Was Stella still in love with him, still running away from her feelings? That would surely explain what Aaron found utterly inexplicable: why she was still single.

A stubborn lump lodged in his chest; it tasted suspiciously like jealousy.

'Would you like to join our team?' Amy asked Aaron, changing the subject. She indicated a man who waved from across at the bar. 'That's my husband, Mike, and it looks like he's found us a table.'

Aaron cast Stella a surprised look. 'You're doing the pub quiz?' He hadn't planned his own team. He knew enough people in the village to just rock up and simply join an existing group.

'Of course. I'm great at general knowledge.' She narrowed her eyes in challenge. 'Why so surprised?'

He grinned, glad she was once more flirting, joking and looking at him with heated stares. 'I thought clubbing was more your style.'

She shrugged, feigning aloofness. 'I'm a woman of many talents.'

'We need a fourth, as my sister can't make it.' Amy said, subtly edging away, drink in hand.

Aaron had all but forgotten that he and Stella weren't alone. They'd worked together all week, each day becoming more fraught with sexual awareness. He felt her interest, too. It spurred his own. But he had to be sure they were on the same page.

'I'd love to join you, thanks. If it's okay with you, Stella.' Aaron searched her eyes.

He found only mischief and sparks as she looked him over as if examining prime horseflesh. 'Mmm…it depends. What are your strengths? Because first prize includes a spa day at Hawthorne Manor, and I'm very competitive.'

Amy chuckled and left to join her husband, leaving him and Stella alone at last.

Deciding that his life could do with a few…temporary complications, he flirted back. 'I also like to win and I have many strengths.' He stepped closer, dipped his head slightly so a flush stained her neck. 'But for the purposes of a quiz, I'm good at history, sport and medicine, of course, not that you need me for that.'

Her breathing kicked up, fast and shallow as she stared up at him. Then she recovered. 'I'm not sure I need you full stop.' She flashed a playful grin, the pulse in her throat visibly hammering away.

'Maybe not, but with you being such a city lover and me being heir to the local manor, I'm also something of an expert on country pursuits.' He let his eyes linger on her lush lips for a second longer than was polite. Away from work and the perceptive eyes of his five-year-old, he felt free to flex the flirting muscles he'd kept in check all week. He was rusty, not dead.

She laughed. 'Is that so? Yes, I recall the weekend bashes at Bennett Manor, the fields littered with wine bottles and poor deceased clay pigeons.' She sipped her drink, her gaze on him over the rim of the glass.

Heat sizzled along his nerves. If she was intent on leaving soon, she would no longer be his trainee. Clearly their age difference didn't bother her, so he shouldn't let it bother him.

'Amy and Mike will cover farming and politics,' she said returning to the matter of the quiz he'd forgotten existed. 'If I take the music and popular culture questions, I suppose you might complement us nicely.'

He grinned at her mock reluctance. 'I'm glad I can be of service.'

Taking his drink from the bar staff member, he followed her to join the rest of their team, his eyes trained away from the sway of her hips.

Sitting close to her around the small table, Aaron struggled to recall any of his general knowledge. Their thighs kept bumping and every time that happened their eyes met, zaps of awareness and small smiles uniting them. She was right; their subjects of strength couldn't be more different, but laughing, competing to be the biggest know-it-all and cheering each other on, it didn't seem to matter in the slightest. Aaron couldn't remember the last time he'd enjoyed a night out as much, and it was Stella who made all the difference.

'Yes!' she cheered as the quiz master announced that their team had won the quiz.

She jumped to her feet with her arms held triumphantly aloft. The other three of them joined her. Stella hugged Amy and Mark in congratulation and then Aaron found himself the next recipient.

Chest to chest, her arms surrounding his shoulders, he could feel the fullness of her breasts, the warmth of her as he rested his hand in the centre of her back, the excited pounding of her heart.

His senses went into overdrive as her scent bathed him.

She pulled back abruptly, laughed nervously as if she hadn't meant to include him in the celebration, had gone too far. But it was too late. His body had reacted to hers, remembered the feel of her and wanted more than a chaste hug.

When she flashed him an embarrassed smile as they retook their seats, he saw the evidence in her eyes; she wanted him too.

Recognition that hadn't been there before filled the

slim space between her body and his. Stella pretended to be unaffected but she could no longer meet his eyes and her hands were tucked under her thighs as if she didn't trust herself not to reach out.

Aaron sighed under his breath, desperate to get her alone. Perhaps he would offer to walk her home later. They needed to acknowledge this rampant chemistry before it burned out of control, before he did something stupid, before she left and he missed his chance.

'Dr Bennett, sorry to disturb you.' Someone tapped Aaron's shoulder.

He turned to see one of the village youngsters, a farmer's son called Ben. 'Can you come and check out Sam? His blood-sugar alarm keeps going off, and he's acting a little bit aggressively.'

Aaron rose to his feet immediately, tilted his head indicating that Stella should follow and strode after Ben. When he reached Sam, an eighteen-year-old diabetic well known at the practice, the teen was pale, sweat beading on his brow.

'Hey, doc,' he said, his speech slurred. The way he slumped against the shoulder of the friend sitting next to him told Aaron he was probably feeling dizzy or confused.

'Sam, have you eaten?' asked Aaron, making a quick calculation of the number of empty shot glasses littering the table and dividing it by the number present in the group.

Sam didn't answer. Instead he rummaged under his shirt to silence the alarm on his blood-sugar monitor, which was alerting him to what Aaron already knew. He was hypoglycaemic, likely a side effect of drinking spirits on an empty stomach.

He heard Stella direct Ben, the kid who had called them over, to fetch a glass of orange juice from the bar.

A girl to Sam's right answered Aaron's question. 'He hasn't eaten. We were going to get some chips later.'

'How many of those has he had?' asked Stella, indicating the shot glasses.

The girl blushed and winced, no doubt feeling somehow responsible. 'About five. It's his eighteenth birthday today.'

'It's okay. It's no one's fault,' Stella said to the girl.

She accepted the glass of juice from Ben and indicated to the others in the group, who now wore matching concerned expressions, to vacate their seats and clear a path to Sam.

While Stella encouraged Sam to sip some juice, Aaron discreetly examined the boy's blood-sugar monitor, adjusting the rate of insulin infusion.

Sam's hand shook on the glass as he sipped, now a docile lamb under Stella's care.

'I don't think he needs to go to hospital,' said Stella. 'But we should take him home.'

Sam stared up at her with grateful eyes as round as saucers.

Aaron nodded, taking in the worried expressions on the faces of his friends. 'He'll be okay, guys. But I think he's had enough partying for the night. What do you say, Sam. Time to go home?'

Sam nodded slowly, rising to his feet and taking Stella's hand to steady his balance.

'I walked here,' said Stella to Aaron, her brow pinched with concern.

'So did I.' Aaron glanced around for a friendly face

who could give them a lift. 'He doesn't live far, but I don't think he should walk.'

'I'll take him. I'm the sober driver tonight,' said the girl Aaron assumed was Sam's girlfriend.

'Thanks. We'll come too,' said Aaron, 'and I'll call ahead and warn his parents to expect us.'

The journey was brief and fortunately uneventful, the silence only punctuated by Sam's repeated mumbled apologies.

'Don't worry—we've all been there,' Aaron said, recalling what it was like to be a teenager growing up in a small village; the urge to push boundaries, experiment, party hard—all under the watchful eyes of people who knew your parents and remembered you as a baby.

'Never drink on an empty stomach,' added Stella. 'Even the pub grub at the Abbotsford Arms is better than nothing.'

She and Aaron shared a secret smile, that of two people with plenty in common, most of all an attraction it was now impossible to deny.

At Sam's address, they escorted the young man inside and spoke briefly to his parents, who were well versed in managing their son's diabetes. Aaron was strangely grateful for Stella's presence. She was young, relatable, and non-judgemental. Was it because she too understood what it was like to grow up in a rural community, where entertainment was scarce and fun was often what you made it? Or was it simply a symptom of his need to know her better?

Back outside, the night had taken on a bitter chill. Aaron turned up the collar of his coat and glanced at Stella, relieved to see her tug a woolly hat from her pocket and pull it on.

'Would you like to go back to the pub?' he asked, too restless to return now that the medical emergency was resolved. 'I'll walk you if you like.'

She shook her head, once again avoiding his eyes. 'No. I think I'll head home. It's been quite a week.'

'Never a dull moment.' He grinned. 'And you thought you'd be coming to a sleepy practice which catered only for minor farming injuries and coughs and colds.'

She laughed, rolled her eyes and bumped her shoulder into his arm. 'Point taken.'

Her touch, deliberate and playful, set his pulse racing.

Then she seemed to sober. 'Abbotsford has changed, or perhaps I've changed.' She kicked at a stone with her toe.

'Maybe both,' he said, knowing no one remained the person they were at eighteen. 'Come on, I'll walk you home.'

He took off in the direction of Stella's parents' house, which was only a few streets away. He didn't want to say goodnight just yet and she'd fallen into a pensive mood he wished he could eliminate.

'It's okay,' she said, catching up in two hurried strides. 'I don't need you to walk me home. I know the way. This isn't some dodgy end of London.'

Aaron shrugged, unperturbed. 'I'll make sure you get home safe, all the same.'

'Very old-school. Thanks.' She acquiesced, falling into step at his side, her smile returned.

'Are you suggesting I'm old?' There were still a few streetlights in this part of Abbotsford, so he could see the way her rosy cheeks matched the shade of her very kissable lips.

'Distinguished and experienced perhaps.' She cast him

a thoughtful glance. 'And definitely responsible. Who'd have thought…?'

He laughed, delight bubbling up in his chest. 'You had fun tonight, despite the lack of dancing. It was good to see you enjoying the quiz.'

'I did.' She grinned, her eyes bright.

He wanted to pull her close and kiss her cold-looking lips until they warmed up. 'So, you definitely still want that transfer, huh?'

Distraction was what he needed. A reminder that, irrespective of his out-of-control attraction, she'd be leaving for London as soon as she could. Only that served to make him want her more. He wasn't looking for a relationship. It could be brief but perfect.

She nodded, but unlike all the previous times, she didn't seem quite as adamant. 'You were right—your practice is busy and varied.'

She smiled up at him in that teasing way of hers. 'You even arranged an extracurricular medical event at the pub to keep me on my toes,' she said about Sam's unfortunate hypoglycaemic attack.

'Well, I think you've settled in very well. You're certainly a hit with our female clients.' He and his partner had often discussed the need to advertise for a female GP to join them. Why could he see Stella fill that post so effortlessly?

A dangerous vision.

'Is there no part of you glad to be back?' he asked, as desperate for her confidences as he was for her kiss.

'There is.' She sighed. 'But I also feel like I've outgrown this place. Last time I lived here I was Sam's age, devastated by my first major break-up, desperate to leave and be in a place where no one knew me.'

'So staying away was easier?'

'I guess. Of course, the last thing I want is to run into an ex who broke my heart. But I got over him a long time ago.' She raised her chin.

Aaron wondered at that. It was certainly something she told herself. But who was he to judge? He still carried his own regrets of the past, unable to let go of the responsibility he felt about his part in Molly's unplanned pregnancy.

'It's just that I built a life for myself in London,' she said wistfully. 'I left here young, naive, someone who thought she knew what love was. Then I grew up.'

Closer to her street, the lights had disappeared, so he couldn't make out her usually expressive eyes, but her body language spoke volumes—hunched shoulders, hands shoved in pockets, head dipped.

'I changed,' she said, glancing in his direction. 'I realised who I wanted to be and what I wouldn't tolerate, and London helped me do that.'

It made sense. Except he had seen how naturally she fitted in here. Was running still working for her, or just holding her back?

'I don't think a city has magical powers.' Aaron stepped closer, lowered his voice. 'I think you would have done those things anyway. You can be who you are wherever you lay down your stethoscope, Stella.'

A small frown pinched her eyebrows together as if she hadn't expected that he saw her so clearly. But she too must feel their connection.

'So you don't believe in love?' he asked, needing to understand the root of Stella's fear. 'Is that why you're still single?'

He was pushing, probing, but what if she was standing in her own way? He saw it in the pub, the change, the lowering of her guard when she hadn't been able to hide her delight at their win, but then, when he'd challenged her view of Abbotsford, she'd withdrawn, as if holding herself remote once more.

Was it just from him and their chemistry, or from this place where she'd experienced the pain of a failed relationship?

'Wow—now I see where Charlie gets his propensity for asking direct questions.' She pretended to be mildly offended but he could see that she was toying with him.

'I'm serious. You're smart. You have a good job, and you're attractive. I would have thought you'd be living with someone by now or engaged, even married.'

She stopped, stared, her eyes alight as if he'd divulged an astonishing secret. 'Attractive? You think I'm attractive, huh?'

He nodded, his feet locked in place to stop himself stepping closer. Sexy, inspiring, funny. 'Beautiful is probably more accurate.' So beautiful his chest sometimes ached when he stared at her unobserved.

That tension he'd now come to expect when she was close wrapped its tentacles around them, the air seeming to pulsate. She swallowed. She must have felt it too. But then she set off walking again, dodging him and his questions.

'I've been career-focused.' She stared down at her boots. 'I don't have time for dating. And you're single too.' She shot him an accusatory look. 'It's not a crime.'

He wanted to laugh, change the subject, allow her to make light of this. But more than that, he wanted to know her, to understand what was in her way.

'No, it's not,' he said. 'But I found love. I've been married.' His reasons for avoiding dating since were complicated.

'But you haven't been in a relationship since Charlie was born?' She glanced at him, the look in those hazel eyes of hers intrigued.

Aaron shook his head. 'As you saw on Tuesday, Charlie's a full-time job, a job I love.' He smiled as an image of Charlie laughing popped into his head. 'He's had a tough enough start in life as it is. I want him to know that he might not have a mother, but he's loved and important, the most important thing in my life. Dating would… complicate that.'

'I understand.'

'Sometimes I imagine that Molly's complications could have happened during the labour, that I might have lost Charlie too.' Now, why had he told her that? It was something he only ever allowed himself to think in the dead of night.

'I'm glad that didn't happen,' she whispered, as if sensing his vulnerability. 'And it's understandable to worry about introducing him to new people. It can be confusing for children to meet a host of prospective partners, not really knowing if they will be around long-term and what importance they hold. He's a fortunate little boy that you put his needs first. Not everyone is so conscientious.' Her mouth turned down, a painful shadow crossing her expression.

Aaron assumed that she would clam up again, but she continued.

'My ex, the one I told you about…he had a son, Angus. He was two when we got together, turned three during our year-long relationship. I spent all of my free time with them. I became very close to Angus.'

'And then...?'Aaron held his breath, an ache forming under his ribs for Stella's pain, because this was the heart of her fear, and he wanted it to have never existed, for her sake.

'And then nothing.' She kept her eyes facing forward. 'The relationship ended abruptly. One day I was collecting Angus from pre-school after I'd finished school myself, playing with him until his father arrived home, the next day I was...discarded as if I had never mattered to either of them.'

Aaron's fingers balled into fists. 'I'm sorry that happened to you, Stella.' How could her ex have been so cruel as to use her like that, throw her away like rubbish after she had given so much of herself to the relationship?

She violently shook her head, as if rejecting his empathy or willing away tears. 'The worst part was that I wasn't even given a chance to say goodbye to Angus, to explain my absence. I just hope that he forgot all about me quickly, that he didn't...pine.'

Because he couldn't stand not touching her any longer, Aaron scooped up her cold hand, tugged it, warmed her frigid fingers with his own body heat. 'You loved this little boy.'

She looked up from their clasped hands. He saw it written all over her face. This was the missing link, the child she had experienced, the reason that failed love affair had cut so deep. She had been doubly invested.

She nodded, her eyes glistening. 'I did. More than I loved his father, as it turned out.' She gave a humourless laugh. 'I worried for a long time after that Angus might have grieved for me the way I grieved for him, that he wouldn't have understood where I had gone and that it had nothing to do with my feelings for him.'

'I'm sorry that you had that experience.' No wonder she had run away emotionally when she left for university. She would have been grieving for the loss of two relationships, confused and rejected and wanting the pain to stop. It wasn't Abbotsford that she feared. It was the pain she'd experienced here.

This Harry guy had clearly used her. Smart, emotionally astute Stella would have realised that, felt the sting of humiliation on top of her heartache.

As if collecting herself from a momentary lapse of weakness, she pulled her hand from his and shoved it inside her coat pocket. 'Well, this is me. Sorry for offloading my sob story onto you. Thanks for walking me home.'

Aaron's heart sank. Of course she would shield herself from this thing brewing between them. She'd been badly hurt. Rejected by a man like him. A man with a young son.

There was a light on in the porch of her parents' cottage, casting an orange glow that illuminated the cobblestone path and reached the small wooden gate, where they paused.

'No problem.' His voice felt thick with emotion. 'Thanks for your help with Sam. We've all been there. Hopefully his hangover tomorrow will give him plenty of time to reflect on his decision to drink on an empty stomach.'

Aaron hated the polite distance in his tone. A part of him wished he'd never discovered the depths of Stella's past heartache, wished for a return of the flirtation, the careless touches, the possibility.

But a bigger part of him wanted to hunt down this Harry fellow who had made a young, heartbroken Stella leave Abbotsford feeling as if she no longer belonged and…

No—Aaron wasn't a man of violence.

'You're welcome.' She placed one hand on the gate and looked up at him, her rapid breaths misting in the damp air as she loitered, saying goodbye but not moving inside. 'I'll…um…see you Monday morning, then.'

Still she hesitated.

Even though he told himself to proceed with caution because he didn't want to hurt her, some invisible force gripped him. Her display of vulnerability, the trust she showed him, the need to comfort her… He just couldn't stop himself.

Without questioning the danger of his action, he swooped in and pressed a chaste peck to her freezing cheek, telling her that he cared, that she hadn't deserved to be treated that way, that he valued the time she had committed to Abbotsford.

It was friendly at best. Only they weren't friends.

Although his lips had left her skin, he lingered in her personal space for a split second longer than was wise, hypnotised by the scent of her perfume. A lock of her hair tickled his cheek.

He was about to stand tall, move away—his apology for crossing a line forming on his tongue—when she turned her face to his and their lips grazed.

It could only have been described as a kiss, no mistake. And she'd instigated it.

Fire consumed his nervous system, his body so rigid he thought he might snap and shatter like an icicle. But he wasn't letting this chance slip by without taking full advantage.

He pressed his lips back to hers, applied some pressure. His stare latched to hers, silently communicating that he'd heard her tiny gasp, that he'd take her mouth graze and raise the stakes, unleashing the desire that had been brewing inside him since he'd called her name in City Hospital's lecture theatre.

Instead of moving away or shoving him aside, Stella stepped closer, fitting into the curve of his body, which was bent over hers, a big spoon to her little spoon.

At the glow of arousal in her eyes, Aaron moved his lips against hers, parting, pursing, pressing home as if their rhythm was the most natural thing in the world.

But this was his first proper passionate kiss in five years. He was kissing Stella.

She whimpered, gripped the lapels of his coat, held him firm. He forgot about the fact that she was his trainee, that he was so much older than her, that he'd just learned what she had been through in the past, forgot everything but the sensation of kissing her and the way his body flared to life, his blood pounding, his hormones raging.

Drunk, high, dazed with desire, he wrapped one arm around her waist and cupped her cold cheek with his other hand, touching his tongue to hers, licking, tasting, deepening the kiss as if life itself depended on their connection.

Stella's fingers dug into his shoulders. Then she moved her hands to his hair, her fingers spearing through the strands and dragging him impossibly closer. Their bodies meshed together, from lips to thighs. He felt every inch of her curves, her breasts, her hips, the heat between her legs. A grunt of satisfaction ripped from his throat. He pressed her up against the gate, the barrier allowing him to grind their bodies closer. His erection surged against her hip. She bucked and writhed, massaging his length between her stomach and his, torturing him to the point of combustion.

His fingers slid under her jumper, finding the soft, warm skin of her lower back. He swallowed her moan. He worried that his hands were cold, but she gripped him tighter, urged her body closer, begging with her body language for more.

And insanely Aaron wanted to give her exactly what she craved, right here on her parents' doorstep.

With a shove and a strangled moan from Stella it was over as quickly as it had begun. Cool air bathed his lips, which were parted to drag in brain-fuelling oxygen. He looked down, confusion dousing his euphoria as if he'd fallen into a waist-high snowdrift.

Stella's eyes were huge in the dark and glazed with passion, but she slipped from his arms and fumbled with the latch of the gate at her back.

'Goodnight, Aaron.' Her eyes spoke a million words—excitement, regret, maybe even a trace of that fear she must have developed after her last run-in with a single dad from Abbotsford.

Similar emotions recoiled inside him, a rush of shocking lust he'd thought he'd never feel again predominant. He should apologise for kissing her, only he wasn't sorry. He was glad that she'd taken the kiss from a friendly goodnight peck, one they could return from, to one that would likely keep him awake all night. His only regret was that he might have misled her with his passionate response, the last thing he wanted to do.

'Goodnight, Stella,' he said, rueful that Monday morning might bring recrimination and awkwardness at work.

He should be grateful that she had withdrawn from

their kiss. Aaron had Charlie to prioritise and he didn't want to hurt Stella when they had no future. He'd had his chance at happiness. Five years ago, as he'd held his days-old son in his arms, he'd made peace with the fact that he didn't deserve another shot.

Except his lips buzzed in remembrance of her kiss, already craving a replay. He waited until she was safely inside before he began the pensive walk home, the conclusion dragging at his heels: that he should keep away from Stella. For her sake.

CHAPTER EIGHT

STELLA HADN'T DREADED a Monday morning as much since she attended Abbotsford Secondary School and all she had wanted was for the weekend to last for ever so she could ride Gertrude. Oh, she was keen to get stuck into a new week at the practice, but a big part of her, the part scared of how shocking and out of control her physical reaction to Aaron had been, wanted to scuttle back to London and hide just to distance herself from the memory of that kiss at her parents' gate. Except denial wouldn't work. The details of every touch, every gasp, every sensation were seared into her brain like a mnemonic she'd had to memorise at med school in order to learn the order of the cranial nerves.

Aaron kissed with the same efficient, unflinching confidence he displayed at work and out of work. She had never wanted it to stop. Only confiding in him about Angus and then kissing him…it had been too much. Too intimate. Too dangerous.

She'd sensed that Aaron too had reservations that went deeper than having to return home for the babysitter, as if they were both wary of crossing that line that would take them from colleagues to lovers. She'd watched him walk away, peeped through her parents' porch window, still haunted and turned on by his expression of both loss and desire, which had been etched into his face as he'd said goodbye.

Stupid Stella. She'd acted on her attraction and now she had to face the consequences.

Sucking in a deep breath, she tentatively tapped on his consulting-room door. There was no avoiding him today or avoiding what she'd done, because she had spent the weekend berating herself for starting that kiss and listing the repercussions for their working relationship. If only he weren't such a good listener, so perceptive and impartial. If only she could stop wanting him with a need that bordered on obsessive.

'Come in,' he called, his voice sounding way too normal for Stella's liking.

Feeling as if her legs were boneless, she entered.

Aaron was alone.

Bad, bad news—she needed as many barriers to temptation as possible.

He looked up, removed his glasses, his smile hesitant but his eyes lighting up.

Stella swallowed past her dry throat. *Act natural.*

'Do you have a minute?' Her voice broke as she tried and failed to stave off the flush of heat that crept up her neck.

Say no. Send me away. Tell me that we made a mistake that can never happen again.

'Of course.' His open, honest smile kicked up at the corners. It had the same effect as the intense, carnal expression he'd worn on Friday night when he'd rocked the ground under her feet and kissed her as if he'd been dreaming of doing so since the first time they spoke.

'As it happens, my ten o'clock cancelled last-minute. Come in.' He stood and Stella closed the door.

With her back to him she could block out the delicious sight he made. Dressed in another fine wool jumper, this one the shade of Scottish heather on a windswept moor, he looked edible. Definitely kissable. Other things too. Tempting, sexy, but ridiculously unwise things.

She turned, cemented her feet to the floor to avoid burying her face in that jumper, inhaling his scent from the soft wool and losing herself in his proximity, masculinity and mastery as she'd done at her parents' gate.

The warm room became vacuum-like and hormone-charged. Stella struggled for breath but tried to focus on the query she had in relation to her patient rather than on the man who had the ability to make her forget all of the reasons that she didn't date. Aaron wasn't the usual type she went for: guys out for a good time without strings. He was still grieving the loss of his wife. He had Charlie to consider. He was her boss.

'I need your advice,' she said. Yes, this was better. Keep things professional, pretend that the kiss to end all kisses hadn't happened and hope that he didn't want to discuss it/fire her/prohibit a rerun.

'I've…um…seen Mrs Cavanagh this morning.' She stared at her phone, the notes she'd made blurring.

'Ah, yes, chronic pain,' said Aaron. 'Tricky case—it was a bit mean of me to give you that on your first day of working independently.' He offered her a seat and then took his own, scooting it forward until their knees almost touched as he gave her his undivided attention. He'd done the same thing many times as they discussed patients or shared the same computer, only now it felt too close. An invasion of her personal space that shredded her peace of mind.

'Not at all.' Stella's stomach turned to jelly. She'd have been happy with only a fraction of his attention; perhaps then she would have been able to think.

So why didn't she scoot her chair back?

'Her history is complex but interesting,' she said, aware of the way her lips formed words and how he watched her talk, his gaze pinging between her eyes and her mouth, as if listening but also distracted by what they'd done on Friday night.

'I saw a similar case as an in-patient at City, actually.' Slightly breathless, she wet her lips, remembering those few soul-searing moments at her parents' gate and how he had made her feel eighteen again. Only it had been better than any kiss she'd experienced back then. Now she was a woman who knew exactly what she wanted.

'Three months ago you changed her medication,' she said, forcing her thoughts away from kissing and back to Mrs Cavanagh. 'She's been in tears this morning because she feels that nothing has helped so far.'

Aaron leaned back slightly and rubbed his chin while he pondered this newest development. Stella had to blink to break the memory of his stubble-rough chin scraping her face in the cold, dark night. Of the way he had groaned with pleasure, such a sexy sound. Of the way his manly body had completely engulfed her until she had wanted to melt into him.

'Do you feel she's becoming clinically depressed?' he asked, clearly faring better than her at keeping his mind on track.

Did that mean he was done with her, with whatever this was? Maybe he'd spent the weekend reconsidering his response to her rash kiss. Maybe it was just she who craved more.

Deflated by that conclusion, Stella nodded. 'I think so. She scores highly on the depression scale and she said that she hasn't been sleeping.'

'Okay, well, she recently lost her sister, so I'm not surprised that her pain has become harder to manage.' He looked at Stella with his Dr Bennett eyes, as if he hadn't kissed her until she'd almost orgasmed on Friday. 'So, what's your management plan?'

Stella hesitated. The kiss had changed their working dynamic. Where last week she'd have been confident to express her opinions, now she felt uncertain, as if she was pushing an agenda, being somehow manipulative.

No. The patient's best interests were all she cared about. Aaron would hear out her suggestions and be objective. He, after all, had been nothing but professional since she entered his room.

Stella pushed her hair from her flushed face. 'There's a newly appointed pain specialist at City Hospital who is having some success with a combination of traditional therapies and alternative approaches, like meditation. I think a referral may be warranted, but I wanted to check what you would do in this situation.'

'I agree—a referral is appropriate.' He quirked an impressed brow that made her feel ten feet tall. 'I didn't know about the new pain clinic, so thanks for the insider knowledge. And how will you manage the depression?'

'I offered her a first-line antidepressant, but she refused. She said she'd like to get the pain under control before she considers taking *any more tablets*. I gave her some information sheets on non-pharmacological remedies, exercise, sleep hygiene, et cetera, but I think she needs more than that. I also suggested that she talk to the practice counsellor, and there are some excellent guided meditations for chronic-pain management online.'

Aaron's smile widened. 'You've done everything I would have suggested. Well done. Make the referral to the pain clinic and mention the mood disturbance in your referral letter. They will re-discuss it with her, I'm sure, as the two so often go hand in hand.'

'Thanks.' Stella stood and made for the door, elated at her clinical management plan but also strangely disappointed that Aaron hadn't ravaged her on his desk.

She needed to get a grip. He wouldn't be unprofessional with a waiting room full of patients beyond the door.

She didn't get very far.

Aaron's deep voice brought her escape to a premature halt. 'I think we should talk about what happened on Friday night.'

Stella froze, turned, cast him a glance full of bravado. 'About Sam?'

Being deliberately obtuse seemed petty, but resisting him was hard enough when they discussed patients. Actually talking about that mind-blowing kiss might trigger another lapse of her judgement. Things were awkward enough. She was in enough trouble, wanted him too much to trust a single idea her weak brain formulated.

Aaron stood and her belly fluttered. 'No, about us.' His voice dropped an octave, his tone husky and intimate. Stella was reminded of the way he'd uttered the word *goodnight*—full of reluctance. Need. Regret.

'About the kissing.' He stepped closer, his eyes moving over her face slowly, thoughtfully, patiently.

Why couldn't she be as cool and collected? As mature and unaffected?

She shrugged, while her heart raced with excitement. 'Do we need to talk about it?'

Did she have the strength to talk about it? She'd prefer to simply launch herself across the room at him and repeat the mistake that had ruined her for all future kisses.

He tilted his head, as if he saw straight through her protective disguise, his stare intent, ducking between her eyes and her mouth as if he remembered her taste and wanted more.

'You're right. We probably should just pretend it didn't happen.' He drew in a controlled breath that Stella wanted to disrupt. She wanted to turn him on, remind him how well they had fitted together on Friday, until he too felt conflicted and needy.

His suggestion was the sensible thing to do. The best way to resume what was left of their working relationship.

Except...

His eyes became so intense, she had to blink and break the connection. 'I don't want to hurt you, Stella.'

His honesty and integrity fanned the flames of her obsession. He was making it so hard to stay rational and detached.

'I wouldn't allow you to hurt me,' she whispered, entranced by the look in his eyes.

He raised a hand and cupped her cheek. The contact made her knees almost buckle, her body sway closer.

'I have a big problem,' he said, his voice full of gravel. 'I'm not looking for a relationship—'

'Neither am I,' she interrupted then gripped his wrist, keeping his warm palm pressed to her face. She knew what she wanted and what she didn't want. She didn't want a relationship, or to be hurt. But she sure as hell didn't want to lose his touch.

His pupils flared, the black swallowing the blue of his irises. 'But I can't help wanting you. Wanting to kiss you again. Wanting more.' His thumb swiped her bottom lip in provocation.

Oh, her too.

She sighed, closed her eyes, enjoyed the moment that felt like that weightless feeling at the top of a swing.

She opened her eyes. 'I want you too, but I'm not sure that it's wise.' The last few words came out as a whisper, totally lacking conviction. How could she be so weak? So led by her hormones? She dropped her hand from his as if to bolster her resolve.

But seriously, who cared about wisdom with chemistry this good? She'd be leaving as soon as her transfer came through. Surely she could indulge in her ultimate fantasy: one night with Aaron Bennett?

Question was: would she survive it?

His hand slid from her face and hung at his side. 'No, it's most definitely unwise.' His lips flattened, and she wanted to snatch back her words. She wanted his touch back, his skin on hers, closeness. Combustion.

'Unless…' he said, one eyebrow quirked in suggestion.

She latched onto that portentous word. 'Unless?' The pleading sound of her voice caused a flush to her skin.

He watched her parted lips in silence for a beat or two, his features shifting through a gamut of emotions as if he too waged an internal battle of sense versus need.

'Unless we both want the same thing.'

She nodded, euphoric that they might be on the same page. 'Just sex.'

Simply saying the word clenched her stomach in anticipation, the memory of his mouth on hers, his thigh between her legs, his hardness pressing into her stomach reawakening her body's aroused reaction.

He conceded with a tilt of his head. 'No emotions. Nothing serious.'

The confirmation was all Stella required for her arguments to crumble. 'After all, I'll soon be leaving.'

'And I only have room in my life for Charlie.'

She wanted to sleep with him. Why not? Neither of them had any interest in a relationship, so they could keep feelings off the table. Her move back to London would physically distance her from any stupid ideas her body might have in craving more than one night in his bed. What was the harm? Their chemistry only grew, day by day. Soon there'd be no containing it. The sexual tension drawing them closer was almost inevitable.

They were going to happen, heaven help her.

He dipped his head, brought his mouth closer as if he could no longer hold back from kissing her, but he kept her waiting, giving her time and options she didn't want.

'Still think it's a bad idea?' His breath feathered her lips, his stare dark and seductive. That look would surely have lured many women under his spell and into his bed.

Stella's heart leapt against her ribs as she tilted her chin up, looked at him from under her lashes, her lips only inches from his. 'Probably,' she shrugged, 'and I'm done with things that are bad for me.'

Despite evidence that he still had the moves that had given him a heartthrob reputation, she could no longer fit him into the same category as her bad-boy ex just to deny how much she wanted him. Younger Aaron might have been a bit of a playboy, but mature Aaron was a community stalwart, a doting father, a diligent and compassionate GP. He was nothing like Harry, who, in starting a relationship with Stella, lying about the fact that things between him and his ex were irretrievably over, had put himself, his feelings and wants above those of both Stella and his own son.

Aaron put Charlie first.

Unable to stop herself, Stella leaned closer as if pulled by gravity, placed her palm in the centre of his chest, her fingertips flexing into his soft jumper registering the pounding of his heart.

A soft groan left him. His gaze slowly traced her features. 'The fact that you're looking at me with glazed eyes, dilated pupils and parted lips tells me that you know we will be so good together.'

The vulnerability haunting his eyes shattered the last of her crumbling resolve. She wanted him and she'd exhausted all of the excuses she used to resist.

She nodded. 'Just one night.'

He reached for her free hand, tugged it and wrapped his arm around her waist, shocking a gasp past her lips. Her breasts grazed his chest, darts of pleasure shooting along her nerves. Their eyes locked.

He dipped his head.

Her chin tilted, mouth raised, ready to surrender to his delirious kiss once more.

A shrill ring tone rent the air.

With a sigh Stella felt against her lips, Aaron dropped his forehead to hers, closed his eyes and growled in frustration.

Stella's breathing came hard. Arousal spiked her blood, its potency draining away as Aaron took the phone from his pocket. He straightened, keeping one hand on her waist, stared deep into her eyes as he answered.

'Yes, Penny,' he said to the receptionist on duty today.

Stella stood transfixed by the heat and desire and promise glimmering in his eyes. They spoke of a similar need ransacking her body, making her weak, needy, heedless of the consequences of wanting this particular man and ready to throw all caution to the wind to be with him one time.

'Your ten-fifteen is here.' Stella heard Penny's side of the conversation and took a step back. The loss of his warmth and the hard comfort of his body physically hurt. Disappointment drained her limbs of energy. She sagged, looked down at her feet and then held up her hands, palms out as she backed towards the door.

What had she been thinking? They were at work. It was mid-morning. There was a waiting room full of patients out there. She'd become almost completely carried away. Without interruption, she'd have kissed him and done who knew what else right here in his room.

As she instructed her desperate, weak libido to get a grip, Aaron ended the call, his eyes still laser-focused on her. That look was trouble, determination and resolve clear in the jut of his jaw.

'To be continued, Stella.'

Without comment, she scarpered, too turned-on and terrified to do more than nod.

By the end of her second week, Aaron was climbing the walls with exasperation to be alone with Stella. It seemed that every member of the local community had gone down with the 'flu, the seasonal spike earlier than expected that year. They had been swamped at the surgery, working late most evenings in order to meet the increased demand for appointments.

Outside of work he'd been busy too. Charlie had extra lessons for a swimming tournament and a mid-week after-school birthday party to attend. When Molly's parents asked if they could have Charlie over to stay on Friday night so they could take him to the car-boot sale two villages over on Saturday, he'd almost wept with relief and gratitude.

His first thought: to invite Stella on a date. A casual, nothing serious date. A drink in a quiet pub out of Abbotsford where they could talk, be alone, explore each other.

He missed her open smile and her playful sense of humour. Not to mention the hot promises they had made with their eyes at the start of the week when, to his utter relief, they had laid down the ground rules for managing their chemistry. And the torture had continued. Just because they skirted big circles around each other at work, succeeded in keeping their hands off each other, it hadn't stopped them practically torching the entire practice with longing stares and knowing looks.

Aaron pulled into the stable yard of Amy's riding school and parked his car. Stella had left work earlier, saying that she was going for a ride. Some of the regular Ability Riding children had missed their class due to the 'flu also ripping through the primary school, but the horses still needed to be exercised.

Instead of bounding from the car in search of Stella, his natural inclination, he paused, gripping the steering wheel as his doubts resurfaced.

As much as he didn't want to hurt Stella, neither did he want to disrupt the sense of contentment he'd finally found for himself and Charlie. He'd been as clear as he could, and she understood that his son came first. If they kept it about sex, as Stella suggested, there could be no misguided expectations.

He snorted, shook his head. He was overthinking.

This thing with Stella had an expiry date; she would soon return to London.

Tired of tying himself up in knots, Aaron headed to the stables and called out a hello. Despite the floodlit gravel car park, the buildings seemed deserted but for the horses quietly chomping hay. Perhaps he'd missed her. She hadn't answered his earlier text, which invited her out this evening, so he'd called in at the stables on the off-chance that she hadn't yet left.

His gut tight with disappointment, Aaron headed to the staff room he knew was at the back of the property. He'd once made a call here to examine an experienced rider who'd taken a fall and had a moderate concussion.

In his haste to see Stella he rounded the corner of the building and smacked right into her. His hands gripped her shoulders, to steady both her and himself as his heart thundered in relief and excitement.

'Hi,' she said, gripping his forearms, looking up at him with that secret smile she'd worn all week. A smile for him, for them.

'Sorry about that.' He smiled, pretended to be unaware of her shudder under his touch. Otherwise he'd want to pick up where they had left off on Monday in his office and kiss her until she was breathless and clinging to him and the restless energy twisting his insides vanished.

Her hair was damp at the ends as if she'd taken a shower. She smelled like a fresh meadow. He wanted to haul her close, kiss her as if the world was ending, put that glazed look of passion on her face and give her a new association with Abbotsford, one that was all about pleasure.

Instead, he slid his hands from her shoulders, down her arms and held both of her hands. 'I texted you. I called in on the off chance that you'd still be here.'

'Sorry,' she said, squeezing his hands. 'I was in the shower. Everyone else has left for the day.' Her eyes were huge in the gloom, expressive and vulnerable and full of questions. He wanted to chase away every one of her demons. But that was a boundary he had no right in breaching, not when they'd vowed to keep this casual.

She gave him a sexy smile, her tongue touching her bottom lip as she gripped his hands tighter and stepped closer so their bodies were flush.

'What did the text say?' she asked, clearly unwilling to release his hands to check her phone.

He let go of one hand to wrap his arm around her waist and dragged her close. Her pupils dilated. 'I wondered if you would like to go for a drink. I know this lovely pub in Little Dunnop. It's quiet and has a roaring fire.'

Her face fell, a frown settling between her brows.

Aaron swallowed, wondering how he'd ruined the mood. Perhaps she was hesitant to be seen alone with him in public.

'It's a couple of villages away,' he cajoled. 'Hopefully none of my patients will be there, so we're almost guaranteed an evening free of medical drama.'

Her stare rose to his. 'It's not that.' Her teeth scraped her bottom lip, and he instinctively relaxed his hold of her, in case she felt that they were rushing into this.

'It's just that my ex is from Little Dunnop.' She lifted

her hand to his chest, her fingers curling into his sweater. 'I don't want to run into him or any of his family.'

Aaron winced, gutted that he hadn't thought of that. 'Of course. I understand. We can go somewhere else.'

'Where's Charlie tonight?' she asked as she looked up at him, her gorgeous eyes pools of desire.

'He's sleeping over at his grandparents' house. They like to take him out on Saturday morning.'

'In that case, no, thanks.' She raised her face, brushed his lips with hers, barely touching but igniting his nervous system. 'I'll give the pub a miss. Do you have a fire at your place?'

'Mmm-hmm,' he said. 'One to rival any pub's in the county.'

Desperate to ravage those tantalising lips of hers, he held back, loving the direction of this conversation.

'Do you have wine?' she asked, her index finger teasing the stubble along his jaw.

'Yes.'

'A condom machine in the bathroom?' She grinned, and he laughed at her sense of humour.

'Not exactly, but we're covered.' He wrapped both of his arms around her waist, what was left of his restraint vanishing. He hauled her into his arms, crushed her chest to his and slanted his mouth over hers at last.

Stella clung to him, parted her lips and returned his heated kiss as if they'd been kissing for years, as if they were made for kissing and nothing else, as if she'd be happy to spend the night in this very spot that smelled of sweet hay and horseflesh and kiss all night long.

When they parted briefly for air, she moaned, dropping her head back and closing her eyes. 'Invite me back to yours,' she said, her voice slurred with passion. Passion he'd inflamed.

'Whatever you say.' He speared his fingers through her glossy hair to angle her head so he could taste the soft skin of her neck in an exploratory journey he wanted never to end.

She moaned, her eyes still closed as she slipped her hands under his sweater, her fingers digging into his back, urging his body closer.

Aaron thanked the universe for his smarts; he wasn't stupid enough to question a woman when she issued a direct order. 'Come back to mine.' He held her face, his stare glued to her, felt her small, definite nod.

He made the four-mile drive home in record time.

CHAPTER NINE

THE MINUTE AARON'S front door closed behind them, banishing the November chill from his farmhouse-style cottage, Stella spun to face him. In unison and without a second's hesitation they reached for each other, tugging off each other's coats and hats while indulging in frantic, breathless kisses. Stella had never felt a fire as intense as the one burning her alive, the urgency almost too much to bear.

How could she need him so much?

It was just sex. That was what she recited over and over. They'd agreed: one night.

With a grunt Aaron swung her around and pressed her back up against some piece of furniture in the hallway, his thigh pushing between her legs. She lost herself, her only coherent thought that she would welcome him taking her right here on the flagstone floor.

Aaron tore his lips from hers, his breath gusting as he trailed kisses over her jaw and down her neck. He groaned, his voracious mouth finding every one of her neck's erogenous zones.

'Do you want that drink?' He pulled away, and Stella almost sagged into a heap.

'Later. I want you.' She heeled off her boots, gripped

the belt loops on his jeans and tugged his hips between her spread thighs.

He cupped her cheek, and then both cheeks, tilting up her chin to stare down into her eyes. 'You are so beautiful, too good to be true. I plan to distract you with so much pleasure that you won't have a chance to come to your senses.'

'I'm not going anywhere.'

'Lucky me.' Something shifted across his expression—a moment of hesitation, a flash of vulnerability she dared not analyse. 'Can you stay all night?'

'Yes.'

He smiled a dazzling smile that made Stella weak.

She tugged at his waist, bringing his mouth back to hers, until their lips fused, their tongues sweeping to meet and tangle. His fingers curled into her hair and Stella hooked her arms over his wide shoulders, clinging tight.

Aaron hoisted her from the floor. She wrapped her legs around his waist and felt his erection between her legs. He carried her across the room to a wide, comfy sofa in front of the hearth, where the fire had burned low, but still gave off an orange glow and waves of heat. Not that she needed the flames; she was on fire for this man.

Aaron sat on the sofa, lowering Stella into his lap, where she straddled his thighs and stared down at his sincere and hungry expression.

He wanted her. Aaron Bennett thought she was beautiful. This must be a dream.

And tomorrow she would need to wake up. But not yet.

She kissed his jaw, his earlobe, down his neck, as all the while she worked on his shirt buttons. When she parted the soft fabric that smelled like washing powder and Aaron, she caught her bottom lip under her teeth to halt a sigh of utter longing.

He was gorgeous under the clothes, better than she'd imagined. Every muscle of his chest and abdomen was defined. Soft golden hair nestled between his pecs and formed a trail that disappeared beneath the waistband of his jeans.

Stella ran her hands over the warm ridges and dips, learning the feel of him, the places that made his eyes darken like a stormy ocean and his hands restlessly fist her hips. She continued her exploration, and he sighed, his head falling back against the sofa.

'I haven't done this for a while,' he said, his eyes ablaze with enough desire to assure Stella that he didn't need to worry.

'Me neither.' Stella wasn't sure that she'd ever done whatever *this* was, but she shuddered to think that it would carry that degree of significance. She couldn't allow that. It was just for tonight, except she'd never before felt this all-consuming obsession, this urgent and confusing need to both slowly study every millimetre of Aaron Bennett and to tear at him until he quenched the fire burning her to ash.

She pushed the shirt from his shoulders and popped the button on his jeans, emboldened by the bulge behind his fly. She was no longer the shy, naive Stella that had once lived here. She was Dr Stella Wright, a strong, resilient woman who created her own destiny.

'Who knew you were hiding all of this under those woolly jumpers?' she teased, sitting back on his muscular thighs.

He laughed, reaching for the hem of her own sweater. She raised it over her head, tossing it to the floor.

'The first time I saw you at the hospital when I interviewed for the lecturing post back in the summer, I almost swallowed my tongue.' He slid his warm hands along her ribs and cupped her breasts through her bra. 'You're a striking woman, but the confident way you carry yourself, your fun, self-possessed attitude... I have to admit I was a little in awe of you that day we first spoke.'

In awe of her?

'Why?' She moved her hands over the smooth skin of his shoulders, too desperate to know every inch of him to pause her exploration.

'I was so attracted to you, but figured I was too old, that you would never look at me this way.' He cupped her cheek, his thumb tracing her lips.

'I happen to find your brand of maturity and responsibility a major turn-on,' she said.

Harry had made a big deal of their few-years age gap at the end. She had always suspected that it was a coward's excuse.

A lump she didn't want to acknowledge tonight lodged in her throat. Aaron was so different from Harry. She was different too. No longer young and lovestruck.

Now she could protect herself, keep her emotions distant.

'And I was wildly attracted to you, too,' she confessed. 'I was so busy ogling you, I almost fell down the auditorium steps.'

The look of wonder and desire on his face made her whimper. Emotion she couldn't name bubbled to the surface.

'Now, stop talking,' she mumbled against his lips. She needed to switch off her thoughts, lose herself in sensation. Tonight belonged to just the two of them, would be their secret to treasure. She'd hold it inside, never tell a soul, relive the memory.

Aaron reached around and popped the clasp of her bra, single-handed. 'Do you want to move upstairs?'

'No. Impressive bra skills, by the way.' Despite the glow of the fire at her back, which bathed Aaron's skin in golden light, Stella's skin pimpled. She wanted to joke, to banter with him to keep things light, but she was already in over her head.

'I still have some moves.' Aaron stroked her back, his fingers lazy and hypnotic where his stare clinging to hers was urgent and voracious.

She nodded, sat up and slipped first one bra strap and then the other from her shoulders and tossed it to the floor. 'Show me,' she said in a breathy voice.

His stare grew intense in that way she'd come to love this week. Every time their eyes met at work, every glance or chance encounter around the health centre, felt deliciously illicit, as if they'd orchestrated a secret rendezvous.

He tugged her waist and she sank into him, their naked torsos burning where they connected. Every inch of his skin was like hot silk. His scent engulfed her until she was certain she'd never eradicate it from her senses. Her head swam with lack of oxygen, but she couldn't tear her mouth away from his wonderful kisses, which were the sweetest, most reckless indulgence she'd ever experienced.

Only she wanted more. She wanted everything he'd give her, for one night. Then she could leave Abbotsford once more knowing that she hadn't been controlled by her fears, that he'd been right: she could be herself any-where she chose.

His warm palms cupped her breasts, and Stella dropped her head back on a moan as he thumbed both of her nipples. Her hips rocked of their own accord, seek-ing out friction to help her weather the storm tossing her body. When Aaron's mouth closed over one nipple, she cried out and tangled her fingers in his hair. Nothing mat-tered but this one precious night. Her fears, her doubts, their pasts, and futures…all irrelevant.

Stella was vaguely aware of the removal of their re-maining clothes, her attention too focused on how Aaron made her feel invincible and beautiful and desired to care about the scramble of limbs and tangle of clothes. She watched him take a condom from his wallet and cover himself, her desperation reaching dizzying heights. And then he was pushing inside her, his eyes locked with hers, his hands cupping her face as if she were a prized posses-sion, and for all she knew the sky might be falling down.

'Stella,' he muttered, the desire in his eyes scorch-ing her skin.

She clung to him, surrounded by his strong arms. She lost herself in returning his every kiss. When he re-treated, she surged to meet him. When he gripped her hands, his fingers laced with hers, she clung tighter, sur-rounded his hips with her legs. When she moaned his name, he urged her on, muttering her name into her hair, the crook of her neck, her ear, his warm breath dancing over her sensitised skin, adding a cascade of shivers to the rapture already taking hold. She shattered, his name on her broken cry, her climax powerful and endless.

Aaron collapsed his weight on top of her with a groan, joining her in bliss, and Stella entered a world where reality exceeded fantasy. A world where she knew exactly what it felt like to be with Aaron Bennett.

A world that she feared was changed for ever.

Aaron drowsily stroked the length of Stella's arm, which was warm from the fire's glow where he'd banked it with fresh logs. They occupied the sofa, their limbs entwined, a blanket covering them. He wove his fingers with hers, unable to stop touching her for even a second. A fleeting rush of panic stalled his breath. What if he couldn't ever stop?

No, they'd agreed on one night. They had hours until dawn, hours until he would shrug off the role of lover he'd donned for the night and resume the most important role of his life: that of Charlie's father.

Only now that he'd met Stella, now that they had crossed that line of physical intimacy, the constant guilt he'd lived with since Molly's death roared back to life, louder than ever.

He swallowed, fighting the urge to take Stella home and retreat into himself. How could he enjoy being with her when he carried so much baggage that made him feel unworthy? There was no need to fear that he was already addicted to Stella. He couldn't allow himself such an amazing privilege. He'd had his chance at love. That was why this one night of passion was all he could justify, all he could permit.

He shifted, tightening his grip on her waist, and asked in a low voice, 'Tell me what happened to turn you against Abbotsford?' It was obviously linked to this no-good ex, the one who'd cruelly used her, lied and then cast her aside. He hated that she denied herself the place she'd grown up.

He expected her small sigh, so he feathered his lips over her bare shoulder in light kisses, letting her know that nothing she told him would matter or alter how he felt about her.

His stomach rolled at the depth of those feelings he had no right to feel. But he could push those down. He would have to. For Stella, for Charlie and for his own sanity.

She turned onto her back, her head resting on his bicep, where she was still tucked into the crook of his arm. He stroked her hair back from her face and kissed her warm cheek.

'It wasn't Abbotsford as such, just the close-knit nature of village life. Everyone knowing your business.' She sighed and Aaron pressed his lips to her temple, willing her to open up. Perhaps he could reassure her that whatever she feared no longer carried the threat she perceived.

'My break-up with Harry was all such a mess at the time. I didn't know until he texted to break things off, but he didn't stop sleeping with his ex, Angus's mum, throughout our entire relationship.'

Aaron stiffened, protective urges welling up inside him. 'He strung you along and broke up with you in a text?'

She nodded, dragging in a fortifying breath, but he saw the pain still there beneath the surface. 'I believed him when he said he loved me,' she whispered. 'He was older than me, more experienced. He was my first, you know. I trusted him.'

Aaron's muscles coiled tight with rage. 'And he betrayed all of that, after he'd allowed you to get close to his son, to care about them both.' How could someone be such a snake? How could he use a person with such a big heart as Stella? She deserved so much better.

'I was so humiliated,' she continued. 'One minute he was professing undying love and including me in his and Angus's daily lives, then all of a sudden he said it was over, that he was going back to his ex. He even had the audacity to say it was for Angus's sake. And I, in my naiveté, believed him. It wasn't until later that I realised Harry always did what was best for Harry.'

Aaron bit his lip to stop himself from asking for more details. Her pain was a gnawing rumble in his gut. But there must be more to the story for her to avoid Abbotsford, avoid people who might have known her back then.

'Then the rumours started,' she said in a whisper he might not have heard if he hadn't been so close.

He froze, his breath stalling. 'What rumours?'

'Mum came home from work one day upset. People were saying that I'd been the reason Harry and his ex had split in the first place. That I was the other woman, the kind of person who thought I could break up a lovely young family for my own selfish reasons.'

'But it wasn't true.' He knew deep down in his bones that she was incapable of selfishness.

She shook her head, but she wouldn't look at him. 'I didn't know about Angus's mother. He told me he was single. He swept me off my feet. When he confessed that he had a son with a shared custody arrangement, I was delighted, already besotted and half in love with him. I was young, stupid. I should have seen through him, realised the spin was too good to be true.'

Outraged on her behalf, Aaron snorted. 'You were young. That doesn't mean you deserved to be treated that way, that you should have been able to read his mind, or that you were in any way responsible for *his* actions.'

She nodded, her eyes sadder than ever. 'I can certainly understand that now, but at the time none of it mattered. I was lost in my grief, crying all the time. Initially I was too heartbroken to care what people thought. I missed Angus. I grieved the loss of both relationships. And then later I became paranoid and anxious, refusing to leave the house in case someone said something to me and I'd break down in the street.'

'And this… Harry. Didn't he deny the rumours, defend you, tell the truth?' What kind of a man would stand by and let an innocent woman he must have cared for a little suffer alone?

'No. That was the most humiliating part of all. It was as if he'd vanished, leaving me to clean up his dirty work.'

He rested his forehead against her temple, breathed in her warm scent. 'I know it would have been cold comfort at the time, but you must know that he never deserved you.'

Could she possibly still be in love with this guy?

Nausea gripped his throat.

She shrugged. 'I know that now. But then I wondered if his ex was responsible for starting the rumours. Or maybe Harry himself to garner sympathy and win her back for good. I don't know. The worst part was that I was so blind to what I thought love was that I truly believed we had a future. That I would go to uni but come home every weekend to be with him and Angus. That one day I'd move back here and we would be a proper family. More fool me.'

'It wasn't your fault.' He stroked her hair, knowing that he'd lost her to her memories of the pain she'd suffered.

'They were already a family,' she continued as if she hadn't heard, 'one that didn't include me.' She met his eyes. 'I was just a discarded side-piece.'

Aaron bit back a litany of curses, seeing red on Stella's behalf. 'I'm sorry that you had that experience, that this Harry guy was too much of a coward to be honest. That he behaved so cruelly.'

She shrugged but he knew a brave face when he saw one. 'It worked out for the best. I was leaving for uni anyway. When I got to London, I kept busy as a distraction, threw myself into being a medical student, worked hard and played hard.'

She smiled her wide smile and winked at him. 'I had a blast, swapped horses for parties and clubbing during any spare time I had. London is good like that—diverting, energetic, always abuzz. Pretty soon I was too busy to even think about Harry.'

'But it stopped you visiting home.' She hadn't dated again. She wasn't over it.

Acid burned behind his sternum.

She shrugged, still holding part of herself aloof, still shielding. 'You know how demanding those years are academically. I spent most of my free time studying, with the occasional party thrown in. Plus my parents often visited London, as all three of their daughters were based there. In fact, they often talk about selling up here and relocating. I suspect they will once either of my sisters starts a family.'

Aaron's heart skipped a beat without reason. 'What about you? Don't you want children one day?' It was none of his business and he shouldn't be invested in her answer. But he cared about her. He wanted her to be happy and fulfilled.

She shook her head. 'It's not something I've really considered, probably because I haven't had a serious relationship since. I love my job. I'm still focused on my career. You know what that's like.'

Silence settled in the room, broken only by the occasional crackle from the fire. Aaron grew inexplicably restless. It shouldn't matter to him that she had no plans to settle down. But he felt as if he'd just been handed a million-pound note, only to discover it was fake.

'What about you?' she said, deflecting the heat away from herself. 'Have you thought about moving on? Getting married again?' She turned onto her stomach, dipped her gaze and toyed with his chest hair, as if she cared about his future happiness. But she was just being thoughtful. She'd just confessed her reasons to fear falling in love again. She only wanted a one-night stand and she still planned to move away, despite her success at the practice.

And her practicality suited him down to the ground. Right…?

'Not really.' Aaron stroked her back, forced his body to relax, because he did care that they had this connection she could clearly take or leave, even though he shouldn't. 'Life is so busy. Charlie takes up all of my free time. I can't imagine there would be too many women willing to settle for the very occasional date sandwiched in between school pick-up and bedtime stories.'

He felt the same as her about relationships, so why was he so…irritated to hear her voice that her intentions hadn't changed just because they'd had amazing sex?

She stroked his hair, her eyes heavy. 'I think you'd be surprised when you do decide to dip your toe back into the dating pool. I witnessed quite the hormonal kerfuffle at the school gate last week. I suspect the single ladies would be lining up to date the Cotswolds' most eligible doctor.'

He laughed at the picture she painted, but the idea made Aaron shudder. Until she'd returned to Abbotsford, he'd had no interest in the local women, in women full stop.

'I can't do it to Charlie,' he said, the old guilt crawling under his skin. 'He needs me at the moment, needs all of my attention. I have to be everything to him, Mum and Dad.'

She seemed taken aback. 'So that's it for you dating-wise? Your personal needs are irrelevant because you became a parent?'

There was no accusation in her tone, just pensive curiosity.

He shrugged, because he'd never actually given it this much consideration. 'Maybe when he's older I'll have time to date.'

But Charlie wasn't the main reason that he kept himself emotionally unavailable. He couldn't trust that he wouldn't let someone he cared for down again in the future, that he would have to relive the pain of loss. He'd rather be alone.

'How old,' she asked, 'like eighteen? When he leaves for uni?' She chuckled softly but there was something watchful, searching in her eyes.

Why was she so interested in his dating life? Had she changed her mind about the one-night rule? Perhaps his moves weren't that rusty.

His silence was the only answer he had. He couldn't seriously contemplate inviting another woman into his and Charlie's life. What if his son formed an attachment and the relationship didn't last? Look at the way Stella had been hurt. Like her, he couldn't bear to think of poor, confused baby Angus. What if a new woman in Aaron's life resurrected all of Charlie's questions about his mother's death, issues he'd dealt with? What if he grew up to resent Aaron for his choice to move on?

He'd never do anything to risk losing his son. He didn't want Molly's death to mean nothing.

At his continued stillness, Stella stroked his cheek. 'I understand. You're the most important person in Charlie's life. Of course you want to protect him. That's as it should be.' She pressed her mouth to his, comprehension in her eyes.

Because she did understand. She'd been on the receiving end of the choices some parents made to put their own, often messed up and selfish feelings first, and she'd been hurt in the crossfire.

But right now, still rocked by their chemistry and the intimacy of having her naked in his arms, Aaron's predominant fear was for himself, for his precious status quo.

Rather than examine his feelings further, he ran with her kiss, turning it from something comforting to something carnal, his body reacting to hers, his mind forgetting all of the reasons this couldn't last beyond tonight as he covered her body with his. They still had a few hours before sunrise. The best way to combat his concerns, to forget why he couldn't date, why Stella, who shared his reservations, was perfect for now?

The distraction of pleasure.

CHAPTER TEN

BY THE END of a busy Wednesday the following week, Stella was enjoying an erotic daydream of Aaron as she had filled every spare moment since her amazing night his bed.

The door swung open, startling her from the emails she had read and reread at least six times. She looked up from the computer, her heart lurching with predictable arousal and excitement at the sight of Aaron.

One look at his serious expression dissolved her desire, her stomach pinching with trepidation.

'There's an emergency on Penwood Hill,' he said of the local beauty spot popular with hikers. 'Community First Responders have been called, but I'm going to assist in case they need help.'

Stella stood, adrenaline shoving her body into action. 'Can I come, too?'

Aaron nodded, his eyes, which carried the glimmer of intimacy, holding hers. 'I hoped you'd want to. Let's go.'

In Stella's mind, a hundred silent communications seemed to pass between them, things they couldn't voice aloud right now, maybe never.

Do you regret what we did?
Have you thought about me since?

Are you, like me, desperate to do it again?

But now was not the time to have any of those conversations and who knew what Aaron was thinking?

As they exited her consultation room, Aaron reached for her hand. A thrill coursed through her at his simple touch, one that had nothing to do with the adrenaline of attending a medical emergency out in the field. This rush was all about the way Aaron didn't seem to care who saw them holding hands as he led her through the surgery where staff were finishing up for the day and the last patient lingered, chatting about his arthritic knee.

Stella tried to breathe through the sensation that people were staring, judging her, gossiping. It was likely all in her head. But she didn't want the locals to think she was making a play for the village's most eligible man.

Perhaps Aaron had acted unconsciously. She should have eased her hand away—the physical side of their relationship was meant to be over. Except the last time she had felt absolutely comfortable holding a man's hand—something she didn't do when she dated casually—was with Harry.

But there was no time to overthink the gesture, or interpret it as the kind of emotional entanglement that she normally avoided. In the utility room at the rear of the practice, Aaron grabbed two high-visibility all-weather jackets from the hooks on the wall and headed out to the car park with Stella in tow.

They climbed into a four-wheel drive emblazoned with the words 'Abbotsford Medical Centre', and Aaron punched an address into the vehicle's GPS.

'Tell me what we're dealing with,' said Stella, focused on the scene they would find as she clicked her seatbelt into place.

'A day tourist has slipped and fallen running the Penwood Track. Possible tib and fib fracture.' Aaron navigated the car from the car park behind the surgery and took a left turn in the direction of the neighbouring village of Penwood.

He glanced her way, his calm-under-pressure confidence as reassuring as his open smile. 'It's complicated by the fact that his wife, who is thirty-six weeks pregnant, was waiting for him in the car. By all accounts, she tried to help him down the track, but started to have strong contractions.'

'So a double emergency?' Stella's mind raced, running through a plan to triage both patients as soon as they reached the scene.

He nodded, his eyes narrowed with urgency. 'Don't worry.' He reached across the central console and squeezed her hand. 'We can do this. The car is equipped with everything we might need.'

At Stella's hesitant nod, he continued. 'The wife became concerned when he didn't come back from his run—he's a fell runner—within his expected time. There's no mobile reception on the track, so she rushed back to the car to sound the alarm.'

He exhaled a controlled breath, a small smile just for her on his lips. 'I told you—never a dull moment around here.'

They shared a second's eye contact that had Stella recalling every touch, every kiss, every cry of their passionate night together.

Face flushed from the erotic memories, she glanced over her shoulder to the well-stocked boot while Aaron focused on the road.

'Do we have Entonox?' she asked.

'Yes. And the community responder is there, but it's his first week without supervision, poor guy.'

Pulse racing, Stella recognised the route Aaron was taking.

'You're not going to follow the road, are you?' she asked as they bumped over a pothole at speed, flicking up gravel.

'Yes. This is the quickest route to Penwood.' He glanced at the GPS, which wouldn't know the short cut over private land that Stella knew like the back of her hand.

She shook her head. 'No, don't go through the village. The fastest way to the start of the Penwood Track is through the Brady farm, you know, Dale Brady's land.'

'Are you sure?' He shot her a searching look before taking a bend in the lane.

'Absolutely. I used to ride that way all the time on Gertrude. The farm track is wide enough for a four-wheel drive and it cuts off the corner taken via the road. Trust me. It's quicker.'

Aaron grinned and then winked. 'Whatever you say. I do trust you. Nothing much changes around this landscape. You probably know the area better than me, as I was more about driving flashy sports cars around Cheltenham than I was about taking a horse or a Land Rover over a farm track in my youth.'

Stella pursed her lips. 'Oh, I recall. You always seemed to have a different pretty female passenger, too.'

He grinned, the moment of lightness punctuating the adrenaline rush seemingly as welcome to him as it was to Stella. He reached for her hand once more, raising it to his mouth to press a kiss across her knuckles. 'Thank you for the insider knowledge. I'm glad that you're here.'

His smile, the touch of his lips to her skin, devastated Stella, who had managed to fool herself that she could move on from their one night, but she'd been sorely deluded. Not that there was time to enjoy the shudders his touch sent through her body, or panic at her realisation that she was in deep trouble where Aaron was concerned.

He was everything she had avoided these past nine years: perfect, a man made just for Stella.

She stared out of the window to stop herself staring at him. Of course he wasn't perfect. No one was. He had as many issues, as many reasons to avoid a serious relationship as she did. She just couldn't decide if that gave her solace or left a sour taste in her mouth.

At Stella's direction, Aaron took a right turn and headed for the Brady farm.

Stella pointed out the dirt road, her stomach now churning with more than adrenaline for the medical scene awaiting them as she replayed their conversation. Aaron was right. In many ways, she too was a local. She'd grown up here, had family here, was a part of local hIstory.

A sharp pain lodged under her ribs. She hadn't realised how much she was enjoying being back in her old stomping ground. How much she'd missed riding and walking this landscape. She had been forced to become another version of herself in this place, one she didn't like: gullible, broken, grieving. Her desire to leave Abbotsford and return to London had nothing to do with the place and everything to do with her aversion to being hurt again. But seeing the village, the people, the community through Aaron's eyes, she realised that the association between place and her past that she'd made was a figment of her imagination. An unhealthy link that kept her bound in fear.

That just wouldn't do.

Before Stella could ponder this momentous realisation, they arrived at the start of the Penwood Track. The single-lane road flared into a small turning circle, which doubled as a makeshift car park for those wanting to hike the track.

Aaron pulled up behind the first responder's vehicle, which was parked next to the only other car. A heavily pregnant woman was leaning against the car, one hand braced on the open driver's side door and the other on the roof of the car.

Aaron had barely engaged the handbrake when Stella flung open the passenger door and ran towards the woman. She was clearly in the middle of a strong contraction, breathing hard through the pain but in a controlled way that told Stella she'd likely laboured before.

Aaron joined them a few seconds later, one medical backpack slung over his shoulder and another which he placed on the ground at Stella's feet. 'I'll go and assist the first responder, who is with the husband. I'll do a quick triage and then I'll come back, okay?'

Stella nodded, wishing they could stick together.

Aaron addressed the woman. 'Don't worry, Mrs Heath, the ambulance is on its way.'

Then he handed Stella a head torch and took the track at a run, disappearing from sight around the bend.

As the woman's contraction passed, Stella rested a hand on her arm. 'My name is Stella, I'm a GP from Abbotsford.' She ignored how naturally that sentence formed. 'What's your first name, Mrs Heath?'

'Abby,' the woman said, gripping Stella's hand with determination bordering on panic.

This wasn't good. Stella needed to transport Abby

somewhere suitable, comfortable and clean. But she had seen that look before during her obstetric post, often when a woman was transitioning into the second stage of labour.

'Can you walk?' Stella asked, glancing over her shoulder to where the practice vehicle was parked only five metres away.

Abby shook her head, her hand gripping Stella's in a vice, her breathing becoming deep and deliberate once more. 'Need to push,' she said, scrunching her eyes closed against the pain of another powerful contraction.

Stella soothed the woman through the worst of it, her mind spinning. Her gaze searched the track for Aaron, but of course he hadn't had enough time to find the husband, let alone return to assist Stella. She had never delivered a baby outside of a hospital before. But nature waited for no one. If baby Heath was on its way, she would have to manage with what they had to hand.

'Could you move into the back of your car?'

At Abby's uncertain nod, Stella guided her the couple of steps, opened the rear door of the car and helped lower her into a sitting position on the edge of the back seat.

Stella rummaged in the backpack, finding all of the basics, but if the baby came before the ambulance arrived she would need to be prepared.

'I need to get some more supplies,' she said to Abby. 'I have gas and air in the car. I'll be thirty seconds, okay?'

Abby nodded and Stella rushed to the four-wheel drive and flung open the boot, scooping up an armful of blankets and a cannister of Entonox. She returned to Abby, her training kicking in, using but also mitigating her own flight response.

She could do this, alone if she had to. She could help

Abby. She could make a difference here. That was why she had wanted to be a GP.

As she searched the contents of the bag in the light from the torch, part of her wanted to laugh at how she'd once foolishly thought working in Abbotsford would be a dull, uneventful, snooze fest. But that had been her fear talking. Another lie she'd believed to protect herself from being as vulnerable as she had once been when she was eighteen.

'I need to push,' said Abby, gripping the driver's headrest with white-knuckle force.

Stella nodded calmly, managed a smile and saw its immediate effect on Abby's wild eyes.

She removed the packaging from a plastic mouthpiece. 'Is this your first baby?' Stella connected the mouthpiece to the cannister of Entonox.

Abby took the mouthpiece from Stella and began sucking on it as another contraction took hold.

'Second,' said Abby when she could next speak. 'The baby's coming. I can't hold on.'

'Okay. It's going to be fine.' Stella pulled on a pair of latex gloves, wishing that she had Aaron's calming presence but also confident that she had been trained for this.

'You and I are going to do this together, okay?' Stella spread a blanket under Abby's legs and another around her shoulders to ward off the cold the dusk brought. Then she eased Abby's clothing down, covering her lap with a clean towel.

'I need to examine you quickly, just to make sure the baby is head first. We'll wait until the next contraction, and I'll be as gentle as I can.'

Abby nodded, her nostrils flaring as a fresh contraction started. Stella quickly established that Abby was fully dilated and indeed in full-blown second-stage labour.

'I can feel your baby's head, Abby. Everything looks great. Are you having a boy or a girl?' She changed her gloves.

'Boy,' Abby panted.

Then there was the scrunch of gravel and an out-of-breath Aaron arrived. Stella all but sagged with relief.

With an expert eye, he took in the scene and, as Abby's contraction passed and she stopped pushing, joined them in the small space the open car door allowed.

'This is Abby and she's having a baby boy,' Stella said, grateful that they'd have the benefit of Aaron's experience and an extra pair of hands.

'Abby, I'm Dr Bennett. I've just examined your husband and he's going to be absolutely fine. He has broken his leg, but I gave him some pain medication and he's warm and comfortable and stable. You don't need to worry about him, okay? He said he loves you and he's going to be with you as soon as help arrives to carry him down the hill.'

'The baby isn't far away,' Stella informed Aaron. 'I've checked and he's a cephalic presentation.'

'Good, well done.' Aaron reached for a pair of gloves, his stare locking with Stella's. She saw his own trace of trepidation. Like her, he was probably thinking of all the things that could go wrong with baby Heath's delivery. Was he also recalling the birth of his own son, the wonderful, much anticipated moment that had rapidly turned to every husband's worst nightmare?

She wanted to hold him, to match their physical closeness to the emotional connection she could no longer deny existed. She wanted to press her lips to the fine frown lines in the corners of his eyes until she had magically chased away any residue of his pain. Instead she smiled, hoping he could read reassurance and togetherness in her eyes in the same way she saw it beaming from his.

'We can do this,' he said, his smile stretching for Stella, and then to Abby said, 'Everything is going to be fine.'

Stella nodded in agreement and returned all her attention to Abby.

Over the next ten minutes the three of them worked as a team, their mutual trust and respect helping ease baby boy Heath into the world. There were tears from both women as Stella placed the tiny newborn in his mother's arms for the first time.

When Stella turned her relieved smile on Aaron she saw that he too was misty-eyed.

Then tears turned to delighted laughter as Aaron and Stella hugged awkwardly over the medical paraphernalia littering the ground. Stella clung to him, breathed in his familiar scent, revelled in the masculine strength of his body, her euphoria latching on to Aaron and their growing bond.

When she pulled away to check on Abby and the baby, out of nowhere chills of doubt attacked her body. Aaron had already experienced all of this with Molly. Aaron had Charlie and wasn't looking for a relationship.

More reconciled than ever that they were right to give their fling a one-night limit, she shakily packed away the equipment, avoiding glancing at Aaron.

In the next few minutes two ambulances arrived, each unloading a stretcher. Stella shoved away her conflicting emotions—fear that she'd begun to feel closer to

Aaron than was wise, and relief that she'd held something back—and helped the paramedics to load Abby and the baby into the back of the ambulance. Once connected to an oxygen saturation monitor, the baby was deemed fine and healthy.

Mr Heath was carried down the hill and placed in the second ambulance, but not before more tears all round as he was introduced to his tiny son.

The minute both ambulances headed back towards Cheltenham, Stella's arms sagged to her sides, the adrenaline that had served her well draining away to nothing. It wasn't until she was seated once more in the passenger seat of the practice four-wheel drive that the tremors began.

'That was incredible,' she said, the memory of the tiny, precious newborn's weight in her arms still fresh.

She glanced at his profile, searching for the impossible, for something she feared and craved simultaneously. that his feelings resembled hers.

All she saw were shadows.

'Thank you.' Her voice broke and her eyes burned, her jumbled emotions expanding.

Had Aaron experienced the wonder she saw on the Heaths' faces when he'd first held Charlie? How quickly had that wonder turned to horror for his wife, and how could he ever get over such a monumental loss?

'What for?' Aaron gripped her hand across the centre console and squeezed. 'You and Abby did all of the work. I'm so proud of you.'

His eyes were haunted. Stella knew him well enough to see his flicker of pain, and she couldn't help the urge to offer comfort, to gently probe and ensure the delivery hadn't brought back bittersweet memories of Charlie's birth and the subsequent trauma of Molly's death.

'Can you pull over?' Stella managed to choke out.

He did so without question, perhaps sensing the unforeseen seismic shift happening inside Stella. Her head labelled it an anticlimax, but her heart perceived a sledgehammer blow of realisation.

Her self-preservation refused to label her feelings. But watching the love and connection of the Heath family and feeling the profound connection to Aaron that went way beyond physical attraction, she knew that she wanted that for herself one day. A partner so in sync with her that they could communicate with their eyes and their smiles alone. A baby that she made with the love of her life. All these years she had told herself that she had the life she wanted, but it had all been lies. She'd been hiding, pretending that she was complete so she could armour her heart.

But sharing that experience with Aaron made her aware just how much she was short-changing herself in life, denying herself its most wondrous experiences: deep love, sharing her life with someone, creating a family of their own with that person.

Aaron turned off the engine and the car filled with silence.

She unclipped her seatbelt and turned to face him, almost deaf from the thundering of her heart. 'Are…are *you* okay?'

The sadness in his expression as he registered the unspoken question behind her question tore through her chest.

She asked it anyway, because she wanted to be there for him. 'Did it bring back memories…of Charlie's birth?'

He swallowed, his gaze shifting. 'A little. I'm just so relieved that they were both okay.' He stared out through the windscreen. Darkness had descended, giving the impression that they were wrapped in their own warm, safe cocoon.

But she couldn't trust impressions.

She ached for Aaron's loss, but at the same time crumpled a little for herself. The irony of her perfect man being in love with someone else, someone ethereal and intangible, someone Stella could never rival, roared in her head, a feral scream of the danger of letting down her guard.

As Aaron stayed silent, Stella switched subjects.

'I want to thank you for everything,' she said, a lump of longing in her throat. 'For bringing me along today. For inviting me to your practice in the first place.' She looked at her hands in her lap. 'I never said thank you for taking me on, even when I disparaged your home, your workplace, your life. But I appreciate everything you've done for me. I appreciate all the opportunities you've given me.'

I appreciate you.

Too close to tears, she couldn't bring herself to utter the last sentiment aloud. She might hurl herself into his arms in search of the heady rush and rightness she knew that she would find there.

'You're welcome.' He tilted his head and seemed to see into her soul. 'Thank *you* for suggesting that short cut and for being your wonderful self back there.' He brushed some hair back from her face. His pupils were wide, swallowing the blue she loved. 'Inviting you here was one of my smarter moves.'

'I'm glad that you did.'

'It's rewarding, isn't it? Making a difference.' He

cupped her cheek, soothing some of the turmoil she carried. 'That's what I love about this job.'

She nodded, frozen by her needs. It had been years since she'd felt a true part of this community. Aaron's patience and persistence had shown her that she could be herself, no matter where she was and be valued, be a part of something bigger than herself. That she mattered, despite the memories tangled up with this place.

And now, for the first time in years, she wanted that in her personal life as well as professionally.

They stared at each other for a handful of heartbeats.

His eyes swooped to her mouth. Tension resonated from him; he was holding back, perhaps both words and actions.

Before she could question the impulse, Stella scrambled into his lap, her knees astride his thighs, and threw her arms around his neck. She couldn't deny her feelings, which hadn't lessened despite their one night as lovers.

She craved him more than ever.

Aaron's hand settled warm and comforting in the middle of her back, his stare dark, vulnerable.

Tired of restraint, she pressed her mouth to his in a cathartic surrender. He returned her kiss with a groan of release, as if he too had held back for too long.

They had broken the rules, which, for Stella, somehow sweetened the addictive kisses.

Aaron's hand curled around the back of her neck, holding her mouth in place as she tangled her fingers into his hair, tilted his head back against the headrest. He gripped her waist, fisting her skirt as she rode his lap. His hardness pressed between her legs as he tilted his hips.

Would anything extinguish this fire scorching her alive?

'What are we doing?' he asked as she let him up for

air, even as his fingers slid under the hem of her sweater
to the naked skin of her back, restlessly flexing, stroking, exploring.

'I don't know.' She feathered kisses over the side of
his neck so the warm scent of his body filled her nostrils
from inside his collar. She couldn't make her lips leave
his skin. 'Perhaps it's just the adrenaline.'

She gripped his face and stared into his eyes. 'I want
you.' Over and over until she'd burned him out of her
system.

He searched her stare, his eyes transparent, showing
her the same needs that paralysed her. 'Me too. Ever
since I woke up on Saturday morning to find you gone. I
couldn't wait for the start of a new week just to see you.'

His words were beyond worrisome to the part of herself she still needed to protect, but she became distracted
by pleasure as his hands skated her sides, cupped her
breasts, zapping her nervous system with sparks that felt
way too good to be wrong.

'This is bad,' she said as he released her from another
soul-searing kiss.

'I know.' He shifted under her, his lips stretching into
that sexy smile she'd come to adore. 'Which is probably
why it feels so fantastic.'

She writhed in his lap, torturing them both with the
friction. 'Like a compulsion. But one night was supposed
to be enough.'

Perhaps her addiction, her weakness for him, was amplified because she couldn't walk away yet. Nothing else
had changed. Her one relationship had ended in enough
desolation to keep her single for nine years, and Aaron
was still in love with his wife and devoted only to his son.

He smiled, the playful delight in his eyes lightening

the mood. 'So I'm a compulsion now? That's a big step up from a crush.'

Stella rolled her eyes, laughter bubbling up from her chest.

Then he sobered, pressed his forehead to hers and exhaled his frustration. 'I have to go—I need to pick up Charlie.'

As if doused in icy water, Stella pulled away. She'd become so carried away by her feelings for him, feelings that she'd vowed she could keep in check, that she'd forgotten his personal obligations.

'Of course.' Mortified, she shifted her weight from his thighs, preparing to retake the passenger seat.

'Wait.' He gripped her hips, stared up at her in heartfelt appeal. 'Can we see each other again? Outside of work?' He smiled, cajoling, his eyes vulnerable and hopeful, and Stella wanted to give him anything. Everything.

She swallowed hard, her throat tight with the ache to say *yes*. But, as he'd just reminded her, Aaron and Charlie were a father-and-son team.

No, Aaron wasn't Harry and Stella was no longer trusting and guileless. But normally, by this stage in a relationship—where things moved from casual towards expectant, attached, romantic—she made her excuses and called it a day.

Before she could become emotionally invested.

Perhaps it was already too late.

'Don't you have Charlie to think about?' She needed to remind herself that Aaron was a package deal, that he would always put Charlie first, and that was a good thing. Given that she had just proved that Aaron alone was temptation enough, there was no way she could risk interacting with Charlie, who, as his father's son, was no doubt equally enchanting. Not if she hoped to keep herself distant enough so she could walk away when the time came.

He nodded, his lips pressed into a flat line. 'Yes.' Regret and realisation that she was right dawned in his eyes.

She reluctantly slid into the passenger seat. 'Let's go back to Abbotsford. It's been a long day.'

He nodded, started the car without comment and drove the four miles in silence. After all, what else was there to say?

CHAPTER ELEVEN

AARON KNEW THE invitation was unwise even as the eager words left his mouth. 'Would you like to join us for dinner?'

He and Charlie had bumped into Stella at the village shop and, try as he might, he couldn't stop himself. She carried a solitary bottle of wine and they hadn't had a moment alone together since he dropped her at home after they had delivered the Heath baby three days ago and kissed in the driver's seat like horny teenagers.

'We're having meatballs and spaghetti.' Charlie beamed, as if the menu might sway her decision. 'It's my favourite. But Dad forgot to buy the pasta sauce, didn't you, Dad?'

'I did.' Aaron met Stella's stare. He was so conflicted that he almost withdrew the invitation. But the deed was done. Charlie had recognised Stella the minute they'd walked into the tiny shop and it was only one home-cooked meal, hardly a grand seduction. It couldn't even really be called a date.

'Um…' She smiled down at Charlie. 'Do you have enough? I don't want to deprive you of your favourite meal.'

'We have lots,' Charlie said dramatically, 'but I'm only

allowed three meatballs, because they are this big.' He made a circle with his thumb and forefinger and looked to Aaron for confirmation.

'We normally have leftovers, but it's no big deal,' Aaron eyed her bottle of wine, 'if you have plans.' None of his business.

Stella flushed. 'My parents are out tonight. I was going to have a glass of this and maybe make some cheese on toast.' She shrugged. 'Actually, I'd love to join you for spaghetti, now that you have the sauce.'

They shared another look that made Aaron think they were both wary of the dynamics and of sharing too much. Was Stella, like him, also running out of resolve against the temptation?

Aaron's cottage was a three-minute walk, door-to-door from the shop. Aaron quickly completed the partially prepared meal with the addition of pasta sauce, Charlie set another place at the table for Stella and she poured two glasses of wine.

'See,' said Charlie, pointing with his fork, 'I have three meatballs, and you have three meatballs.' He offered Stella his happy smile as he showed off his maths skills. 'That makes six. It's a double.'

Stella gave Charlie a high five and an impressed nod. 'You're a very smart young man.'

Aaron's heart swelled with pride as he watched Stella interact with Charlie, even as the instant and easy connection between them caused a lump to press against his lungs and restrict his breath. Just like all the other wonderful things he had learned about her, he immediately knew she would make an amazing mother if she ever chose to have children.

He had an urgent and visceral urge to lean across the

table and kiss her. In fact, he hadn't stopped wanting to kiss her since that very first time their lips met.

He was so doomed…

She had been right. Delivering the Heath baby with Stella had brought up a sickening collision of his past and present. The wonder of holding his son. The love he'd felt watching Molly kiss his downy head. Then the shock and desolation of his wife, Charlie's mother, being snatched away from them both.

When Abby's baby had been safely delivered he'd clung to Stella in that moment of shared joy, wondering how he had become so desperate for her in such a short space of time.

Watching her now with his son, the answer was obvious. How could he not be utterly captivated?

'What's your favourite part of school?' she asked Charlie.

Aaron stifled a laugh, knowing exactly what his son's response would be. He often asked him that very question and usually received the same answer: lunchtime, with home time in second place.

'I like lunchtime,' said Charlie, predictably. 'Today we had veggie pizza.' He stabbed at a meatball with his fork and waggled it around like a cheerleader's pompom, his 'z's lisped adorably since he had lost his first baby tooth last week.

'Yummy—I like pizza too,' said Stella, catching Aaron's eye once more.

Acknowledgement and communication passed silently between them, as if they had been together for years and knew how the other thought.

In his fantasy, he imagined it went something like:
Stella: *Your son is adorable.*

Aaron: *You're so good with him.*

Both in unison: *It makes me want you all the more.*

But the tightening in his gut reminded him to slow down his wild imaginings. Something out of his control was happening. That he craved her company, her smiles, her sharp wit was understandable. The physical compulsions made sense. But this new longing—that the affinity they had for each other extended to Charlie in Stella's case—mystified him.

He was on dangerous ground, craving the cerebral connection as much as the physical, because Stella might have been specifically designed to his specifications.

Only she couldn't be his, just as he wasn't the man for her, neither of them wanting the emotional attachment that sometimes felt as if it was developing without their permission.

Aaron filled his mouth with food, giving himself more time to think. Except he was too out of practice to untangle his emotions, having spent years merely accepting the guilt he lived with and embracing his position.

'Pizza is my favourite,' continued Charlie, oblivious to the adult tension stealing Aaron's appetite and the fact that only half an hour ago he'd declared the same was true for meatballs and spaghetti. 'But Dad always makes the edges too brown and crispy.' His son offered a withering look that spoke of his long suffering under his father's culinary challenges. 'Johnny's mum makes nice, soft edges, like the pizza at school.'

Stella looked away from a sombre Charlie and pressed her lips together, Aaron assumed to hold in a smile.

'Does he?' She flicked a knowing look at Aaron. 'That's not good. But I have an idea. You could help him by setting a timer on his phone that will tell him when the pizza is ready to come out of the oven. I'll show you how to do it after we eat our meatballs if you like.'

Charlie's eyes went wide, impressed, no doubt delighted that he'd have access to Aaron's phone. Like most parents Aaron constantly struggled to police screen time, but this was a practical, even educational skill, so he could hardly object.

His son's face lit up, his dreamy gaze falling on Stella in a way that meant Aaron would likely be peppered with Stella-related questions for the rest of the week.

Aaron mouthed *Thank you* to Stella and gripped his silverware tighter, fresh guilt tightening his shoulders. For everyone's sake, he couldn't let them become too close. Because Charlie had naturally warmed to Stella, as if his life lacked the influence of a sage and wise woman, even if it was simply to ward off burnt pizza in the future.

The sigh Aaron held inside settled like a stitch under his ribs. Why could he see Stella fitting into their lives like the missing piece of a jigsaw? Was his guilt over Molly, the main thing that had held him back from seriously dating all these years, getting in the way of Charlie's development? Did he need a female figure in his life? Had he prevented Charlie from building a wider circle of relationships with his overprotective fears?

Restricting his own life because he didn't deserve another chance at happiness was one thing, but limiting Charlie's life in any way was the opposite of Aaron's intention.

After dinner, while Aaron loaded the dishwasher in contemplative silence, Stella kept her promise and taught Charlie how to set the timer on his dad's phone.

'Now you can show me how good you are with your

numbers,' she said, her fond smile for his son shredding Aaron.

Stella's natural affinity with children and Charlie's awe and trust forced him to admit something he hadn't wanted to explore since the night they'd spent together.

He wanted more than one night.

He probably always had, instinct and the restlessness grumbling away inside telling him this with Stella had never been casual, at least not for him.

But had her desires changed? Perhaps her declaration that she still wanted him in the car had come with the high of successfully delivering the Heath baby. And could he risk exploring this further when Charlie's happiness was at stake?

His feelings might end up putting him in an impossible position: wanting a woman who could disappear at any time and risking that Charlie's feelings might be caught in the crossfire. His son had lost enough.

Charlie let out an excited squeal, alerting Aaron to a change in topic.

'Dad, Dr Stella can ride a horse.' He jumped up on the wooden rocking horse in the corner to show off his skills to their guest. 'Have you got a real horse?' Charlie asked, eyes like saucers. 'I want a pony but Dad will only buy me this one, because it's *dangerless*.' His little shoulders sagged at his dire deprivation.

Stella shot Aaron an apologetic grimace. 'No, I don't have my own horse. They are very expensive and take a lot of looking after,' she said to Charlie. 'I'm just helping other children learn to ride.'

With the dishes done, Aaron needed to usher Charlie upstairs for a bath. Otherwise they could be here all night locked in a plead-denial cycle that they had travelled many times.

'Can you stay a while longer?' he asked Stella after Charlie had reluctantly mumbled goodnight and run upstairs making clip-clop noises. 'I won't be long getting him settled.' She seemed comfortable enough to be here, despite Charlie's energy and constant chatter. And he wanted some alone time with her, to figure out their next move, because his head was scrambled.

'Sure.' She nodded, her smile indulgent despite the lingering reticence in her eyes.

He poured her another glass of wine and took the stairs two at a time. Thirty minutes later, with Charlie bathed, put to bed and a bedtime story read, Aaron came back downstairs to find Stella sitting before the fire. She'd put on an old vinyl from the selection he'd collected over the years, and a pile of Charlie's folded clean laundry sat in the basket on the floor at her feet.

'You didn't need to do that, but thanks.' He grabbed his own wine left over from dinner and took the seat next to her on the sofa.

'Is he asleep?' she asked, tucking her knee underneath her so she faced him.

His head might be all over the place but his body had no hesitations. He took her free hand in his. 'He will be soon. He's exhausted. He didn't even ask for a second story.'

'He's adorable,' she whispered, her face catching the glow from the fire.

Aaron flexed his fingers against hers. 'Did I do the wrong thing by inviting you over?'

She smiled, shook her head, no hint of wariness in

her eyes. 'Did I do the wrong thing with the timer on the phone?'

'No. You've made a fan for life.'

'You're obviously very close,' she said.

Was she thinking about her closeness to Angus? Aaron tugged her hand, pressed his lips to her temple and inhaled the scent of her hair.

'We are.' He cleared a sudden blockage in his throat. 'We've had to be.'

Stella's eyes brimmed with compassion and understanding. For the first time ever Aaron contemplated a different reality for his future. Could he try to have a relationship with someone wonderful like Stella? Someone who respected his and Charlie's relationship but also fitted in as if she had always been a vital component?

'I didn't realise that he worries about me quite so much, you know, with the pizza thing and my concerns about the riding,' Aaron said, scrubbing at his jaw as doubts rattled the convictions that had helped him to survive these past five years. How messed up was it that his young son saw through him and his attempts to provide stability. Safety. Aaron was the grown-up; worrying was supposed to be his job.

Perhaps he needed to back off. He didn't want Charlie to grow up neurotic.

'Children can be very perceptive and intuitive.' Stella stroked his arm. 'Don't beat yourself up. If your worst crime as a parent is a bit of burnt pizza, he'll be absolutely fine.'

Aaron took her hand, grateful that she understood his turmoil. 'Clearly Johnny's family set the gold standard when it comes to all things from procreation to perfect pizza.'

Stella chuckled, her fingers making a lazy path on his skin. Was she aware of how her touch inflamed him, held him captive, redefined how he saw himself? Not just as a father, but also as a man.

'You're a great dad,' she said. 'He's just trying to make sense of his world.' That she saw him so clearly was evident in her next statement. 'It doesn't mean he's lacking anything or missing out.'

Aaron looked away, that persistent trickle of shame heating his blood. Of course Charlie lacked a vital part of his life: his mother. And if anyone was at fault, it was Aaron.

'I blame myself,' he said after a pause where Stella gave him the time he needed.

'For the burnt pizza?' she asked, her small, perceptive smile telling him she was kindly offering him an out clause from exposing his deepest doubt if he needed it. Wonderful, caring woman.

'That too.' He laughed, grateful for her attempt at levity, but trusting her enough to want to voice the fear he suspected would haunt him for ever. 'But mainly for Molly.'

Her stare latched to his, unflinching. Holding. Communicating.

I'm listening.

'We hadn't planned to get pregnant with Charlie when we did,' he said. 'One night we ran out of condoms. Molly thought the ovulation maths meant we'd be okay, but I'm a doctor. I should have known better than to risk such an unreliable form of contraception.'

'You wouldn't be the first married couple to dice with the dates.'

He shrugged, futility a hollow space in his chest. 'I

guess not, but usually the story has a happy outcome, as ours did for a handful of precious minutes. But a part of me can't help but wonder if things would have been different if I'd been more careful. Protected Molly better.'

'What happened to Molly wasn't your fault.' Her tone was firm. 'You know that she suffered a rare but life-threatening complication of pregnancy that could have happened at any time. It's unfair and tragic and heartbreaking.' She cupped his face, holding his gaze. 'But *not* your fault.'

At his silence she continued, 'Is that why you haven't dated anyone? Because you feel…responsible in some way, because of the timing?'

He shrugged, nodded, sighed, all his ugliness spilling out. 'Every time I look at him I wonder if I'm enough, if I'm doing a good enough job. If I can possibly be everything he needs.'

'You are,' she said without hesitation.

'I'm not so sure. I watched the way he interacted with you tonight. It was lovely to see his confidence.' He frowned. 'I thought I was protecting him—he's lost so much—but perhaps I've denied him a woman's influence in his life.'

'You're doing your best out of love, that's all any of us can do. Life isn't a one-size-fits-all, nor are there any guarantees.'

'That's true.' Stella was so easy to talk to, no doubt that was what made her a great doctor. 'Then sometimes I worry that I'm doing too much, being overprotective, like with the horse riding.'

She shook her head. 'My parents used to worry too. He's the most precious thing in the world to you. It's natural.'

He stared, awed by her calm insights and natural humanity. He couldn't become reliant on her compassion and understanding. He couldn't become reliant on her full stop. He needed to keep emotionally distant for his own sake, too.

Just because he'd glimpsed how well she would fit into their lives if she lived in Abbotsford didn't mean that he and Charlie were what she wanted. She planned to leave as soon as she could, head back to her single life in London. His life, Charlie's life was here, a place from which Stella still felt she needed to run in order to outrun herself, her past, her demons.

And he would wish her every happiness and success.

He and Charlie would be fine, but only if he stayed detached. He owed it to Charlie not to mess up again. That meant maintaining their status quo, their boys' club of two, even if he had to forgo his own needs, which right now urged him to hold her tight…indefinitely.

'I'm teaching tomorrow, at the stables,' she said. 'Why don't you bring him along after my last class for a quick ride? I promise I'll take care of him—I'll have my hands on him at all times. We have riding hats and body protectors. I'll choose our most sedate and docile pony. It will be as safe as possible.'

Her concern and reassurance overwhelmed him. He wanted to kiss her so badly he needed an instant distraction.

The song had changed to a nice, slow ballad.

'Dance with me,' he said, standing.

She frowned at his extended hand. Laughed nervously. 'Really? Here?'

He nodded, recalling a pair of high heels and little black dress fit for a chic, city nightclub. Soon she would swap her riding boots for dancing shoes and their lives would return to being different.

'You once invited me to go dancing.'

'And you said your clubbing days were over.' She placed her hand in his, eyes alive as she met his challenge.

He pulled her to her feet and into his arms. 'Yes, but there's more than one way to take a pulse.' He caressed her inner wrist over her radial artery and then touched his fingers to her neck where her carotid beat like a drum. 'This is my kind of dance.'

Falling serious because his senses were filled with her scent and warmth, he pressed her close, one hand gripping hers and the other pressed between her shoulder blades. He caught the soft sigh leaving her lips as she looked up at him from under those long lashes.

Fighting the urge to kiss her, Aaron moved them around the space between the fire and the sofa they'd occupied. This was the way he'd held her in the early hours of Saturday morning when he had willed away the first light of dawn, knowing it would bring their intimate time to an end.

She snuggled closer, dropped her head to his shoulder, reminding him how good they'd been together, how their passion had burned out of control until their reservations and differences hadn't seemed to matter.

She'd admitted that she still wanted him. And now that he was touching her again, her heart banging against his ribs and her eyes filled with what looked like longing, Aaron struggled to find the strength to care that he was risking what he valued most: the predictable stability he'd built these past five years.

If only it was just his feelings at risk, he could live with the liability. How could he have what he wanted, more time with Stella, and protect both her and Charlie from growing too attached? His son would be ecstatic at Stella's offer to show him how to ride, but could Aaron allow it, knowing the emotional risks?

Perhaps if it was a one-off…

'I can hear your mind whirring,' she mumbled into his jumper, her hand stroking his chest.

He released the sigh, tugging at the mental knots in his head. 'I want impossible things.'

'What things?' Her finger traced his jaw.

'You.'

She smiled up at him. 'I'm right here, aren't I?'

He nodded, holding her tighter because her presence back in his arms was everything he had craved since their night together. 'I'm trying to protect everyone's feelings…yours, Charlie's.'

She nodded, her gaze softening, growing more enticing. 'I'm a grown woman. I can protect myself.'

Without waiting for him to process her statement, she reached up on tiptoe, brought her mouth within kissing distance. His lips landed, soft but urgent. She moaned, angled her head, parted her lips to deepen their kiss. He gripped her waist, slid his hands up her back and tangled his fingers in her hair, losing another chunk of his restraint.

She sighed, her whole body collapsing against his chest as if she was exhausted, like him, from fighting this connection that had gone way deeper than either of them expected.

He held her face between his palms and parted from her with a reluctant groan. 'Can you stay the night? Charlie normally sleeps in until seven.' He poured his desires and the unspoken feelings he hadn't yet deciphered into his stare.

How had he gone from content with their one night to being this heavily invested? How would he return to the way he'd been happy with his sexless existence before Stella invaded his world and showed him what was lacking?

Except it wasn't just sex. If he could never sleep with her again he'd still want to see her, to work with her and be on her quiz team. She enriched his existence, and a part of him knew that, if life were different, she would enrich Charlie's too, teach him things that Aaron couldn't.

Her expression shifted through desire to unease. She shook her head. 'I don't want to risk confusing Charlie, but I can stay a while.' She wrapped her arms around his neck, her eyes glazed with passion.

It was a compromise with which he could live.

This time they made it to the privacy of his bedroom, which was at the other end of the landing from Charlie's room, before their passion became overwhelming and undeniable. They stripped in silence, their stares locked, as if both wary, both conscious of what was at stake but unable to fight temptation any longer.

In case this was the last time they would surrender, he commanded every kiss, his passion roaring out of control. He trailed his mouth over her neck, her collarbones, her breasts, every inch of her fragrant skin, learning all of the places that made her fist the sheets and bite her lip to hold in her moans.

Needing more of her, he abandoned her sensitive nipples, pushed her legs wide and covered her with his mouth. Her gasp broke free, her fingers tugging at his hair.

'Aaron.' She whispered his name, a raft of emotions flitting across her expression.

Aaron read every single one. He knew this woman. He wanted to bring her pleasure, soothe her every hurt, make her promises and never let her down the way she had been in the past.

Dangerous wants.

She shattered, riding out her orgasm with her stare lost in his.

He held her in his arms, kissed her, caressed her until she grew restless and needy once more, wrapping her legs around his hips and clinging to his arms, his shoulders, his back. With protection taken care of, she welcomed him inside her body, her passionate cries smothered by their kisses.

Something cataclysmic was happening. Something he couldn't examine too closely in case it changed his life irrevocably.

Unspoken words clogged Aaron's throat. This couldn't be more than sex, no matter how it felt.

He knew that her internal struggles over their fling matched his. She'd been bitterly betrayed, robbed of her relationship with a little boy she had loved, had spent the intervening nine years protecting herself with only casual dating.

He wasn't ready to forgive himself, to lay all of himself on the line in the search for wholeness, happiness. He had nothing to offer beyond his body and this violent connection they both battled. But a part of him wanted Stella to struggle to forget everything they had shared. As he would.

'Stella.' He gripped her tighter as his body reacted on instinct, driving them hard towards the point of no return. She entwined her fingers with his, matched his every move, alongside him on this journey.

They came together, so in sync it was no use kidding himself that he'd successfully managed to keep emotions at bay.

Exhausted and elated, he dragged her close, burrowed his nose in her hair and fought the temptation to ask her to stay in Abbotsford.

When he woke an hour later the bed beside him was cold. He rummaged for his phone, his heart sinking. He found her text, the screen illuminating the dark room.

I didn't want to wake you. Had a wonderful evening.

He should be relieved that, as promised, she had been considerate of Charlie and so pragmatic that she'd slipped out into the night without disturbing him. There were no loose ends he'd need to explain to a curious five-year-old.

Instead, he was more hollow than he had been in years, as if he'd been robbed of something he hadn't realised he cherished until it was gone.

He threw his phone on the bed, the mess of convoluted feelings inside telling him it was way too late for him to emerge from this unscathed.

CHAPTER TWELVE

STELLA HAD JUST stabled all but one of the Ability Riding ponies when she heard the crunch of gravel that announced a vehicle. Her adrenaline spiked, her stomach fluttering. It was them, Aaron and Charlie.

She tucked some stray hair behind her ear and brushed the hay from her mud-splattered jodhpurs, preening for Aaron, even as she lectured herself to stay impervious. But how could she fight her deepening feelings after last night?

Their passion had moved past sex into uncharted territory for Stella as she'd clung to Aaron and sobbed out her pleasure against his sweat-slicked skin. It had been almost impossible to leave his warm bed and creep out into the night.

Almost. Because of course she'd had to leave.

She had known spending any more time with Charlie and Aaron together was a colossal risk. But she'd done it anyway, because she couldn't fight her need for Aaron any longer. Maybe inviting Charlie to ride had been one stupidity too many.

Sick to her stomach at the fear of falling for Charlie's innocent enthusiasm, wide blue eyes and wicked sense of humour, and also breathless with excitement to see his dad, she rounded the corner of the stables, seeking them out like a kid on Christmas morning.

With every step closer to the car park, she recalled Aaron's heartbreaking vulnerability when he had confessed how he blamed himself for Molly's death. It wasn't that he refused to move on, he was just stuck in limbo by his sense of guilt.

Stella had wanted to hold him and never let him go until she somehow made him believe that he didn't deserve the brutality of his own condemnation.

He was human, that was all. Everyone made mistakes.

But the very reason he had avoided dating all these years, the reason he still only wanted a casual fling— because he couldn't forgive himself—placed him out of her reach. He wasn't ready for a relationship and Stella's own state of mind—she could feel herself slipping deeper and deeper under his spell—was far too prudent to tackle that giant obstacle.

She paused, watched Aaron and Charlie cross the yard, hand in hand, while her stomach churned. It shouldn't matter to her that Aaron believed himself undeserving of a second chance at love, but her careless, weak heart lurched into her throat at the beautiful sight the two of them made. The physiological reaction, tell-tale signs of over-investment—dry mouth, sweaty palms, unable to catch a breath—could mean only one thing: she was perilously close to falling, for all of her caution and good sense.

No, no, no.

What was she doing? She might have been able to recover from dinner with Aaron and Charlie. But sharing his bed, disintegrating in his arms, her every need seem-

ingly answered by the emotions on display in his eyes...
It had been too much.

And now her head was full of...terrifying possibilities.

What if she stayed here, in Abbotsford? Could she
explore this relationship with Aaron, take time to get to
know Charlie, see how it evolved? That sounded like a
dream, except she knew from experience that dreams
could turn into nightmares. When just the sight of Aaron
sent her into a spin, could she stay and risk falling in love
with him, with them both?

What if it didn't work out?

They spied her and grinned, waved.

The thought of being that vulnerable, rejected person
again made her want to run away. She slapped a smile on
her face for the delicious duo. She couldn't let either of
them down. Charlie because she had promised him this
adventure, and Aaron because she had vowed to take
care of his little boy.

'Stella!' Charlie tugged free of his father's handhold
and ran the last few paces to her side. 'Can I see the ponies?' He jumped up and down on the spot, his wiry body
struggling to contain his rapture.

Stella crouched down to Charlie's level. 'Of course.
That's why you're here.'

Time to pull herself together and ignore the feelings
she'd stupidly allowed to develop despite all of her warn-
ings. But how could she stay immune to these two men?
They'd wormed their way into her heart with their matching blue eyes and identical dimpled smiles and their beau-
tifully close bond. A bond she wanted to protect as much
as she needed to armour her own heart.

'But,' she said to Charlie, clearing the clog of emotion
from her throat, 'the most important thing about horses,

as you will know, because you're a smart lad, is that we mustn't scare them.'

Charlie nodded, his wide eyes at once solemn and attentive.

Stella stood, her gaze meeting Aaron's, and her heart clenched. This was a big step for him, trusting her with his precious son, who was his entire world.

'Hi,' she said, hot and flustered, because the look on his face said, *I'm thinking about what we did last night*.

That was when she felt Charlie's small hand slide into hers. She gripped his fingers, a giant lump in her chest at his trust, his affection almost her undoing.

'How are you?' Aaron asked, his voice low like a secret, distracting her from the tsunami of feelings that almost knocked her from her feet. 'Are you sure you're not too tired for this?'

His implication adding *after our late night*.

Stella yearned to greet him with a kiss, if only to feel lust instead of all the other emotions she couldn't switch off, but she suspected they would still be there, and probably amplified. 'I'm fine.' *On fire, but fine*.

Then she said to Charlie, 'Let's get you a safety hat and body protector. And then we'll meet Zeus.'

Aaron's eyebrows shot up. 'Zeus?'

Stella nodded, her body aching to touch him, to hold him and reassure him that she'd never let anything happen to Charlie.

'Zeus is our most heroic and kind pony,' she said, as much to Aaron as to Charlie. 'He's special; placid and unshakable. Only very special kids get to ride Zeus.'

She touched Aaron's arm, she couldn't help herself, and shot him an encouraging smile. 'You can sit in the viewing gallery if you want. That's where the parents usually wait and watch.'

Aaron hesitated for a split second, and Stella knew he wanted to be close by in case something happened. 'Have fun.' He ruffled Charlie's hair and backed away, headed for the seating area overlooking the arena. 'I'm going to take lots of pictures so you can show Johnny on Monday.'

Charlie looked up at Stella, awaiting instructions.

Her eyes burned at the trust shown by both of them. At Charlie's innocent excitement and chatter, and Aaron's unspoken belief in her. Tender shoots of hope germinated in her chest. Could she one day be a part of their precious little team? Could she fully commit to a relationship with Aaron, stay here in Abbotsford and give them her all in a way she hadn't done for nine years?

But what if she was once again cast aside, excluded? She'd be back where she was at eighteen: running from her heartache, forced to reinvent herself in order to handle the pain, grieving and alone.

She found Charlie a riding helmet and body protector, ensuring both items fitted correctly.

'Okay,' she said to Charlie, staring into blue eyes so like Aaron's she wanted to hold him too. 'Let's go meet Zeus.'

On Charlie's third lap of the floodlit indoor arena, Aaron's heart settled back into a steady sinus rhythm, each beat forcing him to admit what persisted at the forefront of his mind: his feelings for Stella.

Being with her last night, seeing her with his son, so patient and encouraging, made him admit what was missing from Charlie's life, but more importantly from his own. Yes, he could continue to be everything to his little boy and they would muddle through together, whatever hurdles they faced in life. But he wanted more than that, and perhaps Charlie needed more too.

He wouldn't interfere with her career path, but what if Stella stayed in Abbotsford? They could date, take things as slowly as she needed.

His fingers tightened around the phone in his hand, his heart sore with the sheer volume of emotions coursing through his veins. He'd taken a hundred shots of Charlie riding Zeus, Charlie brushing Zeus, Charlie holding Stella's hand and looking up at both her and Zeus in adoration. But the email waiting in his inbox created a massive distraction to his enjoyment of watching Charlie's dream fulfilled.

Stella's transfer back to a London GP practice had come through an hour ago.

Aaron's first instinct had been to ignore it for a few days, to hide it from Stella and keep her to himself a little bit longer. Because the minute he told her, he would lose her.

But was she his to keep? How did she even feel about him? Would she ever want a proper relationship with dates and sleepovers, shared life occasions and commitment? He understood why she'd wanted to avoid that for nine years, but maybe for her, nothing had changed.

Whereas for him, he no longer recognised himself. He'd try to be okay with casual, but she had destroyed his willpower, bit by bit. Even now, expertly leading the pony by a short rein while walking alongside Charlie, her other hand reassuringly on the back of the saddle, she was still making it impossible for him to resist.

'Dad, I'm doing it, look.' Charlie beamed up at him as he passed the seating for observers on his fourth lap.

'You are awesome,' Aaron said, his gaze tracking to Stella.

Their eyes met. Aaron wanted to leap over the barrier into the arena and kiss her, hold her in his arms and beg her to stay and give them a chance at something real. A new start. A shot at taking their duo and making it a trio.

Try as he might, he couldn't see long-distance working, not with their respective work commitments and Charlie's busy schedule. But there was a growing part of Aaron willing to take the risk, if only Stella felt the same.

As she helped Charlie to dismount correctly, Aaron received a text from Molly's sister, Leah, who had arrived to collect Charlie for his swimming lesson with his cousin, a weekly commitment he and Leah took in turns. Aaron replied and made his way to the stables, his stomach in knots of anticipation.

What if Stella wanted nothing more to do with him and Charlie now that her transfer had been approved? What if she left Abbotsford, left them without a backward glance? On the flip side, could he ask her to give up her city life for a relationship with a single dad tied to a village, who had himself avoided commitment for the past five years?

Charlie was filling the pony's hay net when he arrived.

'Dad,' he said, 'can I take Zeus home? I can brush him and feed him, look.' He held up a handful of hay to prove his utter dedication.

'Zeus does a very important job here,' said Stella, rescuing Aaron from a tricky conversation. 'But, if it's okay with Dad, you can come back and ride him again. Is that a good deal?'

Charlie nodded up at Stella, instantly appeased and

worryingly as enchanted with her as Aaron himself. Then he hugged her legs. 'Thanks, Dr Stella.'

She placed her hand on his back, her eyes meeting Aaron's. 'You can call me Stella.'

Bile burned his throat. She had so much power to hurt him, to hurt Charlie, even though the way she swallowed hard, clearly experiencing some strong emotion, gave Aaron hope.

'Aunt Leah is here, Champ.' Aaron hated to break up the moment, but he needed to talk to Stella alone. He should have told her about the transfer straight away. He should have sussed out her intentions for returning to London before he watched her and Charlie bond over a love of horses. Because what if their boys' club of two wasn't enough for her? She would leave and maybe take more than just a piece of Aaron with her.

They walked Charlie back to the car park together. Stella was quiet, but Charlie's horse-related chatter filled the awkward silence.

Aaron only realised he was holding her hand when they approached the car and he saw the shocked expression on Leah's face. Of course, after five years alone, his in-laws, even his own parents would be stunned that he'd met someone with whom he could see a future. He should have anticipated that and spoken to Leah and Molly's parents before inviting his sister-in-law to meet Stella. He'd been just so caught up in his concern for Charlie, so wrapped up in Stella and his awakened feelings, that he'd forgotten there were people in his life who might be momentarily taken aback by the fact that he was ready to move on.

But only before they got to know Stella, witnessed

the connection the three of them shared and realised that Charlie was safe in her care.

He turned to Stella as Charlie ran ahead and threw himself at his aunt, who had exited the car to open the rear door, where Charlie's booster seat sat next to his four-year-old cousin's.

'Can you give me a second?' He squeezed her hand. He should speak to Leah before she read too much into the simple gesture. Although a part of him acknowledged that, on his side, Leah's assumptions would be correct. He cared about Stella, deeply.

She cast a quick glance at Leah over his shoulder, a frown appearing and then disappearing just as quickly. 'Of course.' She blushed, pulled her hand free of his and stepped back, putting distance between them.

He reached for her again, his hand on her arm, because he didn't want her to leave his side. If he didn't have that email on his phone, burning a guilty hole in his pocket, he'd introduce the two women right now, be open and upfront about his feelings.

'Can I give you a ride back to the village? We need to talk.' At her hesitation, he added, 'Please, it's important.'

His emotions rioted in his chest at the doubt he saw in her eyes, the withdrawal that made his stomach churn. Perhaps she wasn't ready to hear that he'd developed feelings for her.

'Sure,' she said, sounding anything but certain. 'I'll… um…just go grab my bag.'

Heartsick, he watched her walk away. Could he ask her to stay in Abbotsford, stay at the practice, stay a part of his life when it meant asking how she felt about him, and—because they were a package deal—about Charlie?

Aaron approached Leah, catching the way her stare

naturally followed Stella's path over his shoulder. Aaron turned in time to see Stella, who must have been watching their interaction, dip her head and duck around the corner to the stables.

He quickly asked his sister-in-law if she could wait at his place after taking Charlie to his swimming lesson. He was making a mess of this, but Stella took priority. He would enlighten Leah and the rest of his family about his feelings later, explain that he'd found someone important to him and he'd be exploring a relationship going forward.

If she would have him.

But he was getting dangerously ahead of himself. With Charlie's wellbeing also at stake, he should employ some caution until he knew if Stella shared his feelings. And, as Leah's surprise illustrated, Aaron came with plenty of baggage. He would probably need to reassure Stella that he was ready for a new woman in his life, that she wouldn't be competing with a ghost, that she would be welcome in his extended family too.

He followed in her footsteps, nerves eating away at his certainty. Were his feelings—the happiness he'd finally found, the happiness he had tentatively come to believe he deserved—reciprocated, or had he been kidding himself all this time?

CHAPTER THIRTEEN

STELLA SHOVED HER frigid hands into her coat pockets as she crossed the car park at a brisk pace, just ahead of Aaron. Scalding humiliation eroded a cavity in her chest as the old insecurities of being talked about resurfaced. From the look on Molly's sister's face as she'd walked hand in hand with Aaron, a look of wariness and speculation, Stella would soon be the hot topic of conversation around the village again.

Her heart, which had been bursting with pride for what she now thought of as *her two boys*, had stopped dead for a few terrifying seconds as she came to a chilling realisation.

She wasn't simply filled with pride. She was way too heavily invested in Charlie and Aaron. So invested that she'd actually made a promise to Charlie—to be there any time he wanted to ride Zeus—that she'd never have made three weeks ago.

Had she changed so completely? Committed herself to staying in Abbotsford? Committed herself to building a relationship with both father and son? But far worse, she had started to imagine dating Aaron, perhaps becoming a part of his life, long-term. His and Charlie's.

That thought, rather than fill her with the warm and fuzzies, sent shivers through her rigid limbs. What a fool.

She climbed into the passenger seat of Aaron's car and stared out across open farmland towards the village as he rounded the vehicle and took the driver's seat. She couldn't work with him, sleep with him, spend time with him and Charlie and not want more. What if it didn't work out? The pain she experienced last time had had long-reaching consequences.

But the way her chest hurt as Aaron and Leah had talked, clearly about her, each looking over at the same moment, told her it was too late for caution. He'd excluded her, perhaps unintentionally, but it had had the same humiliating effect.

She had once again allowed herself too close to a man who didn't share her feelings.

'So...you wanted to talk,' she asked Aaron, keeping her eyes on the road ahead in case he could see the moisture stinging her eyes.

If she looked at him she'd want to beg to be a part of his little tribe. But she wasn't a member. She was superfluous.

She'd sensed the first signs of his withdrawal the minute he'd arrived at the stables today. She'd convinced herself that he was nervous about Charlie's safety. Then Molly's sister had turned up and he'd become even more of a stranger, the explanation falling into place. She was still an outsider and she'd been stupid to allow great sex with a great guy to lure her into feeling something, feeling as if she belonged with them.

From beside her, he reached for her hand. 'Are you okay?'

She nodded too vigorously, avoiding his searching

stare and sliding her hand from his to press at her temple. 'I just have a slight headache.' It wasn't a complete lie.

Aaron pressed his lips together and returned both hands to the wheel while Stella recoiled further into herself. This must be worse than she'd thought. He was going to tell her they were done. That it was too confusing for Charlie or too soon for him, or that the family didn't approve.

'Okay, I'll just get straight to the point, then,' he said. 'I received an email today, from the college of GPs.'

Hope wrapped cotton wool around her heart. Maybe he wasn't calling this off. Then it was dashed. Since when had she become so needy? So dependent on him for her happiness?

'Your transfer has been approved,' he continued, his face in profile so that she had no idea how he felt about the news that took her aback. She had almost completely forgotten about the transfer. Become so wrapped up in life here, in the practice, in Aaron.

'There's a place for you at King's Park Medical Centre,' he said, his tone infuriatingly neutral. 'You can start as soon as you want.'

A chill took hold. She wanted to wrap herself in a hug.

It was time to leave, exactly what she had wanted—to return to the safety of her London life, to the risk-free version of herself, to the security of being alone. Glamorous bars, meaningless dates and a continuous source of entertainment.

She should feel elated. She could resume the life she'd planned. She could run away from the gossip that would ensue if the village found out that Stella had set her cap at Abbotsford's beloved single-dad GP. She could run away from her feelings.

So why did she no longer have the slightest clue what she wanted?

'It is still what you want, right?' he asked, glancing at her clasped hands as if he wanted to touch her again.

'Of course.' *No. Yes. I don't know any more.*

Tears throbbed at the backs of Stella's eyes. If he touched her while she was this confused she might break down. But he didn't move.

She wouldn't cry. She. Would. Not. Cry.

He nodded, his jaw muscles bunched.

Stella looked away to stop herself from over-interpreting his expression as crestfallen. Perhaps he was simply calculating how her absence would affect the practice, reshuffling the clinics to account for the extra patients.

'I can work a week's notice, if you want.' As long as she didn't touch him again or see him outside of work, she could hold it together for one more week. Five working days. Forty long, temptation-filled hours. Couldn't she?

'I don't want to leave you and Toby in the lurch,' she added.

He frowned, as if about to decline her offer. Then he nodded. 'Only if you can, otherwise we'll manage.'

He drove in silence for a few minutes. Then he pulled up outside her parents' house, killed the engine and turned to face her so she was forced to look into his beautiful eyes.

'I'll be honest, Stella. I hoped that you'd want to stay.' The blue of his irises looked cold in the dim light of the car. She couldn't read his feelings beyond disappointment.

'I hoped you'd want to continue this.' He pointed between them, a frown pinching his eyebrows together.

'Oh?' He meant their physical relationship, their fling,

sneaking around, spending a few hours together whenever the urge overcame them and Charlie was asleep.

A lump lodged in her throat, because they had acted together to protect themselves and Charlie by keeping it casual. She should have known better. A big part of her wanted to see more of Aaron, only she'd broken her own rules and fallen in way over her head. Because now she wanted all or nothing. She couldn't be with him and not want to be a bigger part of his life, to share things with him like lazy Sunday morning walks and quiz nights at the pub. Charlie's Nativity play and Christmas morning.

She had found herself again, here with Aaron, or she had realised that she'd never lost herself in the first place, that she could belong anywhere, that it was her decision.

'Aaron... I...'

'I know,' he said, his voice flat. 'I'm a lot to take on.' Frustration gusted from him on a sigh. 'That's why we could take it slow. See what happens.'

She nodded, her heart made of ice. 'That's a lot to think about.'

She didn't want slow. She'd wasted nine years being afraid, holding back, denying herself.

But clearly Aaron needed more time to get over Molly, his grief, his regrets. He wasn't ready to find love again while he believed himself to be undeserving. Could she really stay, put everything on the line once more for a man who might decide that she wasn't what he wanted after all?

If she stayed, she'd want terrifying things, like a relationship. She hadn't had that since Harry and, given her reaction to Aaron's sister-in-law's curiosity or possessiveness—how she'd felt snubbed—she wasn't sure she was strong enough to take the chance again. Not when the stakes were so high, when she was at risk of falling in love with both Aaron and Charlie.

'I get it,' he said, defeat in his eyes. 'It's been fun, right? But it's not enough to keep you here. Those nightclubs are calling. Time to put away your wellies and dust off your dancing shoes.' There was no malice in his tone, only inevitable sadness, the reminder of their differences.

Stella curled her fingers into fists in her pockets. She wanted to deny his conclusion. To say she had changed, or that she'd never been completely content with that life, she'd just been hiding. But what was the point, if that was what he thought of her? That she'd used him while waiting to return to her real life? Perhaps he didn't know her at all. Clearly she had been the one to become overinvested yet again.

But she refused to be that vulnerable this time. She knew who she was and what she wanted and what she was prepared to tolerate. It was time for some honesty.

'You said it yourself, Aaron; you don't really need me at the practice. You never wanted me there. You have your work, the estate, Charlie, your boys' club.'

She recalled the way he'd rushed over to Leah. Had he been reassuring Molly's sister that nothing had changed in his life, in Charlie's? And if Stella was nothing to him, then why would she stay here, just to be hurt down the track?

He scrubbed his hand through his hair. 'You were the one to say there are no guarantees in life. Who knows what's around the corner? You could stick around for a while. We could try to make this work.' A hesitant smile twitched his lips, his stare softening. He cupped her cheek, the warmth of his hand burning her skin. 'Maybe

I could fall in love with you, Stella. Maybe you could be a part of our boys' club one day.'

If he'd told her she meant less than nothing to him, she would have been less crushed. She'd heard half-promises before. She had been not quite good enough before. Next time she gave her all to a man, she wanted his all in return.

She dragged in a ragged breath. 'That's exactly the kind of declaration a woman wants to hear,' she muttered, her emotions strung taut like piano wire. Could he even hear himself? Only the part of her that cared more than she should understood that this was a big move for him. Starting something. Opening up his life, his son's life to another woman when his heart was still full of Molly.

But did she want to be the other woman, waiting in the wings while he made up his mind to move on from his wife? She couldn't make all of the sacrifices, hang around like a spare stethoscope while he worked on forgiving himself.

She shuddered away from his touch. 'It's not that easy for me, Aaron.'

Maybe if he had fought a bit harder for her, she might have been persuaded to stay; that was the depth of her feelings for him. But she couldn't be the cast-aside one. Not again.

'Why?' The quashed hope in his eyes knocked the breath from her lungs.

'Because I'd be the one to take all of the risk. Your life is here and it's all plotted out. Your job is here, your entire family. You're even going to inherit the manor one day. You are part of this landscape.' She flung her arms wide. 'Part of local history.'

'I can't help that.' His lips thinned.

'What if I stay and this fizzles out, or worse, fails spectacularly? You have Charlie, but I'd be left with nothing again. I'd have uprooted my life for nothing.'

As she spoke the words she realised how much a part of her wanted to be that brave. To give her whole heart to this wonderful man and his little boy, not for them, but for herself. Because she'd found something in Abbotsford she had thought was gone for ever: she'd found herself, her true self.

Aaron's jaw tightened. 'Of course. Everything you've said is true, and I understand your fears. I guess I stupidly hoped that Charlie and I might come to mean more to you than a risk that's just not worth taking.'

Pain lashed Stella so she wanted to bend double. 'Come on, Aaron, don't pretend that a relationship between us would be easy. You have Charlie to consider. He, quite rightly, needs to be your first priority. But as you said, you also have other people to consider. There's Molly's family for a start. I saw the way your sister-in-law looked at me.'

She'd seen the judgement flicker through Leah's eyes. 'How do you think they'd react to a new woman in Charlie's life?'

Aaron sighed, his body rigid. 'I would hope that they'd continue to support me the way they have since Molly died. But they aren't the issue here. You're just scared to admit that you belong here because of some historical gossip that everyone else has forgotten.'

She dropped her gaze, closed her eyes. 'Stop. We need to stop.'

Now they were simply lashing out at each other. And he was right in part; she was scared. But not all of their issues could be laid at Stella's door.

When she looked up, Aaron's eyes were cloaked in regret, but also defeat. 'I told you we were a mistake,' she whispered. 'Neither of us is ready for a relationship this…complicated.'

But oh, how she'd wanted to be ready. If only he'd given some indication that he was ready to commit to her in return, rather than the vague promise of more one day.

The look he gave her cracked Stella's heart clean in two. He gave a sad shrug. 'Perhaps you're right. I'd better let you go inside, take something for that headache.'

Every step she took away from him as she walked to the front door crushed Stella's soul a little more. Sometimes there simply wasn't a cure, a magic pill. Sometimes you had to simply bear the pain.

CHAPTER FOURTEEN

AT THE END of the following week, Stella tucked her stethoscope into her bag and scooped up the tattered fleece jacket she wore at the stables from the hook on the back of the door. She cast a final look around, checking for any personal belongings she might have left behind, only to find the consulting room at Abbotsford Medical Centre wiped clean of her presence.

Her heart clenched. It was as if she had never been here.

Would she be as easily erased from Aaron's mind? When she left for London in the morning, Stella, by contrast, would carry a giant, gaping hole in her chest.

Now that she was leaving, she finally recognised that she had fallen in love with Aaron. It was all such a big mess—they had barely spoken to each other this week—that she welcomed the space, the physical distance in order to think clearly. Because seeing him every day at work, wanting to touch him, to draw him aside and ask where they had gone so wrong, left her overwhelmed. So she had stayed silent.

Stella was about to switch off the lights and leave when she heard a noise beyond the door and froze. No one else was supposed to be in the building; it was nine pm on a Friday night.

She clutched her phone like a weapon. Medical facilities were always being burgled for drugs, although this was the Cotswolds…

Stella peered through the gap in the door to see Aaron enter from the rear of the practice. His cheeks were aglow with the cold as he shrugged off his coat and placed it over a chair in the waiting room.

Stella's knees weakened with relief and longing.

He looked up and their eyes met.

Confusion moved through his expression. 'You're here—I thought you left earlier.'

Was his voice…hopeful?

Stella nodded, reminding herself not to over-interpret anything where Aaron was concerned. She couldn't be objective. 'I did leave, but I popped back to collect my things.'

Stupid, because she had hardly moved in here at the start of her placement, unpacking the bare minimum so she could make a speedy getaway. Only now it felt as if she was leaving behind a vital piece of herself, but that was less to do with this room and more to do with the man staring at her as if they had reverted to being strangers.

'I just called in to collect something I need for a house call first thing in the morning,' he said in explanation, because awkwardness prevailed in their communications now. 'Then I was on my way round to your parents' to say goodbye.'

Stella winced, wanting to scrub the definitive word from his vocabulary. She wasn't sure she had the strength to articulate a final farewell, not after all that they had been through together.

'Well… I'll…um…get out of your way.' She returned to her consultation room, her senses on high alert as he followed her and filled the doorway.

She paused, willing him to say something that would change the inevitable. A selfish thought, because she had no solution to make things right between them.

'Charlie wrote you a goodbye card,' he said, each word a blow to her stomach. 'He made me promise that I would deliver it.' He held out the envelope with her name written in giant, uneven letters on the front.

She took it, her fingers avoiding his, and slid it into her bag. She couldn't read it until she was back in London. She wouldn't break down in front of Aaron.

'Do you have time to go for a last drink at the pub?' He offered an uncertain smile, some of the old dazzle that had helped intoxicate her flashing in his eyes.

She shook her head, too devastated with longing to speak. Why did she feel as if she were on a ledge above a canyon, about to bungee jump? Suspended in that silent moment before the fall and the screams and the terrifying exhilaration? That moment when you wished you could back up, say you had changed your mind, only it was way too late.

'Right, no.' Aaron nodded with understanding that almost made Stella cave. 'Perhaps we can catch up when I'm next at City Hospital, get a drink then.' The hope in his eyes tore gaping holes through her resistance.

No, she had to be strong, to think of her own needs. When she was ready, she deserved to be loved by a man who was all about her, all in, ready to commit. But nor could she leave Aaron thinking that he had done anything wrong. *She* had been the one to change the rules halfway through the game. She was the one who wanted the impossible, wanted more than he could give.

She loved him. If this was goodbye, she could make it genuine and heartfelt.

She stepped close, cupped his cold cheeks in her palms and held his gaze. 'I had a wonderful time here. Thank you for everything. I'll never forget my time back in Abbotsford.'

Pressure pressed down on her chest so she struggled for air. She'd always remember him and Charlie and how close they'd become in such a short period of time. Only not quite close enough.

'Stella…' He groaned her name, regret stark in his eyes. They glittered with emotions. They spoke to her so clearly that she wanted to stare into them all night until dawn.

'Shh.' She pressed her index finger to his lips.

She wasn't strong enough to hear how he wished things had worked out, or how if they had met a year or so in the future the timing might have been better for him.

For an expectant second, his gaze grew intense. Stella's heart thumped. His hands gripped her waist. She thought he intended to push her away. Instead, his stare dipped to her mouth. His fingers clenched. His body became rigid.

Static buzzed in the air, like a storm before the first crack of lightning. She couldn't stop herself. She loved him. Just one last goodbye kiss.

Her finger slid from his mouth, replaced by her lips.

As he had every other time, Aaron commanded their kiss, hauled her body close to his, giving her no room to breathe. Their tongues touched. His fingers fisted her jumper. One hand gripped her neck as if he would never let her break free.

A part of her wanted to be trapped here for ever, physically bewitched with no space for thoughts. But it wasn't enough. Not any more.

To make it last, Stella poured all of the things she was too scared to say, too scared to ask for into kissing Aaron. Their passion escalated more quickly than a dangerously irregular pulse. She wanted him, one last time. Then she would walk away without regret.

As if he'd read her mind, Aaron walked Stella backwards until her thighs hit the desk. She shoved her bag to the floor and perched on the edge, tugging his belt loops to seat his hips between her legs.

Snatching her mouth free of his desperate kisses, she fumbled with his fly. 'Hurry. I want you.'

'Stella...' He trailed kisses down her neck to her clavicle, his hands cupping her buttocks to keep her close.

She shook her head. 'Don't talk.'

She didn't want to hear the question in his tone. She had no answers.

Realising her selfishness, she looked up. 'Do you want to stop?'

He grinned, shook his head. 'Never.' And then he was kissing her again, reminding her how good they were together, how they could shut out the rest of the world, even their own misgivings, when they touched.

Her mind shut down. All her doubts about leaving and fears if she stayed were squashed by the building compulsion. There was a fumbling free of clothes, his trousers shoved down and her skirt hiked up, and from his pocket he produced a condom.

Out of nowhere, he slowed the frantic pace, kissing her

closed eyelids, her neck, the top of her breasts. 'I wish I could take you home, take our time, make it memorable.' His hands caressed her back, pressing them closer, heartbeat to heartbeat.

'Aaron,' she pleaded, because she would never forget one single moment they had shared.

He reared back so their stares locked and all pretence fell away.

She gasped at the vulnerability in his stare. She bit her lip to stop herself from confessing how she felt about him, because for a blissful second she imagined that he felt the same. That he loved her and couldn't spend one second without her, let alone the eighty miles of distance that would be their ongoing reality.

She couldn't trust her intuition. She had been wrong, so wrong before. Seen what she wanted to see. Believed what she wanted to hear. All she could trust was how he made her feel and that would have to be enough to last her a lifetime.

She pressed her mouth to his, kissed him long and deep as she guided him to her entrance.

Fully seated, he groaned, broke free of her kiss, panted.

'Look at me,' he said as her eyes fluttered shut.

She opened them, enslaved by pleasure.

He cupped her cheek, covering her face with kisses that felt like promises. But she needed certainties.

He unbuttoned her blouse, freed her breasts from her bra and took first one and then the other nipple into his mouth. She moaned, slipping deeper and deeper as he held her with such tenderness and passion combined, her throat ached with unshed tears.

She crossed her ankles at his back. His thrusts took

on more determination, and still he held her eye contact, a brand burning into her soul, permanent. Unforgettable.

Stella's orgasm stole her breath, her cries muffled against his chest, against the thudding of his heart, which seemed to say everything that she wanted to hear. Aaron crushed her in his arms as his own climax struck. It seemed that he would hold her for ever as they panted together, coming down from the high.

But she had known it would come to an end.

Aaron withdrew, disposed of the condom and then tugged her close once more, pressing a kiss to her temple and holding her there.

'Stay.' He breathed into her hair. 'I'm falling for you.'

She froze. Suspended. Waiting.

The fine wool of his sweater scratched at her cheek. She was too hot. Or too cold. She couldn't tell.

She just knew that this didn't feel right.

'Don't say that,' she whispered, sliding from the desk and rearranging her clothes.

A tension tightened his swollen mouth 'Why not? It's true.'

'Aaron, please don't.' *It's too late.* 'I'm leaving.'

His stare hardened, a muscle ticking in his jaw. 'That doesn't change how I feel.'

'So you suddenly woke up this morning, my last day in Abbotsford, and realised that maybe one day down the track you might love me, is that it?'

She picked her bag up from the floor rather than look at his hurt expression. He might have strong feelings for her—they were good together physically, mentally in sync, had heaps in common—but that didn't make it love. She'd heard those empty words before. Been manipulated and used by them. She couldn't trust words again, not that he had said those particular three.

'Does it matter when I realised how much I care about you when I never thought I'd care for anyone again?' he asked, frustration in his eyes. 'You don't want to hear it anyway. You're already out of the door.'

Stella shook her head, disbelief and confusion fuelling her flight response and knee-jerk observation. 'The timing feels a little...last-minute.'

Of course he would miss their chemistry after such a long dry spell, as she would. But she'd ruined the sex-only deal with her emotional investment. She couldn't stay, sleep with him over and over and never be certain that her feelings would be reciprocated. She needed to retreat, protect herself. Figure out where she'd gone so spectacularly wrong.

He continued to stare at her. 'You think I would manipulate you to stay with empty words?'

'I don't know.' She was losing her grip on reality. 'I understand, believe me. We have sizzling chemistry. We've just proved that it will be hard to walk away from that.'

She indicated the desk, the keyboard and mouse in disarray.

'But I have to leave. Don't you understand?' She met his eyes, pleading with him to see her point of view. 'I was the worst version of myself here, Aaron. You brought me home and showed me that I've held on to my associations, my fears for too long. That I'm strong. That I can be strong anywhere. But I've also realised that the next time I fall in love, the next time I give my all to someone, I want all of them in return.'

She didn't add that it was too late for next time; she was already in love like never before.

He scrubbed a hand over his face, clearly confused. 'I'm not him, Stella. We can make this work. I'll be in London once a month for my teaching commitments and you can come home for the weekend. It could work. We could make it work.'

'You're right, you're not him, but it could still fail,' she pointed out. 'You know the cruel twists of life better than anyone. You need more time to heal and forgive yourself. You need to focus on Charlie. You don't need a girlfriend who hasn't had a relationship for nine years and lives miles away.'

His jaw clenched. 'So you're suddenly an expert on my needs, are you?'

Stella swallowed hard, fighting tears, because the one thing she did know was that he didn't love her, he only thought that one day he maybe could.

'No…but I understand my own. I need to think about myself. And I need to get out of here. I'm sorry.'

She made it to the car before the first tear fell.

CHAPTER FIFTEEN

AARON GRIPPED CHARLIE'S hand a little tighter on their walk home from school the following Monday. The weather was as grey and dreary as his mood, but he needed to put on a brave face for his son. He'd had lots of practice this weekend.

'So how was school today?' he asked, trying to distract them both from thoughts of Stella.

'Okay.' Charlie looked up at him with a frown. Was his misery, his heartsickness displayed all over his face? He'd relived their demise a thousand times, each time growing more certain of where he'd gone wrong.

He'd messed up. He'd spent so many years living in the past that when Stella turned his world upside down, it had taken him too long to fully let go of his fear. He loved Stella. He should have told her the moment he realised. Instead he'd tried to protect himself by easing into the confession, sussing out her feelings first, telling himself that she needed to take things slowly.

He clenched his jaw. His regrets were piled so high, he felt caged in, claustrophobic, trapped by his own stupidity. Because after everything she had been through, Stella deserved to know how he felt, even if she didn't love him in return.

'Dad…' Charlie tugged his hand.

'Mmm…'

'Johnny said that he's been to London where Dr Stella is,' continued Charlie, 'and there's a giant wheel that spins you around and around,' he made a washing-machine motion with his free arm, 'and a clock called Big Bell.'

'Big Ben,' Aaron corrected, his stomach sinking. He was never going to get away without some searching questions about Stella's relocation.

Charlie nodded, eyes wide at his father's confirmation that, once again, Johnny was the class know-it-all. 'And the Queen lives there in a gold palace. And guess what, Dad?'

'What's that, Champ?' Aaron's gut twisted into knots.

'The Queen has her own horses, hundreds of them.'

He zoned out of his son's exuberant chatter.

He should never have let Stella go. He should have chased after her sooner. By the time he had called at Stella's parents' house horribly early on Saturday morning, she had already left for London. He'd hoped to convince her that his declaration wasn't a trick to keep her here to ensure a steady supply of great sex. That he loved her. That he should have said it sooner, the minute he had started to feel it, but he'd freaked out, telling himself to go slow, that her caution was natural, expected after she had been so badly hurt in the past.

'Perhaps Stella will be able to ride one of the Queen's horses,' said Charlie. 'She likes riding horses, like me, and she went to my school when she was five. Perhaps if I ever go to London, she could help me to ride one of the Queen's horses too.'

Every mention of Stella's name was like a scalpel between the ribs. 'Maybe, although the Queen's horses have very important jobs to do. They are kind of like soldiers.'

Charlie's eyes rounded at the sheer marvellousness of that concept. 'Can we go and see them, Dad? Can we?' He jumped up and down and then galloped off yelling, 'Giddy up!'

Aaron envied his son's ability to bounce back from unmet expectations. If only he could shrug off his regrets so easily. Stella had been right about him: he had carried guilt for letting Molly and Charlie down, a form of penance for being human. But fear of commitment had gone on long enough. He would always love Molly, but he loved Stella too. And unless he showed her that he was ready to take the chance on them as a couple, a family, Stella, him and Charlie, how could he expect her to take the same risk?

His relationship with Stella had popped holes in his fear as if deflating a balloon. If he was happy, Charlie would be happy. He'd met a wonderful woman who understood his work and his life, and most importantly understood him. They shared the same dreams. Yes, they were both scared, both figuring this thing between them out. But was that reason enough to be apart?

Charlie was swinging on the gate, waiting for his father to catch up, when Aaron arrived.

'Will Dr Stella still help me ride Zeus, Dad? 'Cos I really like her and I really like Zeus.'

Aaron's throat constricted. It was time to do everything in his power to make this work. 'I'm not sure, Champ.'

Here came the question Aaron had been expecting since he told Charlie about Stella's transfer over breakfast. 'Don't you need her at your work any more?'

Yes! Of course he needed her, at work and out of work. It didn't matter where, Stella belonged with them, part of their boys' club.

Aaron hesitated. He always strove to tell Charlie the truth.

'I do need her. I need to tell her that.' And more. He scooped Charlie up and kissed the top of his head before placing him back on his feet. 'I really like her too.'

'Then you should kiss her, Dad. Johnny says his dad kisses his mum whenever she's mad, and it makes her smile again.'

How could Charlie with his youthful wisdom and un-complicated vision of the world show him how simple it was to follow your heart?

Aaron's own heart clenched so violently he feared that he might pass out. 'We might need to have Johnny over for tea again some time soon. Clearly I have a lot to learn from that kid. Now, enough about kisses. Let's go and see what Grandma has cooked for dinner, shall we? Because I don't know about you, but I'm starving.'

'I hope it's shepherd's pie. I had shepherd's pie for lunch and it was yum. Johnny says it's made of shep-herds but I know that's not right, is it, Dad?'

'No. Johnny's wrong there.' But he certainly had a point about the kissing.

Stella sat in the crowded Southbank bar with Darcy. They'd attended the nearby winter market, and, rather than fill Stella's heart with festive cheer, as it normally would, she only felt frozen to the core.

Stella had arranged to meet her friends for drinks and dancing in the hope that it would shock her system back to normal. Except every time the door swung open to admit a customer, her stomach swooped with dread. She no more felt like dancing than she felt like taking a plunge in the frigid Thames outside.

To distract herself from the nausea of having made the worst mistake of her life, she looked out at the lights twinkling over the river. Were they dimmer than they had been a month ago?

Everything seemed to have lost its shine.

She wanted to be back in Abbotsford, sitting in the Abbotsford Arms with Aaron in front of the roaring fire. She wanted to wake up on Saturday morning and take Charlie to the stables to see the horses. She wanted to walk across the fields holding the hands of her two boys while they talked about nothing and everything, especially what they would have for dinner.

She had finally opened the letter from Charlie that morning and sobbed her heart out. He'd done a drawing of himself seated majestically on Zeus. The caption read *This was the best day*.

And he was right. In many ways it had been the best day. She had begun to admit her love for Aaron. But it also represented the worst day ever, a day when the rot had set in, destroying all hope.

'You should have stayed,' said Darcy, her gaze sympathetic, despite the bluntness of her message.

'Not this again.' Ever since Stella had returned to the flat they'd shared and she had confessed her dalliance with Aaron, Darcy had been on a mission to point out the glaringly obvious in that way unique to sisters.

Darcy's face crumpled with compassion. 'I know it's terrifying. Believe me, I fought loving Joe with everything in me. But I was just fooling myself.'

'I don't love Aaron.' *Lie*.

Darcy ignored Stella's denial. She knew her too well. 'I understand. It's hard for you after last time. But this is different. Aaron is mature and dependable.'

'He said he was falling for me,' Stella said because she'd drunk two glasses of mulled wine and she had previously omitted that part of the tale.

Darcy's eyes lit up before Stella shook her head.

'You don't believe him,' said Darcy.

Oh, how she wanted to believe him. The need burned inside her like an ember. She shook her head, her cheeks warm with shame. 'I've heard empty words before.'

'And you want actions?' Darcy twirled the stem of her wine glass thoughtfully. 'You want him to prove his love by sky-writing it across the city? Buying you a horse? Moving himself and his son and his practice to London?'

Stella gasped, horrified by the last image. 'No. Of course not.'

The idea of Aaron and Charlie uprooting from Abbotsford was preposterous. Aaron had his job, his family obligations, and Charlie deserved the idyllic childhood both she and Aaron had had growing up in the country. They belonged in Abbotsford.

'So, what did you say?' asked Darcy. 'Did you tell him how *you* feel?'

Stella deflated, crumpling like a paper bag. 'No…' Why hadn't she? She wanted Aaron. She wanted Charlie. She should have told Aaron, fought for him, not run away. What would Charlie think about her broken promise to help him ride Zeus again?

'It sounds to me,' said Darcy, in her eldest sister tone, 'that you were both being cautious, both protecting yourselves.'

'I guess.' Why was everything so clear with a little distance? She didn't want to admit outright that Darcy was correct, but her insides were coiled tight like a spring, desperate to act. Despite all of her talk, Stella had clung to the last shreds of her fear, needing to be certain of Aaron's commitment first.

Neither of them had taken that final leap of faith.

'Of course,' continued Darcy, 'he also has Charlie to think about, so…'

'So I'm going to stop hiding here and tell him how I feel.' She stood, scraping back her stool. 'I belong in Abbotsford with them.'

Darcy grinned. 'That's a relief,' she said, tugging Stella back onto her stool. 'Because Joe has asked me to move in with him, so I'll be moving out too.'

Stella hugged Darcy, her eyes burning. 'I'm so happy for you.'

She just wanted her own happy ending too. She wanted Aaron and Charlie and spaghetti and meatballs.

She pressed a kiss to Darcy's cheek. 'You were right. I do love him. Desperately.'

'Of course you do,' murmured Darcy, squeezing her tight.

Stella laughed, swiping at her damp cheeks. 'Why are you always right?'

Darcy shrugged. 'It's a big-sister thing. Get used to it.'

'I'm leaving now.'

Darcy grabbed her arm. 'You can't drive.'

'I'll take the train.' For her men, she would walk every step back to Abbotsford if she had to, because some risks were worth taking.

CHAPTER SIXTEEN

AARON RAPPED HIS knuckles against the wooden front door, the sting from both the cold and the force of his knock. Impatience pounded at him, so he restlessly paced the front doorstep of Stella's house in London.

She wasn't home.

Frustration choked him until he wanted to punch something. He settled for another attack on the door, although he knew it was futile.

He should have called, but by the time he had fed Charlie and rushed back home for an overnight bag so the boy could stay the night with his grandparents, his desperation levels had reached boiling point. He couldn't live one second longer without Stella in his life, so he'd rushed here to confess. Face to face. Preferably lips to lips and heartbeat to heartbeat. To beg her to listen while he unreservedly poured out his feelings this time, a hundred per cent vulnerable. No more fearful, fumbling *mights*, *shoulds* or *coulds*.

Scrubbing a hand through his hair, he stepped backwards and gazed up at the windows of the house, which were shiny black rectangles of doom, mocking him and his belated declaration.

He dropped his head back in despair and sighed to the

heavens. His breath misted in the cold air while he contemplated his next move and where Stella might be at this time of night. The winter chill permeated his clothing. Where he had been overheated from running here from the car, now he shuddered. Perhaps Stella had already moved on. Perhaps she was out on a date right now, trying to forget him and their connection.

He huffed, shaking his head. She could deny it all she liked, but what they had shared was real and exceptional and he planned to tell her that, date or not.

'Aaron?'

He spun to see Stella on the pavement behind him, his heart climbing into his throat.

'What are you doing here?' she said, her cheeks rosy and her beautiful eyes trying to conceal the flare of what looked like, unless he was mistaken, hope. 'Your lecture is next week. Where's Charlie?' She stepped closer, panic making her voice squeak. 'Is everything okay?'

He nodded, struck dumb by relief. Would she worry if she didn't care? Reciprocal hope surged in his chest like the jolt from a defibrillator.

'He's fine. Everything is fine.' He trailed his eyes over her from head to toe, refamiliarising himself with her outline, her shape, her essence. Had it really only been three days? It felt as if a lifetime had passed since he'd watched her pull away from the practice on Friday night.

'Well, that's a lie actually,' he said, desperate to hold her hands but giving her the space she had said she needed. 'Not everything is fine. I need to talk to you and I'll explain.'

She nodded. 'Come in.'

He followed her up the steps and inside the house— a typical Georgian mid-terrace—his hands twitching to touch her, to pull her into his arms and never let her go again.

They took off their coats and Stella led him into the lounge. 'Have a seat,' she said, her voice high-pitched. With nerves?

He wanted to hold her, to tell her that everything would be okay. Because it would. They'd figure it all out together. But being apart just wasn't an option for him, or for Charlie.

Remembering his son, he pulled the letter from his pocket. 'I brought you this. It's from Charlie. He misses you and wants to know if you have any sway with the Queen or the Horse Guards.' His lips twitched as he handed it over, hoping that Charlie's simplistic view of the world would help Stella to see that nothing was impossible with love on your side.

With his love.

But he was getting ahead of himself.

She looked at the envelope as if it was infectious. At her desperate swallow, her rapid blinking, her choked sob, he snapped and pulled her into his arms. 'Shh,' he soothed. 'It's all going to be okay.'

'I miss him too,' she mumbled into his jumper. Then she laughed, perhaps registering his son's absurd request, finally.

Aaron cupped her cheek and wiped away a tear. 'Stella, I know that you felt you had to leave. I know that you thought I only wanted you to stay for sex. And I know I messed up. I was scared that you wouldn't share my feelings. But I want you to know regardless. I love you.'

He stared into her emotive eyes. Eyes that spoke to him, even in his dreams.

'I'm deeply in love with you.' He cupped her cheeks,

swiped the pads of his thumbs over her cheekbones. 'Head over heels and every other cliché you can think of. I was scared to say it in case you could never love me back. In case you didn't want me and Charlie after what you'd been through. But even if I'm not the man for you, even if you won't ever love me back, I want you to know my feelings. Because I want you to move on from your past and be happy.'

'Aaron—'

He pressed his fingers to her lips. 'Please let me finish what I came here to say, what I should have said before you walked away. I'm yours, ready to move on, ready to give you my all. I'll make this relationship work whichever way I can. I'm fully committed to that. To us. You, me and Charlie, who by the way is desperate to see Big Ben. We'll move here permanently if it makes you feel secure about my love.'

She shook her head, tears beading on her eyelashes. 'No... I don't want that.'

Pain sliced him in two. He'd known it was risky to assume that she could love him back, but he didn't regret coming here tonight.

'I see.' He dropped his hands from her face, stepped back.

'Wait.' She lunged for him, wrapped her arms around his neck, buried her face in his jumper and squeezed him tight. 'What I mean is, I don't want you and Charlie to relocate your lives for me.'

Weak with relief that she wasn't kicking him out, that there was still some hope, he pressed a kiss to the top of her head, inhaled the scent of her hair. 'I understand. I'm a package deal. Two for the price of one.'

'I don't care about that either,' she mumbled.

'So are you just wary of falling in love, or specifically wary of loving *me*?'

She surged up and kissed him, interrupting the speech he'd prepared on the drive here after surgery. 'Aaron,' she pulled back to meet his gaze, 'I already love you. And I love Charlie. I missed my boys. I was on my way back to Abbotsford tonight to tell you.'

Everything that he needed to see shone in the depths of her eyes.

'I should have told you before I left, but I was scared.' She swallowed back emotion, breaking his heart. 'Last time love broke me. But I never loved him as much as I love you. Falling in love with you was twice as terrifying. I had so much more to lose if you decided that you didn't want me.'

'You have no idea how much I want you.' He gripped her tighter. 'I wanted you all along. I just had some stuff to work through, because I never thought I'd have a second chance. I never thought I deserved it. But Charlie and I deserve to be happy and whole. And you make us happy and whole.'

'Yes. We belong together.' Her smile glittered with happiness he wanted to put there every day for the rest of their lives.

He crushed her mouth with his, kissed her as if he'd never have another chance. But he would. He'd take every opportunity to love this woman, to tell her how much he loved her and to show her why he would never stop.

He pulled back, out of breath. 'I want all of you though, not just the incredible sex. I want to hold your hand and sit by the fire folding laundry with you. I want your reminders on my phone—I've made pizza four times since you put that there, just to feel your presence in the house. And when Charlie is asleep, I want to hold you in my arms all night, until you feel as loved as you are.'

She laughed through happy tears.

He tilted up her face and pressed his lips to hers. She tasted like Stella, and salty tears and home. He tangled his fingers in her hair and deepened the kiss, his tongue sliding to meet hers.

'I want you, if you'll have me,' he whispered, his own eyes burning. We'll figure out the geography as long as we're together.'

She cupped his face, pushed her fingers into his hair. 'I want you too. Both of you. And I want to come home, if you'll have me back at the practice.'

'I hoped you'd say that.' He kissed her again and this time they collapsed back onto the sofa so they could do the kissing justice.

'Let's go tonight,' she said when she pulled back for air.

Aaron slid his hand under her jumper, finding the clasp of her bra and popping it open with an expert flick of the wrist. 'The morning is soon enough.'

He pressed a path of kisses down her neck. 'Charlie has a sleepover tonight. I don't want to waste precious hours driving when I could be showing you how much I love you instead.'

'I can't argue with that logic.' She sighed as he divested her of her clothes and found first one nipple and then the other with his lips.

'I must say,' she smiled down at him, her eyes glazed with pleasure, 'this declaration is much better than your previous attempt. Well done.' She gripped his neck and urged his lips back to hers.

All businesslike, he broke free, scooped her up from the sofa and headed for the stairs.

'I've had some coaching from Charlie and Johnny,' he said with a wink. And then he loved her all night long.

EPILOGUE

Three years later

STELLA WATCHED EIGHTEEN-MONTH-OLD Violet chase after
eight-year-old Charlie, who had charged ahead waving
a stick as if to slay the make-believe dragon inhabiting
the woods. Their daughter was never far behind her big
brother. She reminded Stella of herself as a child, always chasing a big sister for fear of being left behind or
missing out.

But fears of that nature were in the past. She had slain
her own personal dragon and joined the boys' club, which
had promptly become the Bennett Club, admitting not
just one, but two girls to even up the dynamic.

Aaron, walking at her side with a similarly watchful
eye on their children, squeezed her hand. 'Are you nervous? About returning to work tomorrow?'

Stella smiled up at her husband, her pulse stirring
at the sight of him in a chunky Aran jumper that she
wanted to strip off the moment they arrived home from
their walk.

Of course, that would be impossible until the kids
were asleep.

'A little. I didn't think my maternity leave would last

this long.' She shrugged and he wrapped his arm around her shoulders, tucking her underneath so they were as close as humanly possible and still able to walk over the rugged path through the woods.

'Well, I didn't think my parents would want to retire early from running Bennett Manor, so it's all worked out perfectly. You and I get to job share and share the childcare while we enjoy our lives together.'

He glanced ahead to where their children walked hand in hand. Then he dragged her close and kissed her under an oak tree, naked of its leaves but filled with the promise of spring.

Stella lost herself in the glide of lips, the touch of tongues, the wash of love.

Charlie was a caring big brother, always looking out for his baby sister, protecting her and standing up to any perceived injustice, which was sometimes a challenge at bedtime and during their frequent trips to the stables.

A cry split the calm. Stella and Aaron broke apart, their parental senses as alert as their doctoring ones.

'Mum…' Charlie staggered back towards them carrying his sobbing sister.

Stella's heart swelled with pride and love that Aaron and Molly's son was comfortable enough to call her Mum. It had happened naturally and at his instigation, and after the first time Stella had crept off to the bedroom to cry.

'She fell over with this in her hand.' Charlie brandished the pine cone Violet had collected at the start of their walk—they had hundreds of similar specimens at home—and carried all the way, as if it was priceless treasure.

And maybe it was priceless. Because it contained miraculous seeds capable of growing a whole new tree, in the same way that Stella, Aaron and Charlie, with the addition of Violet, had grown their precious little family.

With love.

Aaron scooped Violet into his arms and hugged Charlie with his free arm. Violet snuggled into her father's jumper in a way that Stella envied and adored in equal measure.

'Well done, Charlie.' Stella took the pine cone and accepted a mollified, teary-cheeked Violet from Aaron. She raised her daughter's tiny hand to her mouth and kissed her palm, which bore faint pink indentations from the bumps of the pine cone.

And just like that, Violet smiled, the pain forgotten.

Having received comfort from both her parents, and before Stella could hug her properly, Violet squirmed out of her arms and went to her brother.

Charlie made soothing noises as Violet held up her hand for another kiss. He repeated the gesture and they galloped off together along the path.

Aaron sighed at her side, watching his children scamper away. Stella took his hand as they set off after the pair, her heart full of love for this man who had shown her that being vulnerable was not a weakness.

'What are you thinking?' she asked, knowing the signs of his preoccupation well.

'That I hope all of their trials and tribulations, their hurts and heartaches, are as brief and easily remedied as that.'

'They'll be fine.' Stella smiled, because her husband still worried about his parenting skills. Only now twice as much because there were two humans to love and nurture.

'Yes,' he agreed. Then, 'How can you be sure?'

'Because they'll take after you, and you are infamous around these parts for being a bit of a catch—hot dad doc and lord of the manor rolled into one spectacular package.' She pulled him close for a kiss.

'Maybe they'll take after you—wonderful mother, amazing GP, not to mention your dancing skills.' He twirled her under his arm and bent her back into a dip.

She laughed, her wellies almost slipping from under her in the mud.

'Oh, and I forgot, sexy. You are so sexy.' He wrapped his arm around her waist and hauled her close, this kiss turning X-rated.

'They'll take after us,' she said, holding his hand once more.

Aaron raised her hand to his mouth and kissed her knuckles, his eyes communicating so much love that she grew light-headed. 'I love you,' he said.

'I love you too.'

'I couldn't ask for anything more,' he said.

And then they chased after their children.

* * * * *

COMING SOON!

We really hope you enjoyed reading this book.
If you're looking for more romance, be sure to
head to the shops when new books are
available on

Thursday 27th October

To see which titles are coming soon, please visit

millsandboon.co.uk/nextmonth

MILLS & BOON®

Coming next month

CHRISTMAS WITH THE SINGLE DAD DOC
Annie O'Neil

Harry was still on the ground, and although he'd definitely grazed his knee, he somehow seemed entirely unfazed by it. Normally there would be howling by now. But the woman crouching down, face hidden by a sheet of glossy black hair, was somehow engaged in a greeting ritual with his son.

'How do you do, Harry?' She shook his hand in a warm, but formal style. 'It's such a pleasure to meet someone who loves Christmas as much as I do.'

If she was expecting Lucas to join in the I Love Christmas Every Day of the Year Club she was obviously recruiting for, she had another think coming. It was only November. He had enough trouble mustering up excitement for the day of December the twenty-fifth.

Clearly unperturbed by his lack of response, she smiled at Harry and pointed at his grazed knee. 'Now... Important decision to make. Do you think you'd like a plaster with Santa on it? Or elves?'

'Elves!' Harry clapped his hands in delight.

The woman laughed and said she would run into the house and get some, as well as a cloth to clear away the small grass stains Lucas could see were colouring his son's little-boy knees.

Her voice had a mischievous twist to it, and underneath

the bright, child-friendly exchange was a gentle kindness that softened his heart.

'I'm ever so sorry. Harry is just mad for—' Lucas began, but when she looked up and met his gaze anything else he'd planned on saying faded into nothing.

Though he knew beyond a shadow of a doubt that they'd never met, his body felt as if it had been jolted into a reality he'd always been waiting to step into. Every cell in his body was supercharged with a deep, visceral connection as their eyes caught and held. Hers were a warm brown…edging on a jewel-like amber. Her skin was beautiful, with an almost pearlescent hue. Glowing… Cheeks pink. Lips a deep red, as if they'd just received a rush of emotion.

Perhaps it was the unexpected excitement of a three-year-old boy careering into her front garden. Perhaps it was the fresh autumnal weather. Or maybe…just maybe…she was feeling the same thing he was. A strange but electric feeling, surging through him in a way he'd never experienced before.

She blinked once. Then twice. Then, as if the moment had been entirely a fiction of his own creating, realigned her focus so that it was only on Harry.

Continue reading
CHRISTMAS WITH THE SINGLE DAD DOC
Annie O'Neil

Available next month
www.millsandboon.co.uk

MILLS & BOON

THE HEART OF ROMANCE

A ROMANCE FOR EVERY READER

MODERN

Prepare to be swept off your feet by sophisticated, sexy and seductive heroes, in some of the world's most glamourous and romantic locations, where power and passion collide.

HISTORICAL

Escape with historical heroes from time gone by. Whether your passion is for wicked Regency Rakes, muscled Vikings or rugged Highlanders, awaken the romance of the past.

MEDICAL

Set your pulse racing with dedicated, delectable doctors in the high-pressure world of medicine, where emotions run high and passion, comfort and love are the best medicine.

True Love

Celebrate true love with tender stories of heartfelt romance, from the rush of falling in love to the joy a new baby can bring, and a focus on the emotional heart of a relationship.

Desire

Indulge in secrets and scandal, intense drama and plenty of sizzling hot action with powerful and passionate heroes who have it all: wealth, status, good looks…everything but the right woman.

HEROES

Experience all the excitement of a gripping thriller, with an intense romance at its heart. Resourceful, true-to-life women and strong, fearless men face danger and desire - a killer combination!

To see which titles are coming soon, please visit

millsandboon.co.uk/nextmonth